$\mathscr{L}iv$ & *the* PREACHER

Liv & the PREACHER

A Marriage of Convenience for a Good Cause Novel

Mary E Hanks

www.maryehanks.com

Suzanne D. Williams Cover Design

www.feelgoodromance.com

Cover photos:

UserGI15966731 @ istockphoto.com

Kovaleva_Ka @ shutterstock.com

Visit Mary's website:

www.maryehanks.com

You can write Mary at

maryhanks@maryehanks.com.

To Leela

A sweet, generous sister-in-law.

Thanks for your love, faith, and goodness.

To Jason

Thank you for taking this journey with me.

Thanks for being a good sport about my cooking!

You see that his faith and his actions were working together, and his faith was made complete by what he did.

James 2:22

Chapter One

Fall 1988

Olivia Dupont stroked her fingers down her swollen belly in the greasy-spoon diner in downtown Spokane, Washington. "We'll be okay, Little Mister," she whispered to her unborn child, trying to sound reassuring but failing.

She dipped a cold fry in ketchup, then stuffed the soggy food into her mouth to stop herself from weeping. The oily aftertaste of the fry made her want to gag, so she sipped some water from her paper cup.

Paper cup? Cold fries? Crying her eyes out?

How did her life come to this?

At least she owned a car to sleep in tonight. So far, her father hadn't repossessed her cherry red Triumph. Glancing over her shoulder, she peered out the diner's glass door. Her car was still in the parking lot. She was safe.

Safe? The rest area near the freeway on the west side of town where she slept for the last two nights didn't feel one bit safe.

A guy with dark eyes and a thick beard had peered through the windshield at her around three a.m. She pretended to be asleep.

Fortunately, he trudged on. But she kept watch for the rest of the night, teeth clenched, keys in hand, ready to start the engine and take off.

Only, she didn't have much gas. After her long drive from Chicago to Spokane, she didn't have much money left. That's why she was here instead of going on to Seattle like she originally planned.

She stuffed another fry into her mouth and stared at her cold dollar burger. Nothing tasted right. She grabbed a tissue and wiped her eyes which must be five shades of black from her smeared mascara.

A gray-haired guy's sympathetic gaze met hers from another table. She averted her eyes, not wanting anyone to recognize her. But who would suspect she was Olivia Violet Dupont this far from the Midwest?

Surely the elderly couple sitting at the next booth, clinging to cups of coffee like they were the only heat source they'd experienced in a week, wouldn't guess she was the daughter of Richard Dupont III. At least, they had each other. Would she ever have someone who loved her for her? Someone who didn't take advantage of a relationship just to get to her father's fortune?

A monsoon of salty tears soaked Liv's disintegrating tissue. A sob burst from her mouth. The keening noise sounded like a woman in the final throes of labor—like she'd be experiencing in two months. Despite her hand pressed against her mouth, she couldn't subdue the heartache.

"Honey, are you okay?"

Liv glanced up to find a lady in her early fifties with grayish-blond hair settling into the seat opposite her. A compassionate expression on her face, the woman reached across the table and clasped Liv's hand. "I'm so sorry for your loss or whatever you're going through, sweetie. I could sit here with you for a while. Talk, perhaps?"

Liv wiped her nose, her eyes. "I'm sorry. I didn't mean to make so much noise. I'm not usually a crier." She sniffed and hiccupped.

The woman pressed clean tissues into her hand. "I'm Trish North."

"Thank you for your kindness. I'll be okay." Liv bit her lower lip.

"Is there anything I can get for you?" Trish's pale, seafoam-colored eyes and her light hair made her look angelic. "A hot cup of coffee or tea?"

"No, thank you."

"I'll sit with you for as long as you need a friend." Trish patted her hand.

"A friend sounds nice." Liv stroked her stomach as the baby moved beneath her ribs.

"Are you in any kind of trouble?" The woman glanced at her belly.

"Why would you think I'm in trouble?" She was a Dupont. Not a poor person off the streets in need of charity. She gulped. Oh, right. Maybe she was exactly that person.

"I didn't mean any offense. I'm a single mom myself. I may understand your plight more than you imagine."

"I see. I'm Liv, by the way. Olivia Brown." She cringed as the fake last name rolled off her tongue. She'd concocted a phony story. She was a widow, down on her luck, just passing through town.

"Olivia, what a lovely name." Trish's voice was soft and melodic.

"How did your child turn out without a father?"

"Smith? He's thirty-three. Going to be a pastor. I named him after Smith Wigglesworth." The woman peered at Liv as if expecting her to recognize the name.

"Sorry. Who?"

"Someone my husband and I admired as a person of strong faith. Smith was a special name to him and me."

"Ohhh." Liv nodded like she knew what Trish was talking about, but she didn't.

"We wanted to name our kids after people who made a difference for Christ." Trish sighed, placing her hand over her heart. "Unfortunately, we had only one child before my husband passed away. I became a widow when Smith was two."

A widow? Now Liv couldn't tell this woman her fake bio. "I'm so sorry."

"Thank you. His death was heartbreaking."

Trish had probably been married to a wonderful man who adored her and was a loving father. Liv's child would never have that. Liv would probably never have that.

Trish folded her hands on the edge of the table. "Do you believe in Jesus?"

Liv tensed at the personal question. But then, sighing, she responded honestly the way she usually answered questions. "I did once. A long time ago."

Trish leaned forward. "Sweetie, Jesus is still looking out for you. Just now, He sent me to you."

"Sent you, how?" Liv huffed out a hot breath. "I'm pregnant and unmarried. Some would call that sinful. My father did it right to my face." His words of rejection still stung.

Trish's eyes filled with tears. "I'm so sorry for how he treated you. Jesus loves you, Olivia. And I do too."

Liv swallowed down a bitter taste in her throat. "I remember a story in the Bible about a woman who people wanted to stone." Her dad would have been one of those types—an angry control freak.

"True, yet Jesus didn't condemn her." Trish smiled warmly. "He told her to go home and stop sinning. Olivia, can you go home?"

"Not after my dad threw me out. And my mom stood there drinking her martini, watching."

"Their rejection must have hurt terribly."

"It did." Liv tried to hold her composure. No more crying.

"May I buy you something warm to eat?" Trish dug in her pocket, probably searching for change.

"No thanks. I'm not hungry." But she was curious about Trish and her son. "You say your son's going to be a pastor?"

"Yes." A relaxed smile crossed Trish's face. "Next week he'll be heading north to try out for his first church. He's wanted to preach since he felt called to the ministry when he was eight years old."

"I wanted to be a firefighter when I was eight."

Trish laughed. "Fortunately, Smith loves the Lord and has a heart to be a blessing."

"You must be proud of him." Liv would be pleased if her child chose an honorable profession. Anything other than a software engineer with dollar signs in his eyes. She stroked her belly.

"I am proud of him." Trish frowned. "He's . . . engaged."

Why the hesitation? Didn't she approve of her son's fiancée?

"Is she trouble?" Liv knew the kind.

"I'm trying to trust his wisdom. Not meddle." Trish chuckled. "Sometimes, that is."

"You don't like her, huh?"

"It's not that I dislike Katy. It's just—" Trish pressed her lips together as if stopping herself from saying anything unkind. "Opposites attract. It doesn't mean they're wrong for each other."

Liv patted the other woman's hand this time. "Sometimes love is blind."

"True. I trust my son to make the right decision. Really, I do."

"I believe you." Liv withdrew her hand and stuck another fry into her mouth. "I can tell you're a wonderful mother. I hope I'll be as good of a mom."

"Where are you staying?" Trish sat up straighter, eyeing her.

Liv should have had a handy lie ready. She didn't. "In my car at a rest area."

"Oh, my dear, sleeping in your car isn't safe!"

"I'm staying there only until I get a job." The baby moved and Liv adjusted her position to give him more space. "I worked for my dad's company, but when he found out about my condition, I lost my job and my apartment. He even shut down my credit line."

"That settles it." Trish patted the table. "You're coming home with me."

"What? No, I can't."

"Yes, you can." Trish's pale green eyes sparkled. "Please? I could use the company."

"You're serious?" Liv must be out of her mind to even be considering this. Was she considering it? Anything sounded better than sleeping in her car. But going home with a stranger? She couldn't, right?

"Absolutely. I felt led to come in here tonight." Trish tucked her chin-length blondish-gray hair behind her ears. "The Lord nudged me to look inside this café and check on someone."

"Someone?" The word stuck on Liv's tongue. As in God told this woman to check on her? An image of a loving father looking out for his daughter crossed her thoughts. But she'd done too many wrong things for Him to be looking out for her, right?

"You know the nudge in your spirit when you feel like you must do something?" Trish looked at her so earnestly.

"Not really." Liv was bewildered by the woman's willingness to follow an inner nudge.

"I have a small house. I lead a simple life. I don't even own a TV."

She must be a recluse to not have a television. But without one, she wouldn't recognize Rich Dupont's software commercials. That was a plus.

Trish rubbed her palm over Liv's hand in a motherly gesture. "You are welcome to stay with me for as long as you'd like. You and the baby."

Her offer sounded preposterous! Yet strangely inviting. Could Liv simply go home with this stranger who looked like an angel?

Chapter Two

Smith kissed his fiancée, Katy Fleming, goodnight at her apartment door, holding her a little closer in his arms than he usually did. He should leave. Sprint back to his car. The temptation to go inside Katy's living room and continue kissing her hit him stronger each time he dropped her off. As a Christian and a future pastor, he knew better than to give in to such temptations. But he loved Katy so much.

She slid her hands down the back of his sports coat slowly, enticingly.

"I have to go." He broke off the kiss and stepped back, catching his breath.

"Don't you love me?" she asked in a pouty tone.

"Of course, I love you. That's why we should wait for our wedding night like we talked about."

"Your idea. Not mine." She came closer, her palms smoothing over his arms. "Come on, Smithy. I don't want to wait. I doubt you want to either." Her fingers danced up his coat like ballet dancers. Her index fingers twirled sultry pirouettes around his earlobes. Her lips caressed his neck. "Come in for dessert?"

"No." He stepped back again, holding out his palms. "I have to go."

Run. Stay.

The tug-of-war in his mind, in his heart, was a battle between temptation and following God's plan. Of course, he'd follow the Lord. Yet, he yearned to know the things of a married man too.

"You're no fun." She stuck out her tongue at him. "Staying with your mama, doing what she demands. Leaving when you could be cuddled up with me tonight."

Heat rushed up his neck. "I'm staying with my mom to save money for our future. I'm the one who's choosing to not have sex before marriage."

"Like I said, your decision, not mine. But what do you mean about saving money?" She crossed her arms. "You're scrimping for us to live in that shoddy house near the northern border? I hate the cold, Smithy. Don't the temperatures get below zero near Thunder Ridge?"

"Only sometimes."

Her eyelids nearly squeezed shut. "You should have told me about this plan of yours to be a hermit in some decrepit parsonage near Canada before asking me to marry you."

Her harsh tone effectively threw a bucket of icy water over him.

"I wasn't aware of this ministry opportunity *an hour* from the border before I asked you to marry me. But you knew I planned to be a pastor." They'd talked about it enough times.

"I never loved that part about your plans, either."

"Don't tease me. It'll be a nice house for our first pastorate." He softened his tone, trying to keep peace between them. "Three bedrooms are roomy enough."

"One bathroom! How do you imagine a city girl like me will survive with one bathroom? Do you realize how long it takes me to curl my hair and put on makeup?"

Maybe if she didn't put on quite so much makeup and wear her hair so puffy, it wouldn't take her as long. But he wouldn't mention that.

He'd been enamored with Katy for five months. He loved the way she held his hand, gazed into his eyes like everything he said was important, and the way he fell for her so quickly seemed like an answer to prayer for his lonely heart. At thirty-three, he'd longed for a wife and helpmeet.

"We'll be so in love, we'll make it work," he said.

"Make it work? Marriage is supposed to be fun. Not work!"

They had this discussion last night when he said he had to leave, too. He'd been trying to persuade her that Thunder Ridge wasn't at the end of the earth. Off-Broadway shows came through Spokane, a little over an hour's drive. Plus, fabulous art and music shows were scheduled in Sandpoint, a town south of Thunder Ridge.

"Stay with me?" Katy tipped her feathered bangs toward her door. "Please, Smithy?"

"I can't. I'll see you tomorrow."

She stuck her key in the lock. "You don't know what you're missing." Licking her lower lip, she slipped inside and shut the door slowly.

Groaning, he stared at the wooden door with the metal #305B glued slightly off-kilter.

She opened the door two inches. "Change your mind?"

"No. Don't forget, we're having dinner at my mom's tomorrow night. Six o'clock."

"If I must."

"Katy, my mom loves you."

"Hates me, more like."

"It's not in my mom's DNA to hate you." Although, he wished Mom and Katy had more in common. Often, when they got together for dinner or a game night, the evening ended in hurt feelings. Katy's, usually. "I'll pick you up at 5:45."

"Fine." She closed the door.

Smith hustled down the stairs. But all the way to his car he wondered, what would it be like when he never had to leave her again?

Chapter Three

Liv rolled over, shuffling her heavy belly from her back to her side on the hide-a-bed in Trish's living room. The springs in the frame beneath the stiff mattress were uncomfortable. Nothing like the plush pillowtop mattress back in her apartment. But at least she wasn't curled up in her small car.

The sound of voices reached her from the kitchen.

"Smith, I don't understand why you're so alarmed," Trish spoke quietly. "As a pastor, you'll no doubt take in homeless people from time to time."

Was her son upset about Liv being here?

"Sure. But that's different." His voice got louder. "How could you bring a stranger into our house in the middle of the night without telling me?"

"She was tired. We both were."

A few dishes clinked like someone dropped a cup in the sink. Water ran from the faucet.

"Why don't you get some sleep, hon?" Trish said. "You'll meet my guest in the morning."

"How long is she staying?" he asked in a stern-sounding voice.

Wasn't he a gem? Liv knew grouchy coworkers like him in Chicago. He wasn't like his mom at all. Liv snuggled the blanket protectively around herself.

"She can stay as long as she wants."

Thank you, Trish!

"Mom, besides our house being too small for three, this could be a dangerous situation."

Liv snorted. How could she be dangerous? What would she do in her fat-bellied condition? If he kept up this harsh attitude, she'd return to sleeping in her car by morning.

"Let's get some sleep, huh?" It sounded like Trish patted Smith's shoulder. "The Lord directed my meeting with Olivia tonight. Let's leave it at that."

"He directed you to her? For what purpose?"

Try kindness and compassion, *jerk!*

"I couldn't leave her at the café alone." Trish's tone was strong, brooking no argument even from her son.

Trish was one in a million. Smith? Liv dreaded meeting him.

As Trish and Smith shuffled through the living room toward their bedrooms, Liv tugged the blanket over her face, hiding from the man who wanted her gone.

Early the next morning, the sounds of a coffeemaker gurgling and someone walking across the linoleum in the kitchen woke her. The coffee smelled divine. One cup wouldn't hurt. Then she'd hit the road before Trish's crabby son kicked her out.

She pushed off the mattress and made her way to the smallest bathroom she'd ever used. She refused to waddle. Instead, she walked slowly, focusing on her bare feet. After using the facilities, she tried to tone down her frizzy morning hair. She splashed water on her face a couple of times.

Her mom had said she'd be obese and begging for bread before the baby came. The getting large part was inevitable. Begging sounded horrible. Wouldn't she be crazy to turn away from the kindness Trish offered? Even if she had to endure her son? Liv had dealt with troublesome employees before. She knew how to put a snob in his place.

She walked into the kitchen, expecting to find Trish. "The coffee smells amazing!"

A black-haired man stood in front of the drip coffeemaker in pajama bottoms, bare-chested, and barefooted. He pivoted toward her, his eyes wide.

"It's you," she said. "You startled me."

The cup in his hand stalled in midair. "I startled *you*?"

"Yes." She lifted her chin, remembering the ugly way he talked about her last night.

His blackish hair stuck up like he'd been running his fingers through the strands. Did he have a lipstick smear on his cheek? Was he making out with his fiancée last night? What would Trish think of her precious son hot-lipping with the woman she disliked?

Liv couldn't stop staring at Smith's rich dark brown eyes, full brows, and the dimple in his chin to die for—even when he wasn't smiling. Above his baseball-themed pj's, his chest was slightly hairy. She gulped, glancing away.

"Sorry." He smoothed his free hand over his chest. "I didn't expect to see anyone."

She pointed to the coffee machine. "Got decaf?"

"I don't know." He yanked open a cupboard and scrounged through some packages. "Here." He set a container on the green Formica countertop.

"Thanks."

He emptied the remainder of the carafe into a large mug, then swayed his hands toward the machine. "All yours."

She nodded at the navy fabric with the word "Yankees" covering his legs. "Fan?"

"Yep. I'm planning on nine baseball players in my family." He smiled widely.

He had a beautiful smile, too.

"Tall order for your wife." Liv fiddled with putting coffee grounds in the upper compartment of the coffee machine.

He laughed, a husky sound rolling from his throat. "I may not have mentioned that fact to my fiancée."

"No wonder. Nine? Are you kidding me?"

"Not really. So, you're the guest?"

At his deeper tone, perhaps a judgmental tone, she lifted her chin. "Unwanted guest, apparently." She arched an eyebrow. Wouldn't cower before a cad. She'd had a high-powered tenth-story office in her father's software company. Hired and fired her share of lazy workers. Would gladly put this man in his place.

"Oh, um, er." His cheeks darkened. His gaze riveted on her swollen belly.

She wouldn't cover her stomach with her hands or act embarrassed about her pregnancy, either. She'd hidden her condition long enough. "I call him Little Mister."

"A boy?"

"Fifty-fifty chance. Could be one of your nine." She winked teasingly.

Smith spit and sputtered, and she nearly guffawed at his overreaction. He rubbed his hand against the back of his neck. If he moved his fingers, he might wipe the red lipstick off his jawline. If she were more sympathetic to his situation, she might mention the mark before his mother walked in. Nope. She wasn't feeling the least bit sympathetic toward him.

"Just kidding. That was too easy."

"Nearly gave me a heart attack."

"Serves you right for what you said about me last night." She eyed him boldly.

"Oh, sorry." His face hued red.

Did he think she'd let him off the hook so easily?

The coffee pot made a weird whining sound.

"Shut the dial off after it finishes the cycle." He reached forward as if to turn the knob himself.

"I'll do it." She stretched out her hand at the same time, her arm brushing his bare one as she pressed the off button.

Trish swept into the kitchen. Liv and Smith jumped back from each other as if they'd been caught doing something wrong. Silly reaction.

"Olivia, good morning." Trish's gaze rocked back and forth between them. "Smith."

"Morning, Mom. Just making coffee."

Liv filled her cup with the dark liquid. "It's decaf."

"I have some creamer somewhere." Trish opened the fridge and held out a slim bottle. "Here you go, Olivia."

"Thanks. Call me Liv if you want.'"

"I love the name Olivia." Trish smiled, then stared at Smith's face. Busted! She pointed at his cheek. "You have a—" Her jaw dropped. "Is that what I think it is?"

Liv wanted to burst out laughing.

Smith set down his cup and wiped his palm across his face.

"Katy's lips, I'm guessing." Liv smirked.

"Excuse me." He rushed out of the room.

Liv stifled her laughter.

"How did you sleep?" Trish rested her hand briefly on Liv's arm.

"Once I fell asleep, fine." She wouldn't lie about what she heard. Smith had his reasons for not wanting her in the house. Now that she nearly proposed to him, he might have twice the reasons.

"So you met my Smith. What do you think?" Trish poured the rest of the decaf in another cup, then fixed a regular pot of coffee. She was dressed in athletic clothes. Was she a runner?

"I barged in on him. He was flabbergasted."

"It's nice to ruffle his feathers now and then."

Liv laughed. "So, he's a little stuffy?"

"Blame that on his father's side." Trish's voice went softer. "And Pastor Tim's influence."

"A mentor?" Liv sipped her creamy coffee.

"Mmhmm. Are you hungry? What do you like for breakfast? Pancakes? Oatmeal?"

"I need to wake up first. Maybe take a walk."

Trish swayed her hands toward her clothes. "I dance. You're welcome to come along."

"If only I were lighter on my feet. Can you picture me dancing?"

Smiling warmly, Trish grabbed a washcloth and wiped off the counter. "There's a small dance club down the street. I dance for exercise."

Liv smoothed her hand over her stomach. "I'd better stick to walking." She scooted for the doorway. "I'll fold the blankets and put the bed away first."

"Why don't you take care of the blankets and I'll have Smith collapse that ornery hide-a-bed?" Trish poured steaming coffee into her cup. "Stash the blankets on that vintage chair in the corner. Then they'll be ready for you to use this evening."

So she planned on Liv staying even though Smith warned her against an intruder living with them?

"Okay." Maybe she'd hang around for a few days. "Is there anything I can do for you to help out?"

"Smith's girlfriend is coming over for dinner tonight." Trish let out a sigh like she was fortifying herself for the ordeal.

"I could stay away during the visit if that would help."

"Goodness, no." Trish chuckled. "I want you here. Can you cook?"

"Toast and eggs."

"What if I put a list together?"

"Uh, sure."

Hopefully, whatever Trish wanted her to do wouldn't involve doing much in the kitchen. There were a lot of things she was good at—cooking wasn't one of them.

Chapter Four

When Liv reentered the kitchen later, she found a note with her name and a list of chores—dust living room, shine bathroom mirror, sweep the kitchen, make apple pie—propped against a glass on the counter. Make apple pie? She'd never made a pie in her life, let alone one for a dinner with her host's future daughter-in-law. She let out a loud groan.

Smith strolled into the room, his musky scent tickling Liv's senses. "Is there a problem?"

She forced herself not to take a deep breath of his manly scent. Not to swoon at his feet like a love-starved woman.

"Your mom wants me to make a pie."

"Lucky you."

"You don't understand." How much should she explain to the man who already wanted her to leave? Too bad her mother didn't teach her how to cook. Genevieve Dupont had probably never cooked a dish of food in her life. "I don't know how to make a pie," Liv said through clenched teeth.

Smith's chocolaty eyes widened. "This pie doesn't happen to be for tonight's dinner, does it?"

"Bingo!"

He groaned. "My mom's up to something. Did she know you can't cook?"

"I didn't say I can't cook. I can make scrambled eggs."

He bellowed out in laughter.

Her cheeks felt scorched. "We had a cook while I was growing up."

"Thus your lack of cooking skills?" He snickered.

How dare he laugh at her! "I worked in a high-rise building in downtown Chicago. Was about to move into a penthouse. Had all the luxuries—"

"I get the picture. And now?" He swayed both hands toward her baby bump.

"None of your concern." She glared at Smith—this behemoth who might act spiritual one second but was a cad beneath his piety. She'd demoted young hopefuls with one of her powerhouse glares. She'd stand here for an hour pegging him with one of hers if necessary.

"Since you're sleeping on my mother's couch, the matter is my concern."

Oh, he had some nerve.

Smith didn't back down from her intense stare like many employees did in the past. At least, since he put on a blue button-up shirt, she didn't have to stare at his bare chest. "I don't want someone pounding on the door in the middle of the night, hunting for you."

Some of her bluster melted away. "No one is coming to look for me. My car, maybe. Not me." She picked up the list to give her hands a task, otherwise, she might smack him. "You have nothing to worry about. I'm not a criminal. I'm not a fake like some people." She dished him another scowl.

"Ouch. I'm not trying to offend you."

"You could have fooled me." Whatever disaster she made for tonight's meal served him right. "Is this pie-baking scheme an initiation ritual?"

"No. My mother's meddling."

"Meddling, how? Oh, you mean with Miss Kissy Lips?"

His red-hued flush made her smile.

"Two can play her game." He took off his jacket and flung it over the back of a chair. "One of us knows how to make an apple pie."

"You can cook? I mean, I've heard of men cooking, it's not a foreign idea, but—"

"What? I don't look like someone who knows his way around a kitchen?" His smirky mouth tipped up.

"I have no idea what such a man looks like."

"Like this." He spread out his hands. "Thanks to being raised by a single mom who worked, I can cook." He pulled open a cupboard door and flung bowls and measuring cups onto the green counter-top. He pointed toward the sink. "Wash your hands."

"Back off, bossy man." She had enough of his high-handed attitude.

"*Please* wash your hands."

"Fine." Huffing, she turned toward the sink. But when she turned on the water, the spray burst out of the faucet sideways, splattering her face. "Hey!"

Smith guffawed.

Yeah, she wanted to punch him.

She thrust out her hands, blindly trying to shut off the water.

Smith put his arm around her and slid his finger inside the rim of the faucet with his other hand. "There. The washer needs to be replaced."

"You knew this would happen, didn't you?" She pushed away from him and scrubbed water off her cheeks. The rat.

Smith burst out laughing again. She'd never heard a man laugh so much.

"I may have thought it *might* spray you." He shrugged, still apparently fighting a snicker. "Grab a bag of flour out of the pantry, will you? Make yourself useful." He pointed to a narrow closet door.

"I'll be useful, all right." She punched his arm semi-playfully. "Hey!"

She marched over to the mystery cupboard and opened the door carefully. Was Smith setting her up for another trick? When nothing unexpected happened, she glanced back and caught him watching her. What got into her, teasing him like that? When did she ever banter around with a guy she just met? Especially someone judgmental and rude like him?

"Hurry up, will you?"

"Yes, Your Highness." She pushed a few packages aside, looking for a box with the word "flour."

"You don't have to be snide."

"You don't have to be so pompous. And you might as well tell me what a flour box looks like." She clamped down her teeth, hating feeling inferior to anyone.

"It doesn't come in a box. Oh, for goodness' sake." He stomped over to the cupboard. "Well?"

"Well, what?"

"Move your girth!"

"Girth?" He was crossing the line! Elbowing him as hard as she could, she backed up.

He clutched his ribs. "I can't believe you did that."

"No? Why don't you try being nice?"

His jaw dropped as if no one had ever put him in his place before. What a spoiled only child he must have been! Since his mother thought he was perfect, did he expect everyone else to acquiesce to his wishes, too?

"I am nice, usually."

"Just show me the flour."

Trish wanted pie, she was getting pie!

Smith reached around Liv's shoulder and pointed at a white bag right in front of her. "Unbleached flour. You've never seen a ten-pound bag of flour in your kitchen before?"

"You've never seen a Cessna Citation III business jet, hmm?" She smirked. Then scooped up the bag of flour. Unfortunately, the paper wrapping had a hole. A puff of white dust erupted into the air. She coughed and hacked across the room.

Smith laughed and didn't offer to carry the bag. How ungentlemanly of him!

Liv dropped the bag on the counter. More flour puffed into the air like a dust devil over a dry field. "Now what, Your Majesty?"

Smith chuckled.

Before she could stop herself or remind herself this man didn't want her living in his house and thought she might be dangerous, she ripped open the bag. She grabbed a handful of flour in her fist and flung her hand back threateningly.

"Don't you dare!" He lifted his hands, palms out, in mock surrender.

"I dare plenty." In her meanest I'm-the-boss's-daughter gleam, she wanted to let him know she meant business. He'd better not laugh at her again.

"Sorry. Who would have guessed a woman your age didn't know what a bag of flour looks like?"

He didn't know when to quit, did he? She hurled the fistful of flour at his face, his black hair. His dark eyelashes.

He gasped and sputtered and coughed so hard it sounded like he might vomit. She almost felt sorry for him. He stomped out of the kitchen, muttering about her being a pampered princess.

Glancing at the ripped-open bag of flour, horror filled her. Was he leaving her to make the pie alone? They were doomed! Why was she so petulant and stupid?

As quickly as Smith left, he stomped back into the room. He eyed her with contempt and rolled up his green checkered shirt sleeves—he'd changed out of his other shirt—in jerky movements. "You're still going to learn how to make a pie today."

"Fine." She swallowed her pride and the taste of flour in the air. "Don't you have to go to work?"

"My mother knew I wouldn't let tonight's dinner be a disaster. She also probably recognized your—"

"My what?" Clutching another handful of flour, she warned him to shut up.

"Your delicate condition. That you might need my help." He smiled with that chin dimple widening, which sent her heart into overdrive.

She released the flour onto the counter. "If you make the pie, I'll owe you a turn at washing dishes, or something."

"You've washed dishes before?" He raised his thick eyebrows.

"No, but it can't be too hard."

He chortled. "Just like making pie?"

"I'm sure I can follow a recipe." She squinted at him. "But I doubt your precious fiancée wants to eat a burned pie made by some homeless vagrant."

"Touché." He picked up a couple of cubes of butter. "Mom softened these. There's an apron on the hook on the wall." He rocked his thumb, telling her what to do again.

She didn't like anyone telling her what to do or mocking her. He'd done both.

Still, she followed his instructions, since she didn't want to get stuck making the pie alone. She grabbed a plain white apron off a hook by the pantry. The fabric didn't quite fit around her belly.

"Measure two-and-a-half cups of flour."

"Yes, sir." She glanced around at the supplies and picked up a blue plastic measuring cup. She read the fraction on the handle. "Half."

"Grab that one." He pointed at a bigger cup of the same color. "Someone should have taught you how to cook."

"No, duh."

He snickered.

"Stop laughing at me."

"Or you'll douse me in flour again?"

"I know where you sleep. You thought I might be dangerous before. Ever heard of pepper?"

"You wouldn't."

"Don't mess with me." She dipped out three heaping cups of flour and plunked them into the large bowl on the counter. "There."

"You have to measure precisely for the crust to turn out right."

"Seriously?"

"Measure it again."

"You are a cruel taskmaster!" She dumped the flour back into the bag, spilling a pile of it on the counter. Carefully, she measured two-and-a-half cups worth of flour. "Happy?"

"Much better." He pulled the bowl toward himself, shook some salt into his hand, and tossed the granules onto the powder. Then he dropped in the cubes of butter.

His ease at the tasks surprised her.

"How long have you been baking?"

"Most of my life." He pressed a wire thingy into the mix, squashing the chunks of butter into the flour. "Mom always made me help, even when I was a kid."

"Domestic bliss."

"Now, who's the smart-aleck?" He flicked some flour at her face.

"Hey." She wiped dust off her cheeks.

"There's a stool over there if you want to use it." He nodded toward the opposite side of the room.

She was tired of standing, but she didn't want him thinking she'd follow his instructions just because he gave her a command. Nevertheless, she trudged across the small space, grabbed the stool, dragged it back to the counter, and sat down.

"Get a few ice cubes out of the freezer and drop them into a little water."

She glared at him.

"Please?" he said in mock humility. "What?"

"Is this how you treat people? I bet you don't get away with sassing your girlfriend." She slid off the stool. Tromped back to the freezer. Maybe she'd slip a cube of ice down his shirt.

"I'm the one who's helping *you*, don't forget."

Oh, he was smug.

She grabbed three ice cubes, then trudged back to the measuring cup and dropped them in. Following his instructions, she poured water over the top of the ice. "Now what?"

"So this business jet. Have you been in one?"

"Certainly."

"Smooth ride?"

"Barely know you're taking off."

"I wanted to fly planes when I was young." Smith stared out the window as if thinking back on a fond memory.

Liv slid her backside onto the stool, adjusting the weight in her stomach. "What happened?"

"I was called into the ministry."

"Called by whom?"

"God."

"Oh," she dragged out the word. "Are you allowed to decline such a call?"

He had the audacity to laugh at her again.

"Stop! I told you—"

"Sorry. You make me laugh more than anyone I've met."

He stared at her so intently that she wondered if he deemed her a heathen for not understanding stuff about his calling.

Chapter Five

Smith's gaze tangled with Liv's for several moments longer than he should have been staring at her. Not romantically. More like he found himself mesmerized by her feisty playfulness. Even her slightly off-kilter waddle was hilarious. The way they tossed flour at each other like a couple of adolescents? That was nuts! And fun.

When had he felt so comfortable with another person other than his mom? Mom said she felt an instant rapport with Liv. He must be drawn to her in the same way.

Perhaps, her fragile condition invited such caring. What was she? Seven months pregnant? On her own? Although, she didn't act the least bit fragile. Even now she looked like she might grab another fistful of flour and hurl the powder at him. If she did, he'd be tempted to reciprocate.

What did Liv ask? Something about whether he could decline his calling.

"Yes. I could refuse to follow God's will for my life." He swallowed hard. "It's my choice. But I'd never want to disappoint the Lord, even though I've made my share of mistakes." Smith tugged the blending tool through the dough. Liv stared at him, her left eyebrow quirked in curiosity or consternation. "I've spoken at several churches already. But I'm bursting at the seams to pastor my own church, or at least to be an assistant."

"Kind of like becoming the VP of a company?"

He almost laughed at the analogy. "Sort of. Is that what you were?"

"My father was grooming me for that eventuality." She pointed at the bowl. "Anything I can do?"

"Ever peeled apples?"

She gave him an incredulous look. "I thought they came in a can."

He chuckled. Remembering his laughter perturbed her, he pressed his lips together. "Sometimes they come in a can premixed with sugar and cinnamon."

"See, I was right. But not how you do it?"

"Homemade is better." He strolled over to a bowl of Golden Delicious apples his mom left at the end of the counter. He set the whole thing in front of Liv and handed her a paring knife. Did she know how to peel an apple? How could someone get to be in their upper twenties without a basic understanding of baking?

She turned the knife around and around in her hand as if the cold metal felt odd to her.

"Try to trim off the peelings as thinly as possible."

"Yes, Pastor North."

"I'm not that, yet."

Eyebrows pinched together, she plucked an apple from the bowl and stared at the fruit like it had horns.

"Want me to show you how?" He added a little water to the flour mix, pushing the dough back and forth with his fingers.

"I can do it. Don't you dare call me incompetent!"

"Never that." He snickered.

"But you assume I can't do it, right? Maybe I can't do anything?" She lifted her chin, a challenge in her eyes.

He wanted to howl at her sulky expression.

"My mom used to say I could do anything I set my mind to." He nodded toward the apple. "Go for it."

"My dad used to say that too." A sad expression crossed her face, then she pressed the knife against the apple, keeping the sharp part of the blade away from her. A chunk of apple fell to the counter. "Probably not thin enough, huh?"

"Want me to show you how to peel an apple?" he asked again.

"I guess your mom expects a few slices to make it into the pie." She passed him the knife and the fruit.

Tempted to razz her about her lack of skills in the kitchen, he held his tongue. "Hold the apple like so and draw the knife slowly back toward yourself." He trimmed off a long skinny piece of peeling. "Like that."

"Wait. I read you should always keep the knife blade away from yourself."

"Except for when you're paring an apple." He passed both items back to her. "Try again and be careful."

They worked companionably, although the way Liv pared the apples so thickly left a lot to be desired. He made sure not to laugh at her—or maybe he did a few times just to enjoy her comical reaction. The more familiar he became with this spunky woman, the more he understood why Mom was taken with her enough to invite her to stay.

When Liv finished slicing the apples—pulverizing them—he talked her through adding sugar and cinnamon. Even though he told her to stir the mix carefully, half the apples flipped out onto the counter. A few landed on the floor. He snorted and she scowled, threatening to make him clean up the mess by himself if he laughed again.

"Your mom told me you were named after some guy." She wiped the back of her hand across her nose, removing some of the flour. "What's that about?"

"Some parents choose a sports player's name or an actor's name for their child. My folks chose to name me after an evangelist from the early 1900s."

"Is that what you're going to do? Follow in his footsteps?"

"No." Smith dumped the coated apples into the pie crust. "The Lord called me to follow Him into full-time ministry as a pastor. Although, my mom taught me about Smith Wigglesworth's heart for faith. That was something she and my dad planned to do before he died."

"I'm sorry you lost him when you were so young."

A breath caught in his throat. Her humanity and caring touched him. "Thanks." He focused on crimping the edge of the pie crust. "I plan to name my kids after people who had a strong faith in God too."

"Your nine kids?" She flicked a little flour in his direction.

"Or however many Katy and I have." He nodded toward her stomach. "Do you have a name picked out?"

"Just Little Mister for now."

"How about Livingstone?"

Her nose wrinkled. "Who's that?"

"A famous missionary to Africa. Or how about Wilkerson?"

"I know that one." She clicked her fingers. "A guy who helped kids on the streets clean up their act. I saw the movie!"

"God did great things through him."

A shadow crossed her features. "I haven't given much thought to the baby's name. Getting through the day-to-day stuff takes all my effort."

"I understand." He put the pie into the oven. Then tossed Liv a wet washcloth. "Time to clean up."

Moments later, seeing her flicking flour onto the floor with the cloth, he showed her how to hold her hand to catch the crumbs at the edge of the counter. When he washed dishes, he had to demonstrate how to dry them, too. Didn't her parents teach her anything?

Mom entered the house. "Hey, you two. Sorry I'm late." She patted Liv's arm. "How are you?"

"Tired." She wiped the back of her hand over her forehead as if she did all the work herself.

Smith rolled his eyes.

"Let me do that, and you go lay down and rest." Mom took the towel and shooed Liv into the other room.

At the doorway, Liv glanced back at him and winked. The fake. She probably wasn't exhausted at all.

"So, what do you think?" Mom nodded toward the living room. "Isn't she nice?"

"Can't cook. Never pared apples in her life. Unaware of how to wash or dry dishes." He lowered his voice so last night's faux pas wouldn't be repeated. "What were you thinking by having her make a pie for the meal Katy's coming to?" He wouldn't be disrespectful, but he didn't want his mother meddling in his relationship.

"I knew you could help if she got in a jam."

"Oh, she got in a jam, all right." He washed the last glass, feeling manipulated. "She's totally incompetent in the kitchen."

"Hey!" Liv yelped from the other room. "I can hear you guys."

"Sorry." Smith gave his mom an eye roll. "She's plucky."

"Heard that too!"

"Sorry." Smith apologized again, pulling the plug from the sink and wiping his hands on a dish towel.

"I knew you'd like Olivia," Mom said. "I had a good feeling about her."

She'd better not be matchmaking.

"I'm with Katy."

"Of course, you are." Mom shrugged innocently.

"Take the pie out when it's done, will you? I'm heading out for a stroll." He crossed through the living room, noticing Liv resting on the couch with her eyes closed.

"Thanks for bailing me out," she said softly. "I didn't mean to be such a bother about the pie."

He wished she hadn't overheard his discussion with Mom. "No worries." He paused for a moment, glancing back at her. She was watching him through squinty eyelids. "Get some rest."

"Yes, oh Knowledgeable One."

He bit back a chuckle, then left the house.

Chapter Six

"Are you sure I can't skip dinner?" Liv carried a stack of tan ceramic dinner plates with mauve trim to the kitchen table. The small house didn't boast a formal dining room like she was familiar with back at the Dupont residence. But the small setting had a cozy warmth. "I could sit in my car or walk to the library." Anywhere but sitting across the table from Smith and his girlfriend would be fine with her.

"Absolutely not." Trish stirred the gravy fast. "Grab those fake crystal glasses, will you?" She waved her free hand toward a cupboard to the left without glancing up.

"Sure thing." Liv set out the plates, one each on the four sides of the table, then retrieved the glasses. "Smith's fiancée might not like sharing the spotlight with a stranger."

"Nonsense. You're staying here with me, so she might as well meet you. Especially if Smith goes through with his plans." Trish dipped a teaspoon in the brown gravy and licked the edge.

"You think he might not?"

Liv was curious about Smith's girlfriend. Would she make him a good pastor's wife?

Liv sauntered closer to Trish, looking over her shoulder as the older woman tended two pots of food at once. "Everything smells fantastic."

"Thank you." Trish mashed potatoes with one hand and frantically stirred gravy with the other.

"Is there anything I can do?" Even Liv heard the inadequacy in her tone.

A funny look crossed Trish's face. Had Smith told her she didn't know what a bag of flour looked like?

"I'm not good at cooking." There, she admitted it.

"We all start somewhere, Olivia." Trish handed her the whisk. "Why don't you stir this?"

"Really?" Liv felt entrusted with the family fortune. How hard could stirring gravy be?

"About Smith's calling"—Trish continued the conversation as if they hadn't stopped talking—"for most of his life he's dreamed of becoming a pastor. I like to picture his dad smiling down at him from Heaven over such a decision."

"That's cool." Too bad Liv's father wasn't smiling at her, right here on terra firma. His words, "Get out and never come back!" resounded through her brain like a migraine-inducing drumbeat.

Trish pointed to the pan. "Stir faster so the gravy doesn't burn."

"Oh, right." How was she supposed to keep the soupy mixture from burning? "Do you think this church tryout is the right move for him?"

"If God's calling him there, yes." Trish sighed. "It's not that far away, but I wish he'd stay closer to home. Selfish of me. I should be glad he isn't moving to Florida."

"Florida sunshine sounds terrific about now." Liv kept moving the stirring tool, noticing Trish's frown. "Do you have doubts?"

The other woman stared intensely at her for a moment. "I don't mean to be pushy about my faith. Although, I probably already was."

Liv's face warmed. "It's okay."

"Faith is trusting that God's in charge of the situation, even if we don't understand the details." Trish put her hand over Liv's and increased the stirring tempo of the whisk's movement. "Smith is eager to jump into pastoring. Oh, dear." Trish yanked the gravy pan off the burner. "May I?" She held out her hand.

"Sure." Liv passed the utensil to her.

Trish stirred the gravy like her arm was motorized, but even Liv smelled the scorched scent.

"Did I burn it? I'm so sorry."

"Might be salvageable." Trish's tone sounded doubtful.

"If I ruined your dinner, I'll hate myself. Smith will never forgive me." Panic rose in her chest. "He was so concerned about the pie."

The front door opened in the living room. Laughter reached Liv at the same time Trish said, "Such a shame."

Liv wanted to slink away to the bathroom, the only private place where she had access to a lock. But to do so, she'd have to shuffle past Smith and his fiancée.

"Hey, Mom, we're here!"

Trish drew in a long breath. "These things happen." Then, bustling into the living room, she said, "Katy, welcome!"

"Did something burn?" a woman said in a high-pitched tone. "It smells dreadful in here!"

Liv froze. Why had she offered to help at all?

Chapter Seven

How many ways could Liv make herself appear lacking? First, the burned gravy. Then, not closing her eyes during grace. Even clunking her plate with her water glass, nearly spilling the whole thing across Smith's lap. And Katy—the beautiful platinum blond with perfectly ratted hair, slim figure, and flawless femininity—sat across from Liv, staring at her like she was some lost puppy.

Several times throughout the meal, Liv's gaze clashed with Katy's. Was she assessing her threat level? Like Liv might be after Smith? What a laugh. No threat of man-stealing here!

The only thing she wanted to steal was another trip to the bathroom. How many times could she get away with using the facilities during a meal?

She forked a piece of meatloaf into her mouth and accidentally glanced at Smith. His eyes had a merry, sparkling look. She wanted to kick him beneath the table. Shaking pepper on his pillow became an even stronger temptation.

"So, Olivia, what do you do?" Katy's tone implied she doubted Liv did anything.

If only she could tell this snooty-tooty her real last name. "Computer software."

"Oh?" Katy's overdrawn eyebrows rose in a pristine V.

"It's a booming industry."

"One of those fads. Nothing will come of computers." Katy scoffed. "Why anyone works in such a boring field, I have no idea. Here today, gone tomorrow."

Liv felt belittled right down to her canvas tennis shoes. But she didn't defend her father's decade-long opinion that the computer would change industry worldwide. In fact, Richard Dupont III had predicted that computers would become a large asset to businesses, education, and would be used in most homes. Time would tell.

She stuffed a bite of meatloaf into her mouth, nearly choking on the ketchup and her desire to speak up for herself. She coughed, covering her mouth with a napkin. Now she was making a spectacle of herself, beyond the spectacle of obviously being pregnant, her ignorance of cooking, and making a bazillion trips to the bathroom.

Smith pressed his napkin against his lips. Fighting snickers? He deserved a firm shin-kick beneath the table. The only thing keeping her from doing anything rash was not wanting to humiliate Trish, especially after she had to throw out the gravy thanks to Liv's mistake.

"Smith, you want to get the pie?" Trish asked.

"Of course." He strode over to the counter. A minute later he set an amazing-looking golden brown pie in the center of the kitchen table. That Liv had even a tiny part in making this showpiece stunned her.

"Olivia and Smith made the pie." Trish grinned widely as if the duo won an Olympic medal.

Katy scowled in Liv's direction. "After the burned scent in the room, I'm surprised you know how to make homemade pie."

"I don't. Smith made the crust. I chopped apples badly. How this magnificence happened, I have no idea. But it's perfect." She glanced at Smith, catching his smile.

Was he picturing the flour she threw at him? The laughter they shared? Baking with him had been fun. Hearing about his spiritual calling was interesting, too.

A breath caught in her throat. Was she attracted to him? No, of course not. He was with Katy. However, Liv understood why Trish didn't like the hoity-toity woman.

"The first piece of pie is for you, Katy." Smith set a dessert dish with a slice of pie in front of her as if presenting his best to the queen.

She barely glanced at the pie. "Thanks, Smithy."

Blech.

What attracted a man like Smith to this snobbish woman who mostly spoke of fashion, a TV show called Dallas, what Princess Di was doing, and kept patting her puffy hair? All through dinner, Katy picked at her food and criticized Trish's cooking. Then she demeaned Smith's ministry goals and urged him to get a higher paying job. And for some reason, she glared fire darts at Liv.

"Thank you for dinner," Liv spoke to Trish. "I loved the meat-loaf."

"Thank you, hon." She patted Liv's shoulder. "Are you okay?"

"Tired. But what's new?"

"When's the little scamp due?" Katy pulsed her fork toward Liv's belly.

"Two months."

Smith placed a piece of the pie in front of his mom. Then handed one to Liv. Their fingers touched in the exchange. Liv's felt burned. Hopefully, her face didn't show a smidge of fascination with him. If anything, he annoyed her. Any man who chose a woman like Katy for his future wife, especially one he hoped would make a good pastor's wife, had to be a few fuses short of a motherboard.

"Smithy, hurry and eat your dessert." Katy's fork clattered to her plate right next to most of her uneaten pie. "I need you to take me home. I have an early meeting tomorrow."

"Oh. Uh, sure."

Liv tasted a small bite of pie, pleasure and relief rushing through her. "Oh, my goodness. Smith, this is delicious!"

"Yeah?" A big smile crossed his soft-looking lips. "I'm glad our joint efforts meet with your approval." He rocked his eyebrows toward his girlfriend. "What did you think, Katy?"

"I don't like apple pie."

"Oh. Right. I guess I forgot."

An awkward silence filled the room.

"I could eat this all day." Liv took a big bite and exaggerated an "Mmm."

"I just bet you could." Katy stared at Liv's belly. "You might have to go on a diet."

Liv swallowed the bite of pie as if rocks clogged her throat. Then she drank half a glass of water, stopping herself from telling the woman off. Her emotions were hot-wired these days, causing her to fly off the handle and say things she might regret. For Trish's sake, she fought the urge.

"Where's the daddy?" Katy asked pointedly.

"Oh, um—"

"Need more coffee?" Trish asked.

"No, I've had quite enough." Katy gave Smith a pouty look. "Can you drive me home now?"

"Okay." He stuffed more bites into his mouth.

Katy was a piece of work. If Liv never had to be in the same room with her again, she'd be thankful for the rest of her life. What did Smith see in her?

Katy stood, and her hand slowly skidded down the front of Smith's shirt. Staking her claim? Liv understood her loud and clear. And didn't like her for it.

Chapter Eight

A week later, following his tryout sermon at the Thunder Ridge Fellowship, Smith heaved a sigh of relief. His preaching about the Good Samaritan went well. The audience seemed receptive.

But as he sat in front of a panel of three Board members in the church basement, he wondered if his sermon went as well as he thought. None of the men looked pleased. Had he inadvertently said something wrong? Made a doctrinal mistake?

He drank a long swallow of water from his glass. This arrangement of him sitting on one side of the table and the other three men on the opposite side, reminded him of his audition in high school when he tried out for the senior play. He hadn't gotten the part then, either.

Bob Carter, a bald man in his fifties, dressed in a three-piece suit, led the session. His scalp glistened beneath the fluorescent lights as if he'd rubbed oil on his forehead.

The next guy, Arnold Mason, wore a deep frown, but randomly cracked a smile now and then, providing relief to the tension in the room.

The third man, Dennis Vance, barely glanced Smith's way. His pen worked double-time on his notes. He slashed several lines beneath a word, his shoulders curled and tight.

Was there a problem? Did they consider Smith too young and inexperienced? What sections from the Bible would they expect him to explain?

Pastor Tim had groomed him for the pastoral interview process. However, no one could be ready for every scenario.

Bob cleared his throat. "Reverend North, there are some personal things we need to ask you."

"Smith, please. And yes. Ask me anything."

"Why aren't you married?" Bob leaned over the table, staring earnestly at him.

Smith sat speechless for a moment, stymied by the blunt question. "Oh, well, I filled out that section on the interview form." What did his marital status have to do with the job?

"We read what you wrote." Bob eyed him. "I want to hear your explanation."

"Okay. My fiancée and I will be getting married in two weeks."

"So, if we chose you to be our pastor, you would have been married, what, only a couple of weeks? Mere newlyweds?" Bob's lips pursed together.

"Yes. I guess that's right."

"That's troubling to us." Bob glanced at the other two and shook his head. His glum expression said they might as well adjourn this interview now.

"I don't understand. What's the dilemma?" Smith's mouth was desert dry even though he'd nearly finished the glass of water. He swallowed three times.

"Our Board"—Bob swayed his hands toward the other two— "and our congregation are one hundred percent committed to finding a pastor who is a family man. A married man."

"I will be a married man. Plan to have lots of kids," he said lightly.

"Sure, sure. But—" Bob shrugged like he was uncertain how to continue.

"The thing is"—Arnold picked up the dialogue and ran his right hand over his graying hair—"we prefer a husband and wife team. Pastor and pastor's wife. That way we won't run into any unforeseen problems. No impropriety, if you know what I mean." His face flushed.

"Sorry. What are you saying?" Smith's forehead felt furrowed in frown lines. His confusion made his thoughts blur. Were they accusing him of something? "Katy and I will be married. We will be a family. What impropriety are you talking about?"

Bob chuckled. "You're a young man. We've had an older pastor for the last couple of decades. No marital problems. No questionable liaisons."

"Liaisons? I am an honorable man, sir. Ask my pastor."

"Of course. You have excellent references. I've known Pastor Tim for years." Bob cut a smile in Smith's direction, but his pleasant look didn't reach his eyes. "We have a large youth group and an equally active college-aged group. We don't want any difficulties with the young ladies getting the wrong ideas about a bachelor pastor."

"Respectfully, no one is going to get 'wrong ideas' about me." Smith loosened his tie slightly. "There will be no flirtation, no problems like you're implying. I'm crazy about my future wife."

Dennis tapped his pen on the table. "A junior minister in our fellowship was caught in a compromising circumstance with one of our female nursery attendants. We're doing our due diligence to be circumspect and present a unified agreement about this in our fellowship and in our community. Above reproach, as the scripture says."

"I understand." Smith relaxed a little. Their concerns weren't a personal affront on his character. "I get why you're being cautious."

"How did you meet"—Dennis glanced at his notes—"Katy? How long have you been together?"

"We met at work. An insurance company." Smith sighed. "We've been dating for five months."

"Would you say Katy has a strong relationship with the Lord?" Dennis peered at Smith intently.

"Oh, um." The answer caught in his throat.

"Either she is, or she isn't. What would you say, Reverend?"

"Well, I—" For some reason, an answer didn't come quickly to his mind.

"The reason I ask is that her answer on the form is vague."

"Is it?" Smith swallowed hard as he tried recalling Katy's answer.

A few mental snapshots flashed through his thoughts. Things he'd rather not think of here. Katy telling him she didn't want to go to church with him. Her saying she didn't understand his sermon. Her trying to get him to negate his intentions to stay pure until marriage.

Dennis straightened the papers in front of him. "On this form, Katy answered, 'I've attended Smith's church a couple of times. I think he'll make a good pastor. Although, he talks too deeply about spiritual matters for me to understand.'"

Smith cringed. Her innocent-sounding comment hadn't bothered him when he read it before. But in front of these elders, it sounded incriminating. His tie felt like a noose around his neck.

"As far as I can tell"—Dennis stared at the paper—"I can't find where she says anything about believing in Jesus as her Savior. How would you describe her relationship with the Lord?"

Smith had thought this interview would include questions about his life, his walk with the Lord, not his fiancée's.

"She grew up in a Christian home. Has faith-based values." Even he recognized how weak that sounded. Had Katy accepted Jesus for herself? He'd assumed so. "I don't know the details of her faith walk. We've talked about the Bible. We pray over meals. I'm sure there's nothing to worry about."

The three men sent sharp glances in each other's directions.

Smith guzzled his water glass dry.

What if he didn't know Katy well enough? The question twisted something painful in his chest. Anguish or grief. Dread, maybe.

Wait. Of course, he knew her. He loved Katy! She was his first real girlfriend. His first true love. They were getting married in two weeks!

Yet, he couldn't completely ignore her objections to living in a small parsonage. Of her questioning things about the Bible. Didn't his mother ask him about Katy's devotion to the Lord? Pastor Tim might have even mentioned something.

However, he hated that this interview hinged on his fiancée instead of on him.

"So, you're saying you're unsure of her spirituality?" Arnold crossed his arms. "Because if you're not certain about your future wife's salvation, and you've been dating her for five months, you should tell us now."

Smith wiped the back of his hand over his forehead, removing sweat. Man, it was hot in here. "To the best of my knowledge, Katy is a believer. I've never asked her directly about her decision to follow Jesus. I'm sorry I'm not better prepared to answer this question."

"A pretty important question if you ask me." Arnold scratched his nose.

"Me, too." Bob tapped his pencil on the table, joining Dennis's tapping. Each tap created more tension in Smith's neck. A headache pulsed in his temples.

Arnold nudged Dennis's elbow. "You should bring up the other matter."

What else could there be?

"We are a conservative group." Dennis glanced at the ceiling as if pondering something, then faced Smith. "When it comes to the youth of our church, we have high ideals of purity and honor. We want our pastor to share those ideals."

"Sounds admirable."

"I have two teenagers of my own." Dennis puckered his lips in a thoughtful pose. "What would you say to my son if he came to your office and inquired about abstinence until marriage?"

The pencil tapping stopped. All three men stared at Smith.

Was the question about Dennis's son? Or were these men wanting to hear Smith's view, maybe about his experience, in this matter? Pastor Tim warned him there might be inquiries of a personal nature.

"I would speak honorably of marriage and waiting for a Christian spouse. Of remaining pure." Even though Katy was a temptation in this area, he had stayed true to his principles.

After his answer, the men's questions turned to Biblical matters, subjects Smith was more prepared to discuss. However, he felt he had already lost the elders' votes.

Chapter Nine

Liv sat at the kitchen table, searching the classified ads in *The Spokesman-Review* for any job listing sounding the least bit interesting. Who could she use as a reference for a job? She couldn't tell anyone about the high-end position she'd had in her father's company. Or who her employer was. A temp agency might be best, considering her pregnancy. She could explain to the recruiter that she was starting over here and needed to keep her information confidential.

Someone was advertising for a cook. What a joke! A secretary? Far below her paygrade, but she had to start somewhere. A library aide sounded like a possibility.

The phone rang. Liv waited for Trish or Smith to rush into the room and answer. When neither of them did, she picked up the beige receiver. "Hello. North residence."

"This is Bob Carter from the Thunder Ridge Fellowship," a nasally sounding man spoke without greeting her. "Is Reverend North available to talk?"

"Oh, sure, just a sec." Liv set the phone on the table and scurried toward Smith's room.

Three days had passed since he traveled north to preach. He'd been edgy ever since. Would he be happy about this phone call?

She tapped on his door. "Smith, there's a phone call. Some guy from that church."

The door opened swiftly. Wearing a white T-shirt over blue jeans, Smith strode forward. Since she pretty much filled the small space between the bathroom and the two bedroom doors, she backed up against Trish's door.

"Excuse me." His muscled bare arm brushed her belly as he tried to get past her. "I have to—"

"Sorry."

He moved beyond her and ran toward the kitchen. "Hello."

Liv walked slowly into the living room. She'd give him privacy, but other than hiding in the bathroom, she didn't have anywhere in the house out of listening range.

"You want to see both of us?" Smith asked in a high, nervous-sounding voice. "I'll find out if ... what I mean is ... Katy and I will be glad to meet with you." Another pause. "Yes. Thank you for the call. I'm excited to continue with the interview process. God bless you, also."

Smith strode into the living room, his fingers raking through his black hair. Suddenly, he grinned. Liv felt the wonder of his smile all the way to her toes. The sparkle in his eyes was like stars dancing in the midnight sky.

"Good news?"

"The best." He thrust his hands toward the ceiling. "Thank You, God!"

Liv grinned at his exuberance.

Trish entered the living room from her bedroom, tugging the belt tighter around her pink bathrobe. "What is it, Smith?"

He rushed over and hugged her. Liv had a crazy, unfounded wish that his strong arms encircled her, too.

"Bob Carter, the lead elder at the Thunder Ridge Fellowship, wants to speak with Katy and me. Take the interview to the next level."

"Great news! Congratulations, Son." Trish hugged him. "This is what you've been waiting for. What you've been praying about."

"It is. Still more hoops to jump through, but we're moving forward." Smith crossed his arms over the middle of his T-shirt and glanced at Liv, perhaps realizing he didn't have a regular shirt on.

Yeah, she noticed. She stared at the dark hairs beneath his neck that matched those on his head.

"I'll have to ask if Katy's willing to go with me and be questioned." His voice turned somber.

"You doubt she'll go with you?" Trish asked.

Smith took a deep breath, exhaling slowly. "When the Board questioned me, they had concerns about her."

"No wonder." Oops. Did Liv say that aloud? "I'll just—" She rocked her thumb toward the kitchen and scurried to the sink. Water. She needed a glass of cold water.

Running the faucet hard, filling her glass, and guzzling slowly covered the sound of their voices coming from the living room.

So, the Board didn't take Katy at face value, huh? In Liv's book, the overly made-up female wouldn't pass for pastor's wife material. Didn't a candidate have to at least be nice?

But if Smith wanted to marry a prickly woman like her, let him. Liv wouldn't say a word.

Chapter Ten

Smith sat across from Katy in their favorite diner, eating lunch. The joint wasn't fancy, but they made great burgers and fries. The service was fast, which was a bonus.

"So, what's this about?" Katy squinted at him. "Did you get the Sandpoint gig?"

He clenched his jaw at her reference to his ministry as a gig. "Not yet." Sighing, he reached across the table and clasped her soft hand, needing contact between them. "The Board would like to talk with both of us."

"What? Why?" She jerked her hand away from his. "I'm not speaking to them. They're not hiring me!"

"But, Katy, you must talk to them."

"Must? Are you kidding me? No one tells me what I must do, including you." She glared at him. "This church stuff is yours, Smith. Got it?"

"That's not the way it works." He swallowed a wad of saliva alongside his bucket of disappointment. "We'll be married. You and me doing ministry together."

"Doing ministry? Do you hear yourself?" An unexpected smile crossed her lips. "A team in other ways, sure." The toe of her shoe slid up his shin.

He gulped and moved his legs out of her reach.

"Don't imagine for one second I'd sit in front of some old fogies prying into my private affairs." She slapped the table. "If you think I'm not good enough for you, if you can't accept me as I am, then we'd better reconsider this marriage now!"

"Katy—" The air in his lungs whooshed out. Surely, she wasn't backing out of their engagement. "Please, be reasonable. It's not a big ask for us to have a chat with these guys. What would it hurt?"

Her glare could set his hair on fire.

She guzzled her Coke, clearly agitated.

"I'm sorry if talking to the church Board makes you uncomfortable. But it's important. Please go with me?"

"No." She set her glass firmly against the tabletop. "It's your decision to pastor in some northern hick town. I want to continue living in Spokane. Staying in my own apartment."

"What? You don't plan to move with me even after we're married?" They'd never discussed such a preposterous idea. He'd always assumed she would move to the parsonage with him.

"Would that be so bad?" she asked in a whiny voice. "We could live here during the week. You could live in the parsonage on the weekends. Sometimes I'd tag along to church with you. You'd have the best of both worlds."

Lightning striking his chest wouldn't have surprised him as much as her suggestion. She didn't plan to live in the parsonage with him? All the things others—Mom, Pastor Tim, and the church elders— had said to him about her crashed through his thoughts like a flash flood. Katy really wasn't supportive of his calling, his vocation, was she? How had he been so blind to that?

"Living separately after we're married would never work." He thrust out his hands, bumping his glass and spilling his water. Leaping up, he barely missed getting a lapful.

Katy shrieked and stood, the lower part of her sweater dress soaked. "Smith, how could you?" As if he'd done it on purpose, she hurled an expletive at him, then stormed out of the restaurant.

Smith groaned. Between him and the waitress who scurried over with a towel, they cleaned up the table.

His appetite all but gone, he took a couple of bites of his lunch, not even tasting the burger and fries.

He'd been so enraptured with Katy. Infatuated with their relationship and his dreams for their future together. How had he overlooked such a disparity between their personalities and their life's goals?

Chapter Eleven

Smith had always been able to talk with Pastor Tim about anything. But now, as he sat in the pastor's office, he hated opening up to him about his deteriorating relationship with Katy.

"I don't know what to do. Everything within me is fighting against doing what is probably the right thing to do." Smith bit his lip, stopping himself from giving in to the emotional terrors rushing through him. "I've wanted this pastoral position forever. But I love her."

"I'm sorry for what you're going through." Pastor Tim cleared his throat. "Sorry to bring this up, but I have expressed concerns about Katy before. You weren't receptive to my warnings."

Smith tensed, not wanting to hear anything said against the woman he loved.

"I don't mean to sound insensitive or judgmental. But discovering the truth about her plans before you marry her is far better than afterward, don't you think?"

How could anything about this be better? Smith let out a long sigh. Nothing felt right about Katy not wanting to be a pastor's wife. Not wanting to give herself fully to their marriage. Why was God allowing this anguish to happen to him? He'd thought Katy was part of God's plan for his life.

What if he lost this chance to pastor because of his fiancée? Why was the Board so troubled about his upcoming marriage in the first place?

"What are you going to do?" Pastor Tim stroked his thin mustache.

"I don't know."

"You want me to call Bob Carter?"

Why? So the two men could discuss his failed marriage before it even started? He still had to talk with Katy. They hadn't formally ended their engagement. Would she yell curse words at him as she did at the restaurant? Would she weep and beg him to relent and do things her way? What about all the wedding plans?

"No, I'll take care of it myself." Smith wiped the back of his hand across his mouth, wiping away an acidic taste. He might be sick. He should go home and bury his head under a pillow for a month. Not see Katy. Not talk to the Board. Not speak with anyone.

"I'm going to ask you a personal question." Pastor Tim eyed Smith. "How far did things go between you and Katy? Physically, that is?"

Smith coughed. He had the urge to exit the pastor's office without answering. Did Pastor Tim suspect he went too far? He'd vowed he wouldn't let that happen. Still, his face flamed hot over the remembrance of some of their kissing.

"We didn't cross that line."

"Good." Yet the pastor stared at Smith like he suspected there was more he wasn't saying. "Again, I'm sorry this happened. Although—"

Smith hated the segue.

"Everything happens for a reason. You'll make a better pastor, a more compassionate person, because of the things you're going through."

"Even in this?" Smith scoffed, not guarding the derision in his tone. "Losing my future wife and the church I hoped for in one fell swoop?

"Yes. I'm sorry. Even in this."

The words burned through him with agonizing pain in his spirit. "I should go." Smith stood.

"First, let's pray." Standing and settling his hands on Smith's shoulders as he'd done so many times before, Pastor Tim prayed, earnestly asking for God's will to be done. For Smith to find healing and peace.

Yet, as Smith strode to his car, he chewed on the idea of God's will even being what he wanted right this minute. If it meant giving up Katy, did he want to pursue His will at any cost? As soon as the thought crossed his mind, he regretted it. He was supposed to want God's will above his own. Doubly so as a pastor. And yet, he still struggled.

The idea of giving up Katy was just too horrific.

Chapter Twelve

Smith stood outside Katy's apartment, knocking on her door for the second set of raps. The wind and rain howled around him. The gray miserable day matched his spirits. He knocked again.

"Katy, it's me. Smith. We have to talk."

Her Impala was parked in the street below, so she was home. She probably didn't want to talk with him. He didn't want to have this conversation, either. But their breakup had to be faced.

The door opened slightly. Katy peered out at him with red-rimmed, black-mascara smudged eyes. Her hair looked like a ratty mess.

"Hi," he said hoarsely. "Can I come in?"

He hadn't entered her apartment in two months. The physical attraction between them was too strong for him to trust himself to keep his distance from her. Today was different. Unless her heart changed, they had to end things.

She opened the door a little more.

Finding her looking as miserable as he felt, he moaned. "Oh, Katy."

She fell into his arms, sobbing, and he held her. He immediately smelled a tangy scent about her. What had she been eating?

A neighbor opened the next door and stuck his head out, glaring at Smith like he'd caused this emotional outburst. Smith nodded once at the elderly man, trying to reassure him everything was okay. Then he led Katy into her darkened living room and shut the door.

"I'm sorry, Smithy." She hiccupped. "I just can't live that kind of life."

Nearly breaking under the weight of what he had to do, he clasped her hand and drew her to the couch. She tossed a couple of magazines from the cushions onto the floor and toed something around the edge of the couch before they sat down.

"Did you mean it about us not moving to Thunder Ridge together? About you staying here?"

"I love you. But I don't see myself living in a dingy house, having your babies, stuck in Thunder Ridge for the rest of my life! Being a pastor's wife?" She patted her hair and laughed harshly. "Can you honestly see me filling those shoes?"

"I can't give it up." The intense longing in his heart to be a pastor, to reach people with the Gospel, couldn't be ignored. A part of his spirit would die if he did.

"Right. Because the church comes first."

"Not the church." He swallowed. "God. His voice in my heart."

"So, He's first. Then the church. Your someday kids. And somewhere down the line, me?" She rubbed her hands beneath her eyes. "I want to be your Number One, Smithy!"

She obviously didn't understand.

"Jesus is first in my life. But then my devotion would be to you, my wife."

She stared hard at him. "I don't like being second best." In jerky movements, she picked up the magazines she set down earlier and tossed them onto the coffee table. Plunk, plunk, plunk.

"You wouldn't be second best." Smith linked his fingers around his knee, holding them together tightly, holding himself together tightly. He'd never broken up with a woman before. The pain pinching every nerve in his body felt torturous. "If we both love God, our devotion to Him would be a natural thing between us. A beautiful thing."

"I don't understand. Don't give me your holier-than-thou look, either."

"I'm not trying to." He controlled his facial features, hoping she recognized the sincerity in his heart. Even if they didn't get back together, he cared about her eternal soul. "Have you ever asked Jesus into your life?"

"Probably. I pray sometimes."

"When we ask Him to be Lord of our lives, something wonderful happens in our heart." Smith focused on breathing in and out. On not breaking down weeping. "We long for Him. Sort of how we long for food."

"How I long for you," she whispered, running her palm over his arm, then tucking her slim fingers into the hollow between his palms.

"Like that, only spiritually. When I'm focused on Him, I want Him more than anything."

"More than me?" She huffed and pulled her hands away.

"It's just different."

"So, you're really breaking up with me?" Her face crumpled. "I could die." She dove into his arms, wrapping her arms around him like an octopus. Her hands roamed over his back, finding their way up his shirt, nestling against his skin beneath his T-shirt.

"Hey." He stood quickly.

"Come on, Smithy. I know what will make everything better between us. What's been missing in our relationship." She stood next to him and smoothed her palms over his jacket. "Let go of your archaic ideas this once. Spend the night with me, okay?" She kissed him, teasing his lips.

He tasted alcohol on her breath. He set her back from him. "No. That's not going to happen."

"I don't want to lose you. Please, Smithy," she said in a pleading voice. "Why can't we get married and live here in Spokane?"

"As a pastor, as a man, I need my wife to be by my side."

"I love you. You love me. Why should we let this pastoral stuff get in the way of our happiness?"

Her words tore a bigger hole in his heart.

"We can still get married," she said insistently. "Live here. You and me, together, finally."

"No, I couldn't." He sucked in a ragged breath. "And without a wife, they won't accept me for the position."

"That's the only reason you wanted to marry me, wasn't it?" she asked in a shrill tone.

"No, of course not."

But not marrying her would solidify the church Board's decision.

How did someone break up with the person they previously thought they'd spend their life with? "Due to this conflict of interest—"

"Isn't there a compromise?" Her wobbling lips dug at his heart.

Then she was in his arms, clinging to him, kissing his neck, tears running down her face, dripping on his shirt. He held her to him, kissing the side of her head, mourning the loss of what could have been, but now would never be.

Realizing how quickly this embrace could get out of hand, he broke away and strode to the door. "This is goodbye, Katy. Our engagement is off."

"I'll call my family. Notify the florist. You can talk to the preacher. Tell your guests." She bent over and picked up a liquor bottle from the floor. Unscrewing the top, she took a long guzzle. "Goodbye, Smithy."

Chapter Thirteen

Liv returned after her appointment at the temp agency feeling more upbeat than she'd felt in a while. Three positions were available, any of which she could start work at immediately. Then she'd get a cash flow going for her and Little Mister before her delivery date. After he was born, she'd have a foot in the door with the agency so she could pick up more work.

When she entered Trish's house, planning to plop down on the couch and put her feet up, the home seemed quiet for four o'clock in the afternoon. An eerie sound reached her. Moaning? Someone praying?

Both bedroom doors were closed. All the house lights were off. No scents of dinner preparations filled the room. What was going on?

She crossed the room to the couch and lowered herself to her side and closed her eyes. This was what she needed—a few minutes of relaxation.

A click of a door handle awakened her. The room was darker. She peeked an eye open.

Smith shuffled through in his white T-shirt and Yankees pj's. Was he sick? It seemed weird for him to be in his pajamas at five o'clock!

Liv pushed up from the cushions and ran her hands over her long hair, taming her wild look. "What's going on?"

Smith paused. "Just getting some tea." He continued into the kitchen.

Curious, she stood, swaying slightly by the imbalance caused by her bulk, and strode into the kitchen. "Everything all right?" She stood by the table, facing Smith's back, noticing his broad, slumped shoulders. "Is Trish okay?"

"She's fine." His tone sounded muffled like he had a cold. He took the tea kettle off the stove and poured hot water into a cup. "Want some?" He turned to her. His eyes were red, and his face looked blotchy like he'd been bawling his eyes out. Did someone die?

"Yes, please." She lowered herself to a chair at the table. "Are you okay?"

Smith shrugged and finished fixing the tea.

"Honey?"

Um. What did he call her?

"Honey. In your tea?"

"Oh, right." She swallowed a dry lump in her throat. "Yes, thanks."

Moments later, he set a steaming cup of what smelled like peppermint herbal tea in front of her.

"Thanks."

Their gazes met, held.

"If you want to talk"—she was probably stepping in where she didn't belong—"I'm a good listener, or so I've been told."

He took a slow sip of his tea. "Not much to say. How does a fairly intelligent guy face the end of the world as he knew it?"

"I know how bad it feels for the world to crash at your feet. Been there, done that."

Her pregnancy. Nick abandoning her. Dad kicking her out. Mom sipping her martini, watching.

Leaning his back against the sink, Smith continued drinking his tea. She did the same from her seat, stealing glances at him.

"Thanks for the hot drink. It tastes good."

"Sure." His long sigh made him sound weary of life.

"I got a job today." Maybe bringing up a normal discussion might lighten the mood.

"Great." He sounded about as happy as if a special dog got hit by a car.

"I have my pick of three jobs. I'll let them know tomorrow."

"Lucky you."

His uncaring tone was unlike him.

"Not so lucky, I'm afraid."

"I don't mean to be rude." He groaned and dropped into the seat beside her, raking his fingers through his dark hair. "It's been a lousy day."

"No need to apologize." Although she appreciated his candor.

"Katy and I broke up. The wedding's off."

"Oh, no. I'm so sorry." She reached out and patted his hand. Even if she didn't like Katy, she wouldn't wish such a loss on him.

"Thanks." He moved his hand away and stroked his forehead.

She gulped, remembering how desolate she felt after Nick told her he wouldn't be divorcing his wife after all. That he wouldn't be there for Liv during their child's birth. Sadness filled her now for Smith. Weren't he and Katy supposed to get married in two weeks?

"Anything I can do? Cancel invitations? Make dinner?"

He gave her a wry look. "What do you know how to cook?"

"Toast and scrambled eggs." She thought of something. "I'd like to learn how to make an omelet. Will you teach me?"

"Seriously? I've had the worst day of my life and you want to add to it by cooking?"

"When you put it that way, it sounds bad. But I am famished."

She'd learned from her own dark times that sitting around moping didn't help. Nor did trying to bury the pain so deep inside of her she'd never be able to sort it out. Doing something productive was a more powerful remedy than crying and bemoaning her life. Or, in this case, Smith's life.

Liv pushed away from the table and shuffled over to the refrigerator, forcing herself not to waddle. Fortunately, Trish had stocked the egg tray. "What's good for omelets?"

"Cheese." He rubbed his forehead again. "Milk." Another sigh. "Onions and vegetables."

Digging through the fridge, she found a piece of leftover chicken. That could work. She grabbed the chicken, cheese, green onions, and veggies and hauled all of them to the counter. Then she dug out a loaf of white bread.

"How about if I do the prep work, chopping, and fixing the toast? And you do the cooking?"

She met his tortured expression. He looked as smash-faced as she felt the day she met Trish.

"I'm not the best cook, so would you mind helping?"

"I suppose I could," he said in a grudging tone.

"Good." Letting his attitude slide, she found a couple of bowls. One for the veggies. The other one to mix eggs in. "What else?"

"A skillet."

"Right." She dug around in the cupboards without finding the pan. "Where is it?" Swiveling back to Smith, who still sat at the table, she saw his finger extended toward the drawer beneath the oven. She opened it and withdrew a cast iron pan. Smith stayed rooted to his chair.

"What's next, Expert Chef?"

Her teasing didn't get even a slight lifting of his lips.

"Chop everything." He rubbed his hand over his chest like it hurt.

Tenderness rushed through her for him, and she fought her own tears. A mental image of her wrapping her arms around him and letting the big oaf cry on her shoulder flashed through her thoughts. How would she feel with her arms wrapped around his broad chest, and experiencing the warmth that might emanate from his body to hers? Her face flushed. Silly hormones. Good thing he didn't know what she was thinking.

She needed a knife. Rummaging through the drawer below the silverware drawer, she found a knife and preoccupied herself with chopping stuff and throwing it all into a bowl together.

Ten minutes later, Smith stood beside her, gawking at the chopped veggies and meat as if he'd never seen such a disaster before.

"What?"

"The pieces need to be smaller."

"Why?" Because his way was the only way? "Looks fine to me."

"An omelet is thin," he said indulgently as if explaining water to a five-year-old. "The veggies and meat should be thinly sliced. Want me to show you?"

"Not really." What was the big deal about the way she chopped everything?

He tipped his head at her, and she saw the pain still hovering in his eyes.

"Okay. Fine. We'll do it your way, this time."

"My way?"

"Yes, oh Mighty One."

He smirked. "My mom always said chop small enough to make chewing easier."

He washed his hands, then demonstrated how to hold the chunk of broccoli with the tips of his fingers and cut it smaller. She fought the urge to say something sarcastic. *You might think you're smarter than everyone on the planet, but I have a degree in computer science!*

His bare arm brushed hers a couple of times. A butterfly sensation danced up her shoulder and neck, sharpening her awareness of him. She subdued any attraction. He was Trish's son. A man who just experienced a bad breakup. He felt nothing for her. Just two hurt souls chopping veggies.

They worked silently until they had a mound of chicken and vegetables.

Smith searched through a few cupboards. "Here it is." He yanked out a metal grater. "Try this for the cheese." He set the shiny tool in front of her.

She stared at the gadget as if gawking at a sea monster. "What's this for?"

"Do I have to show you how to do everything?"

"Not everything." She smiled before realizing her words might seem flirty.

His chuckle sounded forced. "I'm sure you have proficient skills in the office."

"I can type seventy words per minute."

"Impressive." Grabbing a chunk of cheese and the grater, he showed her how to use the tool. "Keep your fingers out of the way. Those metal edges are like little daggers."

"Yes, sir."

He gave her a sardonic look. Then cracked some eggs. He heated up the skillet while Liv grated the cheese. She scraped her fingers only twice.

"What do we have going on in here?" Eyes red-rimmed, Trish shuffled into the room in her bathrobe and slippers. Her wet hair looked like she just stepped out of the shower.

"We're attempting to make dinner." Liv held up the grater.

"Some are attempting. Some are doing." Smith eyed her with a frown.

"Smith's teaching me how to make omelets. But he's an ogre as a teacher."

"Hey, now."

Trish sniffed like she was near tears.

Liv wished she had a magical fix to make Smith and Trish feel better. She tried to remember what gave her emotional relief. Nothing, really. Except for Trish's kindness. The day she invited Liv to stay with her and even have her baby here, new life began flowing into her veins.

Silently, the three of them sat around the small kitchen table for their meal. When Trish said grace, she included a plea for their hearts to heal. And for God to touch Katy's heart.

Questions churned in Liv's mind. Why would Katy wait until so close to the wedding to end things with Smith? What had been the breaking point between them?

Smith asked Trish to help him call their church friends about the canceled event. Trish somberly agreed.

When they finished eating, Liv volunteered to wash the dishes. Neither Smith nor Trish argued. Both slipped out of the room quietly, and she heard their bedroom doors click shut.

The house was ominously quiet. At least she knew how to wash and dry dishes now. She wished she knew more about prayer. Then she'd ask God to work a miracle in Smith's life.

Maybe not to bring Katy back. But to help him get over the pain of losing her.

Chapter Fourteen

A week after his breakup with Katy, Smith sat down in front of the three elders in the basement of the Thunder Ridge Fellowship and nervously cleared his throat. Since it was mid-week, none of the men were dressed in their Sunday best like last time. Although Dennis wore a tie as if he came here from work. What did he do? Oh, right. A banker.

"We were surprised to get your request for a meeting by yourself." Bob eyed Smith. "You were supposed to bring Katy in for us to speak with her."

"I know. I'm sorry."

The three men leaned forward, arms crossed over the table, matching frowns on their faces.

Smith had endured seven days of misery and contemplation. He wasn't anywhere closer to feeling resolution about giving up the woman he loved than a week ago. A few times in the last couple of days, he almost returned to Katy's house and begged her to take him back.

"Gentlemen, I want to thank you for taking time out of your busy schedules to talk with me." Another throat clearing. "Thank you for the opportunity to speak in your church and to be considered as a candidate for your pastor. That role is the highest calling in my book, something I've looked forward to for a long time."

"We're glad you feel that way." Arnold's stern expression softened. "It can't be easy to sit in front of a congregation, and a Board like this, and put yourself out there for everyone's criticism."

Smith nodded. "It's been an honor. Thank you, gentleman, for the opportunity."

"What's this about?" Dennis grabbed his pen and tapped it on a pad of paper. "Why didn't your fiancée come with you?"

"Katy—" He didn't want to dishonor her, yet a compelling urge to speak the truth came over him. "You were right in your concerns about my … about her not understanding spiritual things. I was blind to it. Not asking her questions about her faith early in our relationship is something I regret."

"Oh?" Dennis met the gazes of the other two men. "What are you saying?"

"She and I are no longer a couple." He blinked fast. "We aren't getting married. It came down to her unwillingness to move here with me if I was chosen for the pastoral position."

"Oh, dear." Arnold cast a compassionate look Smith's way. "How are you holding up, my friend?"

"Not great. But the Lord is faithful."

"Yes, He is." Arnold nodded.

If Smith wasn't trusting God to help him get through this crushing agony, he feared he'd die from grief. An avalanche of doubts had been churning through him, too. He'd been certain God provided him the perfect wife in Katy. How had he been so wrong?

"This changes the whole shooting match." Bob shrugged. "You could have told us this on the phone and saved yourself the trouble of driving up here."

"Yes, I could have." Smith sat up a little taller. "However, I wanted the chance to face you and thank you." There was more he wanted to say, too. Would they listen if he poured his heart out?

"We're sorry things didn't work out differently." Dennis shuffled his shoulders. "I guess this concludes our interview process with you."

"That's right," Bob added. "We'll focus on the next candidate."

"Such a shame." Arnold made a sucking sound through his front teeth.

Bob shoved away from the table. Standing, he stuck his hand out toward Smith. "We wish you the best."

Smith shook the man's hand but remained seated. "Could I trouble you for a few more minutes of your time?" The weight on his chest felt so heavy. He drove an hour and a half for the chance to talk to them. To explain.

Bob glanced at his gold watch. Then, sighing, he dropped back onto his chair. "What is it?"

Smith drew in a long breath. "Ever since I was eight, I've wanted to be a pastor. I've had a calling on my life and have wanted to serve the Lord in ministry."

"Yet you asked a woman to marry you who didn't have a desire to serve alongside you?" Bob shook his head. "Didn't you confess to being blind to her lack of faith?"

"True." Feeling their gazes on him, their possible judgment, he wanted to wilt into the floor. But he needed to say what he came to say. "I've felt a strong urgency to pray for Sandpoint and Thunder Ridge. I believed God was leading me here to serve." He swayed out his hands. "You men have expressed a desire for a pastor who is a family man, something I still hope to be in the future. Would you consider giving me another chance?"

"We are adamant our pastor must be married," Dennis said. "Non-negotiable."

"What if, perchance, it's God's will for me to be here?" He was taking a risk by being bold, but he had to ask the question, or it would plague him in the coming months.

"Then I'd say He would have provided a wife for you." Dennis nodded decisively. "He's aware of our determination to remain true to our bylaws stating a pastor here must be married."

"That's right," Bob said. "I agree with Dennis."

"All right. I understand." Smith heaved a sigh. Pushing his chair back, he stood. "I won't take up any more of your time."

Each of the men shook his hand, but Arnold clapped him on the back too.

"It's a real shame, brother. I'm sorry for your loss."

"Thank you."

Outside the building, Smith trudged to his car, his shoulders stooped. He'd thought his life as a pastor would start here. Why had he felt led to pray for this area? Would another invitation come for him to try out somewhere else?

"Smith!"

He turned toward the voice.

"I just had an idea." Arnold caught up to him, huffing from the run. "This is abrupt. Sorry."

"What is it?"

"I have an unmarried sister." One of his eyebrows raised.

Smith tensed. People had tried to set him up before. He hated the idea of blind dates.

"She's sincere in her faith. Volunteers in a soup kitchen. Even leads the ladies' ministries here at the church. If you were interested in meeting her, I could arrange it." He rocked his thumb toward the church building. "I'd talk with the other two and tell them what was going on. Give you a couple of weeks to … find out if you and Amaryllis are compatible."

"Compatible?" Smith coughed. His heart hurt too much to meet any other woman when he still loved Katy.

"Isn't it worth a try? She isn't ugly." Arnold chuckled.

"It's not that. It's too soon after my breakup."

"Oh, right."

Smith tucked his hands in his coat pockets and stared at the grass.

"But if you married Amaryllis, you'd have my vote for becoming our pastor." Arnold grinned. "As part of my family, I'd have to stick up for you, right?" He clapped Smith on the back.

Smith couldn't believe Arnold was suggesting he marry his sister outside of love. "Are you implying I marry her like an arranged marriage?"

"Mmm … yeah. Something like that." Arnold rubbed his hands together. "Go on a date. See if there's chemistry. What would be the harm in exploring the possibility of you two tolerating each other?" He chuckled.

A lump of dryness in Smith's throat felt like it would choke him. What would be the harm? Even speaking of such a deception felt harmful.

"What do you say?"

"Um, well, I'll pray about it."

"Good. Good. That's a start." Arnold shook his hand fervently. "I'll call you."

"Sure. Thanks."

Marry Arnold's sister for a good cause? What was Smith doing even saying he'd pray about it? He couldn't go through with such a bizarre offer, could he?

Chapter Fifteen

By the time Liv walked to Trish's house from work, her feet were killing her. As soon as she went inside, she plopped onto the couch and groaned. A nap sounded delightful.

Curling up on her side, she adjusted her belly so Little Mister could wiggle to his heart's content and not bother her back. Going to work had been harder than she imagined. Typing was simple, but she had to walk around the three-story facility without the benefit of an elevator.

She must have fallen asleep quickly. An afghan settling over her body awakened her. Opening her eyes slightly, she met Smith's gaze.

"Hi," he said in his gravelly voice.

"Hi, yourself." She closed her eyes again.

It was nice of him to cover her, to care about her. For a week now, he'd been distant, brooding, and sullen. Even Trish commented on it—"Smith isn't himself right now." But who could blame him? Liv remembered the awful depression she went through after breaking up with Nick. Her heart ached for Smith. But his sparkling gaze when he covered her made her smile. He looked happier.

Later, wonderful scents of garlic and chicken reached her. The dim light in the living room let her know she slept longer than she meant to.

"Oh, good, you're awake." Trish stood in the doorway to the kitchen. "Dinner's ready. We already said grace. Are you hungry?"

"Famished."

"When you're ready, come on in."

After using the bathroom, Liv strode into the kitchen. "It smells amazing in here." She sat down, ogling the baked chicken. "It looks like a picture in one of those food magazines."

"Tastes great too. Good job, Mom." Smith lifted a chunk of potato on his fork.

Liv quickly filled her plate.

"So, how did the meeting with the elders go?" Trish set down her fork. "I hope you don't mind my asking. I've been praying about it all afternoon."

"As good as can be expected." Smith grimaced. "They're still determined their pastor must have a wife."

"I'm sorry, Son."

"Yeah, me too."

Other than the clink of forks against ceramic plates, silence permeated the room. If Liv weren't present, would Smith confide in Trish more about his meeting?

"What's the big deal about being married anyway?" she finally asked.

Smith and Trish stared at her.

"Oh, sorry." Too invasive?

Smith sighed. "They had a bad experience with a single assistant pastor having an affair with someone in the church."

"Couldn't that happen with a married man? I mean, it has happened, right?"

"Sure. Marriage isn't a cure-all."

"That's for sure." Her parents' marriage had been far from ideal. Her father's work and business trips kept him away much of the time. Her mom's social schedule and drinking habits kept her equally involved in things away from their supposedly happy home.

Then there was Nick and his cheating.

Smith took a long swallow from his glass of water. "One of the guys, Arnold, has a solution for my unmarried status." He rolled his eyes.

"What's that?" Trish asked.

"He wants to set me up with his sister."

"What?" Liv dropped her fork. "Sorry." But that was the craziest idea she ever heard. Smith just broke up with Katy.

"Are you ready for dating again?" Trish twisted her napkin.

"No. It wouldn't be—" His gaze met Liv's. "It wouldn't be that kind of arrangement."

"Arrangement?" She coughed out.

Smith eyed her like she stepped over the line by commenting.

"Sorry." She bit into her chicken, filling her mouth so she wouldn't say anything else.

"Have you met her?" Trish's voice rose slightly.

"Not yet." Smith strummed his fork tines through his potatoes and gravy. "I'm going to give it a try."

Trish's jaw dropped. "Smith."

Liv's heart pounded ferociously. She hadn't known Smith and Trish long, but she already felt protective toward them, almost like family, or friends, at least. Smith marrying some woman and having an "arrangement" with her so he could become a pastor sounded archaic and ridiculous.

"I can't believe you'd consider such a thing," Trish said.

"Me either," Liv muttered under her breath.

Smith threw her a glare. "It's not ideal." His deep sigh sounded like it came from so far inside him that there couldn't be any breath left. "I thought I'd meet her and find out—" He shrugged.

"If there's compatibility?" Trish finished.

"Yes."

"What about chemistry? Fireworks?" Liv spit out rapid-fire.

"That already got me into trouble."

"Yeah, me too." Liv played with the peas on her plate. "Even so, I wouldn't marry someone without being in love with him."

Smith gazed at her for several seconds.

Her mouth went dry. She was not attracted to Smith North. He was outside of her league spiritually. She was outside of his league in business and worldly things.

"This will be a matter of daily, hourly, prayer for me." Trish buttered a biscuit.

"Thanks, Mom."

The rest of the meal was finished in near-silence, except for Trish asking Liv about her new job. Would Smith seriously consider marrying a woman he didn't love to appease a church Board?

Chapter Sixteen

All the way from Spokane to Sandpoint, Smith's thoughts churned. Was he about to make another terrible decision? He still loved Katy. His desire to be with her hadn't ebbed. Was there any chance her heart had warmed to the idea of them getting back together? Maybe admitting she was wrong about joining him in Thunder Ridge? He groaned. If he saw her again, even to ask, he'd want to kiss her and forget all the reasons he couldn't be with her.

He sighed as he drove past the "Welcome to Sandpoint" sign. If things had worked out with Katy, he'd feel more welcome in this town and the community of Thunder Ridge to the north.

Katy.

For ten days the haunting ache hit him at the most unexpected times. At first, it was simply trying to get through the next minute, breathing in and out. Then the next hour. Finally, his melancholy shifted to how to fill his days productively.

Seeing her from a distance at work had been pure torture. Yesterday, he turned in his resignation letter. He couldn't keep putting himself through the agony of possibly crossing paths with her.

But this step of meeting another woman? That felt traitorous. The betrayal in his own heart hurt. Pulling over into a parking lot at an abandoned-looking building, he rested his forehead against his hands clinging to the steering wheel. *What are you doing?*

Lifting his head, he stared at the graffiti written on the brick wall in front of him. "Get a life." "John and Tonya forever." "Love stinks." He nodded at the last one. Sighed.

Love had been a beautiful thing. Blindingly beautiful. Even when Pastor Tim called on him a couple of days ago, telling him to hold his head up, and reminding him God was in charge, Smith hadn't felt any inspiration in the man's challenge.

He'd observed others in this stage. Watched movies about people drinking and wallowing in their sorrows. Some ate a quart of ice cream in one sitting. But he never experienced the awful reality himself. Until now.

Pastor Tim said what didn't crush him would give him insight into the hearts and souls of others in pain. He'd have better compassion for his fellowman. But what if it did crush him?

He glanced at his wristwatch. If he didn't drive to the restaurant now, he'd be late.

Lord, I want Your will. But couldn't Your will for my life have included Katy?

Smith sucked in a long needy breath. Amaryllis might already be at their meeting place. As lousy as he felt, she didn't deserve for him to not show up.

At the restaurant on the east side of town, Smith entered the family-style establishment. As soon as he reached the dining area, a woman with dark hair finger waved at him. Must be her.

He took a deep breath and forced his mouth into a scant smile. "I'm, uh, Smith."

"Nice to meet you 'Uh Smith.'" She giggled and made a snorting sound. "I'm Amaryllis, Arnold's sister."

They shook hands and Smith sat down across from her.

"I'm so nervous." Her hand bumped her water glass, nearly knocking it over.

"Me too. This is highly irregular."

"I don't know what my brother was thinking."

Smith's chuckle sounded mechanical even to his own ears. "If you don't want to do this—"

"We're both here, aren't we? I'm hungry." She laughed and covered her mouth. "Might as well get lunch out of our meeting, huh?"

"Might as well." Some of his tension eased.

Looking over the menu, he stole a couple of glances at Amaryllis. Her dark eyes—gray or deep blue—sparkled as she perused her menu. She seemed friendly enough. Pretty, too. She acted nervous, but who could blame her?

Maybe he and Amaryllis could have a satisfying life together, serving the Lord in His harvest field, getting along in mutual companionship. There didn't have to be romance. No fireworks, as Liv mentioned. All Smith had to do was befriend this woman, right? Make sure they were well-suited. Then he'd be considered for the pastorate again. But something about this felt wrong.

He swallowed hard.

Eventually, the waitress took their orders. Amaryllis said she was a secretary for a local law firm. She and Arnold grew up in Sandpoint, so this area was home.

"Arnold told me I should tell you I've always wanted to be a pastor's wife." She tittered and her face hued dark pink. "I thought that was too bold. Insensitive. I mean, you and I would never work, would we? Look at us. We don't"—she shrugged—"match, right?"

Heat flamed up Smith's face. "Oh, well, I don't—"

"Never mind. But if I never see you again, Arnold would blame me for not being honest with you." She fluffed her napkin in her lap. "I'm sure you're a nice man, Smith." She said his name like "Smit." "A handsome man who could have your pick of a dozen women. Why don't you hold a contest and pick the lucky winner?" She laughed again, her snort getting louder. "Why choose someone like me?"

Did she expect him to answer that question? He shrugged evasively.

"I am sorry about your fiancée. The canceled wedding and all."

"Thank you."

He could tell Amaryllis was a kind, honest person. Those positive traits would make a great start for a relationship and a fine quality in a pastor's wife.

Was he really considering marrying a woman he didn't love? With his feelings as they were for Katy, how could he? With his desire to be a pastor in Thunder Ridge, how could he not?

Their food arrived and talking with Amaryllis was easier than he thought it would be. Another plus for a possible lifelong friendship between them. She told him about her job and what led to her staying in Sandpoint instead of moving to Spokane or Coeur d'Alene like many of her friends had done.

Even though they both talked about their lives, even chuckling over some humorous anecdotes, Smith drove back to Spokane with a heavy heart. While he and Amaryllis might be able to make a go of a long-term relationship, not once throughout the entire lunch had he felt the tiniest romantic spark. Fireworks? Not even close. Could he live with a wife without that?

Chapter Seventeen

Liv opened the front door and shuffled toward the couch in the semi-darkness, needing to get off her feet. Hearing sniffling, she paused. "Trish?"

"Hello, Olivia." The lamp on the end table near the couch turned on. Trish's face was red and wet.

"What's wrong?" Liv rushed to her and sat down on the couch beside her. "Did something happen to Smith?"

"He—"

Trish's face crumpled, and Liv hugged her. Worry bled through every tender sensor within her. "What's happened to him?"

Trish blew her nose. "I'm being silly." Her shoulders heaved. "He went on that blind date. I hate it. Absolutely hate it."

So did Liv. She shouldn't care what Smith did or who he went out with. But stupidly, for some silly, hormonal-induced reason, she cared about the clod.

"I can't stop crying." Trish whimpered. "My overprotective mothering instincts are kicking in. I'm afraid he's making a dreadful decision. But there's not one thing I can do about it. Other than praying. So I've been sitting here praying and crying."

Liv sniffed back her own emotions.

"I want to trust the Lord." Trish squeezed Liv's hand. "I'm so glad you're here with me. It's easier to face life's difficulties with a friend nearby."

Liv hugged the woman who'd embraced her and welcomed her into her home during a rough time in her life. "I'm glad I'm here too. If there's anything I can do, please tell me. Want me to start dinner?"

Trish met her gaze with a sparkle in her eyes. "What did you have in mind?"

"Eggs and toast are my specialties."

Wiping her eyes with the hanky, Trish smiled, and her mouth wobbled. "Eggs and toast sound perfect."

When Smith entered the house and strode into the kitchen, he paused in the doorway. "I know who cooked this meal." He leaned his shoulder against the doorjamb, a soft smile crossing his lips.

"Because of the great smells?" Liv lifted a piece of toast.

"More like the scent of burned bread."

She snorted. Did his smile mean his date went well? "See if I ever make toast for you again."

"Promise?" He walked to the sink and washed up.

Liv's overdone toast didn't stop him from devouring three pieces and a pile of scrambled eggs with cheese.

"Well?" Trish crossed her arms after they finished eating. "How did it go?"

Smith set his fork down. "Better than expected."

Not what Liv wanted to hear.

"Or worse than expected, whichever way you want to look at it."

"Was she friendly?" Trish asked.

"Very. We had a pleasant lunch. A mix of awkward and companionable moments."

"I was worried." Trish patted his hand.

"I figured. It's in God's hands. I dropped by to talk with Pastor Tim on the way home." Smith scooped up his remaining eggs onto his fork. "He says I made the right decision in meeting with Amaryllis. I'm keeping my heart open to God's leading. Also, it shows the elders I'm trying to submit to their wishes." He held up his free hand. "Not saying I'm jumping into a marriage of convenience."

"I should say not." Trish harrumphed. "Give yourself time. You just ended things with—"

"I know." He stuffed the bite into his mouth.

Liv took a few swallows from her water glass.

"I'm worried about you diving into a permanent liaison you might hate." Trish's eyes filled with tears again. "I don't want that for you."

"Neither do I," Liv muttered.

Smith stared at her.

Maybe she should go and stay in the bathroom for a long time.

"Was Amaryllis"—Trish shrugged like she couldn't find the right words—"tender spiritually?"

"As far as I could tell." He glanced at the ceiling. "She said she always wanted to be a pastor's wife."

Liv nearly choked on the water going down her throat. "Excuse me." She pushed herself up and rushed out of the kitchen as fast as a seven-and-a-half-month pregnant woman could do without waddling. She went straight into the bathroom and shut the door.

Why was she having such a strong emotional reaction to Smith's news? Why should she care if he ruined his life?

Chapter Eighteen

On Saturday morning, Trish asked Liv, "Would you like to take a walk? It's a beautiful fall day. What do you say to getting out and enjoying it?"

"Sounds lovely." Liv sipped her morning decaffeinated coffee. "Give me a few minutes and I'll be ready."

"We should do some shopping for the baby, too."

"I haven't made much money yet." Liv dumped out the dregs of her coffee.

"I have a nest egg I'd like to use to buy a bassinet if you'll let me."

"You've already been so generous."

"Please, let me do this?" Trish smoothed her hand over Liv's shoulder. "You may not have many luxuries for him or her, but the baby needs a bed. A bassinet will be light and movable from the living room to Smith's room after he moves out."

Liv gulped. "Will that be soon?"

"He has an itch to get on with his life. I don't blame him for wanting to fly the coup. However, I have strong opinions about who he goes with." She chuckled.

"He's lucky to have someone as kind and caring as you for a mom."

"Thank you." Trish hugged her. "I'm thankful God brought you into my life. You're the daughter I never had."

"That's sweet of you." Did God bring Liv and Trish together? "I'm thankful for you rescuing me."

"Isn't God good to bring two weary souls together to find peace and help together?" Trish's eyes sparkled.

Liv was relieved to hear she hadn't been a total moocher. Even if she was a big fat nothing when it came to cooking.

"How about that walk?"

"Let me get my tennies on."

A half hour later, Liv and Trish strolled beside the Spokane River, breathing in the late fall cool air. Liv enjoyed the gorgeous view of the river churning beneath the Monroe Street Bridge. They paused to watch a seagull gliding in the air, swooping lower and lower. Must be after a fish.

"I've been wanting to talk with you," Trish said with a slight hesitation in her voice.

"Oh?" Did Trish want her to find other accommodations? Had she done something wrong?

"Don't get such a worried look." Trish put her arm around the crook of Liv's elbow. "You know that day we met? The Lord keeps reminding me of our conversation in the diner."

Liv had become more comfortable with Trish's comments about the Lord. Sometimes, she told Liv about verses she read in the Bible. How a place in John came to life for her. Or how one verse made her want to sing an aria. Liv didn't always understand, but she tried seeing things from Trish's point of view.

"I've been contemplating what you said about knowing Him at some time in your life. Can you tell me about that?" Trish tugged on Liv's arm. "I don't mean to pry, but I am curious."

Liv sighed, relaxing into the stride of their hike, the comfort of walking alongside a friend, the trust they'd built between them almost a tangible thing.

"When I was young, I had a favorite aunt. Auntie Ann." Liv dug into herself for a memory of the dear woman. "We'd go out for breakfast, then she'd bring me to Sunday school and morning worship."

"What happened?"

"I accepted Jesus and faith." A sigh felt like it came from below her ribs where the baby kicked her, a double whammy. "A rift occurred between her and my parents. They forbade me from seeing her."

"I'm so sorry."

"Me too. I was devastated. No more church. No more seeing my aunt—the one person who told me she loved me. I felt so alone." She swallowed hard. "I used to ask my nanny questions about the Bible. She said she didn't know anything about it."

"Did you ever go back to church?"

"No. Slowly, what faith I had faded away."

Trish nodded. "And your aunt?"

"Died of cancer a couple of years later." A sigh deflated Liv's lungs.

"Oh, hon, I'm so sorry." Trish hugged her.

"Thanks. It's been a long time. Still hurts, though."

"The loss of loved ones is like that. Hits you at the strangest times."

As they walked, Liv thought about Trish having lost her husband. How she lived as a single mom for all these years. Trish knew about deep heartache and loss. About how to carry on with life.

"What about now?" Trish asked. "Do you believe in Jesus?"

"For years, I was angry at Him for taking Auntie Ann away from me." Liv smoothed her hands over her swollen abdomen. "Then Little Mister came along. The rest is history, as they say."

"I first believed in Jesus when I was a teenager." Trish smiled at a woman who passed by them. "A girl down the block invited me to church. I went because I needed a friend." She suddenly shifted topics. "Would you like to get some tea? Rest for a bit?"

"Sure." Getting off her feet sounded great.

Seated across from each other in a café that was much nicer than the one they met in originally, they sipped herbal tea and ate blueberry scones.

"Back to my tale," Trish said softly. "Each Sunday, I soaked up everything the preacher said. Finally, I asked Jesus to come into my heart. My life was never the same again." She chuckled. "Not perfect. But peaceful and good in here." She rested her palm over her heart. "If you ever have questions about faith or just want to talk, let me know, okay?"

"Okay. Thanks."

They spent another hour strolling through shops downtown. Liv was interested in all the baby paraphernalia—bassinet, diapers, darling boy's clothes. She'd have to scrimp and save to afford any of it. Trish oohed and aahed over each item, endearing Liv to her even more. When her baby was born, she'd have him call Trish "Granny." She already felt like a part of Liv's family.

Chapter Nineteen

Four days after their first date, and fourteen days since his breakup with Katy, Smith was on his way to meet Amaryllis at a restaurant on the north side of Spokane. What could it hurt to meet with her again? He was lonely. Missing Katy. By the number of calls Amaryllis made to him in the last two days, she wanted to pursue a relationship with him.

He was still undecided.

Arnold called him twice, asking what his intentions were toward his sister. Intentions? How could he make such a permanent decision after one lunch and a couple of phone conversations?

He strode into the restaurant and found Amaryllis sitting at a table by the window overlooking the busy Newport Highway. She'd done her hair in a puffy do and wore more makeup than last time. "Good evening, Amaryllis."

"Hi, Smith."

"How was the drive?" He dropped into the chair opposite her.

"Great." She made a snorty laugh, then covered her mouth with her hand. "Sorry. I'm working on that."

"Working on what?" He picked up his water glass.

"Arnold says I snort like a pig and no man will want me with such a rude laugh." She muffled another laugh. "I can make it stop."

"No worries," Smith said lightly. "You can't believe everything your brother says."

Arnold seemed to be a bit domineering about his sister. Even if Amaryllis had a mildly unusual laugh, she shouldn't try to hide it because Smith, her brother, or some other man, might not like it.

When the server arrived, Smith ordered a steak. Amaryllis chose a chicken salad. He met her glance a couple of times.

"So—"

"I was—"

"You first," he said.

"Have you heard any more about the church's plans for the pastorate?" She clasped her hands together. "I've been praying about it."

"Oh, good." He wiped his sweaty palms down his pant legs. "I spoke with Arnold. Things are at a stalemate since I'm not rushing into anything."

Although, wasn't he rushing into things by going on a second date with Amaryllis?

"How about you? What have you been up to since we last saw each other?" Even the term "each other" bothered him and felt traitorous to Katy.

"I've been a busy bee." Amaryllis chortled. "I've read two books on being a pastor's wife. One on motherhood." Her face reddened. "One on husband and wife things." She winked.

He took a big gulp of water.

"I called a friend of mine in South Carolina who's been a pastor's wife for three years. Getting tips." Her hands fluttered across her neck. "There's so much to learn."

"I'm sure there is, but—"

Should he tell her not to do these things? He couldn't go through with an arranged marriage without a single amount of attraction for the woman, could he?

"Amaryllis, I'm glad we've become friends." He took a breath. "You're a brave woman for being willing to meet me like this. To read books about being a pastor's wife and a mom. Thank you."

"Not brave." She sighed. "Stupid, maybe."

"Why is that?"

"My brother and his crazy ideas." She swept her hand across her forehead. "I'm sorry for putting you through this. For thinking his scheme might work. It won't, right?"

He shook his head slightly, not wanting to hurt her. "I still say you're brave. You have my admiration."

"Admiration." Tears welled in her eyes. "Not what I was hoping for."

"I'm sorry. Even though this probably won't work, I'm thankful you were willing to meet with me a second time."

"You're such a nice man." She stared at the table, not meeting his gaze.

"I hope we can be friends." Although, the "friends" comment probably wouldn't appease her.

"If you do become our pastor, I might have to go to a different church." She huffed out a snorty laugh, not covering it now.

"I doubt that will happen. But if I pastored your church, I hope we wouldn't have to feel awkward around each other." He sighed heavily. "I can't pastor the Thunder Ridge Fellowship unless I'm married. That doesn't appear to be happening."

"If you change your mind—" She looked at him then, shuffling her shoulders with the unfinished offer.

Thankfully, their food arrived.

Chapter Twenty

A month into her stay with Trish, Liv thought she should do something to earn her keep. Surely, she could follow a simple recipe on her own. Propping the cookbook against the toaster, she peered at the instructions for sugar cookies. They didn't look too difficult.

Three batches later, and with a mess of packages, measuring cups, dirty spoons, a collection of broken eggshells, and at least a cup of sugar spilled across the green surface, the countertop was a disaster. She must look equally in disarray due to all the times she brushed her forearm against her hair, wiping wispy strands out of the way, no doubt leaving a trail of flour across her face.

But this one golden sugar cookie with its dark burned edges that she clasped between her fingers was her reward. Biting into the soft doughy middle, the sweet delicacy stirred her taste buds. Pure heaven.

"What's this? What exploded in here?" Smith's voice boomed.

Oh, no. He was home already?

She gulped down the bite. Slowly, she turned to face him, brushing crumbs from her mouth. "Smith."

He glowered. "You made this mess?"

Every muscle in her tired body tensed. "I did."

She took a gander at the space from his perspective. It looked like an explosion, all right. But if only he knew the effort, tears, and determination that went into making this cookie, he wouldn't be standing here scowling at her.

As if it were a perfect piece of art, she tenderly lifted another cookie from the foil she had spread out on the counter. She tore off the burned edges all the way around it. Then, holding the center of the cookie out toward him, she grinned. "Look what this mess and I created."

A tentative smile broke through his scowl. "It's burned."

"Come on. Try it. Just the center." She swayed the middle piece back and forth beneath his nose. "You know you want to."

He rolled his eyes but put the cookie in his mouth.

"Mmm. That's good," he spoke while chewing.

"Told you so."

His eyes lit up, his smile widening. "I'm impressed. Well, not with the burned part."

"Thank you." Her efforts hadn't been in vain.

He wiped his hand over his mouth. "I'm surprised the house smells so bad."

"I had an accident the first time. Well, the second time too."

"Second?" He coughed like he was choking. "How many batches did you make?"

"Three."

A burst of laughter erupted from him.

"It's not funny."

"Yes, it is."

He'd better watch out or she'd punch him in the gut.

All laughter gone, he reached out and his fingers brushed whisper-soft against her cheek, her nose.

She swallowed hard. No man had touched her in such a long time.

Pulling away, she broke their tangled glances and his fingers from brushing her skin. Smith didn't mean anything by it. He had Amaryllis and his pastoral dreams. She had to protect her heart.

The timer went off, and she rushed to the oven and turned the knob. After she used the spatula to remove the cookies, she rolled out more dough, cut it into circles, and put the last sheet of cookies into the oven. When she glanced over her shoulder, Smith was gone.

Gazing around the room, she wished for a maid to come and save her from this disaster. Where should she even begin to restore order? Leaving the kitchen as sparkling as she found it would take her hours.

One item at a time, she put things away. She wasn't familiar with where the utensils and food containers went. But determinedly she cleared the countertop. Unfortunately, she got so involved with cleaning, she forgot about her cookies in the oven.

Smith charged into the room, yanked open the oven, and let out a loud groan as smoke billowed into the air. "Didn't you set the timer?"

"I must have forgotten." She hurried to the door and fanned fresh air in. "I can't believe I did that again!"

Using a hot pad, Smith pulled out the sheet full of charred cookies. Liv hated failure of any kind. Smith standing here judging her as inept rubbed salt into her wounded pride. Tears flooded her eyes. And she hated that too.

Suddenly, he tipped his face to the ceiling and guffawed.

Oh, she wanted to belt him. "Stop that! It's not funny."

"Yes, it is, Liv. Yes, it is." And he laughed again.

Grabbing a damp dish towel she'd been using to wipe her hands, she stomped over to him and flicked his arm with it.

His eyes widened, but he still chortled.

She flicked him again, this time on his backside.

"Hey." Laughingly, he tugged on the dish towel. "None of that."

She yanked back on the wet cloth, jerking with all her might. A playful scuffle ensued. Soon she was snickering, then full out laughing as they tugged at the cloth, prancing around the small table.

"Truce. Truce," Smith said.

Still giggling, she stopped tugging. A wide smile settled on Smith's lips, and his eyes twinkled with merriment or mischief. Suddenly, he jerked the towel away from her.

"No fair!"

"All's fair in—" He froze as if shocked by what he almost said. *Love* and war?

They both stared at each other, breaths heaving.

"I should—" She pointed to the partially messy counters.

"I'll take this outside." He nodded toward the charred cookies.

The magical moment dissipated into a fog of confusion. What just happened, or almost happened, between them?

Chapter Twenty-one

The next morning, after getting up and using the bathroom, Liv folded the blankets. As she pushed the hide-a-bed back into the couch, a book on the end table caught her attention. A Bible. Had Trish left it there for her to read?

Was Trish pushing her beliefs on her? Trying to make Liv behave more like her? She took a breath. No. Trish was a kind and loving person. Surely, she meant well. Besides, what did it matter if she left a Bible for Liv to read? If she read some verses and had questions, she and Trish could talk about them.

Maybe she'd learn some spiritual things she could tell Smith about at the dinner table. He thought he was so smart about cooking. He might have an even higher opinion of his Biblical knowledge. Wasn't that reason enough for her to read up?

After she fixed her morning decaf, she settled onto the couch with the worn-looking Bible in her lap. Where should she start? The words about Jesus were in the New Testament. Flipping through the pages of the second half of the book, she found John. Something her childhood Sunday school teacher said rummaged through her thoughts. "When in doubt, start with the book of John."

Sipping her drink, she read the first few chapters. The more she read, the more interested she became. When she reached chapter three, things Auntie Ann told her about God's love came back.

"God loves you so much, Liv. Even if you were the only person on the planet, He would have sent His son to die for you."

Warmth spread through her.

"Olivia?" Trish strode across the small living room.

"Good morning." Liv lifted the Bible. "I found this and thought I'd read a little."

"That's wonderful." Trish swayed her hand toward the couch. "May I join you?"

"Of course."

"Let me get my coffee and I'll be right back." A few minutes later, Trish sat down with a mug in her hand. "I hope you don't mind my leaving the Bible there. Did anything pique your interest?"

"Some of the verses remind me of when my aunt told me about how to take a faith journey."

"What are you thinking about now?" Trish sipped her drink.

"I suppose that I'm afraid to try again. That I've done too many things wrong." Liv stared into Trish's warm eyes. "If I take the next step, I might fail."

"Oh, hon, we all feel that way sometimes." Trish set her mug on the end table. "The Lord's been looking out for you, whispering your name, waiting for you to answer."

Tears flooded Liv's eyes.

"Would you like me to pray with you?" Trish gave her a quick hug. "I don't want to pressure you. Tell me if you're not ready and I'll be quiet."

Being the recipient of Trish's kindness and grace made Liv feel so peaceful. What would it be like if she believed in God's love as Trish and Smith did? What if she asked Jesus into her life? Was she ready to take such a step?

She closed the Bible and set it on the end table. "I'm open to finding my way back to Him, back to faith, even if I'm only taking baby steps."

"Praise the Lord! That makes me so happy." Trish clasped Liv's hand and prayed, "Please touch Olivia. Help her to believe in You and to take those baby steps of faith."

"I want You in my life, Lord Jesus," Liv whispered.

After they finished praying, Trish said, "Today starts a new chapter for you. If you have any questions, please ask. I'm here for you."

"Thank you." Liv picked up her cup again. "I'll never be able to repay all your generosity and thoughtfulness since I came here."

"You are a blessing to me, too." Trish swept some locks of hair from Liv's face, staring into her eyes like a mother would. "Ready for some breakfast?"

Liv laughed and stroked her tummy. "I'm always ready for food."

"Let's have a celebration breakfast!"

A half hour later, Trish and Liv were eating delicious waffles heaped with strawberries and whipped cream. Smith entered, smoothing back his messed-up hair, and came to a stop. "What are we celebrating today?"

How did he jump to the conclusion they were celebrating anything?

"I forgot to mention that Smith and I have a tradition of eating waffles and fruit for all of our birthdays, good news, and such." Trish smiled.

"Oh?" Liv gulped down her bite of delicious waffle and met Smith's gaze.

"Is it your birthday, Liv?"

She liked the sound of her name on his lips. She shouldn't like it, but she did.

"It's sort of her birthday." Trish pushed the plate of waffles toward the extra plate she left for him. "Have a seat and we'll tell you about it."

Smith trudged over to the coffee pot and fixed a hot drink before sitting down.

"Do you mind, Olivia?" Trish met her gaze with a concerned look. "It's your story. If you want to wait until another time to share, that's okay."

"It's all right." Although, she felt timid mentioning anything of a spiritual nature to Smith yet.

Her baby kicked her in the ribs, and she jerked, laughing. "Oh, my."

"Did he get you?" Trish asked.

"Yeah, in a weirdly forceful way." She smoothed both palms over her stomach.

Smith loaded his waffle with fruit and whipped cream. "So, what's this good news?" He met Liv's glance then turned toward his mom.

"Liv took a step of faith today." Trish smiled proudly.

"A baby step of faith," Liv amended

"We all start somewhere." Smith gave her a quick hug. "Welcome to the family."

"Thanks." She chuckled self-consciously.

"Would you like to go to church with us tomorrow?" Trish asked. "No pressure. But you're more than welcome. I'd love to introduce you to some of our friends there."

"Uh, sure." It had been a long time since she darkened a church door. "With my swelling stomach, I don't have many clothes that fit."

"Our fellowship is a casual bunch. Wear what you have."

What would going to Trish and Smith's church be like? Would the three of them sit together like one happy family?

Chapter Twenty-two

Walking into the medium-sized church the next morning, Liv noticed people gazing curiously at her. Three women who looked in their late twenties/early thirties rushed over to Smith, chatting and grinning, batting their dark-mascaraed eyes at him. Each of the three touched his sports-coat sleeve, one arm hugged him, or leaned up as if to talk to him privately.

Was he flattered by all the feminine attention? Maybe his ego needed a boost after his breakup with Katy. He alternated between grinning and laughing with the trio. Was he flirting with them?

Liv bit back a groan. Not her concern.

Trish tugged on her arm and led her about halfway up the church aisle. A silver-haired man dressed in a dark suit strode toward them.

"Good morning. I'm Pastor Tim." The minister thrust out his hand toward Liv.

"Hello." She returned his handshake. "I'm Liv." She didn't say "Brown." She couldn't lie to the pastor. She'd have to come clean with her name to Trish and Smith soon.

"This is my friend I've told you about," Trish said.

What had she told the pastor? That Liv was mooching off her? She groaned. Smith might grumble about her freeloading off his mother, but Trish wasn't like that.

"Welcome. I hope you make our fellowship your church home."
Pastor Tim smiled widely.

"Thank you." She followed Trish into the cushioned pew. She
was thankful for the softness of the seat. The last church she went
to with Auntie Ann had uncomfortable wooden pews.

Two elderly women stopped by their row. Trish stood and
embraced each of them. Then she turned toward Liv. "I want to
introduce you to my friend, Liv Brown."

Liv gulped at the misrepresentation of her last name. "Hello."

"Good morning. We're glad you could join us," the woman
wearing purple gushed. "I'm Suzie Daily. Been coming to this church
for forty years. Makes me sound old, but I'm not."

"I'm happy to meet you."

"This is Jade Tompkins." Trish tugged the shorter woman closer
to Liv.

Liv shook her hand. "Hi. I'm glad to meet you."

"I'm so happy you are here," Jade said in a soft voice. Her quieter
demeanor made it obvious she was the shier of the two.

"Both of these ladies have been my prayer warriors through the
thick of it." Trish gave Jade a hug.

"We're always here for you, honey," Suzie said.

After the ladies walked on to the next pew, greeting people,
Trish dropped back onto the seat beside Liv. "Aren't they the
sweetest? They're both in their eighties, but they do this every Sunday
morning. Greeting people. Spreading God's love and cheer. I just
love them."

Liv took a big breath, then exhaled slowly, some of her trepidation
about being here easing.

As the opening chords to "Amazing Grace" started, Smith
scooted into the seat on the other side of her. Their gazes met for an
instant. Why didn't he sit with one of his three admirers?

In the next second, everyone stood. Liv nudged her way up
between Smith and Trish. They both held songbooks, so she grabbed

one too. Matching her book's page to theirs, she followed the words to the hymn she remembered from Auntie Ann's church.

Smith sang in a deep bass. Liv enjoyed hearing his throaty timbre. On her other side, Trish sang a soft alto, harmonizing beautifully with her son. Joining in quietly, Liv sang the lyrics, thinking of her own commitment to the Lord yesterday.

Lord, I'm scared about having the baby. Terrified of what I must go through alone. Please, be with me. I'm sorry for how I strayed from You before. Help me walk with You all the days of my life.

After the hymn ended, the congregation sat down. Pastor Tim strode to the pulpit and welcomed newcomers. Fortunately, he didn't make anyone stand and introduce themselves. By the time he began the sermon, Liv had to use the bathroom. Bad timing.

"Where's the restroom?" she whispered to Trish.

Trish gave her directions. "Want me to come with you?"

"No, thanks."

It was bad enough for Liv to waddle down the center aisle to reach the facilities. On second thought, she wouldn't be waddling. Just walking slowly.

As she passed Smith's three admirers in the back pew, they stared at her, taking in her condition. Their curiosity about her was obvious in their raised eyebrows and quick glances toward each other. Did they think she was a visiting relative of Smith's? Or did they, perhaps, consider her a threat? Competition? What a laugh!

Chapter Twenty-three

After church, a call came for Smith from Dennis at the Thunder Ridge Fellowship. The three Board members wanted to speak with him again, today, if possible! What did they want to discuss? Why the rush to meet?

Earlier this week, he called Arnold to tell him things didn't work out with Amaryllis. Arnold graciously thanked Smith for meeting with his sister.

In the nearly three weeks since his breakup with Katy, he'd been nursing his internal wounds. Spending a lot of time in prayer. Having counseling sessions with Pastor Tim. Reading his Bible more. But his heart still hurt.

Dennis's call felt like a lifeline. Even if Smith couldn't become the church's pastor, that someone still saw potential in him gave him hope. Maybe they needed a substitute preacher for a couple of weeks, or something.

Two hours later, he pulled into the church parking lot.

Dennis greeted him at the front door with a firm handshake. "Good to see you, Smith."

"Thanks. It was a great drive into town. The fall colors here are amazing."

"Best place in God's green earth."

Smith chuckled. Wherever people were happy and content with their lives, they seemed to consider it the best place in the world. He used to feel that way about Spokane, especially after falling for Katy. Then, after they broke up, everything shifted as if the earth weirdly rotated off its axis, and even his hometown didn't seem as appealing.

Dennis led him to the basement where he came for the previous interview and meeting. Smith shook the other two men's hands. Bob offered him coffee, and Smith accepted. Surely, it was better to have something to hold in his hands rather than to twiddle his thumbs and appear overly nervous.

"You're probably curious why we asked you to join us today." Dennis swayed his hands toward Arnold and Bob as they all sat down. "The three of us have been meeting and praying about our pastor's replacement every morning at six a.m. for the last two weeks."

"That's good." Smith nodded, clutching the warm mug. Their prayer time coincided with his. He'd been waking up early and praying for weeks now, too.

"The thing is"—Dennis took a deep breath—"we all feel you are the best man to spiritually lead us into the next decade."

"What?" Smith's heart rate accelerated.

"However"—Arnold palmed the air—"we are steadfast in our desire for our pastor to be a family man. Someone our whole body of believers can trust in all areas."

"Right." Smith released a balloon-deflating sigh. "So, why am I here? I still don't have a wife or a fiancée."

Bob, Dennis, and Arnold exchanged glances.

"Each of us has individually felt the leading of the Lord to ask you back to talk with us," Bob said in a confident manner. "That's why Dennis called you."

"I appreciate that, but my circumstances haven't changed."

"I had a dream where I saw you standing in our pulpit preaching." Arnold took a long swallow from his cup. "Sometimes I have dreams of Divine direction."

"So, you're saying you'd still like to offer me the position?" Hope rose in Smith. If only they'd change their minds about him having to be married—

"Well, it's what we'd like to do if things were different," Dennis said.

"Oh. I see."

If Katy had been prepared to be a pastor's wife. *If* Smith proposed to Amaryllis.

Still, he wanted to clarify what they were saying. "So, if I married someone, you'd ask me to be the pastor, right?"

"Yes," Arnold said without hesitation.

The other two murmured agreements.

Inwardly, he groaned. Was this more emotional baggage? Had he come so far only to be left outside in the cold? He wasn't married. Couldn't be the pastor. Why come all this way for nothing?

"Here's what we propose." Dennis leaned forward, his elbows braced against the table. "We'd like you to join us in six days of fasting here at the church. At the end of that time, we'll make our decision based on yours."

"Based on my what?" Smith scratched his scalp.

"During those days of prayer and fasting, if God were to reveal who you should marry," Dennis said, "and you followed through with that decision, we'd ask you to become our pastor."

"Whoa. You're asking God for a miracle?"

Arnold chuckled. "We're praying for guidance. If the Lord grants us a miracle, wouldn't that be wonderful?"

"We're putting it all on the line," Bob said. "We want God to open your spiritual eyes, and ours, about this matter. We're not taking any of this lightly. We're willing to sacrifice by fasting and praying for most of a week. Would you be willing to do the same thing?"

All three gazes fastened on him.

How could he refuse? But finding a wife in six days? That seemed like an impossible feat. Yet if he was going to do this, shouldn't he be filled with faith, expecting an answer?

Chapter Twenty-four

Smith drove back home, puzzling over what he'd agreed to do. Even though it didn't make sense to him, he felt hopeful God was going to do something, possibly revealing His will, in the coming days. That night he prepped a bag of clothes and supplies, then returned to Thunder Ridge early the following morning to spend the week.

Arnold and his wife, Suzette, welcomed him to stay with them. Although, he felt a smidge of pressure by boarding with Amaryllis's brother and sister-in-law—wasn't there an unwritten idea that Amaryllis was available and willing to marry him?—he was thankful for their hospitality.

He slumped into the pink armchair in the corner of the room that was about the same size as his bedroom back home and picked up the book he brought to study. When he was young, he and Mom used to read about the life and sermons of Smith Wigglesworth regularly. Smith devoured everything he could get his hands on about his namesake. This volume of sermons was no exception.

An hour after reading through a couple of the works of Wigglesworth, he jolted awake. Ugh. He hadn't meant to fall asleep.

Suddenly, his desire for food gnawed in his stomach and in his thoughts. Even though it was only his first day of fasting, a distraction might help ease him through the discomfort. Maybe a walk near the lake in Sandpoint?

As soon as he pulled into the parking lot at the beach and hopped out of his car, the view of Lake Pend Oreille drew him closer to the water's edge. Just being here, smelling the fresh clear air, even hearing the squawking of the seagulls, his yearning for food diminished. The expansive lake and the evergreens that seemed to come right down to the edge of the water in the distance were like food for his soul. A comfort to him.

He walked along the sand, and his thoughts turned toward spiritual things. *Lord, I've tried to be submissive to the leadership at Thunder Ridge Fellowship. But the One who I need answers from is You. Should I seek a wife who—*

Who what? Was more spiritual than Katy? Someone who fit his expectations better than Amaryllis did? Guilt washed over him. Had he been too picky when he met with her? Had his wounded heart dictated that he wasn't a tad attracted to her? Maybe if the two of them tried going out again, Smith might find her more … compatible.

He groaned. He knew what true love felt like. Heart pounding, all-consuming, sweet, and passionate. He'd been smitten with Katy. Blindsided by love, it was as if no other woman existed. Isn't that how a relationship should be? How a married man ought to feel toward the woman he planned to spend his life with?

A mental image of Liv throwing flour at him flashed through his thoughts. Totally juvenile. Yet, he'd had fun with her. She was like the kid sister he never had. When she brought the baby home, maybe Smith could be its uncle.

Now, why was he thinking of Liv? He should be focusing on Amaryllis. She had been a Christian for most of her life. She was studying how to be a good pastor's wife.

What about their lack of chemistry?

Why was he toying with the idea of marrying someone else when he still hurt inside over his broken engagement with Katy? And yet, wasn't that why he agreed to spend this week here?

Trudging along the edge of Idaho's biggest lake, and the fifth deepest lake in the United States, he tried picturing what living near here might be like. What would his life be like as a pastor, preaching, doing hospital visitation, ministering in the place he longed to be?

He pictured him and Amaryllis together as husband and wife. Then he groaned again, not liking the image.

He kept hiking along the waterway beneath gray threatening skies. It looked like he might be in for a downpour.

His recent doubts and disappointments pressed down on him, making his shoulders feel inadequate to hold up his head. Pastor Tim's words of advice during his last counseling session brushed through his thoughts. "When you don't know what to do, when the windows of Heaven appear to be slammed shut, keep praying, keep seeking the Lord. God is working even when we don't see it."

The rain fell hard then, the weeping gray skies mirroring his soul.

"God, why did I have to end things with Katy?" he asked aloud. "I loved her. Still love her."

His pastor's words resounded in his thoughts—keep praying, keep seeking.

He licked the wetness from his lips and trudged toward a stand of trees to take refuge until the deluge passed. Squatting in a huddled position, he gazed out over the gray water where the rain splattered against the lake's surface.

Then he prayed more fervently, pouring his heart out to God in a way he hadn't in weeks.

Chapter Twenty-five

Liv and Trish sat at the table eating vegetable soup and dinner rolls, and Liv thought of a topic she wanted to bring up. "You know the verse where it says we can ask anything in Jesus's name, and it will be done for us?" She wiped her lips with her cloth napkin. "Is that true?"

"Yes. If we believe and don't doubt, we can ask for anything and expect an answer." Trish shrugged. "That's the promise I stand on when I pray."

"So if we can pray for anything and receive anything, the world would be a better place if we did that more often, wouldn't it?" She scooped up another bite of soup. "This is delicious."

"Thank you." Trish smiled. "You're right. If we prayed for our neighbors, even strangers, as we should, the world would be more peaceful. Safer. Healthier."

"And Smith would have his answer?"

Trish groaned.

"I'm sorry if that's too personal. Everything will work out. The Lord can do anything, right?"

Trish nodded, but her lips wobbled. "Yes. Your beginning faith touches my heart. I'm glad you mentioned Smith. He hasn't been far from my thoughts all day. He's a grown man, but motherly concerns for our children never go away."

"I'm praying for him, too."

"Thank you. The Lord is faithful to hear our prayers."

They finished their meal in comfortable silence.

As they cleared the table, Trish paused with the soup tureen in her hands. "I think I'll join Smith in fasting and prayer tomorrow. I sense his journey is difficult. My heart aches for him, but there's nothing I can do for him other than pray and intercede on his behalf."

"He's so lucky to have you for a mom." Liv collected the dirty silverware from the table. "I could fast too."

"Oh, no. You have to eat for Little Mister." Trish set the soup bowl down and hugged Liv. "You're a darling for suggesting it, though."

"There must be something I could do."

"Pray." Trish straightened her shoulders and picked up the tureen as if picking up a much weightier item. Like trust or determination.

Liv couldn't say she was sorry Smith wasn't marrying Katy. But she hoped he found someone who deserved a sincere man like him for a husband. Someone who would make a good pastor's wife. And someone who would love Trish for the wonderful mother-in-law and grandmother Liv was certain she would be.

Chapter Twenty-six

Three days into the fast, Smith arrived at the church around six a.m. to pray with the other gentlemen. As was their routine, they spent the first half hour praying in separate areas of the sanctuary. Then they met near the altar and prayed out loud individually. For Smith, hearing each of the men praying and beseeching God for wisdom and guidance gave him insight into their spiritual walk.

Arnold prayed with a bemoaning voice about the need for a "spiritual adviser" for their future.

Smith sighed. Was he such a man? His faith seemed weaker since his breakup with Katy. Maybe even before that. The way he got caught up with a woman who didn't share his faith had, perhaps, blinded him to some of the things of God. That caused deep sorrow in his spirit.

Lord, I'm sorry for wandering away from Your heart. It happened almost without me realizing it.

Dennis prayed in a passionate fashion that startled Smith. "We command these forces of evil that are stopping us from a clear answer to leave in Jesus's name!"

Were forces of evil distracting Smith from God's purposes?

Bob prayed in a softer tone. "Lord, You are amazing. We love You. We are trusting You and relying on Your goodness."

Smith felt a sense of wonder over the Lord working in his life, even when he'd made some knucklehead decisions. His stomach growled noisily, and he hoped no one noticed.

"I thank You for the answer that's coming," Bob continued praying. "Even if it isn't what we planned for, we thank You for it because You are working in our lives."

He wept, and the moment was so poignant, Smith felt teary too. A time of praise and worshiping God followed.

Then came Smith's turn to pray. He felt broken, yet clean, after the other men's prayers. "I want Your will, Lord." His voice cracked. "Not mine, but Yours."

Needing to pray by himself again, Smith knelt on the floor near the front pew. Soon he heard the other men doing the same thing, finding places to pray and seek God longer. As Smith cast upon God all his burdens, his dreams and plans, his hurts over the crisis of losing Katy, a peace he hadn't felt in so long settled in his chest.

The next day, their time of prayer followed a similar pattern. Smith found he wasn't as hungry that day. The broth and tea he drank sustained him. Although, he still longed for a burger and fries. No denying that.

Last night, he read passages from his Smith Wigglesworth book before falling asleep. He felt encouraged by reading about the man's faith. Smith had his own path to walk, but he still wished for a similar faith-filled life as Smith Wigglesworth had.

The thought of calling Mom and assuring her everything was okay crossed his mind. He even thought about Liv. Hopefully, she was taking care of herself and the baby. Since he was trying to stay focused on spiritual things this week, he decided not to call or talk with anyone else.

Now he sat in the sanctuary after the morning prayer time, reading in Ephesians. He flipped back to the book of Matthew. Verses he previously underlined popped out at him. He skim-read those.

Throughout his reading, confirmation of his calling to be a pastor hit him again. But was he supposed to pastor this particular church? If so, what about the church's requirement for him to be married? He still wasn't willing to marry someone just because—

"Smith?"

Amaryllis? He gulped.

"Sorry to intrude." She shuffled onto the pew beside him.

"Good morning."

Moments ago, hadn't he been thinking about how he wouldn't marry just any woman because someone else told him he should? And here Arnold's sister showed up?

Her grayish gaze pulsed toward him. "I hate doing this to you."

"What are you doing?"

"Arnold called at five a.m." Her face turned burgundy. "I like you, Smith."

A hard-to-swallow sensation nearly choked him.

"He says I should talk to you. Try to get you to see things from a different perspective."

"Whose perspective might that be?"

"His, I suppose."

Smith smiled. At least she was being honest about her brother's prying.

"How do you feel about that?" He had to ask, even though he didn't plan to pursue anything with her. Other than that he was supposed to be open to God's leading during this week of fasting.

"For the greater good, and after much prayer, I'm willing to try an unusual marriage in my service to God and His will." She shrugged. "You aren't hard on the eyes."

He ignored her semi-compliment. After four days of fasting and prayer, foremost in his mind was a desire to be honest. "Amaryllis, we wouldn't be 'trying' marriage. We'd be taking vows for life. Possibly jumping into an arrangement we might later regret. I don't want that for you. I don't want that for myself, either."

"Right." She heaved a breath. "Arnold said—"

"Let's not talk about what your brother says, okay?" He gave her hand a friendly squeeze. "This is our lives we're discussing, yours and mine. And our children's."

"About that. I, um, can't have kids."

"Oh?"

"I thought that might not matter in this kind of marriage." She twisted her hands together. "I was sick as a child. I can't carry a baby." Her face turned the deepest red he'd ever seen on another human being.

"I'm so sorry." He wanted to give her a hug, but feared the impropriety of such a move, being alone in the sanctuary as they were. And he didn't want her misconstruing his intentions. "That must have been terribly hard on you."

"Accepting it was difficult." She sniffed a couple of times. "But I'm a modern woman. I don't have to have children for personal fulfillment."

Seeing her tortured-looking expression, Smith felt bad that her brother put her in this situation of having to tell him such a personal detail about her life. That was unfair to her. Why was Arnold so desperate to marry off his sister? Did Amaryllis feel that desperation too? Smith wanted to say something kind and reassuring.

"There's always adoption or foster care."

"Exactly." She met his gaze again. "Would that be okay with you?"

"Sure. I'm fine with adopting. I still hope for a large family."

"Oh. You do?" She frowned.

"Being an only child, and a child from parents who were single children, I've wished for a big family most of my life."

She laughed nervously. "I never imagined being a mom to a lot of kids."

"Do you want to have children?" He watched her reaction carefully.

"One or two. Growing up, it was Arnold and me. That was fine."

Their obvious difference in this matter was a vote against them being together. Was it wrong of him to feel relieved? It wasn't that he disliked Amaryllis. But going into a marriage without some romantic inklings toward a spouse seemed reprehensible. Not that those feelings couldn't develop over time.

They both sat quietly for a few minutes.

"I should leave you to your prayer time." She stood and stuck her hand out toward him. "Smith."

He stood also, accepting her handshake. "Thanks for visiting with me, Amaryllis."

"Thanks for the two dates. Let's call this goodbye for now, shall we?"

"Okay," he agreed. "Sorry it didn't work out."

This meant he had one answer for what he'd been praying about. He would not be marrying Amaryllis.

Chapter Twenty-seven

On the day of Trish's fast, Liv sat at the kitchen table, eating leftover soup. Trish came into the room with her Bible in hand. "Oh, good, you're eating some of that veggie soup."

"Yes, it still tastes delightful." Liv spooned some broth into her mouth.

"I wondered if you and I might have a Bible study this evening." Trish held up her Bible. "I don't want to push you, but I thought we might take a few minutes to read a scripture and talk about it. Maybe you have questions we could discuss?"

"Sounds great."

Later, Liv sat on one end of the couch, a Bible in her lap. Trish sat at the other end, reading glasses on, flipping through some pages.

"This morning I read in First John, and I thought we might start there." Trish smiled at her. "Is that okay with you?"

"Certainly." Liv had to hunt for First John.

Trish read a couple of verses, then shared what she thought it meant. She asked Liv questions, obviously trying to include her.

"I keep thinking about the day we met in the diner. I still believe the Lord led me to you." Trish took off her reading glasses. "It's like He brought us together for a purpose."

Liv wanted to believe that, too. Was it possible God led her across thousands of miles, from Chicago to Spokane, for a reason?

Did He bring her to that diner? It sounded like a leap. But she was thankful to Trish for reaching out to her that night and being so kind.

"Thank you for talking to me in the restaurant. For inviting me to stay with you." She stroked her belly where the baby rubbed his foot against her side. "I don't know where Little Mister and I might have ended up otherwise."

"Oh, hon, of course. I'm glad I listened to the Holy Spirit's nudging." Trish stared at Liv for the longest time, a smile on her face. "You are a blessing to me. And I—" She gulped.

"What is it?"

"I just had a vision, or something like that."

"Like a dream?"

"Sort of, only with my eyes open."

Liv stared down at the words about love in the Bible. Trish was like a walking, living, breathing bundle of love. Her middle name should be love. If only she could be like her. Love like her. Oh, she loved the baby with all her heart. She loved Trish, too. But sharing that with others? Strangers, even, like Trish had done? She couldn't imagine that.

Lord, I want to follow You. I want Your way. Thank You for Trish and Smith. Trish is so worried about him. Please, open his heart to see what he's supposed to do.

When she opened her eyes, Trish was smiling warmly at her.

"What?"

"I have an answer," she said with a tone of awe.

"That's good, right?"

"It's absolutely wonderful."

Trish gave her a big hug, not explaining anything more about whatever the answer was. Then she prayed. "Lord, You have a beautiful plan for each of us—Smith, Liv, and me—and I thank You for what you are doing this week to open all of our eyes to Your love and Your will. I thank You for Your faithfulness and goodness to me and those I love." She clasped Liv's hand. "Bless Olivia's baby, this newest member of my family, too."

Liv liked Trish claiming Little Mister as part of her family. For the rest of the evening, Trish's prayer strummed through her thoughts.

Chapter Twenty-eight

Liv sat cross-legged on the floor along with a dozen other plump pregnant women attending the birthing class at the Women's Health Clinic. They all sat on the floor, even Daria, the fortyish instructor. Trish sat beside Liv, having agreed to be her birthing partner. Daria told them to take a deep cleansing breath and to release it slowly.

Exhaling, Liv thought, if only labor was as simple as this. Deep breaths. Patterned breathing. But the process of delivering a baby as she'd seen in the movies where a woman yelled in agony, sometimes screaming, seemed horrible.

"You okay?" Trish massaged her shoulders.

"Apprehensive about what's coming. All the pain," she whispered.

"You'll do fine. These classes will prepare you for labor."

The library would be a good place for her to grab a few books and study up on the delivery process. She could also use some information on how to take care of an infant, since she'd never even held one before.

She zeroed back in on Daria who was explaining the first stages of labor. "Each of you should practice relaxation in preparation for your exciting day."

Exciting day? Scary, chaotic, and overwhelming were better emotional descriptors for Liv.

After the session ended, she met Carlotta and Willa, second-time moms who appeared to be near her age.

"You'll do fine." Carlotta, a woman with lovely dark skin and hair, smoothed her hand over her large abdomen. "This baby has been doing gymnastics in my belly. I can't wait to get her out and hold her."

"You're having a girl?" Liv asked.

"I have a boy, so I'm calling this one Lacey." She grinned. "Man, the heartburn has been the worst. She better have a ton of hair for what I'm suffering."

"Me too," Willa, a leggy blond with a smaller stomach than Liv's—weird how she was comparing their bellies—laughed with a tinkly sound. "I've been walking the floor in the middle of the night. That never happened with my firstborn."

Liv didn't have it so bad, then, since she hadn't experienced much morning sickness or heartburn. *Good job, Little Mister.* She smoothed her hand over her belly.

After the ladies visited, Trish tugged on Liv's arm. "Would you like to get a snack? I'm famished." She chuckled. "Ever since my fast, my body has been fighting to catch up."

Liv grinned. "How about pie and tea at the diner where we met?"

"That sounds perfect."

Ten minutes later, they sat in the greasy spoon where Liv bawled her eyes out nearly six weeks ago. In a strange way, it felt homey.

Liv took a bite of apple pie, then sipped her tea. "This is great. Thank you so much for coming to the birthing class with me. Not having to face all that alone means the world to me."

"You're welcome. I enjoyed it."

"Was your husband with you during your labor and delivery?"

"Danny wouldn't have it any other way. He was so excited to be welcoming a child into our home." Trish's eyes got misty. "His absence during Smith's growing up years has been hard."

Liv patted her hand. "I'm sorry to bring up sad memories."

"That's okay. He helped me the day Smith was born. I had back labor, so he pressed his fist against my lower back and massaged during the worst of the contractions." She laughed. "Goodness, he worked almost as hard as me. But he loved being a part of the process."

Liv wouldn't have a man who stayed by her. Nick would never have been such a man. He proved that by dumping her after he heard she was pregnant and by cheating on his wife in the first place.

Tension twisted through her. She felt her shoulders and neck tighten up.

"What is it?" Trish met her gaze with concern.

"I thought of the baby's father. Nick." This was the first time she mentioned him since coming to live with Trish.

"Was he a nice man?" Trish sipped her tea.

"I wouldn't say nice. More like too handsome for his own good. Too greedy." She drew in a long breath. "I was caught up in a relationship I shouldn't have been involved in, that's for sure."

"Have you forgiven him?" Trish asked softly.

The question twisted a knot in Liv's chest, making breathing difficult. "No."

"We can pray about that together if you'd like."

"Do I have to forgive him? Is that what God expects?" She pushed her fork away. The pie didn't look as appetizing now.

"Yes," Trish answered softly. "That's probably not what you want to hear right now. But forgiveness is a part of our spiritual journey. Jesus had many wrongs done to him. Terrible atrocities. Yet he forgave everyone."

A soft moan exited Liv's lips. "I guess I'll have to work on that."

Trish smiled kindly. "It's more about releasing it than working on it."

"Oh?"

"Let's say I'm clutching a dirty rag in my hand." Trish acted out clutching an item. "It's filthy and causes an infection, yet I keep gripping the grimy cloth."

"Sounds disgusting."

Liv pictured herself holding that piece of fabric. Not letting go. Oh, not letting go! Just like she'd been holding the pain of Nick's betrayal in her chest. Her parents' betrayal too.

"Do I slowly release one finger, one movement at a time?" Trish acted like she was prying her little finger away from her clenched fist. "Or do I just let go?" She opened her hand delicately as if performing a dance move. Trish sighed. "I was mad at God."

"Huh?"

"I was angry at Him for a year after Danny got sick and died. It was awful." Trish pressed her palm over her chest. "I don't want you to go through such bitterness. I'm going to pray for you to be able to let the past go and forgive. Then you'll truly be free."

Even as Trish said the words, Liv pictured herself letting go of that grimy cloth.

Chapter Twenty-nine

The serene scene Smith walked in on after his return trip from Thunder Ridge made him smile. Mom and Liv both held Bibles in their laps. Liv's face looked nearly radiant.

Mom rose from the couch to greet him. "Smith! You're home. So good to see you." She hugged him tightly.

"Hey, Mom. Good to be back." Something smelled great in the room. "What did you guys have for dinner?"

"Steak and potatoes."

He groaned. Then realizing he hadn't addressed Liv, he lifted his hand toward her. "Hello."

"Hi. Have a good week?"

"Good, bad, ugly, perfect." He chuckled at her flummoxed expression. "It's not every week you get to spend undistracted time with God and other people who are doing the same thing."

"Sounds lovely."

"I'm going to put these away." He lifted his suitcase and brief-case. "Then I'll open a can of soup."

"No steak?" Liv asked teasingly.

"After a week of not eating, I'd better start with something light. Excuse me."

When he strode into the kitchen, Mom had chicken noodle soup simmering in a pan. Smelled both fantastic and awful. His stomach clenched. "Thanks, Mom."

"You look good." Mom patted his arm. "I'm eager to hear all about your week."

"I found peace. Not as much direction as I hoped for, but things are better here." He patted his chest. "I'll tell you all about it." Grabbing a bowl, he filled it with soup and sat down at the table. He wanted to tip the bowl up and guzzle the liquid, but then he stared at the mostly broth-based soup, not even liking how it looked.

"Want any bread to go with it?"

"Not this time." He thanked God for the food, then took slow sips of the hot liquid.

Mom fixed herself a cup of tea and sat down across from him.

Liv shuffled past the doorway, and he heard the tub faucet running a few minutes later. Was she giving him and Mom some privacy to talk?

He finished the bowl of soup and went back for a refill. This time he ate it slower.

"So?" Mom prompted.

They'd been comrades for a long time, chatting about life and God and dreams. Yet, a part of him felt reluctant to share with her about the idea of choosing a wife. Although, he didn't know why. At thirty-three years old, maybe it was his need for independence. Maybe a bit of disappointment, still, that things hadn't worked out with Katy. And Mom hadn't cared for her as much as he'd already seen her acting loving and caring toward Liv.

"I spent a lot of time praying, pondering God's Word, and thinking about my future. Also, reading Wigglesworth's sermons."

"I wondered what you'd bring to read." Mom smiled.

He finished off his second bowl of soup. "This hits the spot. Thanks. Of course, I'd rather eat a burger and fries. But they would probably make me sick."

"How about a cup of hot tea?"

"I drank enough tea over the last week, I might never have another cup." He smoothed his hand over his scruffy face. "How have things been going here?"

"Great. Olivia and I started a Bible study and prayer time in the evenings. She's growing in the Lord. So inquisitive and sincere." She met his gaze, sipping her tea.

It seemed like she was silently saying something to him. Not understanding, he stood and put his dishes in the sink. He was beat. Long drive. Long week.

"I'm going to be her birthing partner."

"Oh?" He swiveled around.

"I went to a class with her. I like the idea of being a fill-in mom and grandma."

"Sounds like something you'd enjoy." If things had gone his way, and if Katy had been willing to start a family, they would have been fulfilling the grandmotherly desires in his mom's heart before long. He needed to stop dwelling on the past. Hadn't his week with God taught him that?

"You don't mind, do you?"

"Why would I mind?" He shrugged.

"When I mentioned it, you got such a somber expression."

"Just tired."

Mom crossed the small kitchen and set her cup in the sink. "What about a wife?" She met his gaze. "Any decision about that?"

"I spoke with Amaryllis again."

"And?"

"We decided not to push for anything to happen. I really didn't—"

Liv shuffled into the room with wet hair and a large bathrobe draped over her protruding belly. Was she twice the size of when he left a week ago? Or hadn't he noticed her girth recently?

"Excuse me." She stopped in the doorway. "I didn't mean to intrude. I was going to get a glass of water."

"Come in, hon." Mom stepped away from the sink.

Smith moved out of Liv's way as she grabbed a glass and then filled it with water. The scent of flowers tickled his nose. Her gaze met his. Then they both glanced away.

It seemed something passed between them. Admiration or caring, most likely. Nothing else.

Chapter Thirty

Following the morning service, Pastor Tim walked by the pew where Smith stood and shook his hand. "After your week of prayer, have you come to a decision?" He patted Smith on the shoulder. "I've been praying for you."

"Thanks. I wish I had something to report. I was on an amazing spiritual journey, but I didn't solve the mystery of having a wife or of pastoring."

"Did the elders have any words of wisdom for you?"

"They each shared what was on their heart." Smith shrugged. "They gave me Bible verses about trusting God."

"Still praying, my friend." The pastor walked on, shaking other people's hands.

"Any plans for the day?" Mom asked.

"Not really. Other than taking a nap." Last night he kept waking up. Once, he sneaked through the darkened living room and made a sandwich. "Where's Liv?" He glanced around the chapel.

"She wanted to walk back to the house."

"Alone? Was it something I said?"

Mom chuckled. "No, she said Little Mister was causing her back pain. It's only a mile."

"And that's okay? For her to walk that far?"

"Sure." Mom raised a brow toward him as they strode down the center aisle.

"What?"

"It's nice to hear you being concerned about her."

"I didn't mean anything personal by it." He heard the defensive tone of his voice, but he didn't try to correct it.

A couple of hours later, Mom paced back and forth across the living room and kept checking her watch. "What's taking Olivia so long?"

"Maybe she stopped somewhere for lunch."

"Maybe. But she said she was walking back here. What if she went into early labor?"

"She knows the phone number, right?"

"Yes." Mom grabbed her coat and purse off the back of a kitchen chair. "I'm going to drive between here and the church and look for her."

"Want me to go with you?"

"No, stay here in case she calls and needs help, will you?" Mom hustled out the door.

Smith settled back into his chair and continued reading. Was Mom just overreacting? Did Liv have a physical crisis with her pregnancy? Pausing his reading, he prayed for her and the baby.

An hour later, he awoke from a nap. His book had fallen on the floor. Liv lay on the couch across from him, curled up with an afghan over her. She looked peaceful in sleep. Sighing, he picked up his book and shuffled into the kitchen.

Mom sat at the table reading a magazine and sipping tea. "You're awake," she said softly.

"I see you found her." He nodded back toward Liv on the couch.

"I did. She was at the restaurant where we met."

"Why didn't she come back like she intended to?" He put coffee grounds into the coffeemaker.

"She was tired and stopped for lunch." Mom heaved a sigh. "I'm a worry-wort. Fatigue was the culprit. Not premature labor."

Smith chuckled. When the coffee was finished, he poured a cup of the dark brew. Then he dropped into the seat beside Mom. "She's lucky to have someone as thoughtful as you to look after her."

"I'm thankful for her too." Tears filled Mom's eyes. "I've come to love her."

Smith sipped his coffee, not commenting.

"She's sweet and caring. I'm so happy she loves the Lord now."

"Yeah. That's wonderful." He took a couple more drinks.

"I don't know when the best time might be to discuss this, but I have something on my heart to share with you."

"Oh?"

They'd had these kinds of talks before. Mom would get a strong feeling of direction during prayer, and she'd tell him about it. Sometimes the warning or concern materialized, sometimes it didn't. But he always tried listening in case God was speaking to him through her.

"Will you pray about us having a talk?"

"You don't want to tell me about it right now?"

"No." She tipped her head toward the living room. "Later, okay?"

Oh. She didn't want Liv overhearing?

"All right." He picked up his cup. What was so important that Mom wanted to tell him, yet she couldn't discuss it within Liv's hearing range?

Chapter Thirty-one

More tired than usual, Liv felt relieved to finally get home from work and put her feet up. She picked up her Bible that she kept next to the couch. She draped a multi-colored afghan over her body, then hunkered down to rest and read some more scripture. "God is love …"

She awoke to the sounds of dinner preparation going on in the kitchen. Pans clinking. Water running. Chopping. Maybe she'd help Trish. After she used the bathroom, she shuffled into the kitchen but came to a stop. Smith, not Trish, worked at the counter.

"Are you fixing dinner?"

"Yep. I won dinner duties."

"Uh-oh. What did you do wrong?"

Smith guffawed. "In this house, it's a shared task. I don't mind."

Should she offer to be a part of that shared task? Or would she be intruding on his culinary privacy?

"Need any help?"

He raised an eyebrow.

"I can stir gravy now, sometimes even without burning it."

He chuckled. "Want to peel potatoes?"

"Okay." Fortunately, Trish recently showed her how to do that.

She grabbed a peeler from the top drawer next to the silverware, then stood in front of the counter and peeled a large potato.

She felt Smith's gaze on her. Was he judging her potato-peeling skills? She, the daughter of Rich Dupont III, who should have been VP of Dupont Software, could peel potatoes. Hot dog! What would her father say about such success? He'd mock her, that's what.

Despite Dad's unjust actions and lack of kindness toward her and Little Mister, she still missed him. She missed working in the Dupont company where she had made a name for herself, too. Sure, having the last name Dupont helped, but she worked hard. At least until she became distracted with Nick. It was a huge mistake she regretted.

But this baby? Her son or daughter? Never a mistake!

Tears filled her eyes. She sniffed, fighting strong emotions. Rotten hormones.

"Hey, now. What's this about?" Smith looked her in the eyes. "You okay?"

"Mmhmm." She nodded, blinking, getting herself under control by washing off the potato.

"It isn't me, is it?" He sniffed near his armpits. "Am I smelly?"

"No." A chuckle broke through her tears.

"I'd apologize for saying something rude—I have been known to do that—but this time I didn't say anything." He squished his fingers into a hamburger mixture, forming it into a meatball. "Is this because I didn't talk to you? Sorry. I'm feeling contemplative."

"You were probably shocked over my offer to help in the kitchen." She went for a lighter mood. "Now, you're stymied by my great achievements?" She held the potato near his nose.

"Miss Brown, I'd say you've mastered the art of potato peeling."

Brown. That lie probably wasn't pleasing to God.

"I might win the blue ribbon for most improved cooking skills."

He snickered. "That's pushing it. Tried making apple pie lately?"

"No. But I bet I could." Now, why did she have to go and brag like that?

He squinted at her like he might take her up on that bet. "It might be tough to leap from potato peeler to champion apple-pie maker overnight."

She felt the challenge in his words. "How about a small wager?"

He moved to the sink and washed his meat-and-sauce-covered hands under the stream of water. "What kind of wager?"

"If I can make an apple pie that's tasty and delicious enough to make you smile—"

"Yes?" Grinning, he wiped his hands on a dish towel.

"Then you have to go on a date with a woman of … of your mother's choosing." That last part came to her like a flash of lightning. His mother wouldn't choose someone like Katy! She'd choose one of those church girls.

He laughed riotously. "Oh, Liv, you are too much."

"Do you agree to my deal?" She stuck her hand out toward him.

"You're serious?" His mouth twitched like he was stopping himself from roaring with laughter. Then he held his clean hand toward her. "You're on."

She shook his hand like they'd closed a million-dollar deal. Now, if only she could make an apple pie to die for. What were the chances of that happening?

Chapter Thirty-two

The next day, Liv stopped by the market on the way home from work and picked up supplies for apple pie. Smith probably considered her an emotional woman who didn't know the first thing about success in the kitchen. Yeah, she'd show him. She could do anything she set her mind to. *Anything.*

However, three hours later, she was a hot mess. Tears ran down her cheeks and dripped off her jaws as she pulled the burned pie from the oven. Everything had been going fine until she forgot to set the timer and dozed off in a pregnancy fog.

"What's going on?" Smith charged into the kitchen as she fanned the back door.

Her nose burning from the acidic scent, she stared at him with the most stubborn glare she could conjure up. "Only a slight setback."

"Slight?" He gawked at the charred pie crust on the counter. Then he broke into deep laughter.

"Stop! Smith, just … stop." She wanted to punch him. Instead, she wiped her face with one hand and kept swinging the door with the other.

"That's not going to help." Smith grabbed the hot pads and scooped up the pie pan. Passing her on his way out the back door, he muttered, "Better luck next time."

She kicked him in the shin.

"Hey! That's not nice."

"Neither is laughing at a girl when the chips are down."

Snickering and coughing, he took the pie out to the garbage can.

She should shut the door and lock it. See if he had better luck next time.

Smith returned and opened both windows in the kitchen. He turned on the fan above the stove. Then he ran water into the pie pan. At least she hadn't ruined Trish's dish.

"Maybe you took on more than you could chew with baking an apple pie on your own." He gave her a cheesy grin.

Oh, he was smug. She wouldn't admit to any such thing!

"You're not getting out of our bet that easily." She trudged across the room, her fury building. "If I want to learn to do something, I will. It may take me a few tries, but I'll make you eat your words."

"Right." Smith covered his hand over his mouth, his shoulders shaking. "Better to eat my words than that pie you ruined." He howled with laughter.

"The pie would have been fine if I hadn't fallen asleep." No reason to tell him she struggled with the crust. That she redid it so many times it felt cardboard stiff. Or that she cut the apple slices too thin. She flipped through the cookbook pages until she found the pie section.

"You're not going to try again today, are you?"

"Why not?"

He stared at her, a crooked smile crossing his face. "Have it your own way."

"Oh, I will. Just watch me."

He stalked out of the room, shaking his head.

Four hours later, nearing exhaustion, Liv sat at the table with a slim piece of pie on a saucer in front of her. She was scared to even try it. Ten o'clock at night, she didn't care if it tasted good—other than to prove to Smith she could do it. And he had already gone to bed.

She ran her fork through the firm crust. Then brought the smallest bite of filling to her mouth. Gag! Yuck! It tasted like she was eating straight salt! She rushed to the sink, spitting and sputtering. She guzzled water from a glass, spit again, and drank again. Why did it turn out like that?

"Something wrong?" Smith's gravelly voice sent chills clambering over her skin.

She froze.

"Looks good." He shuffled over to the counter barefooted and gazed down at the pie. "Want me to taste it?"

"No!" She grabbed the pie and dumped the whole thing in the trash.

"Liv! Why'd you do that?"

"No one is eating it." She ran water into the empty pan.

"What did you do?" He leaned against the counter.

"It tasted atrocious."

"Did you forget to put sugar in it?"

"No."

"Salt?"

"Oh, I put salt in it!"

He strode over to the trash. Leaning over the ruined pie, he put his finger into the filling.

"Don't you dare taste it! I'm warning you!"

His gaze on her, he brought the sauce to his tongue. His eyes widened. He hacked and coughed. "You must ... have measured salt ... instead of sugar." He coughed again.

Her embarrassment escalating, she shut off the light and dashed for the living room where she'd already pulled out the hide-a-bed. Crawling under the covers, she buried her face beneath the sheets. Once again, she proved her ineptness in the kitchen.

What of their wager now?

Chapter Thirty-three

After spending a couple of hours filling out paperwork and applying for jobs, Smith entered the house, dog tired and discouraged. What a long day! Nothing was available in his line of work. He'd have to take a pay cut. Maybe work in retail or food prep.

If only things had worked out with the pastorate.

Surprised to see Mom sitting in the living room, a solemn expression on her face, he asked, "Did something happen? Is Liv okay?" He paused mid-stride, coat in hand.

"Could we talk before she gets back from work?"

"Sure. Let me change first."

The faint smell of burned pie still stained the air, reminding him of Liv's pie-making catastrophes last night.

In his room, he quickly changed into jeans and a navy T-shirt. What did Mom want to speak with him about? Was this about the talk she mentioned before? He strode into the kitchen, grabbed a bottle of tea from the fridge, and carried it into the living room.

"I haven't started dinner yet," she said.

"Want me to fix burgers?" He plopped down on the sofa.

"If you'd like. But let's use this time to talk."

"Okay. Shoot." He opened the peach tea and guzzled half. Was Mom upset about him laughing at Liv last night? He hadn't laughed so hard around anyone in his whole life. Her betting him about making a scrumptious pie in exchange for his mother choosing a date for him was out-of-this-world hilarious. "What's this about?"

Mom drew in a long breath. "I've been talking to the Lord about a specific issue for the last few days. I'd rather not mention this to you at all. You're a grown man who can make his own decisions."

"Thank you. I appreciate that."

"But this thing's been weighing on me so heavily, I feel I must say something."

He had some experience with things weighing him down. "Go on."

"While you were away, I spent a day fasting and praying, too."

"That's great." He took another swig of tea, relaxing a little.

"What I'm going to say may come as a surprise to you." Mom closed her eyes for a moment as if sending up a quick prayer. "I'm honestly not trying to interfere with your plans."

"Okay." He swallowed the dryness in his throat. Took another drink.

"I love you," Mom said quietly. "You're my son. I only want what's best for you. I've prayed for years for you to have a wife who would be a blessing to you, and one who you could be a blessing to also."

Yet she hadn't approved of Katy. Didn't think she'd make a good enough pastor's wife. He tuned back into Mom's words.

"—prayed and believed. My heart felt so full." She held her right palm to her chest. "She's like the daughter I never had. I don't mean to push my ideas on you, but it won't leave my mind."

What had he missed? "What idea was that?"

"Olivia."

"What about her?" He pictured their pregnant houseguest.

"Weren't you listening?"

"I guess not. Sorry." He ran his hand over his forehead. "I've had a rough day. I'm distracted."

"What do you think of Olivia?"

"She's funny. Can't cook worth beans. The things she does are crazy. Why do you ask?"

"What if you"—Mom gulped—"married her?"

"Married her?" The words erupted from him. He dropped his bottle of tea on the coffee table and stood. "Why would you suggest I marry a woman who's carrying another man's child? This is what you wanted to talk with me about?"

"Yes." Mom stood too. "Last week, I prayed for you to have wisdom and clarity about finding a wife. About whether you could accept marrying someone without romance first."

"I can't believe this." He pointed toward her. "You didn't like Katy. She was too worldly. Too lacking in prerequisites for being a pastor's wife. Yet you'd have me think Liv is better qualified to be my wife? When she's a new convert? Unwed and pregnant?"

The front door closed. Liv stood just inside the room, wide-eyed and sickly pale. Acid filled Smith's throat. He hadn't even heard the door open.

Liv shuffled forward then backward as if undecided whether to move into the room or leave the house immediately.

"Olivia." Mom rushed over to her. "I'm so sorry you heard that."

"I should come back later." Liv cast a dark glance at him.

Tension twisted his sinews into knots. A fire of frustration and blame ran through him. Had she known about his mom's idea when she made the pie deal with him? Had she assumed his mother would pick her?

"Please don't leave. Come in." Mom led Liv toward the kitchen.

She held two bags of groceries that appeared to be weighing her down. "I can set these somewhere and come back later to put them away." Her voice sounded high and odd.

Smith crossed the room to her. "Let me help with those."

"No." She clung to the bags. "I'm fine on my own. Have always been fine on my own."

He gulped and watched her shuffle across the room. He met Mom's sad gaze.

Hating himself for having said those things within earshot of Liv, he didn't know what to do. "Excuse me. I'm going to—" He nodded toward his bedroom. *I'm going to bury my head beneath a rock for a few hours.*

In his room, he leaned against the door, squeezing his eyes shut. What was Mom thinking? Marry a pregnant woman? Someone he barely knew? What would the Board of elders think about that? Of course, they'd never agree.

Even if Liv made him laugh like no one else ever had, marrying her was out of the question. He didn't love her any more than he loved Amaryllis. Olivia Brown would never be his wife!

Chapter Thirty-four

The next day after work, Liv stood at the counter peeling apples. She'd already mixed the sugar—making sure it was sugar this time—and the salt and spices. Last night, after the embarrassing conversation she walked in on, she didn't have the heart to attempt another pie. If Smith thought she was hunting for the role of being his pious wife, he was sadly mistaken.

Pregnant and unwed. A new convert.

He could take his stuffy self-righteous, better-than-everyone-else attitude and choke on her apple pie for all she cared. Tears that she abhorred flooded her eyes. She blinked a bunch of times so her tears wouldn't drip over the pile of apple slices. Stinking rotten emotions.

This morning she crept out of the house early enough to miss seeing Smith or Trish and grabbed breakfast at the diner. The weather was cooler, so she drove her car instead of walking. The space between the steering wheel and her stomach was narrow, but thankfully, she could still drive her Triumph.

She stopped peeling apples and turned on the faucet. Then splashed her face with cool water.

A masculine throat-clearing sound made her freeze. She'd hoped to get the pie into the oven before Smith came home. A towel materialized in front of her hands. She pressed it against her wet face.

"Liv," Smith said with a hesitant tone, "I'm so sorry for what you walked in on last night. For what I said to my mom."

She finished drying herself. Went back to peeling the apples, not trusting herself to speak, or to face him. The silence in the room became a roar of the clicking of the knife scraping the apple peels, then the swishing and thudding as pieces plunked into the bowl.

"Need any help?" he asked softly.

"No."

"I'm fixing dinner tonight, so we'll have to share the kitchen space."

"Fine." Grabbing the flour and sugar bags, she shuffled to the pantry shelf and set them down. Walking back, she tried not to waddle. Harder to do in her eight-and-a-half-month condition.

They worked in silence. Soon, the scent of cooking onions and garlic made her mouth water. Focusing on what she was doing, she carefully set the top crust in place. Next, she crimped the edges, praying this pie wouldn't burn. That it would taste fabulous. Even if she didn't care about who Smith dated, she wanted perfection from this pie. She had something to prove.

With the paring knife, she pressed tiny holes to make the shape of an apple in the crust. Stepping back, she admired her work. Not bad for a newbie baker.

"It looks lovely, Liv. Good job."

Internally, Smith probably laughed at her meager efforts, so she rejected his praise.

After hearing what he said to Trish last night, she'd gladly back out of the wager. Even if the pie tasted sensational, she didn't want him thinking she considered herself in the running as his date. Her, a pastor's wife? She was a worse option for the role than Katy had been.

After Liv put the pie in the oven and made sure to set the timer, she cleaned up her mess. Smith continued cooking hamburger meat and frying sliced potatoes. The delicious scents filled the space, but she hadn't met his gaze once since he walked into the room. Finally, she exited the kitchen, glad to not be in the same room as him.

Settling into her favorite spot in the corner of the couch, she pulled an afghan over herself, covering her lower half. She picked up her book on labor and delivery, ignoring the sounds of Smith setting the table. If she weren't so perturbed with him, she'd offer to help. Would tease him about having to go on a date with a woman of his mother's choosing because her pie was going to turn out awesome!

Instead, even if it was the best pie in the world, the kind where the crust melted in her mouth, she wouldn't say a word about who he should date. Let him marry Amaryllis. He deserved an unhappy, unromantic life.

Guilt hit her. Okay. Not an unhappy life. Wasn't she supposed to want good for other people the way she wanted good things for herself?

A couple of minutes later, Smith dropped into the chair opposite her. "Liv?"

She glanced at him over the top of her book.

Not smiling, his face looked red, his eyes droopy. "I'm sorry about yesterday. I don't know how much you heard."

"Enough."

"My mom gave me unwanted advice. I overreacted and said something I shouldn't have." He leaned his elbows on his knees, bracing his hands together. "I hope you can accept my apology."

"I don't want you either," she blurted, heat infusing her face.

His shocked expression satisfied her. Not every woman waited to fall at Smith North's feet like those three women at church did. Like Amaryllis probably did.

"Yes, I'm a new convert," she said determinedly. "That's a good thing, right? Here you are planning to be a pastor. Shouldn't you be glad for a heathen to turn her life around and follow the Lord?"

"Of course." He squirmed in his chair.

"You have an awfully high opinion of Smith North." She glared at him, giving him one of the you're-at-the-bottom-of-the-food-chain glares she used to give insubordinate employees. "I am pregnant and unmarried. But as a Christian, shouldn't you be proud of me for keeping my baby? For valuing life?" She took a sharp breath. "Just shut up about the other judgmental stuff."

She shifted the book so he couldn't see her face. So she could hide behind it and wipe a tear away. *Jerk*. She'd like to yell at him some more, but she said enough.

Even now, Trish would probably come home, hear about what Liv said to Smith and kick their mooching guest out of their house. Where would she sleep tonight? Back at the rest stop in her car?

She felt rather than heard Smith cross the room and squat down in front of her. He slid the book from her hands, a soft smile playing on his lips.

"You're one hundred percent right. I am proud of you for keeping the baby. For trusting God with your life. I'm sorry for how I behaved, Liv. Will you forgive me?" He tipped his head, a humbler expression on his face. "I was judgmental and rude. And cocky, arrogant, and self-righteous, if you want to add those. But I promise to do better." He held his right hand toward her.

Did he expect her to shake hands and forget what he said? *In your dreams, buddy*. Ugh. Wasn't that what forgiveness was all about? Not holding wrongs over someone's head?

She clasped Smith's hand and shook like she would have in a board room with another executive. Not like a wimpy, tearful woman.

"Truce?" he asked.

"I wouldn't go that far."

He chuckled and stood. "Dinner's almost ready. I wonder what's keeping my mom." Crossing the living room, he pulled the curtain back and peered out.

After last night's clash, was Trish avoiding Smith? Or staying away from Liv? Perhaps, dreading having to tell her it was time to leave?

Chapter Thirty-five

Dinner was awkward. Mom arrived just before six, rushing through the doorway saying she stopped by the dance studio for an impromptu workout. She said she needed it, no doubt because of the stress Smith caused. He owed her an apology too.

They sat down to the meal he'd prepared. No one chatted or shared about their day.

Mom glanced at Liv as if she were worried about her, or needing to clear the air, which made Smith feel more like a heel.

"Pie smells wonderful," Mom said tightly.

If only she knew what rested on this pie's outcome. Smith glanced at Liv. She kept her gaze averted and gnawed on her lower lip. He half hoped the pie tasted terrible. If it tasted great, he'd have to stick to his word and go out with whomever his mother chose for his date. By the looks of the golden crust and the shimmering sugar on top, it was Liv's finest baking effort yet. Now that he knew who Mom thought he should marry, the idea of biting into the pie nearly made him sick.

Liv made the wager with him in fun. She hadn't pursued him. Didn't she say she didn't want him? He inwardly chuckled over her heated words.

"Do you still want to have our Bible study after dinner?" Mom glanced at Liv.

"Sure." She didn't elaborate, didn't look Smith's way.

"I'll clean up the kitchen," he offered. Then he'd hide out in his room for the rest of the evening. Give them privacy to talk. Mom would probably explain to Liv why she suggested what she did.

He still wished she hadn't mentioned it. Otherwise, this awkwardness wouldn't exist. He'd be looking forward to trying the pie Liv made, thinking it was something funny between them.

Perhaps, if the pie turned out delicious, Mom would pick someone from church for him to go out with. Gracie Glen or Riley Morrison, ladies he liked to chat with.

Finally, the meal ended.

"Aren't we going to have pie?" Mom asked in a disappointed tone.

"No," Liv said quickly. "It has to cool."

As Smith worked on cleanup chores in the kitchen, he skirted around the delicious-looking pie on the counter. He heard whisperings coming from the other room, but he couldn't tell what Mom and Liv were discussing. After washing and drying the dishes, he quickly strode through the living room, noticing they had their Bibles open. Both glanced at him, but neither smiled.

In his room, he flopped down on the bed, arm over his forehead, and stared at the ceiling. How many stupid things could a guy do? Especially one who spent a week in prayer and fasting? One who should have heard the Holy Spirit cautioning him to not be insensitive. Yet, he hadn't listened to the quiet voice inside. Had lambasted Mom. Hurt Liv, the innocent in this setup.

And it was a setup, right? He'd choose his own wife, thank you very much. He had to tell Liv the bet was off.

Yet, he didn't like backing out of a promise.

Chapter Thirty-six

Liv sliced the pie slowly. The sweet scent of warm apples and cinnamon tickled her senses. Even with the wager looming over her head, she hoped she got this pie right.

Glancing over her shoulder, she whisked her finger through some of the pie filling and brought it to her tongue. Purely divine. If the crust tasted as good, this would seal the deal.

She sliced the knife through the crust. Smooth. Flaky. Using the pie server, she scooped the first piece out of the warm pie pan and set it on a plate. Staring at the single piece of pastry that looked near perfection, her heart hammered in her ears.

Was this pie worth the trouble it might cause?

What if she threw it in the trash the way she did her last pie? That way Smith and Trish could be at peace with each other. She picked up the salt container. All she had to do was sabotage it by sprinkling a layer of salt over the crust. Ready to rid the household of her part in the bet, she lifted the salt container. Aimed.

"Don't do it!" Smith charged into the room and yanked the salt container from her fingers. "You want to ruin the pie? For the deal to be off?"

"Yes," she said, feeling humiliated.

He glared at her for about fifteen seconds, then he opened a cupboard and put the salt and pepper containers high on a shelf, out of her reach.

"Why ruin the dessert you've put so much effort into?"

"I thought it would make things better." She picked up the pie server and put the next piece on a saucer.

"I've been waiting to try that pie." He huffed pretentiously. "If you succeeded in ruining it, I would have gone to bed hungry and upset over the loss."

"And now?"

"If it tastes good, I'll fall asleep a happy man."

"I didn't know apple pie had that much power over you."

"You'd be surprised." He grabbed three forks out of the silverware drawer. Crossing the room, he set the forks and napkins on the table. "Hurry up, woman, I'm eager to see if your pie passes the test."

Nervously, she carried two of the saucers to the table.

Smith ran around her and grabbed the other one. "Mom, the pie's ready!" he shouted. Then he leaned toward Liv. "We don't have to tell her what you almost did."

She sat down and took a bite of pie. The crust melted in her mouth. *Mmm.*

"I'm so glad you didn't ruin it," Smith said around a bite.

Liv cleared her throat loudly.

"What are you saying?" Trish asked as she sat down.

"A private joke." He winked at Liv.

She put another bite of the baked apple in her mouth and sighed. This was a masterpiece! The best thing she'd ever made!

Smith jumped up and dished himself another piece. Apparently, he liked it, too.

Whether he followed through on dating someone of his mother's choosing or not, she was grateful the pie turned out well.

Little Mister kicked against her, and she jumped.

"What's wrong?" Smith asked.

"The baby's kick surprised me." Liv smoothed her hand over her belly. "Want to feel him?" She glanced across the table at Smith's slack-jawed expression. "I thought you might like to feel a baby kick, that's all."

He nodded hesitantly.

"I want to feel it." Trish leaned over and put her hand on Liv's stomach, moving her palm slowly. "There it is. My, he is strong."

Liv glanced at Smith again. "Do you want to?"

"Okay." He squatted beside her and held out his hand, obviously unsure what to do.

She took his hand and laid his palm gently on the place where Trish's hand had been.

"Whoa."

"Crazy, huh?" She moved his fingers toward the center of her belly.

He chuckled. "That's something. He is strong." Smith returned to his seat. "Thank you."

"Of course."

She was thankful for the peace that filled the room while they enjoyed apple pie and a baby's kicking. Even if Little Mister wasn't arriving under the best of circumstances, a baby was a blessing, no matter what. And so was a mouthwatering piece of apple pie!

Chapter Thirty-seven

Smith woke up suddenly out of a sound sleep. Heaving in gulps of air, he shoved the blankets off. He'd just had the strangest dream! All the pie he consumed must be the cause.

He strode into the kitchen, poured a glass of cold water, and brought it back to his room, trying not to make a sound that might disturb Liv. Maybe he'd read a few Bible verses before he fell back to sleep. Sitting on the bed, he flipped the pages to Matthew where Joseph was warned in a dream to flee Bethlehem and go to Nazareth. Then to a couple of instances where God directed other people through dreams.

Leaning against his pillow, he pondered his dream. In it, he'd been kissing Liv! Not a blasé brush of their lips either. It was more of an I'm-madly-in-love-with-you kiss. Then there seemed to be a time shift, and she wasn't pregnant. They stood in a garden. In fact, he recognized the parsonage at Thunder Ridge in the background. Turning, he'd watched three little boys run straight for them. One, a toddler. The others, maybe five and six.

Him and Liv kissing? Having kids together? Why would he dream about such things?

A nearly unswallowable gulp choked him.

What if God was directing him to look at Liv … like a woman he might be interested in? What if Mom's words about giving Liv a chance were another way God was guiding him?

By morning, a migraine throbbed in his temples. He called in sick to the temp agency. He needed a day of contemplation and prayer anyway.

Maybe he should go by and talk with Pastor Tim. His mentor often helped him see things more clearly. Although, he'd be embarrassed to tell him about the romantic nature of his dream. Did that aspect of his night vision disqualify it from being from God?

While he ate his oatmeal with brown sugar, he read from the Psalms. Filling himself with spiritual words, he tried to stop remembering what kissing Liv and having a family with her had felt like in his dream. He thought of what Mom said about him marrying Liv. That was still a crazy idea, right?

How could he get past the fact she was pregnant with another man's child? Didn't he want to marry someone pure? Someone as new to lovemaking as he would be?

With the way Katy pushed for intimacy, had she been innocent? Maybe she had more experience than she let on. He groaned.

He'd better give Pastor Tim a call.

Two hours later, Smith sat in his mentor's office, sharing his dream with Pastor Tim, still trying to make sense of it. His pastor nodded empathetically, but he seemed puzzled too.

"So, let me get this straight. What you're asking is … is it possible for God to direct you through dreams? Of course, it's possible."

"I need to know if He is guiding me." Smith clenched his hands together. "Not whether it's possible."

"You're the only one who can decide that. Verify it through prayer. Through reading the Word." Pastor Tim ran his fingers over his worn Bible. "You've prayed and asked God for guidance, right?"

"Yes. I spent a week fasting and praying."

"Yet, you are shocked when an answer came to you in a way you weren't expecting?" Pastor Tim chuckled. "When it comes to spiritual things, you have to learn to expect the unexpected."

"But Liv is pregnant!"

Pastor Tim smoothed his palm over his clean-shaven chin. "That would be a leap for you, wouldn't it?"

"Yes." Smith expelled a breath. "I like her. She's fun to be around. But marriage? I can't fathom that."

They sat in silence for a minute.

"How does she feel?"

"Who?"

"Olivia. How does she feel about you?"

Smith snorted. "I have no idea."

"You must have some idea. Does she flirt with you? She's living in your house."

"We might have flirted about making a pie." Smith briefly explained their pie wager.

"Hmm."

Smith leaned forward, anticipating some words of advice or spiritual direction.

A merry-looking expression crossed the pastor's face. Chuckling, he said, "It never hurts to marry a woman who can make a good pie!"

Chapter Thirty-eight

Mom stared at Smith as if he'd gone mad. "You want me to tell you who to go on a date with?"

"That's right." He should have waited until she took off her coat and relaxed for a few minutes. Instead, as soon as she walked in the door, he cornered her with the question.

"If you were to choose someone for me to go on a date with, who would you pick?"

"You're serious?" She gawked at him.

No wonder. Hadn't he nearly bitten her head off the night before last?

Mom slipped out of her jacket and sat down in the easy chair. "I don't understand."

Smith dropped onto the couch across from her. "I'm sorry for overreacting to your thoughts about Liv before. I value your input in my life." He took a breath. "I visited with Pastor Tim today."

"Did you get some direction?"

"Just this. I want you to tell me who you'd have me go out on a date with if you were to choose."

"Really, Smith."

"Who would it be?"

"Olivia." She tossed up her hands. "There. I'd choose Olivia."

He knew it. He closed his eyes for a moment.

"But as you said, she's pregnant." Her voice turned into a whisper like Liv might be hiding around the corner. "She has a past. But she's trusting in Jesus. I love her like a daughter. How can we hold anything against her when our Lord does not?"

He couldn't disagree with anything she said. "I had a dream about her last night."

"You did?" She rested her palm over her heart.

"I don't know if it means anything. Pastor Tim says I shouldn't be surprised by God's revelation after I've spent time praying and fasting about my future."

"True."

"Yet I can't fully accept it. That it's a dream from God, I mean." He thrust out his hands. "I had such high ideals about marriage."

"I know." Mom sighed. "What now?"

"I asked you about the dating stuff because of a challenge I accepted from Liv."

Mom's eyebrows rose. "What kind of challenge?"

"If she made a good-tasting pie, which I doubted she could do, I'd let you, well, I'd let you pick a date for me."

"You're kidding!" Mom covered her mouth with both hands. "She didn't know who I'd pick, did she?" She lowered her hands and grinned.

"No, she didn't."

The front door opened, and Liv entered, ending their conversation.

As Smith prepped their dinner, he felt a flicker of hope. What if he and Liv were meant to be together? What if God had directed Liv and Mom into the same restaurant the day they met like Mom thought? What if his dream had been the Lord guiding him? Could Smith accept Liv as his wife? Accept that she might be God's plan for his life, and he for hers?

After dinner, Mom disappeared into her bedroom, saying she was beat. Her gaze met his with a warning. Was she telling him to be nice when he spoke to Liv?

Carrying two cups of peppermint tea into the living room, Smith set one on the coffee table in front of Liv.

"What's this?" She glanced up from her maternity book.

"I thought you might like a hot drink. I fixed one for myself too."

"Thanks."

"Sure." He dropped into the chair, sipping his tea. He'd been nervous about this conversation for hours.

Liv picked up her cup and kept thumbing through her book. She was lovely in this soft, evening light. Her hazel eyes met his gaze. "What?"

She had a nice smile too.

He took a deep breath. "I have a question to ask you."

"Okay." She lowered her book and set down her cup. "What is it?"

"Would you"—he set down his cup on the end table and scooted forward on his chair—"would you go out to dinner with me tomorrow night?"

"What? Why?" Her eyes widened.

He couldn't tell if she was shocked by the idea or abhorred by it. "Would you be my dinner date?"

"Look at me!" She swayed her hands toward her stomach. "With me being this size, why on earth would I go out on a date with you?"

Her reaction solidified his opinion that she didn't see him as a potential date or a possible spouse.

"I'm following through on our wager." Partly, anyway. After her cool reaction to his question, he wasn't mentioning his dream.

"Can't find a real date, huh?" she asked with a smirk. "Go ask your mother. She'll pick one of those girls who have been drooling over you at church."

"I did ask her." He grinned. "She chose you."

"Your mother is sweet." Her face turned a couple of shades of pink. "As you can see, I'm not in a place to be dating a future pastor. Thank you for asking, though."

"How would it be if we went out as friends?"

She met his gaze, not agreeing. Not turning him down either.

"Your pie was amazing, Liv." With his palms together, he made a pleading gesture. "Can we go out for a nice dinner together?"

"Shall we ask your mom to join us?"

He held in the urge to burst out laughing. His mom on a date with him and Liv? "Not this time."

Chapter Thirty-nine

Liv followed the host to their table, hoping Smith, walking behind her, didn't notice her waddle. Not even the billowing midnight blue dress she purchased for the occasion could hide her shape or her movements.

Smith assisted her with her chair, which made her feel only more cumbersome and conspicuous. She eyed the expanse of tables and guests to locate a restroom sign in the far corner. Rats. She'd have to parade across the whole restaurant to reach it.

After getting situated and ordering hot tea, Liv perused the menu. Several entries intrigued her. But she couldn't wait another minute. "Excuse me." She pushed away from the table.

"Need help?" Smith stood.

She wished he wouldn't do that. She gave him a look. Slowly, he sat back down.

"I'll be right back." She made her way across the expanse of the restaurant to get to the restroom. "Find anything spectacular?" she asked when she returned, nodding toward Smith's menu.

"I'll have the salmon and rice. What about you?"

"Chicken, maybe. Or soup." That should go down smoothly and not choke her due to her nervousness. She set her menu on the table.

"Liv—"

She met his gaze as the server arrived and took their orders.

Smith stared warmly at her, his face looking flushed. What had he almost said to her?

She cleared her throat self-consciously. Goodness, they ate across from each other plenty of times in the seven weeks she lived at Trish's house. Why was this so awkward? Because of the conversation she overheard? What led to them being here on a pseudo date?

"I'm glad we got the chance to go out like this," he said.

Right. Like he was glad to be out on a date with a whale?

"Thanks for inviting me. It was fun to get dressed up, even if I look like Shamu."

"Hey, now. None of that." He smiled, his chin dimple widening. "Why don't you tell me a little about yourself?"

"What's to know?"

Did he suspect she hadn't explained her past honestly to his mother? Did he plan to uncover who the real Olivia Dupont, er, Liv Brown, was?

"Sorry if that's too intrusive. Shall I tell you about me?"

"All right."

Soon she was laughing over his tales of growing up in a neighborhood of rapscallions, and how his mom must have wanted to pull her hair out over his shenanigans. He said Trish dragged him to Sunday school week after week until his heart grew tender toward the Lord. Even at eight years old, he wanted to become a pastor like Pastor Tim.

"How did your mom cope with this rowdy boy changing into a God-fearing adolescent?"

"Somehow she survived."

Their meals arrived during Smith's storytelling. Thankfully, she didn't choke on a single bite.

"Dessert?" Smith's eyes twinkled after they both finished their meals.

"That sounds like a perfect ending to a lovely outing." She avoided the word "date."

Smith ordered two pieces of apple pie.

"Now, tell me about you." He reached across the table and tapped her hand resting beside her dessert fork. His request didn't feel as much like prying as earlier.

"I was raised in a household of four—my parents, brother, Russel, and me—and a plethora of maids and cooks who never pleased my mother long enough to remain."

"Thus your lack of expertise in the kitchen." He winked.

She snorted as their slices of pie arrived.

Smith took a bite and made a face. "Yours was better."

Already full, she took a small taste of pie. It was quite good.

"And you worked in software?"

"Mmhmm. A family business."

"Did you enjoy it?"

His questions were innocent enough. But how much could she tell him? She still hadn't disclosed her real name, something she'd have to do before going into the hospital.

"I loved it. For a while, it was my whole world."

He smiled as if he understood, but curiosity sparkled in his eyes. No doubt, he wanted her to explain about the baby. About her previous life. Yet why should she get into any of that with him? What did it matter who she'd been involved with? They weren't dating. And that was in her past. She didn't even want to think about it herself.

"Sorry. I didn't mean to pry."

She sighed. "I was involved with someone I shouldn't have been. Someone who deceived me."

Smith nodded and didn't show any signs of condemnation. "And the father. Will he be involved in—" He waved his empty fork toward her. "What did you call him, Little Mister's life?"

"Yes, that's what I call him. No, Nick won't be involved. Not even listed on the birth certificate. His choice."

"I see." He leaned forward again. "You really should fix that."

"Fix what?"

"The baby's name. How about Lake?" He nodded as if the word explained everything. "John G. Lake was a traveling preacher whom God used in healings. He's a part of the spiritual history in Spokane."

"Lake, huh?"

"Yes." His smile spread wide. "You could name him after a man of faith like I was."

"I'll have to think about that."

Once their pie plates were empty, Smith stood and offered Liv his arm. She let him help her stand then slipped her hand into the crook of his elbow. Just a friend escorting her to his car, but she couldn't help noting her heart pounding hard against her ribs. Must be her romance-starved brain. Nothing else. Surely, nothing else.

Chapter Forty

When Smith escorted Liv into the house, Mom sat in the living room. "Welcome home, you two." Her gaze met his with questions he couldn't answer with Liv present.

Liv went straight into the bathroom, and Smith traipsed into the kitchen and filled a glass with water.

"Well?" Mom followed him. "How'd it go?"

"Fine. No shooting sparks, if that's what you're asking."

"Nothing?" She looked so disappointed, he almost laughed.

"I don't know what you expected."

"Yes, you do." She gave him one of her motherly looks.

"Wedding bells? Not likely." He guzzled the water glass empty.

Liv shuffled into the room. "Thanks for a lovely evening, Smith."

"You're welcome. Need any help with the sofa?"

"I can still do it. Thanks." She moved out of his line of sight.

Around three a.m., Smith awoke with an urgency to pray. He turned on the light and sat up. He prayed for Mom, Pastor Tim, people in the church who he knew needed physical healings, and wisdom for the Board members in Thunder Ridge.

Katy came to mind. *Lord, please touch Katy.*

Forgive her.

What? He thought he had forgiven her. Wanting to follow the Lord in everything, he prayed silently, *Lord, I forgive Katy for her part in the hurts and emotional brokenness between us. Please, touch her heart. Help her to find Your love.*

The longing for the woman he'd loved still churned in his heart at unexpected moments. He couldn't pretend he didn't miss her.

Another name came to mind.

In his list of people he cared about and prayed for, he overlooked Liv. Why was that?

He thought of the way they laughed and teased about her pie-baking calamities. The times she made a joke about some aspect of her life or work. Her smile. Her beautiful eyes. Her terrible cooking—other than that last pie. The way they flicked each other with the towel. All their shared laughter.

Lord, You know what Mom said about Liv and me. After Katy, it's hard to imagine loving anyone else. Sure, Liv's cute. But she's—

The Lord knew. Smith didn't have to spell it out to Him. Yet—

She's nearly nine months pregnant. How can that work with the expectations of the church Board? What would they say if I married her?

Married her? He coughed.

But wasn't that what going through with the pie challenge was about? To see if maybe Mom was right about God bringing Liv into their lives for a reason?

He checked his alarm. Nearly four a.m. Shutting off the light, he hunkered down under the covers.

His thoughts turned prayerful again. *Lord, if it is Your will for Liv and me to be together, could You show me? I need a sign. Help me to hear Your voice.*

Chapter Forty-one

Liv shuffled around the kitchen, prepping toast and cold cereal to eat before she left for work. After she lowered herself to the chair, she bowed her head and thanked God for the food.

Just as she bit into her toast, Smith stepped into the room. He was already dressed in his suit coat and slacks. "Good morning, Liv."

She finished chewing. "Morning. I'm surprised to find you awake so early."

"Rough night's sleep." He strode over to the counter and fixed his coffee.

She continued eating, needing to leave for work shortly.

Steaming cup between his hands, he dropped into the chair next to her. "Can we talk?"

"Yes." She sipped her hot tea to clear her throat. "What's going on?"

His face looked pale. "This is going to sound crazy. I had a strange dream for the second night in a row."

"Oh?"

"About you."

"Yeah, I'd say that's crazy. Why would you be dreaming about me?" She stuffed a bite of cereal in her mouth.

"It wasn't a bad dream. Sometimes God gives people direction through dreams." He met her gaze. "I was praying in the night. Then I fell asleep and had the dream."

"About me?"

"Us, actually."

"Us? There is no 'us.'" She took a bite of toast and chewed fast.

"Liv, how strange would it be if I asked you to marry me?"

"What?" she coughed out. Then took a long drink of water.

"You're shocked by the suggestion. I don't blame you."

Shocked. Stymied. Gobsmacked.

"Why would you even consider such a thing? We barely know each other." She smoothed her hand down her large belly, feeling Little Mister move. "I'm pregnant. Like twelve days from birthing a baby."

"This arrangement would benefit both of us. We get along, don't we?" He spoke quickly. "I'm in need of a wife who loves the Lord. Maybe I could be a strength in your life. Yours and the baby's."

"This arrangement? A strength?"

"I'm not expressing myself well." He ran his hands over his black hair. "Sorry."

Why would Smith propose a, what, marriage of convenience to her? Did she appear that desperate? She hardly needed him to be a strength for her. Wasn't he still in love with Katy?

"I have to go to work." She stood and scooped up the breakfast dishes. The faster she got out of the house, the better.

"Could I drive you?"

"No," she said abruptly. "I prefer to walk."

"I meant, so we could keep talking."

"About what?" She gave him the crankiest facial expression she could conjure up. She'd had enough of this discussion. Smith had to be crazy, and a bit desperate himself, to even be suggesting such a thing. "Do you mean to say you'd ask me to marry you—although your proposal had to be the worst one on record—so you can pastor a church?"

"Sorry for the insensitive proposal. I can do better." He heaved a sigh. "I feel rushed to come to a decision. I went out with Amaryllis to see if we were compatible. And my mom—" He stopped abruptly.

"Trish knows about this idea? And approves?"

His Adam's apple bobbed up and down. "She suggested it."

"Whaaaat?" Embarrassment heated up her core.

"She's sensitive to the things of God."

"I know that. But marriage between us? That is insane!" Liv carried her dishes across the kitchen and felt like hurling them into the sink.

Suddenly, Smith stood beside her. "Please, Liv. Will you consider marrying me for a good cause?"

"The only reason I'd marry you, or any man, is because of love. We don't have that."

"Not yet." He brushed a brief kiss over her cheek.

At his touch, hot flashes spread up her arms and over her neck.

"I like you, Liv. You make me laugh."

"Smith—"

"Think about it, that's all I'm asking, okay?"

She held his gaze for a few moments. Was he serious?

Chapter Forty-two

The call Liv answered that afternoon took her by surprise, although with a week and a half to go until Little Mister's birth, she should have expected it. "Miss Brown, your temporary position at Clark and Clark ends today. You are close to your baby's due date, correct?"

"Yes."

"Feel free to stop by and talk to us again afterward."

Liv wanted to groan. Instead, she politely finished the call.

Her last day on the job, and she hadn't set aside enough funds to cover hospital costs. Who knew what else she and Little Mister might need in the coming months? Hadn't she mooched off Trish long enough?

Smith's ridiculous proposal tumbled through her thoughts. Marry him for a good cause? That persnickety church Board would take one look at her and laugh their heads off. If they didn't approve of Katy, they certainly wouldn't approve of her.

Why would Smith, a good-looking man in his early thirties, contemplate a marriage of convenience to her when he could have the real deal with one of those church girls? What did he think she was? His very last resort to getting the job he wanted?

A loud groan erupted from her this time.

For the rest of the afternoon, her thoughts ran amuck as she entertained thoughts of what marriage to a pastor might be like.

A few people said goodbye to Liv on their way out the door. Sadly, no one said she'd done a great job or that they appreciated her work. Oh, the life of a temp!

This morning she walked to the job site. Now, it was raining hard. Maybe she could dash into the diner. Well, not quite dash in her condition. But after the day she had, comfort food sounded appealing.

A car pulled to the curb beside her and honked. Smith?

He jumped out of the car, squinting into the raindrops. "I thought you might be getting soaked in this." He held up his hand as if to catch droplets.

"Might be. I was thinking about getting some pie."

"Oh?" He grinned.

Did he think she was flirting? "I meant, I thought I'd head for the diner." She pointed down the block.

"Mind some company? Get in." He opened the passenger door.

"Um. All right." Getting out of the rain was probably wise. She slid her bulky torso onto the seat.

Smith shut the door and jogged around to the other side.

"Thanks for the ride."

"Sure. I was worried about you." He pulled into traffic. "Still want to stop for pie?"

Suddenly, she didn't want to be at another restaurant with him alone. Didn't want to rehash this morning's conversation, either. "We can just go home. Wouldn't want to ruin dinner."

"If you're sure. Another time, perhaps?"

"Maybe." She wasn't agreeing to anything.

At the house, Smith turned up the car heater and didn't shut off the engine. "Could we talk for a few minutes before we go inside?"

"Is that necessary?" Now she felt even more cornered and put on the spot. She was tired and wanted to put her feet up. Maybe get something hot to drink.

"Have you thought any more about my question?"

"Look, Smith, I got the ax today, so I'm not in the mood—"

"You got fired? I'm sorry." He clasped her hands as if he had the right to do that.

She withdrew her hands from his. "Nothing's changed. You and I would never work."

"Why not?" he asked softly. "I would be a good husband for you. A kind dad for your son."

"I'm sure you would be that, but—" She liked him wanting to be a dad to Little Mister. He told her before how much he wanted a big family. "What about love?" She wouldn't back down from the main issue stopping her from even considering his proposal.

"I'm sure love would come in time. We're already friends. We'd wait for love before … doing husband and wife things."

Husband and wife things? That wasn't a subject she wanted to contemplate with the man sitting beside her. Heat rushed to her cheeks. "We should go in."

"If we wait a few more minutes, the rain might let up."

The windshield wipers swishing back and forth made a steady rhythm in the car.

Smith still had his gaze locked on hers. "We get along, don't we?"

"I suppose." She smoothed her hand over the baby's elbow or a heel pushing against her stomach.

"How do you feel about having more kids?"

"Asking a pregnant woman that question is bad timing." She squinted at him.

"Sorry."

"You want a big family. Nine is out of the question."

He chuckled.

"Not that I'm agreeing to anything, because I'm not."

"Okay." Smith moved his hands over the steering wheel. "What's the biggest hindrance in your mind to us being together?"

"Other than not being in love? My past."

"'Though my sins be as scarlet, they shall be washed white as snow,'" he quoted softly.

Liv's heart thumped louder in her chest. Could he overlook her past?

"Liv? I can't say I love you like a woman being proposed to wants to hear," he said in a tender tone. "But someday, I will love you. I promise you I will pursue your heart."

Heat raced through her. But she still felt compelled to say, "I don't love you either."

He chuckled. "I'm glad you're honest enough to say that. When you say, 'I love you,' to me, and I say the words to you, it will make them all the sweeter." He stroked her cheek with the back of his fingers. "Would you be willing to take an adventure with me, Liv? A lifelong adventure?"

Tingles streaked up her spine and neck.

"Would you marry me?" he asked softly.

Could she marry him when she didn't love him? Then she was nodding. *Nodding!* Why was she agreeing to—

"Oh, Liv—"

"I have a stipulation," she said as a thought came to her.

"Okay."

"I'll go along with marrying you before we love each other if we are honest with the church Board. They have to agree to the whole thing."

"You're serious?" He tipped his head, staring intently at her. "You want them to know we're not marrying for love?"

"That's right. Complete transparency. We should tell them about my past, too."

"Liv—"

"I mean it. No secrets from them. They are getting a package deal. One they might not want."

"Ah, Liv." He groaned.

"If they decline to accept our irregular union, I won't hold you to anything. The proposal will be off." She said they had to be completely honest with the church, but what about her honesty with Smith and Trish? "I need to tell you something, too."

"You don't owe me any explanations. The past is in the past."

"You're sweet to say so." She sighed. "But there are things you should know."

"Okay." He clenched his jaw as if preparing for the worst.

"My last name isn't Brown."

"Oh?" His brows formed a V.

"I'm Olivia Dupont, daughter of Richard Dupont III." She touched her stomach. "Because of my father's embarrassment about the baby, he disowned me. I invented the last name of Brown."

"Dupont, huh?" He scratched his scalp.

"Mmhmm. I didn't want anyone to try to take advantage of my family connections."

Smith let out a loud guffaw.

"Why are you laughing?"

"I thought you were going to tell me some horrible secret. Like you were dying of cancer." He reached across the console and gave her a brief hug. "Instead, you're rich."

"No, I'm not." She pushed back from him. "When your mom found me, I was broke as a bum. All ties with my family have been severed."

"Olivia Brown Dupont"—he clasped both of her hands gently between his—"you are my family now. And my mom's family. We'll be a family for this baby too."

She'd heard of people marrying for money and prestige. What about matrimony in exchange for a family?

Chapter Forty-three

Liv stood next to Smith, clenching her hands together, as they faced Trish. How would marrying without being in love even work?

"Mom, Liv and I have decided to get married," he said calmly.

Trish's jaw dropped, her gaze flitting between them. "Really?"

They both nodded.

"Oh, my goodness!" Trish hugged Liv, then Smith. "This is wonderful news. Just wonderful. I'm so proud of both of you."

Liv chuckled in the awkward way that made her sound ten years old. "Thanks."

"Tell me all about it. Sit. Sit." Trish palmed the air with her hands and sat down in her easy chair.

Smith nodded toward the couch, and Liv followed his lead. She sat about a foot away from him.

"This is what I hoped and prayed would happen. Now, Little Mister will truly be my grandchild." Trish grinned and clapped.

"I want you to know that I've put a stipulation on Smith's proposal," Liv said.

"Oh?"

Smith's eyelids closed to half-mast. A tic throbbed in his jaw. What? Didn't he want her to tell his mom the truth?

"I'll only agree to move forward with this marriage if we tell the church Board about our plans. And if they accept our arrangement." Liv took a gulping breath. "There's no reason for us to marry if Smith still won't be chosen as their pastor."

"That sounds reasonable." Trish glanced at her son. "What do you think the elders will say?"

"Hard to guess. I'll call one of them tonight." Smith's expression turned somber.

Was he having second thoughts already?

"There is one other thing," Liv said.

"She won't care about your name." Smith gripped his hands together

"It's not that. Although, I will tell her about that." She faced Trish. "If the Board, by some miracle, accepts our proposed idea, would you come live with us in Thunder Ridge?"

"What do you mean?" Smith's jaw dropped.

They hadn't discussed it, but Liv focused on Trish. "Would you be a chaperone for us for however long it takes for us to fall in love?"

"Liv—" Smith groaned. "I will be a complete gentleman. I promise you." A softer expression crossed his face. "I care about you already."

"I know." She smoothed her hand over his coat sleeve. Realizing what she did, she pulled back. "This would be a sign of our attempt to do things in the right way, in the proper way, to the church Board and your future congregation."

"I would gladly move into the parsonage with you if you're both comfortable with that." Trish swayed her hands toward them. "Until the time comes when you are both ready to be fully married, I will be a chaperone, bottle washer, nanny, whatever."

"Thank you." Not only was Liv not ready to live in a house alone with Smith, but she would have missed the other woman's company dreadfully.

"Smith?" One of Trish's eyebrows lifted. "What do you think? I don't want to impose."

"You wouldn't be imposing. Your presence in our home when we haven't fallen for each other would be wise. Thank you, Liv, for suggesting it." He gave her a reassuring smile. "It will all work out, you'll see."

She hoped so. But what would they have to go through, how many hurdles might they have to cross, until they truly loved each other as husband and wife?

Chapter Forty-four

The next day, Liv sat down at Bob Carter's invitation, but Smith saw her hands moving nervously over her stomach. Hopefully, she'd relax and not feel like this meeting in the church basement was an inquisition. They all wanted the Lord's will. Smith knew this because of the in-depth conversations he'd had with Arnold, Bob, and Dennis over the course of his interviewing process and their time of fasting. He respected all three men.

Of course, he wished this requirement about him being married didn't hang over his and Liv's heads. But he felt at peace with his decision to marry her. And he was thankful she agreed to his proposal.

"Let's get started," Dennis said. Then he led them in a prayer for God's will to be done. "Smith, why don't you briefly explain what's happened since we last spoke."

"All right." He glanced at Liv, making sure she was okay.

With her past business meetings, high-powered luncheons, and helping lead a software company, he figured she could hold her own with these three guys sitting around a table, sipping coffee.

"Since our time of fasting and prayer, I've continued seeking the Lord about the future."

"As have we." Arnold nodded. "We're glad you're here today. Thank you for continuing to pray about solutions."

"You're welcome. I've sought counsel about this with Pastor Tim, and my mom, a woman who seeks the Lord daily."

"You're a blessed man." Dennis nodded.

"I am. A confused man some of the time."

A chuckle went up around the table.

"So, what have you decided?" Dennis asked, glancing at the wall clock.

Smith cleared his throat. "My mom believes, as do I, that the Lord brought Liv into our lives for a reason. Two months ago, Mom felt led to go into a restaurant to talk to someone. She was drawn to Liv's table." Smith told the story of her bringing Liv home and how she became like a daughter to her.

The men's gazes were aimed at Smith. Occasionally, they glanced at Liv, especially when he explained about her conversion. When he got to the part about asking her to marry him, he clasped her hand beneath the table. Whether for her support or for his own peace of mind, he was uncertain.

"Liv," Dennis addressed her, "you've been quiet through Smith's explanation. Is there anything you want to add?"

"Yes." She released Smith's hand. "I'm so thankful the Lord brought Trish to me that day. It was life-changing for me. She's shown me nothing but God's love through my time of living in her home. That's what has drawn me back to God."

Smith turned to watch Liv, intrigued by her sparkling eyes, and her sincere sharing of her faith.

"What Smith failed to tell you is vital to me that you know."

Dennis braced his elbows against the table, his chin resting against his fists. Arnold set his cup down with a clink. Bob cleared his throat. The men stared at Liv with worry lining their faces. What were they expecting her to say?

"I'm pregnant." She gave a soft laugh. "And not with Smith's child."

His face heating up, Smith gulped. Had she shocked the other men into silence? None of them chuckled or spoke.

"I have a past," she said quietly. "But the Lord has graciously forgiven me. Trish and Smith have forgiven me and offered me grace. I ask that each of you will do that also. Forgive as Jesus forgave me."

At her humble request, Smith sighed.

"Yes. I certainly do," Dennis said.

Bob nodded. "Absolutely."

"We all need forgiveness and grace," Arnold said.

"Thank you." She smiled. "I want us to be completely honest here. While Smith and I will marry, and we plan to honor our vows, we are not romantically in love at this time."

Her honesty was killing Smith. She told him they had to explain the whole matter to the Board. But waiting to hear the men's reaction made his next swallow feel like an eternity.

Arnold glanced at Bob. Both men exchanged questioning glances.

"That isn't to say we won't fall in love. I expect Smith to love me someday." She grinned cheekily. "I'm not a great cook. So, he doesn't have that to look forward to. Although, I can make a mean apple pie!"

Smith's face heated up again. But a peacefulness filled his heart, too. She was right in saying they weren't romantically involved. However, his wanting to wrap her in his arms right now had to be a genuine start toward that happening.

"Honesty and transparency are vital to us." Liv's voice altered from sweetness to a more confident tone, giving him an insight into her business persona. "We've all had trials and difficulties to face in life. Those make us stronger, don't they?"

The men shrugged and nodded.

"I made a bad choice in being with a dishonest man in my past." She huffed. "But Smith is honorable and kind. He was raised by a godly woman. I have no doubt he'd make you a fantastic pastor with a strong work ethic and a depth of integrity unrivaled by any man I've known." She met Smith's gaze. "In that same level of belief, I'm sure he'll make a great husband for me and a fabulous father for our children. If you'll give us a chance."

Grinning at her use of the word "children," Smith felt his backbone tighten. Liv's words about his calling soothed in him what Katy's doubts about his pastoral future had sabotaged.

"That's all I want to say. Thank you for your time, gentlemen." She clasped her hands together and sagged against the chair.

"Thank you, Liv." Dennis smiled at her. "Or is it Olivia?"

"Either." She pulsed her finger in the air. "One other thing. If you decide Smith is the man you want as pastor here, you don't have to worry about anything untoward happening before he and I are truly married."

Smith bit back a groan.

"His mom, Trish, will be moving into the parsonage with us as our chaperone." She met each man's gaze with a serious expression. "You have my word that I plan to be a loving wife to Smith. I can't guarantee I'll be a great pastor's wife, because I don't know what that job entails yet. But Trish will teach me. Like Ruth stayed with Naomi, I will be that person with Trish."

An almost holy silence filled the room.

Arnold wiped his eyes as if moved by Liv's words. "You've given us much to think about."

Fortunately, no one asked if they'd still go through with the marriage if Smith wasn't asked to be their pastor.

"Gentlemen. Thank you for your time." Smith stood and extended his hand toward each of the other men. Whatever they decided, they knew the truth about him and Liv.

He helped her stand and she chuckled, making a joke about trying not to waddle. Her humor, and her poise while she expressed herself in a humble way, impressed him.

"What now?" Liv asked as soon as she exited the ladies' room. "Grab some lunch?"

"Sounds good." A mischievous expression crossed her face. "Shall we celebrate with pie?"

"Always!"

Chapter Forty-five

Two days later when the phone rang, Smith hesitated to answer it. This might be the call that changed everything. His future. His relationship with Liv. His next step. Not that he doubted God's plan. But he might doubt himself if all his planning and taking a leap of faith fell through. Hadn't he reacted badly when things fell through with Katy?

Lord, help me. I want to completely trust You to work things out in my life.

He picked up the receiver. "Hello. This is Smith."

"Good morning. Dennis, here. The Board came to a decision late last night," he spoke quickly. "We'd like you to be our pastor."

"Really?"

"Yes, we talked until we had a unanimous vote. Will you move to Thunder Ridge and be our pastor, Reverend North?"

"Absolutely! Thank you." *Thank You, Lord!* "I've been praying about this since our meeting."

"As were we. God was good to give us the assurance we needed."

"What was that, if you don't mind my asking?"

"Actually, Olivia's expressed confidence in you as a minister and about her faith showed we could trust her." Dennis chuckled lightly. "Any woman who can speak so respectfully and confidently about her future husband is a rare gem. We'd be honored to have her as our pastor's wife."

The weighty words settled on Smith's shoulders like a mantle. The Board accepted him largely because of Liv? What a twist!

He thanked God anew for Liv's willingness to marry him. To begin a life with him together.

"About the details of your marriage, we've agreed to keep that to ourselves. No one else needs to know the intricacies of your private lives." Dennis paused. "Should you or Olivia choose to discuss it with the congregation in the future, that's up to you."

"I appreciate that. We both appreciate it."

"When will you marry? The sooner the better, I'd say." Dennis chuckled.

"I agree. When do you want me to begin as pastor?"

"As soon as possible. The congregation has been without a leader long enough. Folks are begging," Dennis said in a wry tone, "for someone other than Bob to speak on Sunday."

"Shall I plan on being there Sunday, then?"

"That would be great! We'll have a potluck dinner following the service to welcome you and Olivia."

"Thank you so much for the honor you've given me. Given us."

"You're welcome. See you both on Sunday. The parsonage is ready whenever you want to move in."

"Perfect. I'll let you know."

Smith said goodbye, hung up the phone, and since he was alone, shouted, "Hallelujah!" God had answered his prayers. He was going to be a pastor! He was going to be a husband and a dad, too!

Thank You, Lord!

Chapter Forty-six

Liv stood next to Smith in front of Pastor Tim, feeling nervous, uncomfortable, and gigantic in her midnight blue dress. But she was here with her husband-to-be, and Trish and Terri Jo, Pastor Tim's wife, as witnesses.

"Are you both ready for this?" the pastor asked with a twinkle in his eyes.

"I'm ready." Smith smiled.

Liv nodded and shrugged tiredly. As soon as this and their celebration lunch were over, she was going home and resting.

Smith looked handsome dressed in a gray sports coat and black slacks. His dark tie was slightly askew, and she was tempted to straighten it.

Trish beamed at her son, then at Liv.

"Do you, Smith North, take Olivia Dupont to be your wedded wife?" Pastor Tim asked.

Smith smiled at Liv, but the skin around his eyes looked tight. Was he nervous? Was he thinking of the vows he should have been taking with Katy?

"I do," he said huskily.

"Do you, Olivia, take Smith to be your wedded husband?"

Smith met her gaze with a raised eyebrow. Did she want to promise to "take him" to be hers? Last night, he told her they would stay married, be great friends, and someday be lovers. That it would take time, but they would fall in love. He'd spoken so confidently then.

"I do." She made her voice say the words with more confidence than she felt.

"By the power vested in me, I pronounce you husband and wife." Pastor Tim grinned like a proud father. "You may kiss your bride, Smith."

Kiss her? They hadn't discussed this part. A kiss was probably expected in a wedding ceremony. She automatically wet her lower lip. They turned awkwardly toward each other, her stomach bumping into his hand.

He leaned toward her, his eyes blinking slowly.

What should she do? Offer him her cheek? Some wedding kiss, huh?

But then his soft fingers gently cupped her cheeks, stilling her unease. Her face burned in every place his fingertips brushed her already hot skin. He gazed meaningfully into her eyes as if asking her if it was okay to kiss her. She nodded slightly.

"Thank you for marrying me, Liv."

His lips brushed hers with whisper softness, his gentleness taking her by surprise. Then he stepped back.

Liv released a slow breath.

Trish hugged her and kissed her cheek. "Welcome to our family, Olivia. You're already a part of our family, but this makes it official. You're a North too."

No longer a Dupont. No longer a Brown.

"Thank you."

Trish hugged Smith and spoke privately to him. Then they went to their favorite diner for a meal and, of course, apple pie for dessert.

As soon as they arrived home, Liv curled up on the couch and fell asleep. A couple of hours later, she awoke to a startling backache. She gasped at the intensity. Oh, no. Was she in labor on her wedding day?

"Trish?" she called weakly. Her stomach spasmed and she gritted her teeth before remembering she was supposed to relax and breathe during contractions. Relax? Yeah, right.

When the pain subsided, she pushed herself into a sitting position. Somehow, she had to get off the couch.

"Smith?" She hated to bother him.

No one seemed to be hearing her. Shuffling to the bathroom, she paused outside the bedroom doors. "Trish?"

A sound of movement. The door opened.

"What is it—" Trish gasped. "Is it time?"

"I think so." Another contraction hit. She grabbed hold of the doorframe. "Yesssss." She groaned loudly, clenching her teeth. "My back—"

Trish maneuvered around her and pressed her palm against Liv's lower back. "Breathe, hon. You're doing fine. It'll pass soon."

Smith's bedroom door opened, his eyes wide. "Is she okay?"

"She will be," Trish answered.

The contraction dissipated and Liv blew out deep breaths. "I have to use the bathroom."

"Then we'll take you to the hospital."

"This might be false labor." Fake marriage. False labor.

"I don't think so," Trish said.

With difficulty, Liv went into the bathroom and used the facilities. While she washed her hands, another contraction hit. Five minutes since the last one? Yikes.

When she opened the door, Trish stood there with her coat on and the bag of baby necessities they'd packed hanging over her shoulder.

Smith strode toward her from the front door. "Car's ready. What can I do?"

"Hold her arm," Trish told him. "I'll support her other side." She looked closely into Liv's eyes. "Did you have a contraction in the bathroom?"

Liv nodded. "A bad one."

"Let's hurry."

"Shall I carry you?" Smith offered gallantly.

"I'd like to see you try." Liv pelted him with a glare, not finding any humor in the situation. "Hold onto my arm if a contraction hits. I'll walk slowly. Don't want Little Mister to be born on the porch."

Smith and Trish supported her arms. She made it to the car without a contraction. How to climb inside, lowering herself into a seated position, while she felt so achy, remained a mystery. Trish, anticipating her needs, ran around to the driver's side, crawled across the console, and helped ease Liv into the seat.

Another contraction shot pain through her. Unprepared, she gritted her teeth and growled as her body spasmed.

Smith squatted beside her, his face filled with worry. "I'm so sorry for what you're going through. I wish I could help."

Contraction finished, Liv breathed hard then went limp against his shoulder.

"Smith, close the door and get in." Trish buckled up behind the steering wheel.

Smith helped Liv lean back against the seat. Then he shut the door, climbed into the backseat, and slammed the door.

Trish drove slowly to the hospital, but Liv wished she'd hurry faster. Sitting upright in the passenger seat was pure agony, especially when another contraction took her by surprise. Smith reached his arm through the gap over the console and clasped her hand. She squeezed his fingers as hard as she could until the spasm ended.

At the emergency entrance, getting out of the car and into the wheelchair was a miserable experience. Liv felt like she was losing her mind. How could she keep going through this intense pain? And it was going to worsen?

Finally, two nurses helped her into a bed in the birthing room. A doctor examined her and said it wouldn't be long. What a relief!

Trish stood in place beside Liv, ready to administer strong back rubs as needed. Drugs were offered and Liv desperately wanted to take them. But for some reason, must be all those natural birthing videos Daria showed them, she refused. It was going to be only a little while longer, right?

Shocked and awed by the process of labor, she felt her body kick in as if it was trained to get Little Mister out of the birth canal quickly. On the final push, with the glory and beauty of delivering a child into the world—and the sweet relief of labor being over—the moment she saw her boy, her heart melted into a puddle of love. Tears flooded her eyes. The widest smile she ever grinned crossed her face as she sagged against her pillow and the nurse placed the cuddly bundle in her arms. This was her first time holding a baby. Her baby.

"Oh, Olivia, he's beautiful," Trish whispered.

"Hey, Little Mister. Nice to meet you." Liv stroked his dark hair that would be a perfect match to Smith's. Her heart hiccupped. She stroked her baby's cheek. "Wait until you meet your daddy."

She glanced at Trish. A poignant moment passed between them. Trish's eyes filled with tears, and she leaned down and kissed Liv's cheek. "He's going to love him."

"I know." She kissed the baby's forehead. "You are loved, Little Mister."

The nurse took the baby to clean him up. Exhausted, Liv wanted to go to sleep. The doctor and nurse had other ideas. But finally, she closed her eyes and dozed, thankful she'd made it through her ordeal. "Labor" had a different meaning for her now.

When she woke up, Trish sat in the chair next to her bed, a soft smile on her face. "How are you doing, hon?"

"Better. Thirsty."

Trish hopped up, grabbed a glass of apple juice, and leaned a straw toward Liv's lips.

"Thanks." She guzzled most of the glass of juice. "Where's the baby?"

"In the nursery."

"Smith?"

"Last I saw him, he stood outside the nursery window gazing down at your baby. His son. Fatherhood suits him."

Liv chuckled. "Can I see him?"

"Smith?"

"Little Mister."

"Let's ring for the nurse." Trish pushed a button resting on Liv's bed.

"I wouldn't mind talking with Smith later."

Trish smiled, seemingly pleased with that.

Was Smith really watching over the baby already?

Chapter Forty-seven

Smith stood outside Liv's hospital door and took a deep breath. He'd become a husband and a dad on the same day. He was about to see his wife—*his wife*—following the birth of her—no, their—first child. A mix of gratitude, joy, shock, and weariness strummed through him.

He still couldn't get over the changes in his life. Getting married, taking on the new pastorate, moving to Thunder Ridge, and now, becoming a dad. This had been one tension-filled day as he married Liv, then waited, pacing and praying, in the waiting room for news of the baby's arrival and his wife's well-being.

The door opened.

"Smith, you're here." Mom took hold of his arm and drew him into the room. "Come in."

His gaze sought Liv's. A warm, but tired, look crossed her face. She lifted her arms slightly, showing him the tiny bundle wrapped in a blue blanket.

"He's here," she said softly.

Smith rushed to her side, gazing down on the little guy he'd been observing in the nursery already. "He's amazing."

"He has dark hair like yours." Her eyes twinkled up at him.

Smith leaned over and pressed his lips to the sleeping baby's forehead. Then he did the same to Liv. Pausing inches from her face, he smiled. "You did good, Livvy."

"Thanks. But no one calls me Livvy."

"No one, huh? Is that a challenge?"

"You feel that too? Every time I say something?"

Her words were teasing, but she said them slowly like she was fatigued. He wouldn't push his nickname for her, right now.

"Something like that."

"Trish says you've been here the whole time. That was nice of you."

"Just waiting. Nervous for you two."

Mom put her arm around Smith's back. "He wouldn't have missed this for the world, would you, Son?"

"Nope."

"Can you believe it?" Liv chuckled and a little color blossomed in her cheeks. "Marriage and a baby on the same day. Want to hold him?" Her eyes darkened. "I mean, do you?"

"Uh, yeah." He felt tongue-tied. "I do."

"Why don't you have a seat?" Mom directed him to a chair next to the bed.

He sat down and she settled the baby gently in his arms. Such small features. Tiny fingers. A slight yawn stretched across the newborn's mouth as he nestled into the crook of Smith's arm. Awestruck, he gazed at the little fellow for several minutes without saying anything.

"What are you going to name him?" He glanced at Liv.

She looked so tired, her eyes droopy, her shoulders sagging.

"Are you okay?"

Mom hurried to Liv's other side. "How are you, hon? Doing okay?"

"Just sleepy." She looked like she could barely keep her eyes open.

"Maybe I should go." But Smith didn't want to leave. He wanted to stay right here with his son ... and his wife.

"You don't have to leave." Liv met his gaze beneath heavy eyelids.

"Okay." He'd sit right here with Little Mister all night, if necessary.

The sounds of Liv's deep breathing reached him. He watched her sleep. So lovely. Precious.

Thank You, Lord, for bringing this woman to me. And for this little boy, our first son. Help us to become a real family.

"You okay?" Mom whispered. "I'll take him if you're tired."

"I'm fine. Better than fine." He snuggled the baby closer to his chest, to his heart.

Mom snapped a picture with her camera. Fortunately, she didn't use a flash that might awaken Liv.

Smith held the little guy for an hour, inwardly whispering truths to his heart. *You are dedicated to the Lord, young sir. You are going to be a blessing to our family. You have a loving grandma. A fabulous mommy. A dad who will always support and guide you the best he can. And while I don't know your name yet, you are my firstborn son. I love you.*

Chapter Forty-eight

Liv awoke groggy and thirsty. She opened her eyes and smiled when she saw Smith holding Little Mister, gazing down at him as if conversing with him. Dad and son. Tears filled her eyes.

Thank You, God, for giving my baby and me this man to be a part of our lives. He'll be a good dad. A good husband ...

"You're awake." Smith met her gaze. "I've been talking with our little guy."

"Lake."

"Really? You're calling him Lake?"

"Uh-huh." She reached for the glass on the portable tray, but Trish jumped up and helped her get the straw to her mouth.

"Hi there, Lake," Smith whispered. "Lake North. I like it."

"So do I." Trish smiled and leaned over the baby. " Hi, Lake. I'm Granny Trish."

Nostalgia whisked through Liv. If only her own parents had been as warm and accepting of her having a son as Trish was. She shook her head, squeezing negative thoughts out of her mind. She needed to move on. Wasn't marrying Smith a part of that moving-on process?

"May I hold him now?" She reached out her arms.

"Certainly." Trish took Lake from Smith's arms and put him into Liv's. "There you go. Here's your mommy."

"Hi, Lake." Liv touched his forehead, smoothing her fingers down the sides of his face and shoulders like she'd imagined doing when he was in her womb. "Boy, have I waited a long time to see you."

"It's probably time for a feeding," Trish said. "Smith? Maybe you could get us some coffee while Olivia feeds Lake."

"Oh, sure." He nodded in Liv's direction and then exited the door, shutting it quietly behind him.

"Thanks." Liv adjusted the baby blanket over her shoulder. "This will take some getting used to."

"In no time, it will be easy-peasy."

About fifteen minutes later, a tap at the door sounded and Trish scurried to answer.

"I have coffee." Smith's husky voice came through the crack in the door. "Is it too soon?"

Trish glanced back at Liv.

"It's fine. He's done eating and is asleep." She pulled her nightgown over her shoulder.

Trish opened the door wider and accepted a to-go cup of coffee. "Thank you."

Smith entered the room hesitantly. "Everything okay in here?"

"Yes. We're doing good." Liv smiled down at her sleeping baby, so glad she could hold him in her arms now.

"He's awesome." Smith grinned. "That was the first time I ever held a newborn."

"Not your last!" She chuckled. "Although, I'm not saying I agree with having nine kids. Especially now that I know what labor is like."

"No doubt." Smith laughed and settled back on the chair he'd vacated.

Trish dropped into the other chair, sighing like she was exhausted.

"Trish, you should go home and get some sleep," Liv said. "You worked hard today too."

"I will. Thank you so much for letting me be part of this miracle."

"You're welcome. I couldn't have done it without you." She met Smith's gaze briefly. "Maybe we'll all meet and do this again someday in the future."

"Sounds like a plan." Smith smiled, his cheeks turning ruddy. "Sorry I couldn't bring you one of these." He lifted his cup. "I would have but since you're nursing—"

"They have juice galore here." Liv looked over the options on her portable tray.

"What happens next?" Smith crossed his leg over his other knee, settling into his chair.

"If everything's fine, we'll be released after the doctor's morning rounds."

"We'll come back and pick you up then." Trish stood and grabbed her coat.

"Actually"—Smith glanced from his mother to Liv—"I thought I'd stay here tonight."

"You don't have to do that." Liv swallowed a lump in her throat.

"It's our wedding day. You're a first-time mom. I want to be here with you."

His smile sent tingles all through her. That's right. It was their wedding day.

"Looks like a hard chair to sit in all night."

"I'll be all right."

Yawning, Trish leaned over and kissed Liv's cheek, then Lake's. "Sleep well, my lovelies."

"Goodnight, Granny. Thanks for those contraction back rubs."

"You're welcome, hon." Trish waved then left the room.

"Need anything?" Smith asked.

"Could you hand me some grape juice?"

"Sure thing." He gave her a glass of juice with a straw.

After she drank her fill, she passed him the glass and he set it down.

"Have you decided on Lake's middle name?"

"He needs one that works with Lake and North." Liv tilted her head from side to side, looking at the baby from different angles. "Maybe Daniel after your dad."

"What about Richard after yours?"

"I want a name that will be special to Trish," Liv said determinedly. "She changed the course of my life."

"That's sweet of you. Whatever you choose will be perfect. Do you want me to put him in the bassinet?" He nodded toward the clear mobile baby bed.

"That would be great. Thanks."

He took the baby from her, obviously more confident about holding a newborn now. "Sleep well, Lake." He kissed his forehead.

Smith was being so gentle and kind. So daddy-like. Liv wanted to store this memory of father and son in her heart, but her heavy eyelids wouldn't stay open.

Chapter Forty-nine

A week after Lake's birth, Smith and a couple of buddies from church loaded up a rental truck with all their furniture and household belongings. Mom had emptied the kitchen items into boxes. Liv offered to help with packing, but Smith and Mom kept telling her no. Her red Triumph was on a tow dolly ready to be attached to the truck.

"Are you doing okay?" he asked as he strode through the living room and saw Liv rocking Lake in the rocking chair, the only piece of furniture left in the house.

"I'm okay. You probably want to put this in the truck."

"It can wait until you're done." He pressed his lips against Lake's forehead. "We're going on an adventure, buddy."

"A week old and he's getting a second home already." Liv's tired smile said she probably did too much work today, even with him and Mom trying to keep her from doing so.

He stroked a wisp of blond hair out of her face. By her wide eyes, his touch startled her. Clearing his throat, he stepped back and jammed his fingers into his jeans pocket.

"I'll move so you can load this."

"Don't worry about it. I'm going to get some water first." He strode into the kitchen and found Mom cleaning the interior of the fridge. "Sorry for all the work this move has caused you." He filled a disposable cup with water.

"Nonsense. The place needed a good cleaning before we left." She stood and met his gaze. "It's been a lovely home for us. I'm glad we found a renter to live here until we figure out what to do with it." She smoothed her hand over the green countertop. "Lots of tears and laughter were shared here."

"That's the truth! Your moving up to Thunder Ridge with us means a lot to Liv and me. Thanks for agreeing to be our chaperones." He felt silly saying that, but he appreciated her willingness to do anything to help him and Liv segue into marriage.

Mom hugged him. "Things are going to work out. Be patient and you'll see."

He knew she meant he and Liv would eventually have a real marriage. Considering the surprised look on Liv's face when he skimmed his fingers over her cheek, it wouldn't be a quick courtship.

He guzzled his water cup dry. "Better get a move on."

"The bathroom needs a going over before we leave."

"I'll do that."

"Good." She handed him the cleaning supplies. "Otherwise, I'm afraid Olivia will. I don't want her doing any more work today."

"I agree."

"I hear you guys!" Liv called from the other room.

Smith chuckled, thinking of other times when she yelled at them about hearing what they were talking about. "Sorry."

Mom opened the refrigerator door and continued cleaning the inside.

Smith took the cleaning supplies into the bathroom and scrubbed the toilet, sink, and tub. He felt a little sad to be leaving his childhood home, the only home he ever knew. But Mom, Liv, Lake, and he were embarking on a new journey and would be making memories in the parsonage.

Hearing a shuffling at the doorway, he turned.

Liv held the baby, a perplexed look on her face. "Katy's here."

"Katy?" His heart pounded faster.

"She's in the living room. Appears troubled."

"Okay." He stood, wiping his hands down his damp shirt, wet from where he'd been reaching across the edge of the tub.

"I'll, uh, give you some privacy."

Before he could object, she turned toward his old bedroom, shuffled inside, and closed the door.

Why did Katy show up today? Taking a deep breath and fortifying himself to face his ex-fiancée, he strode into the bare living room, minus the lone rocker.

Mom stood in the doorway to the kitchen, arms crossed, frowning.

Katy looked pale, lacking her usual makeup and peppiness. "Smithy, I'm so glad to see you." She lunged into his arms.

"Katy, hello." He patted her shoulder awkwardly.

Mom sent him a warning look then swiveled into the kitchen.

"What's happened?" He extricated Katy from his arms. Even though he'd been married to Liv for only a week, and their marriage was far from normal, hugging his ex felt wrong.

"I had to talk with you." Her gaze darted around the sparse room. "I've made a terrible mistake. I haven't been able to sleep or eat."

She looked frail. Had she lost weight?

"Are you okay?"

"I'm heartsick over the decision I made about us." She swayed out her hands toward him. "I heard about your move from someone in the office. I had to talk to you. To appeal to you one more time."

"Appeal to me about what?"

"I still love you, Smithy." She fell against him again, her arms coming around his middle.

He glanced up, meeting Mom's disapproving expression from the kitchen doorway.

Untangling Katy's arms from his waist, he held her away from him. Agony and doubt assailed him. Why was she telling him she still loved him now?

"I'm willing to go with you, to be a pastor's wife, or whatever, if you'll still have me." Tears filled her eyes. "What's my life without you?"

"Katy—"

"I mean it. What we had—"

"Stop." He strode behind the rocking chair, putting a solid object between them. "Things have changed."

"I know. We split up because I hurt you," she said in a throaty voice. "I know you still love me. I'll do anything you want. Be whoever you need me to be."

His jaw dropped. But his shock probably wasn't as great as the look of horror crossing Liv's face as she came into the room.

"I needed to get—" She pointed toward the bulging diaper bag on the floor. "Excuse me for interrupting." With Lake wiggling in her arms, she whisked up the diaper bag and turned toward the bedroom.

"Wait." This was Smith's moment of truth. His freedom rested with Liv. Despite what Katy said about still loving him, he'd broken free of that burden. Sure, for just a moment having her in his arms had felt like coming home again. But he knew what accepting her on her terms meant. She might say she'd do anything to be with him, but he knew her better than that.

And he'd made vows to Liv in front of Mom and God. His heart was in Liv's hands. He nearly ran across the room to her.

"Smithy?" Katy called after him.

He slid his arm over Liv's shoulder, and whispered, "Please, help me."

She met his gaze. Nodded.

Turning toward Katy with Liv nestled beneath his arm, he appreciated Liv more now in this moment of solidarity than he'd appreciated her helping him become a pastor.

"Katy, I want to introduce you to my wife, Liv North." He cuddled Liv closer to his side, whether he held her, or she leaned into him, he couldn't be sure. "And our son, Lake."

"But, how, when—"

"A week ago." He didn't let go of Liv.

"We're moving to Thunder Ridge today," Liv said and sagged against his side. "Smith and I are moving into the parsonage. It's such a lovely cottage. We can't wait to begin our lives there together— Smith and me, the baby, and Trish."

Smith swallowed hard, proud of Liv for standing up for him, for them.

"Trish is going with you?" Katy screeched.

"That's right. She's the best mother-in-law a girl could wish for. A fabulous Granny for our children."

"May I talk with you alone, Smith? Now!" Katy demanded.

"I'm sorry, that won't be possible." Liv settled Lake into his arms.

He was momentarily flummoxed by her taking charge, but he asked for her help. She appeared to be taking that request seriously.

Liv crossed the room and linked her arm with Katy's. Katy wore a jaw-dropped expression, but she walked out onto the porch with Liv guiding her. Smith followed them to the doorway, holding Lake.

"Thank you for stopping by to wish us well," Liv said. "As you can see, our truck is filled. My car is ready to go. Smith and I are about to embark on our journey as newlyweds."

"I can't believe this." Katy twirled back, disengaging her arm from Liv's. "You married her?"

He smiled tenderly at Liv. "I did."

"This needs to be goodbye between both of you." Liv met Smith's gaze with a serious expression. Then she shook Katy's hand as if closing a business deal. "This ends your association with my husband."

"Your husband—"

Smith wanted to laugh at the horror on Katy's face. He doubted anyone had ever spoken to her so forthrightly before.

Liv scooped up Lake from Smith's arms, and without meeting his gaze, rushed into the kitchen.

Smith had the strongest urge to go after her and thank her profusely.

"Are you going to let her get away with talking to me like that?" Katy demanded.

"Yes, in fact, I am. You and I are done, just as she said." This final conversation between them had been difficult. Thanks to Liv's intervention, he could say goodbye to Katy and mean it.

"But Smithy—"

"Goodbye, Katy. Have a great life." He would have hugged her farewell but thought better of it.

"If she's the type of person you want to be married to—" She snorted. "After all that high and mighty stuff about how a pastor and his wife ought to behave, and now you marry an unwed mother?"

"Not unwed. She and I are married for life." Saying the words felt good and right.

"I still don't understand," Katy whimpered and trudged down the steps. She turned back, her eyes sizing him up. "Do you love her as you loved me?"

Gritting his teeth, he glanced at the sky. He wasn't ready to answer that question. "I'll always think fondly of you."

"Fondly." She barked a laugh.

Smith let out the longest sigh in history and watched Katy get into her car. This officially ended a bittersweet chapter in his life.

But he was ready to face a promising future with Liv by his side.

Chapter Fifty

On Sunday morning, Liv sat next to Trish in the back pew at the Thunder Ridge Fellowship. Their first two days in the parsonage had been exhausting as they unpacked everything, but they'd settled in as well as could be expected in the small three-bedroom cottage. Liv was so thankful for her mother-in-law who had done the lion's share of the work.

When Liv came into the church a few minutes ago, several women greeted her with oohs and aahs over Lake. It was fun having so many people smiling at her little bundle and offering heartwarming congratulations.

Smith sat on the front pew beside Arnold, the elder she met in the meeting she and Smith attended before their marriage. During the singing, Liv caught several curious glances sent in her direction. It was only natural that people would have questions about her and Smith. Hopefully, no one in the congregation would find out right away that they'd been married for only ten days.

Not that they'd keep it a secret forever. But how and why she and Smith chose to marry, and what happened in the privacy of the parsonage—separate bedrooms, for now—wasn't anyone's business but their own.

Lord, please don't let anything bad come of our decision to marry hastily.

The song Liv didn't recognize ended and everyone sat down. While a woman made announcements, Liv's thoughts wandered back to when Katy came by the house a couple of days ago. The embrace she witnessed between Katy and Smith annoyed her. Did he still struggle with feelings for his ex? Of course, he did. She sighed.

At least he asked for her help in getting Katy off the property. Ousting her diplomatically had been satisfying. Not that Liv hadn't felt bad for the woman, because she did. But Katy must accept that she and Smith were finished. That part of their lives was over because Liv and Smith had vowed to make an honest attempt at a real marriage.

"Are you okay?" Trish whispered.

"I'm okay." Liv smiled sheepishly. She hadn't been paying attention to what was going on at the front of the church.

Arnold stepped behind the podium, a wide smile on his face. "We're so glad to have Pastor North and Olivia, his mom, Trish, and the newest arrival, Lake, with us today. Let's give a Thunder Ridge Fellowship welcome to our new pastor and his family."

A long hand-clapping followed. Many glanced back at Liv and Trish with wide smiles.

Trish squeezed her hand, whether showing her support or sharing in the joy and pride she felt over her son's appointment as head pastor, Liv didn't know.

Smith strode to the pulpit, looking handsome in his three-piece gray corduroy suit. "Thank you for that warm welcome. My bride and I are thankful for the opportunity to be here this morning. It's been a journey getting here."

A smattering of chuckles followed.

Liv felt herself blush over his endearment—his bride. Is that how he thought of her?

"We're so thankful to all of you for opening your hearts and welcoming us into your fellowship. Over the coming weeks, we'll get to know each other better." He opened his Bible. "Thank you to everyone who helped with painting the parsonage and giving it a facelift. We love our new home."

Liv sighed, letting go of some of the tension in her shoulders.

"Let's open our Bibles to Psalm forty-six." Smith's gaze reached across the length of the church and met hers. He smiled briefly.

Would he always do that? Single her out? A fluttering of butter-flies in her tummy told her she had some womanly feelings toward her husband. Not love. Maybe admiration. Maybe hope for something more between them. He was a kind man. An honorable one—even if he hadn't quite gotten over Katy yet. In the days ahead, or months, that would change, right? Like she eventually got over Nick, Smith would heal and release the emotional ties that bound him to his ex-fiancée.

Liv shut her eyes as Smith led them in a prayer for God's blessing over the Word to their hearts. While he prayed for everyone in the room to "hear with spiritual ears," Liv prayed for his heart to be healed, and for love to find its way into the parsonage at Thunder Ridge.

Chapter Fifty-one

After church, Smith crashed in the recliner in the parsonage living room, mulling over his first service as pastor. From people's greetings when he arrived to Arnold's encouraging introduction of him and Liv, to the way the sermon came out of him powerfully and smoothly, to Liv standing beside him at the exit telling people goodbye and wishing them well, everything went so great he hardly knew what to think. Other than to be eternally grateful ... to God, to Liv, and to his mom who'd been supportive throughout the transition.

As soon as they ate the soup someone sent over yesterday, Liv and Mom had gone to their rooms to take a nap. An evening service meant a long night ahead. Smith would have to gear up for that in a couple of hours. For now, he wanted to relax and doze in this chair.

But instead of falling asleep, his mind wouldn't turn off. He owed much of this day's happiness to Liv. If she hadn't been willing to take a risk with him, to be willing to marry him without romance and love first, he'd still be sitting back at the other house lacking any plans for his future. Now he had a pastorate, a wife, and a son.

Thank You, Lord, for Your blessings and goodness.

Liv's bedroom door creaked open, and he heard her walking quietly to the bathroom. After a few minutes, she reentered the main area of the house and, since he watched her through barely opened eyelids, he saw her glance his way then creep into the kitchen. The water ran.

As she walked back, holding a tall glass of water, he cleared his throat quietly. "Thank you, Liv."

She paused. "For?"

"Being there today. Smiling and greeting people. Standing by me." He seriously doubted, now, that Katy would ever have done that. He must stop comparing the two, yet their differences lingered in his mind.

"You're welcome." She continued toward her room.

"Would you like to go out with me? Maybe tomorrow?"

"Oh, um." She paused, hand on the doorknob. "Lake is still so young. Maybe in another week?"

"Sure. That'll be fine." A zing of disappointment cut through him.

She entered her room and the door clicked closed.

How old was Lake? Ten days old? Yeah, Liv was probably still fatigued. Smith had been preoccupied for much of the time since he spent that first night with her in the hospital. He hadn't done much to help with Lake in the interim, either. Not like he would have if he and Liv slept in the same room and the baby cried in their shared space.

Lord, help me be a good dad, graceful and loving to Lake and all the children You bless us with in the future. And could you help me be a better husband to Liv too?

In the middle of the night, Smith awoke to the sounds of Lake crying and Liv walking back and forth across the squeaky living room floor. He pushed off the mattress and threw a sweatshirt on. He wore pajama bottoms and was barefooted as he strode into the living room.

Crossing the room in the semi-darkness, he held out his arms to the baby. "Mind if I try?"

Liv's hair fell around her face. Dark puffy shadows lined her eyes. "Are you sure?" She jostled Lake while eyeing Smith.

"I'm sure." He took the crying baby into his arms. "Hey, there, Lake." He smiled at Liv. "Try to go back to sleep, okay? Let me do this to help you."

"Okay." She stared at him for several moments. "Call if you need anything."

"I will. Leave your door open a smidge," he said over the baby's whimpering. "I'll lay him down when he falls asleep."

"Fine." She yawned. "Thanks."

Alone with Lake, Smith paced and patted his back. When a couple of small burps came out, he chuckled. "Now, you'll feel better, buddy." He kept walking slowly around the perimeter of the room, talking quietly. "This is our house. You're going to have fun here, exploring, climbing the trees in the backyard. Playing catch with your brothers." He kissed the baby's warm forehead. "You'll learn about Jesus here too." He sang "Amazing Grace" in whispered tones.

Lake stopped whimpering and settled against his chest. Smith sat down in the rocking chair and rocked for a while. Finally, the baby succumbed to sleep. Still smoothing his hand over the little guy's back, he quietly told him a story of his namesake. By the time he finished with the preacher's journey to Africa with his family, and the small amount of money they had upon arrival, Smith was almost falling asleep too.

Not wanting to risk Lake sliding off his chest, he stood and walked quietly into Liv's room. He carried the baby to his bassinet and whispered a prayer of blessing over him.

Before leaving the bedroom, he glanced in Liv's direction. A glow from the night-light cast a faint light over her face. She was beautiful even in sleep.

A wisp of breath caught in his throat.

God had blessed him with this funny, feisty, strong woman to be his wife. One day he'd love her with his whole heart. Until then, he'd better stay out of her bedroom.

Chapter Fifty-two

Lake was two-and-a-half weeks old on the day Liv agreed to go on a date with Smith. She wore a plum-colored loose-fitting dress, something she brought with her from Chicago, and put on makeup for the first time since the wedding. There was nothing she could do about her frumpy feelings. Or her tired exhaustion after running on little sleep for a couple of weeks.

She scrunched her slightly wavy hair, trying to get it to look better than it did. Why did her eyes look so droopy? Must be fatigue.

Smith knocked softly on her door. "I'm ready when you are, Livvy."

Livvy? Were they close enough to have pet names? Hadn't she told him no one called her that?

"Okay." She touched up her mascara, then grabbed her slim black purse before heading into the living room.

"You look lovely." Trish held Lake and rocked him in the chair.

"Thank you." Liv didn't meet Smith's gaze. She went right to her baby and kissed his sweet cheek. "See you soon, Little Mister." She patted Trish's arm. "Thanks for watching him, Granny."

"No problem. You go and have fun." Trish met her gaze. "I mean it. Relax. Don't worry."

"Right." Liv smiled tightly. Not worrying about leaving her newborn baby seemed impossible.

"Our reservation is—"

She glanced at Smith and tuned him out. The reservation could wait! She needed to say goodbye to her son. But her husband, dressed in a navy sports coat over dark slacks, a navy tie with white polka dots, and his hair slicked down, took her breath away. Took away whatever anxiety she was feeling, too. He looked model gorgeous!

She followed him out the door. He opened the car door for her, and she slid in. The children's nursery rhyme "first comes love, then comes marriage" pranced through her thoughts. Mentally, she reversed the words. "First comes marriage, then comes baby, then comes love, maybe."

She wouldn't lie to herself and say she wasn't attracted to the man she married. He'd shown himself to be an attentive father, always sweet and caring to Lake. And the night he walked the floor with the baby and let Liv sleep had been especially endearing.

But husbandly stuff? This was the first hint of any romantic effort on Smith's part since their nuptials. But, in all fairness, they'd both been hyper-focused on settling in—him with his pastorate, and her with motherhood.

"You look nice," he said huskily. "Mom was right about that."

"Thanks. You look good too."

He grinned.

She glanced at his profile as he drove toward Sandpoint, taking in his ski-slope nose, his soft lips, dark ebony hair, and long side-burns. That to-die-for chin dimple! He met her gaze and she gulped. What would this night, or their future for that matter, hold? Romance? Love? Or years of regret?

Sigh.

At the candlelit table in the Diamond Liz Restaurant, Smith helped her into her seat. He sat down and leaned forward as if to tell her a secret. "You look even more lovely in this candlelight."

"Everyone does." Calming her throbbing heart, she grinned. "That's why they use them. In fact, if you put candles all around your church, everyone would appear much lovelier too."

He guffawed. Hearing him laugh again was nice.

Smith ordered steak and potatoes. She chose a chef's salad.

"One other thing," Smith told the waiter.

"Yes, sir?"

"We'll have apple pie afterward." He winked at Liv in the candle-light.

Her heart melted toward him a little.

"Yes, sir. I'll bring dessert after you've finished dinner."

Throughout their meal, they chatted about Lake, Smith's new responsibilities in the church, and how she could make one side of her small room into a nursery. Just friendly conversation. Nothing personal. Which was fine with her. She was too tired for any serious discussions.

After they finished eating, Liv felt too full for pie but wouldn't say so. Gazing at the piece of apple pie the server set down, she silenced a groan. One bite. Maybe two. That's all.

Smith's eyes sparkled in the candlelight's glow. She really liked him. Not loved. But talking and laughing together gave her hope for the possibility of a happy future together.

"What do you think?" His eyebrows rose after he took a bite of pie.

She bit into the filling. "Delicious. Thanks for this. It feels nice to get out, even for a short break."

"You're welcome." He wiped his lips with the cloth napkin. "We'll have to do this more often. Get out. Talk. Have some fun together."

"I'd like that."

"There was something I wanted to ask you."

"Oh?" A tightness spread across her middle.

"How can we bring our relationship up a notch?" His face hued ruddy but his gaze stayed steady on her. "I don't mean move in together. We sort of already did that. I mean—" He sighed like this turn in the conversation was difficult for him too. "How can I help you feel more relaxed around me at the house? At the church?"

At the church? She tensed. She thought she'd pulled off that part of being a pastor's wife quite well. The smiling and greeting people, standing by Smith's side as his supportive wife. What more did he expect?

"I don't mean any offense."

"No?" She set her napkin on the table and her knuckles hit the surface with a thud. "How else did you mean it?"

"Livvy—"

"Don't call me that."

"Why not?"

"I don't want you calling me nicknames until you and I are"— she avoided saying "in love"—"are on more stable footing as a couple. Can we leave now?"

"I'm sorry if I called you a pet name prematurely." He groaned. "Look, when we visit like this and laugh, I love being with you."

She inhaled sharply. He said "love," but probably did so without realizing it. Why was she getting upset with him, anyway? He was trying to get them to interact with each other more like husband and wife instead of strangers. What was wrong with that?

"I enjoyed myself too," she said quietly.

"Then what is it? A wall went right up around you."

While shoving her feelings under the proverbial carpet was tempting, she preferred honesty. "I'm not going to accept one iota of blame for not being the perfect pastor's wife."

"What?"

"I mean it. You knew what you were getting when you asked me to join you in this arrangement." She wouldn't hedge the truth. "If you wanted a wonder-woman pastor's wife, you should have chosen Amaryllis."

However, as soon as she spoke the woman's name, she wished she hadn't.

His eyes pulsed wide. His Adam's apple bobbed up and down.

A minute of awkward silence passed.

Letting out a slow breath, Smith reached across the table and clasped her hand loosely. "Liv, I don't expect that. You've done remarkably well adjusting to our lives here. At the church, too. I just wanted to know what I could do to make things better for you. To help you be more comfortable with"—he lifted her hand—"me. That's all."

While tempted to jerk away from his touch, the anger that rose easily within her, maybe from fatigue and hormones, was ebbing away.

"Is there anything I can do?" He seemed determined to have this conversation. "Can you tell me one thing I could work on?" He gave her a soft smile.

Someday she'd love this man. Not right now. But that awareness of him being her future husband, her future lover, as he stroked his thumb against her palm stirred warm feelings within her. Not her boyfriend, and just barely her spouse, he was becoming someone special to her.

Only one thing came to mind as she pulled her hand away from his and clasped her hands in her lap. "Will you bake with me again?"

"Apple pie?"

"No." She chuckled, glad for a lighter mood. "Something else."

"You like it when we bake?" A wide smile crossed his lips.

"I do."

"Me too. How about trying cookies?"

"I love chocolate chip cookies."

"They are my favorite." He moved his empty plate out of the way. "Tomorrow I'll get supplies for making a lot of chocolate chip cookies."

"Why a lot?"

"You and I need lots of practice together." He winked.

Was he talking about baking cookies or something else entirely?

Chapter Fifty-three

Liv had just finished nursing and burping Lake when a knock sounded at the door.

Trish hurried across the room to answer. "Liv, we have company," she announced.

A dark-haired woman dressed in bright blues and reds entered carrying a cellophane-wrapped platter. "Hello, Mrs. North. I'm Amaryllis. I wanted to bring these cinnamon rolls by and meet you."

Amaryllis? Liv gulped and wished she'd had time to tidy up before this visit. Her lounge pants and long T-shirt must look like she just got out of bed.

"Thank you. It's nice to meet you. I'm Liv."

Amaryllis chuckled in a nervous tone. "Where should I—?"

"Let me take those," Trish intervened. "My, my. They look scrumptious."

"Thanks. Just an old family recipe."

Amaryllis was probably a knowledgeable baker. Would this woman have made a better match for Smith? Would Liv always be comparing herself with Amaryllis, Katy, and other women from the church? She swallowed down a groan and the troubling questions.

"Would you like some hot tea?" Trish asked their guest.

Liv appreciated Trish taking over hostess duties.

"Yes, please. Two sugars."

"Coming right up. Have a seat." Trish met Liv's gaze then carried the pastries into the kitchen.

"May I see the baby?" Amaryllis's wide eyes sparkled toward Lake.

"Of course." Liv adjusted him in her arms. He'd already closed his eyes.

Amaryllis tiptoed across the room and peered down. "He's so sweet. I always wanted a baby. But I couldn't—" She shrugged.

"I'm sorry." Liv's heart went out to her. "I didn't know."

"How could you unless Smith told you?"

"No, he didn't. Please, have a seat." Liv swayed her hand toward the couch.

"Thank you." Amaryllis settled on the cushion and wiped her fingers beneath her eyes. "Sorry to get emotional. That happens to me whenever I'm around babies."

"It's okay." Liv rocked Lake gently.

Amaryllis stared up at the walls. "I heard about the painting party. Under the circumstances, I didn't want to participate. I would have painted the house myself if Smith and I—" A nervous machine-gun laugh erupted from her. Amaryllis covered her mouth. "Sorry."

"You don't have to keep apologizing. This is awkward. I get it," Liv said, trying to be honest and polite. "I am glad you came by, though."

"Thank you. I've been visiting another church." Amaryllis rushed her next words. "You don't have to worry about me telling anyone I was Smith's first choice."

Liv gasped softly.

"Well, not his first choice. Second choice, according to my brother."

Which made Liv what? His third choice? Could she make her excuses and go hide in her room? This conversation was going from awkward to awful fast. But gritting her teeth and forcing a smile like she'd learned to do in uncomfortable board meetings at her father's company, she faced Amaryllis with the most pleasant expression she could muster.

Trish carried a tray with three teacups on it. She set the tray on the coffee table and handed a cup to Amaryllis. "We're glad to hear you're going to keep Smith and Olivia's personal business private until they're ready to share, aren't we, Olivia?" Trish met Liv's gaze, her eyebrows lifting.

"Yes, we are. If you'll excuse me." Liv stood slowly. "I'll be right back." She carried Lake into the bedroom, set him down in the bassinet, and arranged the blanket over him without him waking up. Then she pulled a sweater over her T-shirt and tidied herself.

Reentering the living room, she took the cup Trish held out to her and sat back down in the rocking chair.

The silence in the room was painful, but Liv wouldn't avoid a topic needing to be addressed. Amaryllis was a Board member's sister who could, theoretically, cause trouble for Smith. Had he considered that when he met with this woman to consider her as a bride candidate?

Amaryllis glanced back and forth between the bedrooms. "I see you chose Mrs. Turner's sewing room as the nursery. She always loved her craft room." She pointed toward Smith's door. "That was Pastor and Mrs. Turner's room."

By Amaryllis's lifted eyebrows, Liv wondered if she was curious about Smith's and her sleeping arrangements.

"Why are you going to another church?" Liv returned to that topic.

Amaryllis's skin tone went from pale to wine-colored. "Why, the obvious, of course."

"If it were obvious, I wouldn't be asking."

Trish glanced at her curiously. "More tea, anyone?"

"No, thanks," Amaryllis said.

Liv shook her head. "Why would you leave the church where you and your brother have attended for … how many years?"

"Our whole lives."

"See there. That doesn't make sense. You showed bravery by coming here today and even mentioning you were Smith's possible choice for a wife before me." Liv eyed the woman the way she would have an employee being questioned about tardiness. "You've faced me, even though you knew it might be difficult for both of us. Smith is a fair man. Didn't he treat you with kindness and respect?"

"Oh, he did," Amaryllis gushed. "For a while, I thought we would go forward with the marriage."

"Of course, you did." Liv inhaled a painful breath. "Why else would you have kept meeting with him?"

"Exactly. And like you said, he's kind. And so handsome! He can't help that." She snorted. "How comforting his laugh was to hear."

Liv held the hot air in her mouth for a few extra seconds. She wasn't in love with Smith. But she didn't like someone else talking about her husband as if they were.

"But you both prayed about it, right?" Trish asked. "You both knew it wasn't meant to be, if I've heard the story correctly?"

Amaryllis nodded. "He didn't have feelings for me." She heaved a sigh. "Especially after I told him I couldn't have kids. But I cared for him. Would have tried my best to please him."

Acid crept into Liv's throat. Maybe Amaryllis was right about going to another church. Somewhere she wouldn't be reminded of what might have been between her and Smith every time she walked through the foyer. Liv didn't want to be thinking about that, either. Waiting for him to get over his attraction for Katy was weird enough.

But was it right for her to let Amaryllis leave her house without saying something loving that might bring peace to her wounded spirit?

Help me, Lord. I want to live in Your grace and kindness.

She zoned back in on the conversation going on between Trish and Amaryllis. The older woman's arm rested over their guest's shoulders. "I'm sure he never meant to hurt you."

"I know." Amaryllis sniffled and wiped her eyes with a tissue. "It's been difficult."

"I hope"—Liv scooted forward on the rocker—"we can be friends."

"You do?" Amaryllis's eyes widened. "Even when I'm the other woman?"

"I wouldn't call you that." Liv forced herself to relax and not take offense. "Smith wanted God's will for his life. The same as you did, right?"

"Yes."

"It was part of all of our journeys." Liv crossed the small space between them. Squatting in front of Amaryllis, she took her hand between both of hers. "Please continue coming to our church. We need you in our fellowship. I've heard you've been a wonderful leader to the ladies. We want you here."

Trish gasped slightly like she was moved by her comment.

"I'll have to think about it." Amaryllis blinked fast. "But thank you."

"We ladies have to stick together." She patted Amaryllis's hand then stood.

Amaryllis stood also. "I didn't anticipate such kindness from you."

Trish led her to the door. "Thank you for stopping by, Amaryllis. We'll have your cinnamon rolls for dessert tonight."

"Tell Smith I made them, okay?"

"I certainly will." Trish held the door open until Amaryllis had been gone a few moments. Then she strode right over to Liv and embraced her. "I'm so proud of you, hon. Thank you for being willing to let the things she said go and for being loving toward her. I'm sorry for what she mentioned about her and Smith nearly going through with a marriage. I don't know if they ever came close to that."

Liv appreciated her kind words and the hug, although her heart felt a little bruised by some of the things Amaryllis said.

Chapter Fifty-four

Smith entered the parsonage carrying a full bag of groceries. He'd chosen plenty of ingredients. With Liv's baking record, they might have to throw away a few dozen cookies before they succeeded at a winning batch. But that was okay. They'd be spending time together, and that's what mattered.

Mom strolled into the kitchen smiling. "What do we have here?"

"Liv and I are going to make cookies tonight." He pulled packages of chocolate chips, butter, and brown sugar out of the bag and made a pile on the counter. "A stay-home date."

"I guess I should sit out here in the living room then."

"Why is that?" Smith paused with a bag of flour in his hands.

"My chaperone duties, of course."

"Right. I almost forgot."

"Unless you want me to be scarce." She raised one eyebrow.

Did he want that? "Nah. It's fine. Whatever makes Liv more comfortable."

"Do you—" Mom stared at the ceiling for a moment. "Do you have feelings for her?"

"Mom." He set the flour down with a thud. A puff of flour dust morphed into a mushroom cloud. He coughed and waved his hand to clear the air. "That's personal."

"Sorry." She opened the cupboard and pulled out a glass. "If you are, it's okay. She's your wife."

"Leave it be, will you? We're moving slowly. There's nothing to report yet."

She squeezed his arm. "Sorry for intruding."

"Yeah, thanks." He nodded toward Liv's room. "You live here. You'll be the first to know when things progress to us 'having feelings' for each other."

What would it be like to hold Liv like a woman he was attracted to and cared for when he'd thought Katy would be the only one for him? He sighed.

"So you're going to teach her how to bake chocolate chip cookies?" Mom took some milk out of the fridge and filled her glass.

"Uh-huh. Chocolate should be good for encouraging romance, huh?"

"I'm sure it is." Mom winked then took her glass back into her room.

After their dinner that included the delicious cinnamon rolls Amaryllis had given them, Mom held the baby while Liv read the cookie recipe. Smith washed his hands and grabbed a large bowl.

"Did you get walnuts?" Liv glanced over the pile of ingredients.

"No."

"The recipe calls for it."

"That's okay. I don't like walnuts." He strode over to the pile of things he purchased today and lifted a bag of sliced almonds. "I like almonds or pecans better."

"And that's okay? To replace items in the recipe, I mean?" She gnawed her lower lip.

His gaze lingered on her rosy mouth and the softness of her smile. The way she looked insecure about following the recipe was cute.

"It's okay to replace the nuts or to not include them. Do you like almonds?"

"Sure. I'm fine with walnuts too."

He gave her a teasing glare. "In this house, there'll be no cooking with walnuts!"

"Yes, sir. The king has spoken!"

He guffawed. "About walnuts, yes."

"We might as well get started then."

"You sound about as eager as if we were cleaning fish."

She grimaced. "Are you going to teach me how to clean fish also?"

He burst out laughing. Even Mom chuckled from across the room.

"Stop laughing at me."

"But you're funny." He snickered, subduing another hearty laugh.

"What should I do first?"

"Unwrap the butter cubes." He pointed at the package. "There's half a cup in each one."

She read the recipe. "Two cups of butter, so four cubes." She opened the butter container and unwrapped four cubes, dropping each one into the bowl. "Why'd you get so much butter? How many batches are we going to make?"

"As many as it takes for you to get it right."

"Hey. That's not nice."

He snickered. "Next, measure the brown sugar. Then add eggs."

Liv did what he said, following each step in the recipe.

Smith watched her work, observing her frown of concentration as she added flour, trying to get the dough thick enough, but not too thick. Occasionally, she gnawed on her lower lip, and he imagined what her lips might taste like. What would it be like to press his mouth against hers? To taste the chocolate chips on her breath?

"Something wrong?" She stared back at him.

Flour speckles peppered her nose and cheeks. He wanted to smooth the pads of his fingers down her cute cheeks. Maybe brush his thumb gently over her lips.

"Nothing's wrong."

"You had an odd look on your face."

"I'm just watching you."

Their gazes met and held.

She glanced away first. "How's this?" She held out the bowl to him. "Pass inspection?"

"The dough looks great." He squeezed a little of the light brown dough between his fingers. "Texture's right."

The phone rang and he moved across the room to answer it. "Hello. Pastor Smith."

"Pastor, this is Arnold. Got a minute?"

"Sure." Smith shrugged apologetically at Liv and strode into the laundry room, bringing the phone receiver and its long cord with him. He closed the door behind him the best he could. "What's up, Arnold?"

* * * *

Liv didn't need Smith showing her every step of the recipe. He already preheated the oven, so she scooped out twenty round globs onto the cookie sheet.

Once she put the sheet in the oven, she checked on Lake sleeping peacefully in Trish's arms. "Shall I put him down for you?"

"Okay."

Loving the expression on her baby's face, she sighed. "Sweet Lake, how I love you," she whispered as she carried him to his bassinet. She nestled him in his bed and cozied the blanket around him. Leaning over, she pressed a kiss to his cheek.

She stood there for a few minutes watching him, amazed by the loving emotions of motherhood swirling through her. Being a software exec hadn't prepared her for the middle-of-the-night feedings and washing diapers, nor for the recovery period after having pushed a boy child out of her body. But it might have prepared her for the long haul. For sticking to a thing, or in this case, to a human being, no matter what happened.

How many other babies would use this bassinet? Maybe it was too soon after labor and delivery to picture going through that again. Too soon to think of her and Smith sharing a bedroom, too. Still, she wondered.

"Liv?" Trish called from the other room.

The scent of burned food reached Liv's nostrils. "Not again." Charging out of the bedroom, she ran to the kitchen where Trish was pulling out the cookie sheet bearing twenty blackened cookies. "Terrible day."

Trish strode to the door. "I'll take these out to the trash."

Smith rushed into the room, his eyes wide. "What happened?"

"You know what happened." She sighed in defeat.

He set down the receiver. "Sorry, that call couldn't be helped." He strode across the room and opened the kitchen window.

Liv pulled another cookie sheet out of the cupboard. "I'll try again."

Trish returned and washed the pan.

Fifteen minutes later, Liv stood on guard by the stove, prepared to stop the timer the second it dinged. She didn't want it bothering Lake, but she also wanted to prove to Smith and Trish that she could make cookies successfully this one time!

The buzzer sounded. She turned it off and grabbed the potholder. Eagerly pulling out the cookie sheet, she immediately saw the cookies looked too flat.

She groaned. "What did I do wrong now?" She set the pan on the stovetop and stared at the disappointing baked goods.

Smith leaned over her shoulder, making a choking noise that sounded suspiciously of subdued laughter. "Good thing I bought plenty of ingredients."

Oh, she wanted to elbow him in the gut.

"Do you know what you forgot?"

"No. How could I?"

He grabbed the spatula and ran it beneath some cookies. "No baking soda."

"I'm sure I followed the recipe." She grabbed the empty chocolate chip package and smoothed her finger down the list of ingredients.

Smith held out a little piece of cookie to her. She popped it in her mouth. "Dry."

He nodded then dumped her efforts in the trash. "Want to try again?"

"Yes." She let out a long sigh. Why did she have such brain fog when it came to cooking?

Smith washed out the bowl and wooden spoon. "Need any help?"

"Uh-huh. Why don't you take a long walk off a short dock?"

"That's not nice."

"Neither is mocking my baking attempts."

"Sorry." Yet he still snickered.

"You're asking for it." She remembered another time when she threw flour at him. Maybe he needed a little reminder. "I am going to triumph over this recipe."

"Sure you are." Smith chortled.

"Go. Get out of here, will you?" Liv shoved his arm, his muscles tensing beneath her fingers. "I'm sure you have things to do other than standing here watching me make a fool of myself."

"You look cute with a dusting of flour on your nose."

She wiped the back of her hand over her face.

"Here." He lifted her chin and ran his fingers over the sides of her nose, across her forehead, and down her cheeks. His fingers' touch was cool against her burning skin.

She gazed into his eyes that still twinkled but less merrily. His fingers weren't touching her face now, but his gaze seemed to be caressing her skin.

She swallowed the dryness in her throat. "I should—"

"Can I watch you make the next batch?"

"Only if you don't laugh. Even if I burn more cookies, no laughing."

"But I want us to laugh together." He smoothed a wisp of hair back from her face. "Laughter makes our house a home."

"Amen," Trish said quietly from the rocking chair.

"Laughing *together* is fine. Just don't keep laughing at me."

"Okay. I'm sorry." At least, he sounded more humble this time.

He embraced her in a friendly hug. Although, the gentle touch of his hands across her back made her heart hammer in her ears.

"How about if we make the cookies together?" His soft words and the way his eyes glistened toward her seemed more like he'd asked her on a date. "You don't have to prove anything to me, Liv."

"Yes, I do." She had to prove it to herself also.

"You'll get the hang of cooking, eventually."

He had to say "eventually!"

"The next time you taste one of my cookies, you will be assured of my improved skills."

He grinned. "I'll look forward to it. Until then, let's do this together."

"Together" sounded good. Like he was promising her something she couldn't live without.

Chapter Fifty-five

A week later, Smith came home for a late lunch feeling irate. A parishioner's accusations from that morning pulsed through his thoughts like a hammer beating against a rock. "You're not preaching the Word! If you knew the truth, you'd preach better. Spend more time in prayer!"

The angst rushing through his veins had to be the reason for his insensitivity when he greeted Liv. He saw her nursing Lake in the rocking chair, her upper torso slightly uncovered, and he spoke sharply. "Can't you do that in your room?"

Liv's face turned a few shades of red and she tugged the blanket over her shoulder in jerky movements. "I didn't know you were coming home. I'm sorry if finding me feeding my son makes you uncomfortable." She stood abruptly and carried Lake across the room. Then slammed her bedroom door.

Oh, man. What had he done? Oaf! Idiot!

Mom entered the living room from her bedroom. "What was that about? Is Olivia okay?"

He raked his fingers through his hair. "I don't know. Is there anything to eat in this house?" Boy, he was in a mood. He pivoted toward the fridge, hoping to find sandwich makings.

"There's leftover roast beef from dinner last night. Want me to fix it for you?"

"No, I'll fend for myself." He heard the gruff tone in his voice, but he didn't rectify it.

He yanked the meat and mayonnaise from the fridge. A few minutes later, he bit into the hastily made sandwich and chewed. It didn't even taste good. Nothing had gone right today.

"Anything I can help with?" Mom asked quietly. If she heard his comment to Liv, she probably feared getting her head bit off too.

"No. I've made a fine mess of it on my own."

"I'm sure you'll do what's right." Mom turned and walked toward Liv's door.

What did she expect him to do? He couldn't explain to his mother how he snapped at his wife who was simply feeding their baby. She hadn't been undressed. Nor was she doing anything provocative or indecent. It was his own mind that jumped to thoughts he shouldn't have been thinking.

He tore off bites of his sandwich that felt too dry, swallowing in gulps. He searched for one of the chocolate chip cookies they made. After he downed two with milk, his stomach was satisfied, but guilt took up residence where his irritation previously sat. What an imbecile he was to blast Liv when what he wanted to do was rail at the church member for chewing him out!

Mom slipped out of Liv's room, not glancing in his direction. She went straight to her room and closed the door behind her.

He had no one to blame but himself. He owed Liv an apology. Yet thinking of what he needed to say churned in his gut as if the meat he ate in his sandwich had already spoiled.

As a pastor, wasn't he supposed to be humble and grace-filled toward everyone? Hadn't he exhibited tolerance to the person who criticized him? He hadn't spouted off angrily at the guy. No, he came home and did that to his wife. *His wife*. He sighed.

Because they had an unusual married life didn't give him the right to treat her in any way other than how a loving husband should. A loving groom of, what, almost four weeks? Groan.

First, he'd use the bathroom. After he straightened his hair and brushed his teeth twice, he clutched the edges of the sink and stared at himself.

"You're a pastor, a man of God, yet you flew off the handle like an idiot." Yep. He deserved a personal lecture. *Go in there and apologize. Liv's a lovely person who's agreed to walk this uneven road with you. God gave her to you to love and encourage and support. And she'll do the same for you if you let her.*

After another long sigh, he strode to Liv's closed door and rapped softly.

No answer.

He knocked lightly again. "Liv? I need to talk with you."

Thirty seconds later, the door opened a couple of inches. Her red face told the ugly tale. She had been crying. This was all his fault.

"Oh, Liv, I'm so, so sorry."

She stared at the floor, not meeting his gaze.

"Please, can you step out here for a minute?"

Glancing back into the room, probably checking on Lake, she nodded.

He wanted to tug her into his arms and hold her, comfort her. But he didn't have that right, especially after what he said. Her crossed arms as she stood in front of him proved she didn't want him touching her.

"I'm sorry for what I said." He gulped. "It's perfectly natural and beautiful for you to be feeding the baby."

"I didn't expect you to come home when you did."

"I know. None of this was your fault. Please forgive my bad behavior. I was a clod. An absolute clod. I've had a bad morning, but that's no excuse for taking it out on you. I'm sorry." He covered his face with his hands for a moment and groaned.

"Thank you for apologizing." She drew in a long breath. "I thought you wanted me to go."

"Go where?"

"To leave. If you don't want me nursing Lake, I can't stay here."
She lifted her chin.

"Liv. I don't want you to leave. I don't want you to stop nursing
the baby either."

"I wasn't indecent when you walked in," she said strongly. "You'd
see more cleavage at the beach on a Saturday in the summer."

"I overreacted. It's just—" Heat infused his face, but honesty
prevailed. "We, uh, haven't been intimate yet. I'm a man. My thoughts
roamed to—" He groaned. "Look, I'm sorry."

She blinked slowly. "So you weren't appalled or horrified?"

"Heavens, no." A smile broke through all the turmoil and tension
he felt for the last few hours. "You're a lovely woman." Wanting to
add some levity, he said, "If I were a caveman, you'd be in my room
right now."

"Why, Pastor North, you surprise me!"

"You and me, both. Sometimes I'm going to react stupidly." He
shrugged deeply. "I never want you to leave or feel unwanted. We're
on this journey together for the rest of our lives. I mean that."

"Thank you. My thoughts went in a million directions."

And his thoughts had gone in only one direction.

"I take full responsibility for my bad reaction. Can you forgive
me?"

"Of course." She sighed. "Do you have time for a walk?"

"Really? I mean, you want to take a walk with me?"

"It seems like we should spend a few minutes together if you
have the time. I'm sure Trish will watch Lake."

"That would be great." It was a relief to him that they'd gone
from near disaster to her being willing to take a walk with him.

"Give me a second." Liv crossed to his mom's door and knocked
softly. "Trish, could you listen in on Lake while Smith and I take a
short walk?"

The door opened. "Sure." Mom's face looked red too. She'd probably been crying and praying for him and Liv.

"Thanks, Mom." Smith raised his hand in a wave, trying to reassure her that everything was going to be okay.

Chapter Fifty-six

Liv matched her stride to Smith's as they walked down the sidewalk in front of the residential area. After what happened back at the parsonage, his rudeness and her stomping off mad, ready to pack her bags, she was glad they could spend time together before he had to go back to work.

"You're quiet." Smith met her gaze. "Are we okay?"

"Yeah. I'm just thinking."

"Do you want to talk about what happened?"

"Not really." His confession and honesty had been sweet. "Are you okay?"

He took in a long draw of air and released it slowly. "Stuff at the church this morning knocked the wind out of me." His stride increased. "I've had a super frustrating day."

"I'm sorry." She walked faster too. "Want to talk about it?"

A pained expression crossed his face and he shrugged.

"I know about your confidentiality agreements as a pastor. Trish explained it to me." When he didn't say anything, she continued, "We had confidentiality agreements at our software company too. But sometimes we spoke among ourselves in disguised conversations."

"Such as?" He slowed down their pace and met her gaze.

"I might say something like the cookies have become difficult to work with today." She smiled conspiratorially. "Or Cookie #1 said Cookie #2 is stale. Cookie #2 replied that Cookie #1 is full of flour."

Smith chuckled. "Are you suggesting we have a secret language? Cookie talk?"

"Yes. Something like that." She took a risk in pushing things a little between them, especially after what happened earlier, and linked her hand around the crook of his elbow. "So, did you have a cookie disagreement today?"

"I did. One cookie claimed the oven wasn't to his liking."

"Those cookies are the worst." She made a mocking scowl.

"The cookie wanted a comfier oven and a more helpful care-taker."

"Having to listen to disgruntled cookies who want to be served at finer tables must be hard." She gave him a sympathetic look.

He sighed. "It is."

"It takes time to get cookies to turn out right." She grinned. "I know that from experience. In fact, cookies take gentle care. Some-times you have to start over with a fresh batch."

He paused on the sidewalk, staring at her.

"Did I say something wrong?"

"No, it was perfect. You gave me a different perspective about the cookies in my care." His shoulders weren't as slumped, and a more relaxed expression crossed his face. "You're quite amazing, Liv. If things were different between us, I'd kiss you right now."

The moment felt tense with expectations and possibilities. She didn't lean toward him in anticipation of a kiss. But that didn't stop her from imagining what his lips falling over hers might be like.

Chapter Fifty-seven

Three days later, the weather turned icy cold. Trish said a north wind brought in winter like an unexpected visit from a mother-in-law. Fortunately, the parsonage had a woodstove that kept the house warm as long as Liv and Trish fed it all day. With these cold temps, someone would have to do it during the night too.

Smith arrived at lunchtime with a bouquet of pink, red, and delicate white flowers in his hands and a layer of snow coating his hair and jacket. He held the flowers out to her. "Happy one-month anniversary, Liv."

"Thanks." She took the flowers. "I didn't even remember." This meant Lake was one month old today, too.

Smith smoothed his hand over his hair, scattering snowflakes on the floor. "What would you say to us going out for dinner? It would be nice to celebrate."

"What about the storm?"

"I could pick up pizza instead. I think we should celebrate all our monthly anniversaries."

"Really?" Didn't people joke about how men often forgot one-year anniversaries? How was he going to remember them every month? Still, it was a sweet idea. "Celebrating every month sounds nice."

"Good. It's a date." He strode to the woodstove in the corner of the living room. Squatting down, he added a couple of pieces of wood to the fire. "Are you adjusting to this kind of heat?"

"Keeping it going, you mean?" She hunted in the cupboards for a vase.

"Yeah, it's a beast. Hungry all the time."

Their gazes tangled. Was he talking about the woodstove and its hunger for wood? Or his hunger for romance between them?

"Under the sink," Smith said softly.

"Thanks." She bent down and peered into the caverns of the space beneath the sink and found two vases.

While Smith finished building up the fire, she put water in the bigger vase and arranged the flowers. He rejoined her in the kitchen and opened the fridge.

"There's leftover chicken. It would make a great sandwich."

"Sounds good."

Thankfully, he didn't expect her to make his lunch. Since he'd been a bachelor for years and liked working in the kitchen, that made her life easier.

Hearing a sound coming from her bedroom, she hurried to check on Lake. He was awake and wet, so she changed his diaper. Recalling Smith's reaction to her nursing the other day, she was undecided whether she should stay in her room to feed Lake or go out to the rocker.

He whimpered and she made a quick decision. Walking to the door, she called softly, "See you later, Smith. I'm going to feed Lake."

"No problem."

She closed the door and sat down on her bed. Starting to undo her blouse, a soft knock made her hand still.

"Liv?" The door opened a crack. "You don't have to hide in here."

"It's easier this way." She didn't want him to feel uncomfortable around her while she fed the baby, especially until they were more relaxed around each other.

"This is your house. Feed Lake wherever you want. The rocker is probably more comfortable for both of you."

She could tell he was trying to help them ease beyond the tension of what happened.

"It's up to you." He smiled and shut the door.

Now what? Stay here in her sanctuary? Or sit in the living room and try not to hold Smith's previous actions against him?

Lake fussed again. Grabbing a baby blanket, she carried him into the living room and settled into the rocker. Then she made sure she was well-covered before nursing him.

Smith cleaned up his lunch dishes and put things back in the refrigerator. "How's he doing today?"

"Hungry as always."

Smith laughed. "Hunger is always a healthy sign."

He met her gaze with an intense look. It had been so long since anyone flirted with her, she was uncertain if that's what was happening now.

Did this mean he was finally over Katy? Smith and Liv hardly knew each other. Yet, she had been living with him and Trish for three months.

He settled into the chair opposite her. "What would you like on your pizza tonight?"

She pulled the blanket up higher over her shoulder. "Get whatever you and Trish want. I'll pick off the pepperoni, or whatever is spicy."

"All right. I'll see you two later." His gaze lingered a moment on her blanket then he stared into her eyes. "I want this to work between us, Liv. It's weird for both of us. But I want you to know I want it to work."

"Okay."

Okay? What was she, twelve?

He strode to the door.

"Smith? I want it to work too."

"Glad to hear it. And you're a great mom. I admire that about you."

"And you're a great pastor."

"Thanks." He inhaled deeply. "Someday, I hope I'll be a good husband and dad, too."

"For those nine sons, huh?"

Smith guffawed. "I'm surprised you'd mention that."

"You have a right to your dreams. There's always adoption."

"Yes, there is. Talk to you later." He put on his winter coat, hat, and gloves, then left the house, whistling.

Chapter Fifty-eight

A week later, Liv was going stir-crazy with being confined to the house. Trish called it cabin fever. Two feet of snow fell in last week's storm, and with the single-digit temps this week, the snow was going to stick around for a while. No going outside with Lake. No taking any walks.

She crossed the room, glancing out a window into the white world, then crossing over to another window. She certainly felt the winter blues today.

Seeing her red Triumph covered in two feet of snow in the driveway didn't help, either. Not being able to use it made her feel even more trapped indoors. In the spring, she'd have to consider trading it in for a baby-friendly vehicle—maybe a station wagon or a minivan—that was better for wintertime driving in Thunder Ridge.

She sighed.

Trish entered the living area from her room with a book in her hand. "Would you be interested in doing a study with me?"

"Like a Bible study?"

"Sort of. We haven't resumed our studies as we were doing before our move." Trish sat on the couch, setting the book in her lap. "We could read a few pages each day and talk about it. That would give us something to do while we're waiting for spring."

Spring felt so far away.

"Yeah, sure. I'm game," she said without much enthusiasm. "Smith has his pastoral work. Preparations for Sunday. Talking with people. While I—" She swallowed hard. "I'm sorry. That sounds so ungrateful."

Trish chuckled. "Olivia, you can say anything to me. I'm not shocked or disappointed in you. Remember, I was a single mom. I had a lot of alone time on my hands, too." She inhaled sharply. "Not to say you are a single mom. You have Smith. And me."

"I'm so thankful for you, Trish. Smith too. It's just all this"— she swayed her hands around the room—is sort of weird." She dropped into the chair.

"How about a hobby?"

"Like?" She gazed at her mother-in-law skeptically.

"Knitting? Drawing? Cooking?"

"I'm a bad cook. I can't imagine knitting. Drawing never worked for me in school."

"You might be adept at knitting once you get the hang of it. Lake could use a winter hat." Trish grinned as if her idea was a good one.

Liv pictured an explosion of yarn coming out of a hat in a bazillion directions. "Might get a few laughs out of that at church."

"Speaking of church"—Trish held up the book—"this is a book about service. I read it many years ago."

"Service to whom?"

"God. Others. Even to your husband."

"My—"

Wait. Was Trish going to lecture her on how to be a better wife to her son? Was she implying she was lacking in this area? Every muscle in Liv's body tensed. She'd never been angry with Trish before. Why did her mother-in-law's comment bring about such a sudden rush of irritation? Emotions hit her at once—failure, anger, loss, then shame at harboring unkind thoughts toward the loving woman she knew Trish to be.

"What's wrong?" Trish asked. "What did I say?"

Liv drew in a breath. "I've failed at so many things. I hate the idea of you thinking I've failed at being your son's wife too. Honestly, he and I hardly know each other."

"Oh, Olivia," Trish said in an anguished tone. "That's not it at all. You and Smith must work out your marriage on your own terms with lots of grace for each other. You are doing fine. Fabulous, in fact. I'm here to help or offer advice only if you want it."

Okay. That sounded better. Trish wasn't sticking up for Smith and putting Liv down.

"You're doing wonderful at being a mom and marrying a man you don't love yet. Not to mention Smith being a pastor, too. That's a lot for you to take on all at once."

Her sympathetic words melted the residue of Liv's angst. "Thank you."

"You never have to worry about not being good enough or failing in my sight." Trish smiled warmly. "This is a lifelong journey. Not a speed race." She chuckled again. "My son isn't perfect. But even marriage to a man you're smitten with has its challenges, especially in the first year."

Trish crossed the small distance between them. She wrapped her arms gently around Liv and hugged her. "Shall we skip the book for now, hon?"

"No. That's okay. Let's try it until Lake wakes up."

"Okay. If you're sure."

For the next week, the two of them spent a half hour each day after lunch taking turns reading from the book, much like they previously did with Bible studies at the other house. Liv learned some things about the author's view on having a servant's heart. She'd had experience with prideful behavior in her job and the family-owned software business. Humility and servanthood had never been discussed in the board meetings she attended.

"How does being a servant fit into the role of a leader?" Liv asked. "I thought strength and pride were necessary parts of being in charge."

"I'd say that's where worldly leadership and the things of Christ separate paths." Trish gazed out the window for a moment. "For a pastor, at times he must make tough decisions, like a business leader, or a parent might do. But he always tries to be loving and caring • toward his congregation. After all, he could be tempted or fall, also. Because of that awareness, he doesn't think more highly of himself than he ought to, even when dealing with people who have made mistakes."

"So Smith doesn't want to step up and direct the church?"

"Direct as in guide, yes. Direct as in 'I'm the man in charge,' no."

Liv pictured her father and how he demanded the highest work ethic from his leaders, often taking employees to task in front of other workers, showing his dominance. The way he'd ousted her from his home and heart made her shudder. Maybe her dad had been a poor leader all along.

"Smith will make errors." Trish chuckled lightly. "A pastor and a pastor's wife both make mistakes."

"And that's okay?"

"It's life. It's humanity." Trish shrugged. "We give grace often and without measure. That's servanthood in a nutshell. It's a humble spiritual mindset."

Liv pondered that idea for the rest of the afternoon.

Chapter Fifty-nine

On the day Lake turned two months old, which meant it was Liv and Smith's second-month anniversary too, Liv remembered how Smith brought her flowers and pizza to mark their first month of being married. Did he remember today was their second special day?

Should she cook something for him? Scrambled eggs and toast? How about if she baked a batch of chocolate chip cookies and carried them over to his office? That would surprise him!

Since she'd put Lake down for a nap, she hurried into the kitchen, eager to try baking cookies again. In the pantry, she found enough ingredients for a batch or two. This would be her chance to show Smith how well she could follow a recipe on her own.

She gathered all the supplies, a large bowl, a cookie sheet, and a cookbook. Trish had gone to meet someone for coffee, so Liv had the kitchen to herself.

Wishing she'd set out butter for this project last night, she contemplated what to do. The microwave oven could soften the four hard cubes. She dropped them in a bowl, put them in the microwave, and hit the timer.

The phone rang and she quickly answered so it didn't disturb Lake. "Hello. Liv North."

"Hi. This is Amaryllis. Got a minute?"

"Uh, sure." Liv glanced at the microwave. Did she set it for two or three minutes?

"I wanted to tell you about a ladies' meeting I'd love for you to attend."

"Oh?" Liv heard the butter making popping sounds. Was it melting into a puddle?

"It's so exciting. We're meeting to sew children's clothes for a mission in Africa."

Sewing, huh? Count her out.

"Even if you don't sew, I'm sure there's something you could do to contribute."

"Oh, like what?"

Trish had warned her about groups in the church who might want her to participate, but ones she didn't feel like being involved with. That even with a servant's heart, she had to use her time wisely and do what was right for her and Lake, and for Smith too.

"Would you be interested in helping us? I heard you mention knitting on Sunday."

Liv gulped. "Just booties for Lake."

"That's perfect! Booties, a blanket, whatever."

A blanket sounded ominous.

"There are five of us and we're each inviting one person to join us. Will you come to our meeting as my guest?"

Amaryllis sounded so upbeat and welcoming, Liv hated to refuse.

"I could probably do that." Mostly, she wanted to check on the butter and get back to her baking.

"Excellent. Thank you." Amaryllis chuckled. "You sound distracted. Are you busy?"

"Sort of. Sorry."

"No worries. The meeting is on Friday."

"Okay. Thanks for the invitation."

Amaryllis talked a little more about the project and then ended the call.

Liv rushed over to the microwave. Melted butter lined the bottom of the glass bowl. Splatters of yellow speckled the interior of the microwave. She groaned.

She'd have to use the melted butter anyway. After she cleaned the mess in the microwave, she followed the instructions for the recipe precisely. But the whole thing turned into a gooey mess. She dumped more flour into the dough to make it thicker. Maybe too much.

Hoping her surprise for Smith turned out okay, she dropped spoons of the sweet brown mixture onto the cookie sheet. Then placed the pan in the oven and set the timer.

It took nearly the whole cooking time to put the ingredients back in the cupboards and clean up the countertop. Wouldn't Smith be surprised when she presented him with the cookies she made? This would be a personal victory for her.

When the timer sounded, she removed the pan from the oven. The cookies smelled delicious but looked overdone. For the next sheet of cookies, she reduced the time by a minute.

During the third round, Lake cried, and Liv ran to the bedroom to scoop him up. "There, there, Little Mister." She cuddled him against her, loving his sweet smell of babyhood.

She changed his diaper and brought him to the rocking chair, settling in to nurse him. That's when she smelled a familiar, horrible scent. "Oh, no! Not again."

Lake jerked and cried at her loud voice.

"Sorry." She jumped up and ran to the bassinet and set him down. "I'll be right back."

He continued crying, wailing, as she dashed into the kitchen. Grabbing a hot pad, she yanked the tray of charred cookies out of the oven. A billow of smoke filled the room.

Lake's cries reached a zenith as Trish burst through the door, groceries in hand. "Oh, my goodness. What happened?"

"Another baking casualty."

"Go, go. Take care of the baby. I'll see to this." Trish shooed her out of the kitchen.

"Thank you." By the time she scooped up Lake and returned to the rocker, Trish had a window open and was fanning the smoke with a towel.

"Were you hungry for cookies?"

"It's Smith's and my two-month anniversary. I thought I'd bake something for him."

"What a sweet idea."

Liv stared at the ceiling while rocking back and forth with her foot. "One tray turned out okay. At least, I think it did."

Trish groaned like she was in terrible pain.

"What is it?"

Her mother-in-law clutched one hand to her jaw and held up one of Liv's "okay" cookies with her other hand. "I cracked a tooth." She moaned.

"Oh, no. Trish, I'm so sorry. My cookies are hard enough to crack your tooth?"

"Don't worry. I'll call a dentist." She took the phone into the laundry room and closed the door.

So much for making Smith a treat to celebrate their two-month anniversary.

"I'm finished with baking!" Liv gnawed on the inside of her cheek, far from the relaxed state she should be in while nursing her baby.

Trish reentered the room, her hand still at her jaw. "Praise God, they have an opening at two-fifteen. I'm going to lie down until then."

"I'm so sorry."

"Really, it's okay." Trish's smile wobbled as she slipped into her room.

Even from here, Liv saw the grocery bags on the counter. Thankfully, Trish had dumped the burned cookies into the trash outside. The acrid smell of smoke diminished, but the room was freezing. Trish must be in awful pain to have left the groceries out and the window wide open.

Liv finished feeding Lake, burped him, and nestled him into his bassinet.

She hurried into the kitchen and closed the window. Then she put the groceries away and folded the brown bags. All that remained was trying one of the cookies for herself.

Carefully, so as not to break one of her own teeth, she picked up a cookie and nibbled it. Dry as cardboard. The chocolate chips were hard as rocks.

Poor Trish.

Chapter Sixty

During a lull in Smith's afternoon schedule, he dropped into the chair in his office and thought about calling Liv. How had another month passed so quickly?

Should he bring a meal home for dinner? Maybe he'd call and see what she'd like to do to celebrate their second month of marriage. Someday when they were really in love with each other, they'd look back fondly on these beginning days. It was important to him that they celebrate each month together.

He felt a little impatient that things weren't progressing toward romance faster between them. But he wasn't going to push for intimacy until he and Liv knew they loved each other. He cared for her already. When would he experience deeper feelings for her? How long would it take for them to fall in love?

Pastoring kept him busy and preoccupied most of the time. Last night he sat in the hospital with a middle-aged husband waiting for his wife to come out of surgery for a uterus tumor removal. Earlier he prayed with a couple who were barren and begging God to heal them.

Soon, a couple who he was counseling about marriage problems would be here. In those cases, he felt inept as a pastor. What did he know about keeping a marriage working properly?

Once Lake was older, and the extreme winter weather passed, he and Liv could go out on more dates and make their relationship a priority. Maybe they'd attend a play or a concert. He picked up the phone to try to get a call in before his next counseling session.

On the third ring, Liv answered, "Hello. This is Liv North. How may I help you?" Her voice sounded pleasant and welcoming.

"Hey, Liv." He deepened his tone to a husky sound. "I've been thinking about you, and us, this morning."

"Smith?" Her voice rose.

"Does any other man call and talk to you like that?" He chuckled.

Silence greeted him.

"Liv?" All playfulness aside, he sat up straighter. "Are you okay?"

She made a swallowing sound like she was stuffing down her emotions. "It's been a rough day."

"Sorry to hear that. What's going on?"

His secretary, Mrs. Scarlett, opened the door and made hand gestures toward the reception area. Apparently, the couple for his next appointment had arrived. He held up his hand to show her he needed a few more minutes. Mrs. Scarlett nodded and closed the door.

"The surprise cookies I made for you got ruined." Liv talked fast. "Amaryllis called. Melted butter. Too much flour. Burned one batch. Another was rock hard."

While he listened to her choppy explanation, his mind locked onto her words about the cookies being a surprise for him. Liv had gone to all that effort for him?

"Your mom broke her tooth on one!"

"Oh, no. Is she okay?"

"She had to go to the dentist. It's all my fault." She made a quiet sob. "How can I ever keep nine boys alive when I can't bake a simple batch of cookies? We might need to hire a chef for the rest of our lives. I'll have to get a full-time job to pay for her!"

He bit back a chuckle, but her mentioning them having nine boys spun around in his mind, flinging joy and hope all through his system.

"You were making those cookies for me?" he asked softly.

"Yes." She sniffed.

"That was nice of you." He glanced at his watch. "Liv, what would you like to do for our celebration today?"

"I'm not making you any more cookies, that's for sure."

"Okay." He laughed at her vehemence. "What, then?"

"A week of sleep would be nice."

Heat infused his face. He knew what she meant. She was probably exhausted. But the idea of them sharing a room, sleeping together for a week, sent his thoughts to places he shouldn't be daydreaming about right now.

He cleared his throat. "How about pizza again?"

"That works. It's nice of you to want to do something with me."

"I do. Would you go out with me, Liv?" All the vulnerability in him over their tenuous relationship had to be obvious in his tone.

"You mean like a real date? As if we weren't already married?"

"Yeah, something like that. What do you think?"

"Sure. I'd like us to go out. But I doubt your mom feels like watching Lake tonight, after her tooth emergency, and all. Another day would be better."

"All right." He glanced at the large calendar on his desk. So many things were scribbled into the spaces, he could hardly see any free time. "How about if I bring home pizza tonight? Then we could go out on Friday night. Does that work?"

"Okay."

"It's a date then."

"Thank you. Oh, and Smith?"

"Yeah?"

"Can you help me with cookie baking?" She gulped. "I told myself I'd never try it again. But I hate failing at anything."

"I'd love to make cookies with you, Liv." Even as he said the words about making cookies, his thoughts leaped to other things he'd like to do with her … like holding hands and kissing.

He glanced at his watch again. His five minutes were up. "I have to go. Sorry."

"See you later."

He set down the phone, his hand trembling a little at his recent thoughts. Maybe he'd spend a minute praying before he told Mrs. Scarlett to bring the next couple into his office. He had to get his own thoughts, his own wishes for a happy, satisfying marriage, under control first.

Chapter Sixty-one

From the moment Smith came home, he seemed different to Liv. His eyes sparkled in her direction. He kept smiling at her, almost as if he were already falling for her. But that wasn't possible, right? They'd been so busy with Lake, the move, and Smith becoming a pastor they barely spoke to each other, let alone had strong feelings for one another.

Trish sat with them at the table, the three of them chuckling over the happenings of the day, including Liv's cookie mishap and Trish's broken tooth.

"It was probably due to the melted butter," Trish said. "When that happens the tendency is to add more flour than the recipe calls for."

"That's exactly what I did." Liv bit into the cheesy pizza. "This is great pizza, by the way."

Smith took a bite. "Mmhmm. Happy second-month anniversary!"

"Thanks. You, too."

"If you want to try again tomorrow," Trish continued the previous topic, "I'd be glad to help. We could have a cookie baking time while Lake's napping. In fact, we could make enough cookies to fill up the freezer."

Liv's gaze met Smith's. His sparkling eyes seemed to be saying he wanted to be the one to teach her how to make cookies. Maybe he wished they were already closer. Is that what he was silently saying? Or was that what she wanted to hear him say?

Liv blinked, breaking the visual hold he had on her, and heard Trish still talking.

"—that's how it was when I first learned to cook. Good thing my husband loved me since he had to eat plenty of burned dinners in our first year of marriage."

Liv snickered.

Smith chuckled too.

"What's so funny?" Trish asked.

They laughed again.

Lake saved the day by crying in the bedroom. Liv jumped up and ran to get him. After she changed his diaper and sat down in the rocker in the living room, she nursed him. But her thoughts kept replaying the moment she and Smith found what Trish said so mutually funny. *"Good thing my husband loved me since he had to eat plenty of burned dinners."*

Liv imagined Smith might be doomed with such a fate too!

After she finished feeding Lake, Smith held out his hands toward the baby. "May I?"

"Yes. Certainly."

He scooped him up and walked around the living room and kitchen, murmuring softly. "She's a fantastic mama." Smith's gaze met hers across the room. "You're a lucky fellow to have a sweet mama like her. Pretty too."

He shuffled across the open space, smoothing his hand over the baby's back. "Jesus loves you, Lake. Your mama and daddy, and Granny Trish, love you too." He hummed "Jesus Loves Me" and kept walking.

Liv closed her eyes. She must have dozed off. When she awoke, Smith sat on the couch across from her, reading his Bible. The room was dimly lit other than the light coming from the lamp on the end table.

"What time is it?" she asked in a croaky voice.

"Almost eight."

She sat up. "Wow. I slept for a couple of hours."

"You must have needed it."

"And Lake?"

"Sleeping ever since I walked and sang to him."

Now, she remembered. "Thank you for doing that." She eased back against the chair. She should get up and throw a load of clothes in the wash. Peek in on Lake. But she felt so cozy sitting here with Smith smiling at her. "What? Do I have spinach between my teeth?"

"Hardly." He set his Bible on the end table. "I'm so thankful for you."

"You mean because our marriage enabled you to have the pastorate you wanted?"

"That, too. But it goes beyond our agreement." His voice turned husky. "In the last two months, I've observed the kind person and the wonderful mom you are."

"Even if I can't make chocolate chip cookies?" She smirked, seeking a lighter tone.

"Even then. You are someone special, Liv North. I like saying your first name with my last name." His eyes sparkled as they had earlier. He sure was acting more romantic than he usually did. "I have a couple of questions for you."

"Okay." She smoothed her hand down her blouse, whisking away possible baby drool and making sure her shirt was buttoned.

"Would you like to bake cookies with me tomorrow?"

"Yes."

"And"—Smith scooted to the edge of the couch, clasping his hands together—"what do you think about us holding hands?"

"Right now?" She felt a frumpy mess, having just woken up. Had she even showered today?

"Not right this minute, unless you want to."

"Okay, good." At his frown, she added, "I don't mean good as in I hate the idea. I haven't thought about it is all."

"No? How do you feel about us taking our relationship up a notch by holding hands? Showing a little affection to each other."

"Well—" She wasn't one to back down from asking hard questions. "Is this because you feel more romantic toward me? Or is this request because there's a timeline you plan to keep?"

He lifted his chin but kept his gaze on hers. Some men she knew wouldn't meet her eyes if she mentioned a difficult topic. Fortunately, Smith didn't seem intimidated by a woman asking questions or having an opinion.

"There's no timeline, sweetheart."

She gulped at his husky tone and his use of a romantic endearment for her. "Okay, good."

"Love will come as it comes." He leaned back on the cushion. "Listen, I'm not trying to push you into anything you're not ready to do. But I am asking. Are you okay with me holding your hand sometimes? About us moving forward in our relationship as a married couple?" The soft look he gave her melted her emotions to pudding. "If you're not, that's okay. In time—"

"I am. It would be nice to hold hands with you. Sometimes."

"Good." A wide smile crossed his lips. He reached across the coffee table, extending his hands palms up, his gaze locked on hers.

Slowly, she set her hands over his, feeling the smoothness of his palms. She sighed as he clasped her hands.

And with that simple action, it seemed they took their relationship up a notch.

Chapter Sixty-two

The next day, Smith asked Mrs. Scarlett to rearrange his afternoon appointments. He was eager to move the dial forward a smidge on his and Liv's relationship. Starting today, that meant doing two things. Holding his wife's hand. And teaching her how to make his favorite cookies.

While he had held Katy's hand, they never baked together. That was something he and Liv were doing exclusively as part of their courtship.

Comparing Katy and Liv was dangerous territory, especially since he hadn't fallen in love with Liv yet. But for some reason, the contrast kept coming to mind. If he let himself dwell on thoughts of Katy too long, he could stir up old emotions that might cause him and Liv grief. But the day she showed up at his house and Liv stepped in and helped him get her to leave, he had experienced an emotional turning point. One that bound him closer to his bride.

He took a big breath and exhaled. Katy was in his past. He needed to let go of any emotions her name conjured up. Perhaps, easier said than done, but he was determined.

Later, he entered the parsonage with his arms loaded down with grocery bags to hear the phone ringing, the stove buzzer going off, Lake sobbing, Mom charging into Liv's room, and the shower running in the bathroom. Unused to such chaos in the house, he dropped the bags on the counter, clicked off the buzzer, and lifted the phone to his ear. "Hello. Smith North."

"Oh, Pastor," a woman sobbed. "I-I'm so glad to f-find you at h-home."

"How can I help?" Frowning, he unzipped his jacket.

"It's my husband—"

"Excuse me, but who am I speaking to?" Smith stretched the cord as far as it would go around the corner and into the laundry room, trying to get away from Lake's crying and Mom's cooing as she tried to console him.

"It's Tally Sherman." She took a stuttering breath. "I've come to this church for nine years. Both me and my husband. My dirty, lowdown, rat of a husband!" She wailed.

"I'm sorry for whatever you're going through, Tally."

The woman on the line spouted off a litany of her husband's failings, going into detail over her grievances against him.

Suddenly, Liv barged into the laundry room with a towel wrapped around her torso and another towel draped around her head. She came to an abrupt halt, eyes wide, her jaw dropping open. She obviously didn't know he was in here.

He lifted the phone. "Sorry," he mouthed.

Cringing, she opened the dryer and yanked out a couple of cloth diapers, then ran barefooted out of the laundry room.

He pressed his lips together, fighting a chuckle. If he weren't on the phone with a parishioner, he would have cracked a joke about them meeting like that in the laundry room—especially with her wearing only a towel.

Tally discussing her husband's faults pulled Smith back into the conversation. He wished he didn't have to hear about the man who'd slept in a hotel for the last three nights. Or that Tally was considering filing for divorce.

"Do you think … what was his name?"

"Randal," she huffed.

"Can you and Randal come to my office tomorrow?"

"No, it must be today. Another day with that woman and he'll be lost to me forever."

Smith glanced at his watch. "Okay. See if Randal will meet at my office at two, okay?"

"Thank you, Pastor." She sniffled.

Smith strode into the kitchen and dropped the phone into its cradle. Then covering his face with both hands, he moaned. His afternoon was not going to include any romantic time between him and Liv. Instead, he had to try salvaging someone else's marriage. But his calling as a pastor included him being willing to do whatever he could to help others, no matter his own schedule or personal wishes.

"Smith?"

"Hey, Mom."

She glanced between him and the groceries spilling out of the bags on the counter. "Has something happened?"

"That phone call was someone in need of immediate counseling." He sighed heavily. "Duty calls. Can you tell Liv I'll have to postpone our date?"

"No. She's picking out clothes to—" Mom shut her mouth firmly.

"She's picking out clothes to wear for baking cookies with me?" He grinned—until he remembered he had to cancel their time together.

"Forget I said anything." Mom dipped a tea bag in and out of a cup in agitated movements

Smith crossed the space in two strides and kissed her cheek. "Thanks, Mom. That's the best news I've heard all day."

"Then tell her yourself."

"Tell her it's the best news?"

"I mean, tell her yourself you won't be having a baking session with her." Moisture filled Mom's eyes. "I won't be a go-between for either of you."

"Okay. Fine." He tossed his coat over the back of a kitchen chair. Then he put the baking supplies he'd purchased in the pantry.

"There's leftover pizza if you want any."

"I do." He grabbed two slices out of the fridge, set them on a plate, and put them in the microwave.

After eating the warmed-up pizza, it was time to face the music with Liv so he could get back to his office. By Tally's accusations, it was going to be a heated argument between her and her husband.

He knocked softly on Liv's door, waiting for her to object to him entering her room. When she didn't answer, he opened the door and peeked in. She sat on the edge of the bed, rocking Lake slightly while she nursed him. She tugged the blanket over her shoulder.

"Hey, Liv," he said quietly.

"Hi." She adjusted Lake's position. She was dressed now, but the towel was still wrapped around her head. Standing, she leaned over the bassinet and set the baby down.

"Sorry, but I have to cancel our afternoon baking," he whispered.

"You do? Oh, uh. That's okay."

He appreciated her first reaction was a kind one, not pouty or grumpy.

When they entered the living room and she closed the bedroom door, he said, "An emergency counseling situation came up."

"I understand." Her hands shot up to the towel on her head. Her face turned red. "Sorry for barging in on you earlier."

"No problem." He'd rather enjoyed that.

She removed the towel and ran her fingers through her lovely long blond hair. He had a strong urge to run his hands through her hair also.

"I must look like a disaster."

"Not even close." A breath caught in his throat. "You look—" What could he say with his mother standing in the kitchen, near enough to hear? "Beautiful." He smiled at Liv.

"Thank you."

"I have to go, but can I have a raincheck on baking with you?"

"Certainly."

He clasped her hands, squeezing them slightly. "See you later, Liv."

They were taking tiny steps toward a real relationship, and he was going to make sure they held hands often.

On his way out, he saw his mom smiling.

Chapter Sixty-three

By the time Smith arrived home last night, Liv was too tired to bake anything. Lake had been fussy all day, and she called it a night by eight p.m. Smith seemed zonked too. He said the counseling session went long, followed by two unexpected hospital visits.

He joked about a pastor always being on call. For some reason, that troubled her. Not that she expected him to drop everything and spend time with her. Then again, maybe that was exactly what she hoped he would do—prioritize her.

Was she selfish to want her husband to value their time together? Perhaps when they were truly husband and wife, this aspect of their marriage would realign. Then he'd tell people to set up an appointment with him the following day because he had an important date with his wife. The thought made her smile.

The next day, Smith postponed their baking session again. The couple he was counseling the day before had a brawl involving the police, and he was summoned to help with the crisis.

He came home looking exhausted, his hair poking up like he repeatedly raked his fingers through the dark strands. He barely met her gaze before reheating a plate of food Trish made, then traipsing into his bedroom. When his door shut with a soft click, Liv groaned.

She recognized a heavy burden when she saw it. She wished they were close enough for Smith to share his emotional load with her.

He had to cancel their date on Friday.

A week passed, and one thing or another kept them from baking together or spending time as a couple. The weather turned to sub-zero temps, keeping her locked in the house. If she had cabin fever before, she had something like cabin-fever delirium now. On top of her internal frustrations, Lake was fussier than usual.

Liv got up with him at two a.m., then three a.m. Fatigued and weary, she walked the floors, shushing him so he wouldn't awaken Smith and Trish. "There, there. You're okay."

Lake's crying, then whimpering, then crying continued. Liv sang a muffled lullaby, hoping her tune might bring her baby some comfort. He bunched up in her arms like he had painful gas in his stomach and squalled.

A door creaked open. Liv turned, expecting to find Trish coming to offer aid. Instead, Smith, wearing a T-shirt and pajama bottoms, trudged toward her. His hair poked up. His tired gaze met hers.

"Sorry for disturbing you," she said over Lake's cries.

"It's okay. Can I give it a try?"

His low rumble washed over her tired senses.

"Sure. If you want to."

"Hey there, buddy," Smith said as he took Lake into his arms and snuggled him against his chest. He walked away from her, bouncing Lake, singing a song about Jesus.

Lake quieted so quickly. Was it possible he'd missed Smith?

Liv watched and listened as Smith shuffled around the room, singing, then saying soothing words to the baby. The peaceful way he took care of Lake settled over her too. She sank into her rocker and covered herself with an afghan.

"You're exhausted, Liv." Smith's gentle tones awakened her. "Sorry I haven't been here for you." He stroked some hair away from her face. She liked his fingers tangling slightly with her hair, touching her cheek.

She pried her heavy eyelids apart. He squatted next to her chair, his gaze meeting hers.

"You should go to bed and get some rest now that Lake's sleeping." He stood and held out his hand to her.

Did he want to hold her hand in the middle of the night?

She let him pull her to her feet. "Thanks for calming him. Nothing I did helped."

"He needed his daddy," he said without letting go of her hand.

"I guess he did." Warmth spread through her. All her frustration toward him from the last week of his being physically and emotionally absent melted. Thankfulness welled up inside of her that he was here being Lake's daddy, and now, was here with her too.

He held her hand as they walked across the living room to her bedroom door.

"I'm sorry I've been so busy." He took a broken gulp of air. "Things have gotten out of hand as far as my time management goes. I didn't mean to neglect you or Lake."

"Oh, well—"

"I mean it. I'm sorry, Liv."

She nodded, thankful for his humble admission.

"Cookie baking tomorrow, no matter what?" He drew her hand to his lips and brushed a soft kiss over her skin.

Ticklish sensations cascaded up and down her neck and arms. "Smith, you don't have to—"

"I want to. Some emergencies can't be helped. But I must figure out how to triage the rest of the stuff." He let go of her hand and gently stroked her shoulders. "You and Lake are the center of my world. I'm still learning how to be a good pastor and a decent husband and dad. It may take some time and juggling skills, but I promise I'll get there."

"Okay. Thanks."

She had the urge to lean up on tiptoe and kiss his oh, so soft-looking lips. What would he do if she did? She didn't follow the impulse. But did he feel the electrified currents zapping the air between them? The way his eyes blinked slowly, the way he glanced at her lips a couple of times, maybe he did.

Chapter Sixty-four

"No, I can't see Amaryllis or Arnold today." Smith watched his secretary scratch out words on her yellow legal pad.

"And the Carletons?" Mrs. Scarlett frowned.

"Can you reschedule them for tomorrow?"

"They were adamant they required an appointment with you today."

Groaning, Smith pressed his fingers against his forehead. Why were so many people in need of counseling and encouragement right now? Was the freezing weather that kept so many locked up in their homes causing all this dissension in marriages and relationships?

"Please call and reschedule, if possible. I'll trust you to take their emotional temperature." He sighed. "If it must be today, so be it. Honestly, I just need some time with my family."

"Of course. I'll do what I can." Mrs. Scarlett closed the door.

Smith leaned back in his swivel chair and pondered his time with Liv and Lake in the middle of the night. He'd recognized the exhausted look in Liv's eyes. The emotional distance between them was obvious too.

Something needed to change. Otherwise, it felt like their platonic friendship would go on and on. If he weren't married to her but wanted to get to know her better, what would he do? What had he done with Katy? He groaned at the off-limits topic.

In a dating situation, he'd ask his girlfriend out, and spend time talking and flirting with her. Had he done anything with Liv that showed her he wanted to be with her romantically?

He walked the floors with Lake last night. Called Liv "sweetheart." But what were those compared to not doing much of anything to advance their relationship in ten weeks?

They hadn't laughed much lately. Flirting was nonexistent. His schedule kept him flying by the seat of his pants. He felt like he had to be everything to everyone, which often left him with little to no energy or desire to do anything other than veg out on the couch in the evenings, or else retire to his bedroom altogether.

He hadn't been doing his part to nurture his marriage. If he didn't wise up and do things differently, he and Liv would be the ones seeking marital counseling.

Mrs. Scarlett tapped on the door. "The sun is shining on you today, Pastor. All three sessions were moved to tomorrow. You're free for today."

"Excellent. Thank you, Mrs. Scarlett!"

When he entered the parsonage, the delicious scents of garlic and onions reached him. Liv and Mom were working side by side, chopping vegetables.

"Smells heavenly in here," he said as he removed his outerwear and hung them on hooks in the entryway.

Liv met his gaze with a gentle smile that made him even more glad he came home early.

"We're making stew," Mom said, holding up a carrot.

"Sounds great. Especially on a blustery day like today." He shivered, thinking of the sideways blowing snow he walked through to get from his car to the front door. He marched straight to the woodstove and held his hands out toward it.

"I'm surprised to see you." Liv joined him at the stove, holding her hands out too.

"Why? I told you—" He took a breath. "Right. Because I've canceled so many things lately?"

She shrugged. "I didn't grow up around woodstove heat." She was obviously changing the topic. "I like it, though."

"It's a pain to keep going, but the intense warmth when you need it is amazing."

Their gazes met and held. His words "intense warmth" replayed in his mind. Had her thoughts leaped to romantic heat between them? Or was it only his thoughts doing that?

He smoothed his hands around hers and smiled at her look of surprise. He'd warned her he would be doing this more often. They stood by the fire for a few minutes, holding hands. He liked being close to Liv. He liked holding her hands, too.

"How was your morning?" she asked, sounding wifely.

"Okay. I almost had to cancel this afternoon. Mrs. Scarlett did some scrambling and worked it out for me to escape early."

"I'll have to thank her next time I see her." There was that lovely smile on her face again.

The water ran in the kitchen, reminding him Mom was nearby.

"Are you ready to do some baking with me?"

"All set. Chocolate chip cookies, or die?"

"Nothing quite so drastic." He chuckled.

"I have to warn you, I have a reputation for burning things."

"I'll watch out for that!"

He held her hand as they walked from the woodstove into the kitchen.

After they pulled all the supplies out of the cupboards and fridge, he said, "I want you to make this first batch on your own. I'll just watch if that's okay."

"I thought we were doing this together." She sounded disappointed.

"We are. You asked me to help you learn how to bake. Doing it yourself is the best way."

"I've failed so many times on my own already." She groaned and swayed her hand toward the oven. "I don't want to burn anything else in my life!"

"I'll be a good supervisor." He pulled a chair over to the counter and sat down. "What's first?"

"Butter. Not melted butter!"

"See. You learned by your mistake."

"Maybe you should watch and not talk." She flicked a little flour at him.

"Hey." He wiped his nose. "None of that." But his thoughts roamed back to the other house, the first time they baked together, and how she bespeckled him with flour.

She leaned over the cookbook, her arms crossed on the counter. She looked cute. And slimmer already. *Eyes on her cute face. Nowhere else!*

"What?" She glanced at him. "Did I get flour on me already?"

"Not yet." He smiled, tempted to throw a little on her face to do his part in their flirting.

She peeled the wrappers off two cubes of butter.

"Why only two?"

"I'm going to make half a recipe." She pointed at the cookbook. "Then there'll be enough to try again if I wreck the first batch."

"Liv—"

"I have to prepare for the worst." A glint in her eyes warned him not to say anything contrary about her decision.

"Fine." He lifted his hands in surrender.

She added brown sugar and eggs. When she scooped up a cup of flour, he held out his hands. "Hold it right there."

"What's wrong?"

"Mix the wet ingredients first."

"Why's that, oh Knowledgeable One?" she said in a smirky tone. "It's all going into the same dough."

"Do you have to challenge everything I say?"

"Yeah, I guess I do." She tossed a grin in his direction.

"Did you read the instructions?" He tapped the open book.

She heaved a sigh. "No."

Standing, he lifted the book and read aloud, "Add the butter, sugar, eggs, and vanilla and mix until blended."

"But Smith, it's not going to make any difference."

"Trust me, it does, okay?" He swept a strand of her hair out of her eyes.

"Okay. Trust is a two-way street."

Was she talking about cookie baking or their relationship now?

"I know it is."

She met his gaze with a challenge still in her eyes. He half expected her to throw the cup of flour over him. But a moment later, the tension sieved from the air as she put the wooden spoon to work mixing the wet ingredients.

Smith leaned against the edge of the sink and watched her, enjoying the look of consternation on her face. He mentally checked each of her ingredients and her half-measures. This batch ought to be delicious. His mouth watered at the thought of biting into warm chocolate chip cookies.

When all that remained was adding the chocolate, he asked, "Have you double-checked the recipe, including the instructions?"

"No. Why would I?"

"You're a new baker. It's best to double-check."

"Okay," she said in a long-suffering tone. With the bag of chocolate chips in her hand, she peered down at the recipe. "Yep. I did everything."

He knew she'd forgotten a step. "If you're sure."

She cut him a glare. "If I'm doing something wrong, tell me."

"This is about you learning the art of cooking and following a recipe."

Steam spilled out from the stewpot on the front burner. He quickly adjusted the lid. That pot being in front of the dials may have kept Liv from realizing the oven wasn't turned on yet.

She dumped half a bag of chocolate chips into the mixing bowl, then stirred. Lake fussed and she turned toward the bedroom door as if to see to him. But Mom scurried from her room into the baby's room, obviously tending to him.

Liv faced the bowl again. "I'm sure I've got it right."

"Check the texture. You'll get used to how this cookie dough feels over time. Our sons will thank you for it someday." He gave her a thumbs-up.

She pressed her lips together as if squelching a comment and squeezed a little dough between her fingers. She picked out a chocolate chip and tossed it in her mouth. "Mmm. Want one?"

"Why, yes, I do." He opened his mouth.

Grinning, she picked up a chocolate chip from the bag and tossed it gently in the air. Like a fish gobbling food, Smith caught the chocolate piece.

Liv laughed.

"See. I have skills." He let the candy melt in his mouth.

"Because you're adept at catching chocolate?"

"That's right."

They both grinned.

After Liv dropped bite-sized chunks of dough onto the cookie sheet, she opened the oven door and pushed the tray onto the middle shelf.

Smith fought the urge to laugh.

Maybe she felt the heat coming from the stewpot. When she quickly shut the door and set the buzzer, Smith couldn't hold back his snickering any longer.

"Why are you laughing at me?" She clasped some flour and tossed it at his face. Coughing, he lunged forward and grabbed a small handful of flour.

She backed up. "Don't you dare!"

"I dare plenty!" He rained flour over her head.

"Smith! Stop!"

Squealing, she ran to the other side of the kitchen where he easily caught her by one wrist and sprinkled the rest of the flour over her hair. Flour covered her face and eyelashes too.

"Stop now or I'll—"

"Or you'll what?" He grinned down at her, wanting to kiss her rosy lips.

"Or I'll—"

Their gazes meshed, tangled, noses almost touching. He leaned in a fraction of an inch, watching her hazel eyes pulse wide. What would it be like to kiss her flour-dusted mouth?

Mom cleared her throat from the living room.

Smith jerked back as if he touched a hot iron.

"Sorry to intrude but Lake needs his mommy."

Liv batted her flour-coated eyelashes at him, then skittered around him and ran for her bedroom.

Smith blew out a long breath. Sometimes having his mother in the house wasn't helpful at all.

Chapter Sixty-five

As Liv nursed Lake, she watched Smith cleaning up the kitchen. He still had some flour in his hair. She probably did too. Occasionally, he glanced at her, and their gazes met.

Had he almost kissed her a few minutes ago? He leaned in toward her like he was going to, glancing at her mouth like he enjoyed what he saw. She must have leaned toward him, too. Unless she imagined the whole thing.

Would their first post-wedding kiss be sweet and tender? Or passionate and powerful?

The buzzer rang and Liv jerked, which caused Lake to whimper. "Can you get that for me, Smith?"

He eyed her with a humorous look.

"Please?"

"Okay. It's your call." He lifted a hot pad in the air as if showing her he was using one, which was weird. Then he pulled the cookie sheet out of the oven and set it on the stove.

Liv inhaled, trying to detect the aroma of chocolate chip cookies. She couldn't smell a thing. "How do they look?"

Smith shrugged, his back to her. By the way his shoulders shook, he was suppressing laughter. The cookies must have turned out terrible. Yet she couldn't smell the horrible scent of burned chocolate.

"What's going on?" She adjusted Lake to her shoulder and patted his back gently. Getting up from the chair and crossing the room, she expected to find charred or disgusting cookies. Instead, the dozen cookies on the sheet looked like clumps of raw dough. "What happened?"

Smith burst into laughter. "Sorry. Sorry."

"What did I do wrong? Oh, no. I forgot to preheat the oven, didn't I?"

"Yes." He bit back a snicker.

"You knew? Yet you used the hot pad! Why? Just to make fun of me?"

"No." His face red, moisture filled his eyes. "I couldn't help myself. I suggested you reread the instructions, but you refused."

"You could have given me a hint. Stop laughing!"

"I wanted to see your reaction when you opened the oven door. That's why I couldn't face you."

"Laughing at my expense? You know I hate that!"

"I'm sorry." He smoothed his hand over her hand on Lake's back, not sounding sorry at all. "Don't be mad at me, okay?"

"I don't get mad. I get even." She squinted at him. "You better watch out!"

"Pepper up my nose in my sleep, if I recall correctly? This means you'll have to sneak into my bedroom at night."

"Not necessarily." She moved Lake higher onto her shoulder. "Can you watch him while I finish the cookies?"

"Absolutely." He took Lake, but his gaze still sparkled with subdued humor.

Twenty minutes later, the tray of cookies came out of the oven looking perfectly golden. The shiny chocolate chunks peeking out the tops looked melted and delicious.

Smith put Lake down in his bassinet and then joined her. "Do I dare?" He reached for a cookie that was cooling on a sheet of foil.

She swatted his hand. "Say anything bad about my cookies and you'll be sorry."

"I wouldn't think of it." He winked at her. "Flirting with you is fun, Liv."

"Is that what you call this? Flirting?"

"Sure. What would you call it?"

The phone rang, stopping her from answering him.

As he took the receiver into the laundry room, Liv perused her cookies. An idea crossed her mind. Smith deserved a good prank he wouldn't forget.

* * * *

Fifteen minutes later, Smith hung up the phone, shaking his head. Many of his congregants called on him, torn up by marriage problems and life's trials, desperate for solutions. Yet, sometimes, he felt helpless to offer encouragement or wisdom. *Lord, help them,* he prayed as he turned to find Liv watching him.

"Sorry about the long call."

"Don't be. You're a kind man. Doing a good thing."

Her words bolstered his spirit. He walked straight to her and hugged her. Not a passionate embrace like he might have given her earlier. But this one felt meaningful. A husband and wife sharing a heartfelt moment.

She stepped back, her eyes sparkling toward him. "Ready for a cookie?"

"Sure am. Maybe two." His mouth watered at the thought of biting into the melted chocolate inside the cookies. Maybe he'd have some milk too. He grabbed a tall glass and filled it full of the cold liquid.

Liv handed him a saucer with two cookies on it. How sweet of her to do this for him, handing him a plate, standing here smiling at him. Was she eager to see what he thought of her cookies? Even if they didn't taste perfect, he'd school his features.

"Try it." She pointed at the cookie closest to him.

Hungrily, he bit into half of it and chomped. His eyes watered. A fire burned up his throat. He dashed for the sink and spit, then spit again. Running the faucet, he gulped big swallows of cold water. What had she done?

Liv's laughter echoed in the kitchen. Wiping his mouth, he spun around and found her holding out his glass of milk. He guzzled it dry, his throat still burning.

"What was that?" he choked out.

"A tiny added ingredient." She grinned cheekily.

"What ingredient might that be?"

"Hot sauce," she said innocently.

"As in you grabbed hot sauce instead of vanilla? You ruined the whole batch?"

"No. I prepared that cookie especially for you. You should have seen your face." She burst out laughing again.

He pressed the back of his hand against his tingling lips.

"Liv—" Then it hit him. He'd pulled a prank on her. She warned him about payback. "I see I'm going to have to watch my back around you."

"Or at least what you put in your mouth."

Her gaze tangled with his in a breathtaking way that brought his attention to her soft lips again. Lips he'd like to try kissing.

She made a gulping sound. "Do you want any more cookies?"

"Not if they're like the one I just ate."

She picked up the second cookie from the plate and held it out. "Come on, Smith. Try it. It's good. Trust me."

He liked the way she said his name. Liked the way she implored him to trust her. He imagined what it might sound like if she whispered his name during a kiss.

Opening his mouth slightly, he leaned forward. She touched the cookie to his lips. His gaze meshed with hers, and he bit into the soft cookie, his lips brushing her fingers. The chocolaty taste scrambling across his taste buds soothed the tempest leftover from the last spicy bite. "Mmm. That's great." He took the cookie from her fingers and stuffed it in his mouth.

"See. I made cookies without them being a national disaster!"

"Well—" His brain replayed the horror he felt when he bit into the other cookie.

However, another thought came to mind replacing the bad with good. He'd never forget how they tossed flour at each other earlier—and what almost happened between them afterward.

Chapter Sixty-six

One thing or another kept Liv from going to the ladies' meeting Amaryllis had invited her to. Today, she was going to give it a try. Leaving Lake in Trish's care, she shoveled out her car—a huge task in itself—and carefully drove along the snowy streets to the church.

What would the women expect of the pastor's wife at one of these meetings? Would the Board member's wives think she should know all about Biblical topics? Would they want to know personal information about her? She groaned.

At the church parking lot, she shut off the engine and grabbed her bag of knitting supplies—two skeins of yarn and her size six needles. She'd knit and purl as Trish taught her, keeping it simple. Hopefully, she didn't tangle the threads and reveal how little she knew about knitting!

"We're so glad you've joined us, Mrs. North," Amaryllis gushed when Liv entered the Sunday school classroom where a dozen ladies surrounded two long tables. "Come in." She waved Liv to an empty seat.

"Thank you."

"Hello." Jenn Carter, Bob's wife, waved from across the table. "Glad you could join us." The woman with a long braid down her back focused on the hand sewing in her lap.

"Everyone," Amaryllis announced, "if you haven't met our pastor's wife yet, this is Mrs. North." She swayed her hand toward Liv.

"Liv, please." She smiled at the other ladies.

A few greetings followed.

"Our first box of baby clothes has reached the mission in Uganda." Amaryllis beamed. "They're looking forward to more shipments in the future. So keep those knitting needles humming."

Cheers and "Praise the Lord" rang out. Amaryllis sat down and picked up what looked like a blue baby blanket, then chattering ensued as the ladies worked on handcraft projects and visited with each other.

Taking it all in, Liv pulled out the soft yellow skein of yarn and glanced at the younger woman next to her. "I don't think we've met yet. I'm Liv."

"Hi. I'm Candy Martin, Marla's daughter."

"Marla?"

Candy nodded toward the other table. "Mama is Pastor Smith's secretary."

"Oh, you're Mrs. Scarlett's daughter!"

"Yes, that's right." She laughed.

"What do you do?" Liv asked.

"Do?"

"Do you work outside the home?"

Candy laughed again. "I have twins. That explains everything I do."

"Wow. Twins. A double blessing."

"Double the fun. Double the exhaustion." Candy rolled her eyes.

"How old?" Liv set up the first row of stitches for a bootie.

"Two months."

"Oh. Your babies are close to the same age as my son, Lake."

"Mom mentioned you had an infant." Candy let out a long sigh. "I've been so busy and tired, I haven't been back to a church service since the twins' arrival."

"I understand."

"Mrs. North, we've met before but I'm Jubilee," a woman with partially gray hair said from across the table. "I've been dying to ask, how did you and Pastor North meet? We're all aware you have a 'unique' marriage." She snickered behind her hand. "We're curious to hear how it came about, aren't we, ladies?"

A few giggles followed.

Liv's face felt on fire. These women knew about Smith's and her unconventional marriage? Who told them? The Board members said they'd keep it confidential until she and Smith were ready to tell people. Who blabbed? Amaryllis?

Liv wanted to walk straight out of this little gathering. She had no intention of discussing her marriage with any of these women. And she had a few choice words to say to Amaryllis!

"Now, Jubilee," Jenn spoke up, "we don't want to put Olivia on the spot."

"All I meant was it's a charming but antiquated idea—marrying someone you don't love." Jubilee made jerky movements as she turned away from Liv. "Surely, they're not ashamed of their choice."

Ashamed? A breath caught in Liv's throat. *Run for the door!*

But a warm hand clasped hers, stilling the agitated movement of her fingers around the knitting needles.

Candy's gaze met hers kindly. "I think it's beautiful. Falling in love after the wedding. Marrying Pastor North so both of you could come and be our pastor's family. I love you so much for doing that."

Warmth flooded Liv's heart. "Thank you." She'd be indebted to Candy for the rest of her life for sticking up for her, rescuing her, the way she just did.

"I didn't mean any offense," Jubilee said in a huffy tone.

Liv cast on a few more stitches, avoiding anyone's gaze. Had Amaryllis told these women that Smith considered her as a bride before Liv?

Chatter about other topics picked up around her, but Liv continued stewing on what Amaryllis may have told Jubilee, and the others, and debating whether she should leave. Smith wouldn't expect her to stay, would he?

"How do you like Sandpoint, Olivia?" Jenn asked.

"Oh, uh. Between taking care of Lake and staying inside due to the cold weather, I've mostly been at home. Schweitzer Mountain looks gorgeous from my window."

"Wait until spring. You'll love the lake." Jenn met Liv's gaze with an understanding smile then resumed her hand sewing.

"We should plan a ladies' picnic up on the mountain this summer," someone else said.

Liv was thankful for the discussion that followed as various ladies offered suggestions and opinions about picnicking locations and what time of year would be best for such an event. Any topic leading away from her and Smith's romance, or lack thereof, was appreciated.

Amaryllis read the letter from the missionary in Africa where they sent baby items. While the needles flew, and gazes were focused on projects, opinions and ideas got tossed around about how to do more than crafting ventures. What could they do to raise more money for the mission?

Liv had an idea, but she didn't want to say anything, didn't want to put herself out there for anyone to say something disparaging toward her. Then she thought of all the training she had in computers and presentations. Why not suggest something useful?

"We could put together a presentation with graphic design on transparencies to show during a service." When no one else spoke, she continued, "Also, if we had a few pictures from the mission, maybe some of the babies wearing your homemade garments, and a map of where the mission is, we could showcase them on cardboard displays. Possibly garnering more funds."

The room was silent as if she'd taken everyone by surprise with her input.

"That's a lovely idea," Candy said.

"Yes," Jenn agreed. "Does anyone know how to put something like that together?"

"I do," Liv said. "I've done company presentations, both with transparencies and storyboards, in the past."

"You have?" Amaryllis's mouth dropped open.

Another buzz went up around the room.

"If we put together a nice program, not only for our church, but to engage with some large businesses and foundations about the mission, some might allocate funding." Liv felt more confident discussing something she had knowledge about. "It's worth a shot."

"Really?" Candy's eyes widened. "I've never thought of companies being so generous."

"My—" No need to mention her father's company. "I've known companies who have an annual budget for giving to charities."

Sharing something from her business experience made her feel more valuable to this group. Now, if only she could forget about Jubilee's prying question from before.

Chapter Sixty-seven

Smith came home early and handed Liv a bag from the bakery. His expression looked strained, although she didn't know him well enough to figure out if it was work-related troubles or fatigue.

"What's this?" She peered inside the bag and saw a chocolate éclair. Her mouth watered.

"Comfort food."

"Do I need comfort food?"

"I thought you might." He eyed her somberly.

"Oh. You heard about the ladies' meeting, didn't you?" She let out a long sigh.

"Mrs. Scarlett told me." He clasped her hand. "I'm so sorry, Liv. Our marriage should not have come up for discussion in a group of church ladies. You've done a beautiful thing by marrying me before we fell in love so I could pastor this church. So we could be a family. Those ladies should not have brought you to task like that."

"It was awkward. I felt so humiliated I almost left." She flushed at the remembrance. "But I'm glad I stayed. I'm going to help by making a computer presentation for the mission's project we're doing."

"We're doing?"

"Sure. Maybe I can make cookies for a bake sale, huh?" She chuckled, trying for some levity.

He smiled. "Maybe we could work on that together."

"The presentation or the cookies?"

"I'm sure you're better at any computer project than me. But I might be more adept in the cookie-making department."

"Last I checked, the cookies I made were gone." She squinted at him. "Someone ate them all."

He held up his hand. "Guilty as charged. They were good."

"But?"

He chuckled. "I don't want you to be mad at me."

"Do I go around being mad at you?" She crossed her arms, enjoying the banter between them.

"No." The merriment left his eyes. "I appreciate your even temperament. I'm glad you don't pout and act mad about everything like some women do. That was something—" He clamped his lips together.

"Something that bothered you about Katy?"

"Sorry to bring it up." He glanced at the ceiling. "Even to be thinking about her."

"Why? She's part of your past. You'll think of her sometimes." Although, the woman continuing to come up in their discussions was grating on her. Wasn't Smith supposed to be moving on from that relationship? Still, determined to face their unusual situation with optimism, she said, "We both have a past. It's not like it got swept away. Washed clean, yes. Disappeared, no."

"So you think of Nick sometimes?"

"Yes. But not in a good way. My thoughts of him usually include words like ratfink, louse, or deadbeat human." She shrugged. "Trish says I have to forgive him."

"I understand." Smith whisked a few strands of her hair off her cheek. "I haven't pondered those things about Katy as much since my thoughts have been more centered on you."

"Nice to hear, since you're my husband." She grinned, not sure if Smith was being flirtatious or downright honest with her.

"I am your husband." He smoothed his palm over her knuckles. "A man who wants to get to know his wife better."

He was being flirtatious with her!

"Are you asking me out?" She winked. "Because I might be able to fit you into my schedule. What with baby feedings, and now with the expectations of the ladies' group, my cup might be getting full."

He laughed boisterously. "Didn't I warn you to watch out for ladies' groups and their expectations of the pastor's wife?"

"No, in fact, you didn't." She tugged on his hand for emphasis. "Your mom did though. I went today to visit with the ladies. When the topic of our love life came up, I was blindsided."

"I'm sorry." Suddenly he smiled. "Do we have a love life to talk about?"

She smacked his arm. "Pastor North, you shock me."

"Do I now?"

He took her in his arms, the gentle move surprising her. His gaze darted toward her lips, and warmth spread through her veins.

"You know what, Liv?"

"What?" The word came out breathy.

"You're lovely. And while we aren't at the falling in love phase, I do have strong feelings for you. I think of you as my wife all the time."

"You do?" She gulped.

He nodded slowly. "And I want—"

"Smith?" Trish's voice, coming from her room, broke into whatever he'd been about to say.

Liv scrambled back from his arms.

"Can you help me?" Trish called. "This picture keeps falling down."

"Sure thing, Mom." Smith stared at Liv, a slight smile crossing his lips. He leaned near her ear. "Stop looking so guilty. We're married." He winked at her then walked into the other room.

Chapter Sixty-eight

The next evening, Smith set his napkin down at the restaurant where he and Liv were having dinner out. Their lighthearted conversation revolved around Lake, the women's group, and humorous anecdotes he'd come across in his sermon preparation. However, all through the meal, he looked for ways to bring them into a more serious discussion about their relationship.

Liv seemed relaxed around him. And she was so beautiful. Even if he couldn't say he loved her yet, he enjoyed her smile, her warmth, her endearing way of making things light and easy between them. Whereas Katy—

Ugh. He shouldn't be thinking of her. Even if Liv was okay with a passing thought of his ex-fiancée coming into his mind, he wanted to avoid it. He'd prefer she wasn't dwelling on Nick, either.

He took a long guzzle from his water glass. Was his not being completely healed about Katy the reason he couldn't tell Liv he loved her? Wasn't being able to say those words essential before closeness and intimacy? He needed to make this a matter of daily prayer.

"You turned quiet." Liv clasped her hands at the edge of the table.

"Sorry. My brain went off in another direction."

"Thinking about church stuff?"

"No. But I was pondering something I shouldn't be thinking about right now."

"Oh. Her?" She made a face like she was disappointed.

A pain in his chest felt like a knife wound. How could she read him so easily already?

"Let's focus on us tonight." He leaned forward, hoping she followed his lead. "Why don't you tell me one thing about you I don't know already?"

"How about if we make a rule first? When we're on a date"— she swayed her hands toward the lovely table setting—"no dwelling on past romantic interests, all right? It's a real mood killer."

She didn't frown at him, didn't glare, just asked in a way that seemed honest and sincere. And right then he knew he didn't want her assuming he was pining for Katy.

"I agree. But let's get one thing straight." He reached across the tablecloth and clasped her hand, toying with the ring he placed on her finger on their wedding day. "Sometimes my mind wanders back to her, but I am committed to you, to us, and our future. And I am"—he took a swallow—"very attracted to you, Liv."

Her mouth opened and momentarily froze.

"I've been thinking a lot about kissing you. I almost did yesterday before my mom called for my help."

Liv closed her mouth and licked her lower lip. He was aware of her every move.

"Would you have let me kiss you?"

"Yes." She smiled. "I'm not sure if I'm ready. Although, I was drawn to you in that moment, too."

He loved how she spoke her mind. How he didn't have to second-guess her thoughts.

"I'm glad to hear it."

"You know before when you asked if you could hold my hand? Should we talk about kissing first, too?"

"Isn't that what we're doing? Talking and flirting about it?" He smiled.

"Okay, then." She put her other hand over his. "Why do you want to kiss me?"

"Why?" Her question stymied him.

"You say you're attracted to me. How attracted?"

The air whooshed out of him. They were in a restaurant where anyone walking past might hear them.

"I'm serious. You've admitted to still thinking about Katy."

He gulped.

"You're a good and an honest man." Her gaze remained steady on him. "Are you attracted to me for me? Because you want to fall in love with me?"

He felt the heat of a thousand-watt bulb burning his face.

"Or are you attracted to me because you're forcing yourself to have feelings for me instead of Katy?"

"No, that's not it at all."

"Then, what? You've said you don't love me like a husband loves a wife."

Man, she seemed determined to nail his hide to the chair.

"Liv—" He peered around at some of the other diners. No one he knew stared back at him, thank goodness. But he felt cornered by Liv's questions. "Why is this so important? Knowing my intentions?"

"It just is." Some color came into her cheeks. "Maybe I'm afraid you're going to push for more from me before I'm ready. Or before either of us are ready, just because we took the official step of getting married."

"Trust me, Liv. I won't push for anything you don't want to freely participate in. Yes, we are married, so if we wanted to become more"—he lowered his voice—"intimate, it would be okay."

"Are you ready for that ... with me?"

A tender look of insecurity crossed her features and his heart melted.

He hunkered closer to her, as close as he could get with the table still between them, gazing intently into her moist eyes. "Liv, there's no one else I'd want to be ready to take that step with than you. You are the only woman I imagine myself with as my wife. But if you're asking if I'm ready for you to move into my bedroom yet, the answer is no."

She nodded slowly. "Thank you. I need to hear how you feel."

Her eyes stared deeply into his. His gaze zeroed in on her soft red mouth that looked kissable in this light. He forced himself to meet her gaze again.

"Liv, we aren't madly in love with each other yet." He smoothed his hand over hers, pressing his fingers against her palm. "But we're on a journey toward loving each other." He let his fingers slide up her wrist, smoothing over her warm, delicate skin. "While I care for you as a … as a friend and my wife—"

"Yes?"

"There are times when I want you because of the manly attractions I have for you, too."

She grinned widely. "So, you are a mortal after all?"

He burst out laughing, letting go of her hand. How could she pop a joke right in the middle of such an intense topic? She'd be a wonder at softening tempers in some of his tougher meetings with parishioners.

"The way you soothe my heart with a lighthearted comment attracts me to you and makes me want to get to know you even more."

She smiled. "Thank you for being honest with me about your thoughts."

The waiter arrived at their table. "Dessert?"

"Yes!" They answered simultaneously, then burst into laughter.

Chapter Sixty-nine

Smith couldn't get last night's conversation with Liv off his mind. While Mrs. Scarlett read the day's schedule and reminded him why each person had planned a meeting with him, he kept picturing his wife's smiling face over dinner. The way her eyes sparkled at him. The way he wanted to kiss her so badly.

Later, during a phone call where septuagenarian Dottie Barker made a counseling session via phone and plied him with a rundown of her ills, his thoughts roamed to Liv's question. *"Why are you attracted to me?"*

He reined in the answers—because you're beautiful, I can't stop thinking about you, you make me laugh—and focused on Dottie's problems.

Now, he sat opposite Clay and Jubilee Taggart, two staunch—or so he'd thought—members of his church, trying to pay attention to their argument. The personal topic Jubilee had brought up with Liv in the ladies' group still riled him, but he subdued those feelings.

"I thought you loved me!" Jubilee spoke sharply.

"I do." Clay, a burly, redheaded city worker, glanced at Smith as if he were at his wit's end. "Why you involved Pastor North in our disagreement is beyond my understanding."

"Exactly. You have no understanding of a woman's feelings!" Jubilee threw the barb then faced the wall.

Smith sighed. "Let's take a breather. You both need to be heard by your spouse. How about if you tell me what attracted you to each other in the first place?"

Clay squinted at Smith like he thought he was out of his mind. Jubilee kept her gaze aimed at the wall.

"Clay, why don't you begin? Why did you choose to be with Jubilee?"

"Too long ago to remember. That's what thirty-two years of marriage and a lifetime of nagging does to a man."

"Thirty-three!" Jubilee yelped.

Smith hoped he and Liv never felt as frustrated and at the end of their tether with each other as Jubilee and Clay did.

"Why are you attracted to me?"

Focus.

"Clay? Why don't you think back to when you were first interested in Jubilee? Why did you choose her?"

Clay sighed wearily. "She and her sister pestered me to pick one of them. So I did."

Jubilee's shoulders stiffened like she'd been hit.

Smith sucked in a long breath. Maybe his question was the wrong one.

"Jubilee was prettier. Kinder." Clay thrust his hand through his red hair. "More interesting to talk to. I liked that."

"Is that why you never listen to me now?" Jubilee nearly shouted. "Because I'm not interesting?"

"Woman, you drive me nuts!"

Inwardly, Smith groaned. Why did Jubilee have to take offense to every word her husband said? The answer hit him. Her emotional pain was so great everything Clay said added salt to her wound, making her sharp-tongued and spewing unloving words. The revelation made it difficult for Smith to even go on asking questions.

"We're done here," Clay said. "This talk isn't getting us any closer to meeting in the middle."

"Is that what you want?" Smith asked. "Are you willing to do anything to meet in the middle?"

"I'm here, aren't I? When I should be working." Clay glared at his wife.

Jubilee turned a pain-filled glance toward Smith.

"Jubilee," Smith said softly, "are you willing to do anything to meet Clay in the middle?"

"I'm trying." She drew in a stuttered breath. "I'm not perfect. We've had our share of problems. But I don't want to give up on our marriage."

"That's good to hear."

The couple glanced at each other with almost shy expressions. Thirty-three years together and they still felt uncertain meeting each other's gazes?

"I'd like you to have a seven-day no-arguing clause," Smith said quietly.

"What?" Clay asked incredulously.

"What do you mean?" Jubilee stared at Smith.

"For seven days, I want you to agree that there will be no arguing between you." He held up his hand to stop either of them from commenting until he finished. "Instead of grumbling or complaining about each other, I want you to imagine what it was like when you were courting. Consider what drew you to the other, what you might say to your girlfriend or boyfriend, not your spouse of thirty-three years." He made sure to say the appropriate number of years.

"What good will thinking of the past do?" Clay shuffled his shoulders. "We're here today."

"Right. And you're stuck in a rut of deep hurts. Both of you." He glanced back and forth between them. "Perhaps, things have been meanly said, or concerns haven't been addressed, and you are hurting so badly, you don't even want to look at, let alone talk to, the person you vowed to spend the rest of your life with. The one you promised to love."

Jubilee's gaze fixated on her clenched hands in her lap.

Clay gnawed on his lower lip, staring out the window.

"For seven days, neither of you are to ignore the other, nor are you to speak unkindly. Instead, think loving thoughts about your spouse." Smith paused, praying about what to say next. "One other thing. I want you to pray together daily. Hold hands or don't, but I want you to pray for each other and for your family."

They stared at him as if he'd asked them to fly.

"Will you agree to my terms, Jubilee?"

She shrugged, shooting inquisitive glances at her husband.

"Clay?"

"I don't see how any of this will remedy the gnarly thing between us. There are thirty-three years of trash in here." He thumped his breastbone with his knuckles. "In her too."

Jubilee wiped her eyes with a tissue.

"Please, do what I've asked." Smith smiled at both. "We'll meet again in a week and discuss how it's going. I promise to walk through this valley with you. I'll be praying daily for you too." He stood, as did the couple, and he shook their hands.

"Thank you, Pastor." Jubilee walked stiffly out of the office.

"Still don't see how this helps," Clay muttered.

"Your marriage needs healing, Clay." Smith clapped his shoulder. "God is right here to help you. Call on Him. And be kind to your wife this week, okay?"

"Yeah, yeah."

After Clay left the room, Smith dropped to his knees. He stayed there praying for Clay and Jubilee until Mrs. Scarlett knocked on the door and told him it was time for his next appointment.

Chapter Seventy

During the next week, Liv spent Lake's nap times working on the presentation for the ladies' program. Smith had brought home a boxy computer from the church and set it up on the kitchen table. Liv felt like she was back in her glory days in her father's company.

Hopefully, her efforts here would help bring in money for the orphanage. She planned to make several document pages using bullet points and bold fonts, like the ones she'd done with Dad's presentation software back in Chicago. Then she'd copy everything onto a floppy disk. At an office supply store in Sandpoint that she'd already contacted, she'd have the pages transferred onto transparencies.

She tried making the letters and fonts just right to be pleasing to the viewer. Remembering Dad's adage, "You have three seconds to grab someone's attention," she did her best to make a presentation even Richard Dupont would approve of.

But thinking of her father brought back bittersweet memories of how lovingly he treated her when she was a girl. How proud he acted when she graduated college and came to work for the family business. How he urged her to excel as she made her way up the company ranks. Then how cruelly he treated her when he discovered her pregnancy, especially when he found out about Nick, a man who was trying to finagle his way up the corporate ladder.

Dad's hurtful words and actions made her feel orphaned. Not like the needy children in the photos Amaryllis gave her. But orphaned, nonetheless. In her preoccupation with Lake, marrying Smith, and moving here, she'd stuffed the pain of her parents' rejection down deep inside of her. But it was there, the anguish simmering in her heart.

Had anyone tried finding her? Or did they just write her off like a business expense and never think of her again?

Lord, I don't want to feel bitterness toward Dad and Mom. They are my parents, even if they don't claim me right now. I read in Your Word that I'm supposed to honor them. Then there's Nick.

Why did she have to think of him? Why mention him to God?

Taking a deep breath, she looked over the photos of babies and children for the storyboard. Some wore homemade clothing, knitted booties, and were lying on blankets the women had made. Yet, with each photo of the children, her heart grieved a little more.

Trish bustled into the house with grocery bags in hand, kicking the door closed. "It's freezing out there!" She plopped the bags on the counter, then turned the burner on beneath the tea kettle. "It's below zero again."

"I'll add a few pieces of wood to the fire." Liv jumped up and fed the stove. Then she helped Trish with putting the groceries away. She liked working alongside her mother-in-law in the kitchen, but she also wanted to talk with her.

"Do you have something on your mind?" Trish asked when the bags were nearly empty. "Is Lake okay?"

"He's fine." Liv set a box of crackers in the cupboard. "Looking at the photos of the orphans stirred up some angst in me about my parents."

"I see." Trish pulled out two mugs, dropped tea bags into them, then poured hot water into each. "What troubles you about your family?"

"Seeing the condition of the children brought back thoughts of the way my dad threw me out." Liv wiped away moisture from beneath her eyes. "We talked about letting hurts go already. And I've been pondering forgiveness. It's just hard."

Trish added a teaspoon of honey to each cup and then brought them into the living room.

They both sat down on the couch.

A deep ache burned in Liv's chest. "How Dad treated me still bothers me."

"Honey, I'm sorry for the pain he caused you." Trish clutched her hand for a moment. "But your dad is human, flawed, and sinful."

"He'd be offended if he heard anyone say he was flawed."

"Yet he is." Trish sipped her tea. "We all are. That's why you can forgive him. Focusing on what he did, what he said, what you wish you would have said—I've struggled with those thoughts too—makes forgiveness more difficult. But picturing a person being flawed like I'm flawed and prone to mistakes, makes giving grace and forgiveness easier."

Liv sipped her tea, pondering what Trish said. On the day her father cast her out, he had been flawed. Did he ever regret his actions?

"When I remember my sins, I can't dangle someone else's over their head." Trish turned toward Liv. "You aren't in this alone. Each of us has issues we must forgive. I'm a widow. I agonized over why God let that happen to me. Why did my son have to grow up without a father?"

"You've done so well. I thought—"

"That it was easy?"

Liv nodded. "But you've had a plate of burdens to carry alone."

"Not alone, because the Lord sent wonderful people to help me."

Liv felt a welling up of strength and thankfulness within herself. God was with her. And He had sent Trish and Smith to help her.

"Do you mind if I pray with you?" Trish asked.

"Not at all."

Her mother-in-law prayed a heartwarming petition for God to help Liv overcome the hurts of the past and to be able to forgive her parents. And Nick too.

Touched by her prayer, truly wanting to release the past, Liv silently prayed for Smith. That he'd be able to forgive Katy. And that he'd be ready to start a new life with Liv and Lake soon.

Chapter Seventy-one

Liv awoke to Lake crying hard in the night. Scooping him up, she held him against her chest, whispering, "What's wrong? Are you hungry already?" She glanced at the alarm clock. Only midnight? It hadn't been that long since he ate. "Do you have a bellyache, Little Mister?" She walked back and forth patting his back. No burps came up.

She grabbed a blanket and headed out to the rocker to nurse him. Still fussing, he scrunched up his body and wailed even louder.

"Poor boy." Adjusting her clothes, she stood again, traipsing across the floor. "There, there."

"Can I help?"

She hadn't heard Smith come in. "Um, sure, I guess."

He shuffled across the floor to her, his dark hair sticking up in tufts, his cheeks shadowy. "What's the problem?" he asked over Lake's whimpers.

She kept bouncing the baby. "I ate chili last night. It might have made him gassy."

"Let's see what I can do." Meeting her gaze in the semi-darkness, he held out his hands.

She slid Lake into his arms. "Thanks."

"You're welcome." He clutched Lake against his T-shirt and walked toward the kitchen, shushing and whispering to him.

What should she do? She was so tired, but she hated leaving Smith with the baby if he wouldn't settle down. She stood there listening for a few minutes.

Lake whimpered, but not as loudly as before. Smith continued walking, murmuring assurances. He sang "Amazing Grace" in subdued tones.

Liv smiled, remembering how he sang songs to Lake before. Someday he'd be singing songs to their other children, too. She met his gaze across the dimness. A soft smile crossed his mouth.

Thank You for giving me someone to share moments like these with. For giving me a man like Smith to be my husband and my children's father.

"You should try to get some rest," he said.

"Okay. Thanks."

Yet, she didn't want to go back to her room and sink into a deep sleep where she might not hear Lake if he needed her. Sighing, she dropped onto the couch and lay her cheek on a pillow, closing her eyes.

Smith continued walking with Lake. His shushing and singing got quieter. Or her awareness faded.

Sometime later, he nudged her arm and stroked some hair away from her face. "Liv?"

"Hmm?" She opened her eyes, searching for Lake. He wasn't in Smith's arms.

"I put him in the bassinet." He nodded over his shoulder. "I'm going to catch a little sleep."

"Okay. Thank you for helping with him." He was so sweet and kind. How could she not fall in love with this man? Soon. Surely, it would happen soon.

"You're welcome. You should head to bed too. You'll rest better in your room."

She pushed up from the couch and Smith took her hand, helping her stand. They stared at each other, his tired eyes sparkling back toward her.

"I should probably—" She slipped her hand away from his.

"Oh, right." As if in a daze, he stepped back and yawned. "Goodnight, Liv." Hurrying to his room, he didn't glance back at her.

The soft click of his bedroom door reached her, then Liv scurried to her room. Sighing, she climbed into her cool bed and thought about the expression she'd seen on Smith's face. The soft look in his eyes when he met her gaze.

Was she ready for more to happen between them? Not sharing a bed. But kissing? Being more romantic? Maybe she was ready for that.

Chapter Seventy-two

At the next ladies' meeting, Liv showed the women the presentation she made about the orphans and the mission's work. She used a projector and screen to display the transparencies as she explained how a presenter could share about the project. Then she pointed out the photos on the storyboard, describing how the speaker could encourage attendees to have open hearts for giving.

"That's it." She shrugged.

"That was amazing!" Candy said.

Other women chimed in with positive notes of approval and clapping.

"It looked professionally done," Jenn said, smiling. "We'll have to incorporate your computer skills into all our media work for the church from here on out."

"I don't know about that." Liv shrugged, not wanting to commit to anything. "I was glad to help with this. The kids touched my heart."

"Your fine work shows how much you care," Mrs. Scarlett said with a smile. "Your husband tells me you've been up with a fussy baby this week, too."

"Yeah. Just one of those things."

"Sounds familiar," Candy said with a moan. "I have double the midnight trouble at my house."

The ladies chuckled.

"Who's going to speak to the congregation during the program?" Candy asked.

"I can do it." Amaryllis beamed.

"Maybe Liv should do it." Candy nodded toward her. "She has experience with presentations."

"I agree." Mrs. Scarlett raised her hand.

"I don't know." Amaryllis frowned in Liv's direction.

Why was she looking at her so grumpily?

"Mrs. North is new here," Jubilee said in a condescending tone. "Some in the congregation might not approve of her situation, and therefore might not give money to this worthy cause. We're supposed to be above reproach."

"That's right!" Amaryllis said emphatically.

Wait. What were they talking about? Heat rushed up Liv's face. Was Jubilee referring to her getting pregnant before meeting Smith? She gritted her teeth, subduing her fight-or-flight response. Despite her effort, anger flamed livid within her alongside a mountain of embarrassment.

"Jubilee," Brittany, Dennis's wife, said, "I hardly think that's appropriate for you to mention here. Olivia is our pastor's wife. All our pasts are forgiven because of what Jesus did for us."

"Sure." Jubilee glanced from one side of the table to the other as if garnering support. "But we're talking about the goodwill of our congregants. The goodwill of the orphans, too. How can we encourage folks to dig deep into their pockets when some might begrudge the speaker?"

Begrudge her? Liv clenched her hands together so tightly her fingernails dug into her skin. She held her tongue, but she wanted to stand up and defend herself. To tell Jubilee off! Who did she think she was?

"Is Mrs. North the right one to appeal to our congregation when she's so recently become converted and had a child outside of marriage?" Jubilee asked.

"Jubilee!" Candy said in a shocked tone.

Liv wanted to disappear into the floor. After all the work she did for this group, how could anyone treat her so insensitively?

"She has a heart for orphans," Jenn spoke up kindly. "She lovingly put together this program. She's Pastor North's wife."

God bless Jenn.

"Someone else should present it is all I'm saying." Jubilee crossed her arms. "Why don't you do the honors, Amaryllis? You're an elder's sister. Or Mrs. Scarlett who has the pastor's ear?"

The room fell uncomfortably silent.

No one else spoke up for Liv. Each lady stared at her handcraft in her lap as if avoiding the discussion, or else avoiding meeting Liv's gaze.

She might as well gather her supplies and leave. She wasn't returning to one of these meetings again! But then, Trish's comments about people's flaws and weaknesses, and how they should all have grace toward each other, came back to Liv. Jubilee was flawed like Liv was flawed. She'd made her share of wrong choices. Maybe, someday, Jubilee would regret what she said here today.

Lord, help me to have grace and love like You.

Liv didn't want to be the cause of dissension among these ladies. Not that she agreed with Jubilee's bitter-sounding words and attitude. Nor did she appreciate the other women seemingly ignoring what Jubilee said and going on with their knitting and handcrafts.

Taking a deep breath, she forced herself to speak politely. "It's fine with me if someone else speaks during the presentation. Goodness. I have my hands full with Lake."

"That's what I wanted to hear." Jubilee smiled smugly.

"Thank you, Mrs. North," Amaryllis said.

For the rest of the meeting, Liv didn't say a word.

She'd been home a half hour and had just finished feeding Lake when Smith stormed into the house, brushing snowflakes off his coat. "I'm so sorry, Liv."

At his caring tone, tears flooded her eyes. Rotten tears. She blinked rapidly. "It's okay. Thanks, though."

"No, it's not okay." He ran his hands down her arms, causing a chill to skitter up her neck. "Mrs. Scarlett told me about the meeting. What those catty women said was out of line!" He skipped right over their cookie talk and went straight to the issue. "I plan to have a serious discussion with Jubilee and Amaryllis later today."

"Please don't. You're not responsible for fighting my battles." Even with her teary emotions, she'd sat in tenser board meetings than the awkward women's group today.

"Liv—"

"I mean it. The meeting was awful. Jubilee got all worked up. But she had a valid point."

"Like it's okay for her to bring up your past as a reason for you not to serve in our church?" His eyes grew wide as golf balls. "I won't let this slide. She acted rude and unloving to you, and I plan to tell her how I feel about that. Amaryllis has a place of leadership among those women. She should have stood up for you!"

"I agree with that. But I think she's still hurting, or miffed, about you overlooking her as a wife." Liv cringed, hating to mention it.

Smith groaned and dropped down on the couch, raking his fingers through his hair. "I have to do something."

"I'm trying to fit in. So, please, just let it go, okay?"

"But you're my wife."

Lake whimpered and she jostled him. "Thank you for being willing to stick up for me. But you and I have enough things to work through without bringing church troubles into our relationship."

He stared at her for a long while, his cheeks turning red like he was waging an inner battle.

"I'll be right back." She hurried into the bedroom and grabbed the infant seat. Returning, she put a blanket in it and set Lake down on the couch next to Smith.

"Hey, buddy." He smoothed his fingers over the baby's hand.

Liv sank into the rocker, deciding to be honest. "We both know I have a past."

"We all have a past." He leaned forward, elbows on his knees. "No one has the right to throw it in our face. The Lord forgave all of us. Jubilee included. And she's far too—" He bit his lip and closed his eyes like he'd almost said something he shouldn't have.

"Cookies can be so difficult at times," she said.

"Isn't that the truth? Sometimes cookies burn and make a stench to high heaven."

Liv chuckled.

Smith leaned back against the cushions and whispered to Lake, "You have a wise mama." He winked at Liv.

Smiling, she settled more fully into the rocking chair. "Do you want me to fix your lunch?"

"Nah, I'll grab leftovers." He nodded toward Trish's room. "Is my mom here?"

"No. She's visiting a dance studio. She said it was time."

"She's always participated in some form of exercise group or dancing. Always active."

"I hope I'm like that when I get older."

"We can walk together when the weather warms up. Push the stroller and be a happy little family." A dark look crossed his face. "Can you imagine yourself happy with me, Liv?"

"Sure. I'm content."

"But with me?" He sounded so vulnerable.

"I think so." She couldn't say she was in love with him, if that's what he was hinting at.

"Our third-month anniversary is coming up." He interlaced his fingers and set them over his knee. "When I heard about what happened today, I wanted to make things right between us. I don't want anything hampering our baby steps forward."

His frown troubled her. Was he unhappy? Three months was a long time to have been married, living together, and yet not kissing or doing other husband and wife things most newlyweds would be doing.

"What about you, Smith? Are you unhappy?" She heard the insecure sound of her tone but didn't alter it. Maybe she didn't really want to know if he was unhappy with her.

"The pastoral tasks have their challenges. But, no, I wouldn't say I'm unhappy, exactly."

"I meant with us. With me." She kept her gaze on his. "It's unusual that we're living together but not being closer."

"I'd like that part of our lives to improve. I still believe it will in time." He took a full breath. "I appreciate what you've done in letting us be married, in taking such a giant step with me."

"But?" She could tell one was coming.

"How do we take it to the next level? I hear squabbling couples—"

"Cookies, you mean?"

"Yes. One set of cookies has me extremely perplexed." He tossed up his hands. "There's so much discord between them I can hardly breathe when I'm around them."

"Do their troubles make you wonder if you and I will squabble like that?"

"Maybe. After our last date and discussion, I hoped we might have moved closer to—"

"Sleeping together?" Her heart rate accelerated.

His face turned dark red again. Her bluntness probably shocked him.

"Not that necessarily." He met her gaze without glancing away. "I still haven't kissed you."

"Is that what you want? For us to start kissing?"

"Yes." He tipped his head, staring at her. "How do you feel about that?"

It was sweet of him to ask. How did she feel about kissing Smith? The thought of him taking her in his arms and holding her like a man who wanted romance and emotional attachment between them sent warm butterflies cascading through her whole physical and emotional core.

Yet, how could she know what kissing him would be like until they tried it?

"If the timing's right, it'll be fine."

"So you're open to us kissing if the timing's right?" He smiled.

"Yes," she whispered.

"This is good news." His eyebrows quirked. "What if the timing is right for me, but it's not for you?"

"If you lean in and I don't," she said in a flirty tone, "that'll be the first clue."

"And the second?"

"If my eyes keep sparkling up into yours, you won't be able to look away."

"Liv, that happens already." He clapped his hand against his knee.

"Well, then?"

He scooted forward on the couch. Was he planning to kiss her right now?

One thing nagged at her, stopping her from moving forward too. "You want to kiss me for more than obligation, right?"

"Much more than obligation."

"Okay, good."

"Do you ever think of kissing me?" he asked quietly. "About sleeping in my room?"

"Yes, to the first. No, to the second."

"Ah. I see."

In her usual honesty, she added, "I need time for things to develop romantically between us before I'll be ready for the other stuff. I'm waiting for love to grow in both our hearts."

He nodded as if he understood, but she wondered what else he might be thinking. Was he disappointed in her reply?

Chapter Seventy-three

After canceling their session twice, Jubilee and Clay sat across from Smith with angry expressions on their faces, barely looking at each other. Apparently, Smith's assignment was an utter failure.

Since he knew what Jubilee said about Liv in the recent ladies' meeting, he fought a powerful urge to reprimand her. But Liv asked him not to. And he was supposed to be loving and helpful to all his congregants. Jubilee and Clay needed healing in their relationship. That's what mattered right now.

Lord? I might need an extra serving of grace in my life today.

"How was the week of prayer?" he asked.

Clay groaned and rolled his eyes.

Jubilee bit her lip and stared at the wall behind Smith.

"Did you pray together?"

"Some," Clay answered.

"So, you didn't pray together every day?" Smith rested his forearms on the desk.

"He refused." Jubilee eyed Clay accusingly.

"Every time we prayed, she yammered incessantly." Clay blasted out a noisy breath. "Blaming me for everything. 'You know how he is, God,'" he mimicked Jubilee's voice. "She had a bucket of offenses against me she brought up in prayer—with me sitting right there! A man can only take so much."

Smith tried picturing these two ever having felt affection for each other. With their outraged demeanors, what could he say to help bring healing or peace to their marriage? Prayer still stuck in his head as the answer. "Okay. Let's pray."

"What?" Clay's shoulders bunched up to his ears. "We tried. Didn't work."

"I'll say," Jubilee muttered.

"My trust is still in the Lord." Smith should have prayed as soon as this couple entered his office. "Lord, You are so good to us. Thank You for working in Clay and Jubilee's marriage." Smith thanked God for all the things He already did for them. He called out their children's names that Mrs. Scarlett had helped him remember. "Bless this family. Please give us wisdom as we talk together."

After the prayer, Jubilee wiped her face with a tissue. Clay still wore a begrudging expression.

"The Bible says we should 'speak the truth in love.' Let's do that today, hmm?" Smith met Clay's gaze. "What hurts the most between you and Jubilee? I'm sorry if I'm off base here, but I get the sense you have a gaping wound in your heart." He was going for the pain point, but with the way these two could barely look at each other, he doubted they'd stay together another week.

"What do you mean?" Clay growled.

"Your hurt or grief is obvious in the way you avoid looking at Jubilee." Smith spread out his hands. "I'm not experienced in a long marriage like you two are, but I recognize hurt when I see it. I've had my share of pain and loss. The temptation to feed on injustices and let bitterness dwell in me was strong, too."

"What about her?" Clay nodded his chin at Jubilee.

"I'll address her shortly. You're the man of the house. I asked you to pray with your wife every day. Yet, here you are, telling me you couldn't." He sighed empathetically. "It hurts in your heart, doesn't it? Your wounded spirit needs healing. So, please, let's cut to the chase and address the heartache. I'm putting you on the spot, but I care for you as a brother in Christ."

He glanced between the two, neither meeting his gaze or each other's. "I care for both of you. I admire the years you've clung together and held onto your marriage." He waited a moment, letting Clay catch his breath. "What are you the most angry about?"

Jubilee nudged her husband's arm. "What have I done, Clay?"

Smith was thankful for a woman's softer side. Even if she had said something hurtful, she wanted to know what it was and to help their hearts be mended.

"I—" Clay pressed his lips together and shook his head.

"You're in safe territory here," Smith said. "What froths in your throat every time you look at your wife?"

"Her harping. If she complains to me about one more thing, I'll explode."

Jubilee tensed.

"In coming to these sessions, have you hardened yourself to hearing any criticisms?" Smith asked.

"Yes." Clay stared at his hands.

Lord, help these two find healing and help in You.

"I wasn't aware that I was harping." Jubilee huffed. "It's just how I am."

What? Is that why she put Liv on the spot about her past, because that's just how she was? Anger, and his desire to defend his wife, infused Smith. But just as quickly, his hotheaded reaction fizzled. This couple's need for healing must remain foremost in his thoughts.

"Jubilee"—he made sure his voice was calm—"what hurts you most about Clay's words and actions toward you?"

"The way he shuts me out. Walks away. Like the prayer business. I thought we were bringing our supplications to the Lord. I told Him how I felt. Not railing at Clay. I'm … sorry." She reached out and clasped Clay's hand.

He turned a startled gaze toward her. "The Lord knows my faults, woman! You don't have to tell Him what they are like a giant to-do list."

"Okay," Jubilee said in a perturbed tone and let go of his hand.

"We both need fixing. Not just me."

"I know that."

After a few more minutes of discussion, Clay asked, "Any other assignment, Pastor? I have to get back to work."

"Since the last homework didn't get finished, why don't you try that again?" Smith said. "This week when you pray, I want you to focus on thanking God for your spouse. Thank Him for all the blessings He's done in your family. In your children's lives. Let it be a time of praise and thankfulness."

Clay and Jubilee nodded.

Smith escorted them to the door. Then he sank onto his chair, wishing he could drive home and spend some time nurturing his relationship with his wife.

Chapter Seventy-four

Smith stared into the bathroom mirror and tweaked his tie, getting ready for his and Liv's third-month-anniversary date. In the last few days, his thoughts hadn't been far from his conversation with her about kissing and taking their relationship further. He recalled what Liv said about wanting to wait for both of them to be in love.

He cared for her. Was attracted to her. But being in love with her? He let out a long sigh.

Later, they sat in the high school auditorium for a theatrical production. Coming to a local play to support the kids had been Liv's idea. Smith would have rather gone somewhere more romantic, but their dinner before the show had been nice. However, they probably talked too much about church stuff and Lake. Not the personal subjects he wished to bring up.

Experiencing some disappointment over the platonic atmosphere between them, about twenty minutes into *Cheaper by the Dozen*, a story that appealed to him about a large family, Liv's fingers touching his palm surprised him. He gazed into her shining eyes in the semi-darkness. She smiled at him, and his heart pounded a chaotic beat.

He linked their fingers and rested their hands against his thigh. Liv scooted a little closer to him, probably getting more comfortable, but he liked how her arm leaned against his.

The only relationship he had to compare to this was his and Katy's courtship. Honestly, he wished he wouldn't compare the two. But when he met Katy, he'd been swept off his feet. Walked around gaga over her for days. Of course, she pushed for things he couldn't give into almost from the start. He should have been wiser about that.

On the other hand, he and Liv were going snail slow in their relationship, and they were already married. He shuffled in his uncomfortable seat and felt Liv's gaze on him. Her eyes sparkling toward him nearly took his breath away.

Inside and out, she was like a light in the dark. A light in his darkness. Three months ago, Liv risked everything to marry him and help him become the pastor he longed to be, and to give Lake a stable home with a mom, dad, and a grandmother. And he loved the little guy so much—Lake Daniel North.

He focused on the play, watching the high school actor portraying the father of a dozen kids. Someday Smith hoped he'd be a dad to a bunch of children, too.

But first things first. How could he get Liv to want to be closer to him? Wasn't the way she slipped her hand into his a good sign? Was she feeling more romantic toward him already?

Chapter Seventy-five

After the play, even though she'd enjoyed the production, Liv was in a hurry to get back to Lake. This was the longest she'd been away from him.

"Any chance you'd like to stop and get a piece of pie?" Smith's lighthearted tone brushed over her as they walked hand in hand toward the car.

"I should probably get back."

"Oh. Okay." He sounded disappointed.

"It's time to feed Lake, otherwise—"

"Of course. I understand." He helped her into the car then shut her door.

She hated to end the evening on anything but a pleasant note. As soon as he climbed into his side and started the heater, she asked, "How about if we pick up something at the store before we head home? A pie, maybe?"

"That would be great."

They made a quick stop at the market. No apple pies in stock, but they had cherry, which was a fine second option.

At the house, Liv changed into comfier clothes, took a fussy Lake from Trish's arms, and fed him. Relieved the evening went so well, and with the way she and Smith held hands during the play floating through her thoughts, she sighed.

In the kitchen, Trish asked Smith about the performance. Liv enjoyed hearing the two of them talking, mother and son. Someday, she and Lake would be like that, sharing concerns. Talking about his dates. She smiled at the thought.

Later, with Lake contentedly asleep and Trish heading off to bed, Liv sat beside Smith at their small kitchen table eating the cherry pie he heated up.

"Mmm. This is great."

"Yes, it is." He forked a bite into his mouth.

Her gaze was drawn to his moist lips where a tiny dab of cherry sauce rested in the crease of his mouth. A longing to sweep away the red juice, to test what his lips felt like, teased her senses. She broke her preoccupation with staring at his lips and took a couple of bites. "What did you like best about the play?"

"The twelve kids." He chuckled and wiped his mouth with his napkin.

"No doubt." She toyed with her fork over the remainder of her pie. "I guess you still want that, huh?"

"Sure do." He smiled warmly and clasped her free hand.

She liked his smooth skin touching hers. Surely his lips moving over hers would be as enjoyable, as satisfying.

"What did you like best?" He released her hand and continued eating.

"I thought the high school students, especially the ones portraying the dad and the older kids, did a superb job. It drew me into their reality."

"Me too. Although, I may have been a tad distracted."

"Oh?" She grinned playfully. "By what?"

"By the lovely woman holding my hand." He set his fork and napkin down. Scooting his chair closer to hers, he took her hand in his again. "Do you realize how besotted I am with you?"

"Besotted? Goodness." A flush swept up her face.

"You, sweetheart"—he gulped on the word as if it had never crossed his lips before—"are becoming very dear to me."

Becoming. His endearment lacked the tender emotion she longed to hear in his voice. They weren't in love yet, but she wanted it to be so. He was trying to get closer to her, she could tell. Maybe forcing the issue? Should they be working so hard to make romance happen between them? Shouldn't it come naturally?

He'd been in love with Katy. And Liv had been besotted, to use Smith's word, with Nick. What if she and Smith moved on to kissing, even intimacy, yet true love evaded them? How long would they stay together in a loveless marriage? Would they have an endless "'til death do us part" of trying and never succeeding at finding real love again?

Now she was depressing herself.

"What's wrong?" he asked.

"Just some dark thoughts. Sorry."

"Dark thoughts like—?"

Did she dare tell him and dash his hopes? Honesty prevailed like it usually did with her. "I care a lot about you, Smith."

"I care about you, too," he said in those husky tones she enjoyed.

She liked the way he leaned toward her as if he wanted to hear everything she said. When he smiled and his chin dimple widened, sparks of attraction shot through her.

"But I"—she forced herself to continue—"that is, you and I aren't deeply in love with each other yet."

"Are you saying you want to wait for that to happen before you kiss me?" He glanced at her mouth a couple of times.

"Not necessarily."

"Then what's troubling you?"

"I don't want us to try to force love to happen."

He slumped back against his chair. "Did you feel I was forcing something tonight? A kiss, perhaps?"

"I'm not worried about us kissing. I'm worried about us pushing what might follow a kiss if we lip-lock before you're free of your past."

His eyes shuttered to half-mast. "I'm not holding onto the past."

"Are you sure?"

He met her gaze with a startled look.

"Sometimes when we look into each other's eyes, and I imagine we might kiss—"

"Yes?" he said breathily.

"It's like you think of a memory and a wall goes up. I imagine you're picturing her." She shrugged. "Your heart must be torn. Partly wanting to let her go. Partly clinging to her memory."

He blew out a breath. "I don't mean to do that."

"You loved her deeply. Thought you would marry her."

Smith nodded slowly. "I care deeply for you. We are married. I'm determined to put all thoughts of Katy aside and focus on you. On us." He smoothed his hand over hers.

"Determined" flashed through her brain like a warning light. If he'd fallen in love with her, he wouldn't have to be determined to forget another woman, would he?

"I think I'll head to bed." Smith scooped up their dessert dishes and carried them to the sink.

Liv stood, feeling awkward. Like she hurt him. Or was too blunt.

Maybe he was right about them going ahead and kissing. Something needed to nudge them toward a more passionate relationship. Would a kiss do that?

Smith turned off the kitchen light. "Goodnight, Liv."

"Goodnight. Thanks for the date." Disappointment raked through her. "Wait, Smith."

He stopped in the middle of the living room, his back to her. "What is it?"

"I'm sorry for bringing up Katy. For sharing my thoughts too honestly."

He pivoted toward her, not crossing the space. "Don't ever be sorry for being honest. I appreciate that about you. I just need to ponder what you said." He drew in a long breath. "I could use your help though."

"Okay."

"We are married. I want to be married to you."

She swallowed a wad of dryness in her throat. "I want to be married to you too."

Their gazes met and tangled like a dance. She desired to get to know her husband better. To help him get over his past the way he and Trish helped her mend and get over hers. She wanted to be here for Smith, caring for him all her days on this earth. Was that love? Or simply affection?

She took a step toward him. He must have taken a step too. Then she was in his arms and his mouth was caressing hers, his soft lips moving against hers with sweet intensity. She kissed him back hungrily, completely lost in the moment and the passion simmering between them. He pulled her against him, holding her close against his chest.

A throat clearing broke them apart. They both stumbled backward.

"So sorry," Trish said from her doorway. "Do you mind if I walk through to get something out of the dryer?"

Smith groaned. "Of course, Mom."

Even in the dim lighting, his face hued deep red.

As if they were young teenagers caught kissing, she and Smith stared at each other wide-eyed and silent.

Then she smiled. He grinned too.

Trish caught them kissing. So what? It would probably happen again, because now that they'd kissed, Liv was definitely going to kiss her husband again!

Chapter Seventy-six

Smith sat in his office the next morning, trying to pray, but his thoughts kept roaming to him kissing Liv last night. That had been one spectacular kiss! Until his mother entered the room. He groaned. Kissing Liv made his pulse hammer like it hadn't since— He didn't want to compare it to his experiences with Katy. But his first real kiss with Liv was fabulous! He couldn't wait to go home and kiss her again.

However, what she said about not wanting them to force love resonated in his heart, too. Did that mean he should slow things down between them? He didn't want to do that!

He truly cared for her. He loved her as a friend and a co-believer in Christ. He appreciated all she'd been willing to do to marry him and come to Thunder Ridge with him. But he couldn't say he was wholeheartedly in love with her. Even with their amazing kiss, he had to be honest with himself and her about his feelings. Liv had been right to say what she did about his tied-up emotions for Katy standing in their way.

What was he going to do about it? How to get over his ex-fiancée would be a matter of serious prayer for him in the days ahead. Maybe he should speak with Pastor Tim. His mentor would surely have some spiritual insight or wisdom to share.

He pushed the intercom button for Mrs. Scarlett.

"Yes, Pastor North?"

"What does my schedule look like this afternoon?"

"Two counseling sessions."

"Could you try to reschedule those for me?"

"Will do. Anything else?" Mrs. Scarlett asked in her efficient voice.

"Would you call Pastor Tim and set up an appointment for me? I'll drive over to Spokane at his convenience."

"Yes, I will do that."

Later, Smith sat at the desk across from Pastor Tim, a man whose advice he greatly respected. Yet, he felt reluctant to share his innermost thoughts about Liv and what she asked him about Katy.

After catching up on each other's lives, Pastor Tim eyed Smith. "What brings you here today? What's troubling you, my friend?"

Smith's throat tightened.

"How's married life treating you?"

"It's—" Smith sighed. "It's good and weird and confusing."

Pastor Tim chuckled. "That's life and marriage in a nutshell. Sometimes good, sometimes confusing."

"And weird?" Smith asked half-heartedly.

"I get that." Pastor Tim crossed his arms over the desk. "What has you confused today?"

"Love." He peered into his mentor's kind eyes. "I love Liv as a friend and a believer in Christ, but not in the way she wants me to love her. Not yet anyway. I want to move things toward normal married stuff, but she wants us to be in love first."

"I see." Pastor Tim scratched his chin. "You're saying you haven't consummated your marriage yet?"

Smith felt embarrassed by the question. "That's right." He sighed and his chest hurt.

"How long since the wedding?" Pastor Tim glanced at the ceiling as if counting back months.

"Three months. But she gave birth on that day too."

"Right." Pastor Tim nodded. "No doubt, she's preoccupied with the child. You're preoccupied with being a new pastor?"

"Yes. But the question in my heart is how do I let go of my past experiences?"

"What do you mean exactly?"

"Liv thinks I'm still imagining Katy when I'm with her. Even pining for her."

"Are you?"

Smith gulped. "Not intentionally."

"But Olivia sees a lack of something in your romantic attention toward her?"

"I guess."

"A wife is sensitive to her husband's interest and devotion, or lack thereof, to her." Pastor Tim interlaced his fingers over a closed book on his desk. "Have you two kissed? I'm sorry if that's too personal of a question, but I have a reason for asking."

"Yes. Once, other than during our vows."

"Were you kissing Olivia?"

Smith sat up straighter, his face creasing in a frown. "Of course, I was kissing her."

"I mean in your thoughts, were you kissing your wife? Engaging with her?"

"Yes. Oh. You mean, was I thinking of Katy?"

"Reliving memories, perhaps?"

"I wasn't. I have honest feelings for Liv."

"That's good." After a thoughtful pause, Pastor Tim continued, "Do you still find yourself daydreaming about Katy?"

"Sometimes." Smith hated such a confession. "Not by choice or because I'm drumming up reasons to not fall for Liv."

"No, I wouldn't think that of you."

"I want a real marriage with her. One that will last for our whole lives."

"Then I'd recommend you do a few things differently." Pastor Tim closed his eyes for a moment, possibly praying for direction. "Your wife needs to feel safe with you, assured your thoughts are with her, before moving forward in your relationship. Not on a woman you previously loved."

"I haven't tried to ponder another woman."

"Yet you have?"

"Yes." He had to be honest about this.

"Can you see the problem between you and Olivia?"

"I do now." Smith groaned, almost wishing he hadn't driven into Spokane today. Yet he needed this. The accountability of another man in ministry was essential to his growth as a pastor and, apparently, as a husband lacking the ability to bridge the gap between him and the woman he wanted to love fully.

"In the past, you told me Katy pushed for things to happen intimately between you."

"That's right." Heat bled up his neck and across his face.

"Those experiences are ingrained in your mind and your emotional responses. You need to replace those thoughts and feelings with devotion and tenderness for Olivia." Pastor Tim met Smith's gaze with the look of authority he'd come to expect. "God wants you to be victorious in this. And you will be! Whenever you have a thought of Katy, or of you kissing her, I want you to do a couple of things. One, immediately pray. We can trust God with every aspect of our lives."

"Okay."

"Secondly, redirect your thoughts by taking authority over any imagination that rises up against the plan of God for your life."

"I will." Smith felt his spirit getting stronger as he planned an attack against this problem.

"Finally, after you pray and take authority, saturate your thoughts with the beautiful and endearing parts of yours and Olivia's marriage that are good." Pastor Smith chuckled. "Even without the benefits of intimacy, are there things about her you like? Things you could fill your mind with, replacing the old with the new?"

"Absolutely." Smith pictured the way Liv made him laugh. How she was determined to learn how to cook. Of their pie and cookie-making escapades. Their cookie conversations! Her sweet smile. The way she nursed Lake and stared at their child with so much devotion. "Yes," he said more emphatically. "There are a lot of good things to think about my wife." Including last night's doozy of a kiss.

"Then let's pray and give this situation to the Lord." Pastor Tim prayed a powerful prayer for Smith and Liv to follow the Lord's leading and to be open to every prodding of His Holy Spirit.

Smith drove back to Thunder Ridge with thoughts of Liv, and only Liv, strumming through his mind. He couldn't wait to see her and kiss her again!

Chapter Seventy-seven

On Sunday morning, Liv sat in the back row at church holding Lake. Trish sat next to her as they listened to Amaryllis giving the presentation Liv had prepared. Not once did she feel slighted or thought Amaryllis didn't do a good enough job. Neither did she wish she would have been chosen for the task. In fact, sitting here with her son in her arms, sitting next to her best friend, she felt relaxed and content.

If she'd been the one speaking, she might have felt apprehensive talking in front of the congregation, especially after what Jubilee said about her. Did people in Smith's church condemn her for marrying him the way she did? What if they thought badly of him for marrying a woman before he was head-over-heels in love with her?

Goodness. She imagined there were a lot of pastors and their wives in cold or barely-loving marriages. Who were any of these people to judge her and Smith when they'd only just started on their journey together?

Tension knotted up the muscles in her shoulders. She pressed her free hand against the tightness in her neck and kneaded it.

"You okay?" Trish whispered.

Liv nodded but didn't want to explain.

After Amaryllis's presentation, the congregation clapped. A couple of ladies passed baskets around for donations. For those who were interested in a long-term investment in the needs of the orphans, and for those who wanted to hear more through a newsletter, cards were passed out.

Liv hoped she could still help with that process, even if some of the women didn't want her representing them.

She closed her eyes. *Lord, I want to trust You with everything in my life. Help me not to feel badly toward Jubilee and some of the other ladies who quietly agreed with her about me. I want to forgive and live free of strife. Also, I'd like to do something meaningful here in Smith's church.*

When she opened her eyes, she met Trish's kind gaze. Her mother-in-law squeezed her hand as if she understood.

After the service ended, several of the women from the ladies' group came by and told her how wonderful the program had been. How they loved the storyboard. Some thanked her for her work on it.

Smith stood by her longer than usual as folks left the building.

"Any chance I could take you ladies out to lunch?" he asked, glancing between Liv and Trish.

"Fine with me." Liv smoothed her hand over Lake's back.

"Me, too," Trish agreed.

"Great." Smith held out his hands toward Lake. "May I?"

"Sure."

Every time his gleaming gaze met hers, Liv's thoughts tumbled back to two nights ago when they kissed. Her cheeks heated up. He chuckled. Was he imagining the moment when Trish burst in on them, too?

Smith carried the baby toward the exit, showing him to parishioners as any proud daddy would do. Liv was thankful for the way he'd stepped up and become a father to Lake. And now, he was stepping up to make them into more of a couple. But she was still worried it might be a little forced.

At the restaurant, Liv carried the infant seat in and placed it in the booth beside her. Trish and Smith sat on the other side. They ordered lunch and chatted about the presentation at church.

"Didn't Liv do a great job?" Trish elbowed Smith's arm.

Why was Trish pushing him to compliment her? Liv would rather he did that on his own if he was going to.

"Oh, yes. Good job, Liv." Smith met his mom's gaze, and a look passed between them.

Disappointment rushed through Liv. She didn't want him taking his cues about how to interact with her from Trish. Then she sighed. Smith didn't know how to be a supportive husband any more than she knew how to be an encouraging wife. It would take time for both to adapt and get used to what each other needed.

"Your closing remarks were kind." She smiled at him. "I appreciate your including me in the credits."

"You worked hard. And we, I, appreciate your help." He reached across the table and clasped her hand. "I mean it, Liv. I'm sure you're the reason people opened their hearts and their wallets to this important ministry. Thank you."

There, his words sounded sincere and more like the Smith she knew.

"I'm glad I could help."

"I have an idea I want to run by you," he said after their meals arrived.

"Okay." She set down her salad fork.

"Would you be interested in driving to Spokane with me tomorrow afternoon? I asked Mom if she'd watch Lake." Another look passed between him and Trish. "I thought we could use a day away. Just the two of us. What do you say?"

"I'd like that." Although her response wasn't as enthusiastic as it would have been if she thought he'd come up with the idea himself.

A drive sounded great, and so did being alone with her husband. But had Trish put Smith up to asking her out like she'd hinted for him to compliment her?

Chapter Seventy-eight

Smith had finished showering and was dressed in casual clothes of jeans, a dark green sweater, and comfortable shoes. He was glad his mom suggested he take Liv away from the house and for him to get away from church duties for a few hours. He'd contemplated several things he and Liv could do that he hadn't done with Katy, since they needed new experiences to share together.

Of course, his mind leapfrogged to things he had gone to with his ex—the ballet, the symphony, plays, and various restaurants in Spokane. He asked her to marry him outside of Higgins Restaurant and she—

Wait. Why did his thoughts do that? Staring at himself in the mirror, he recalled Pastor Tim's instructions. First, prayer.

Lord, help me focus on Liv and our relationship. I don't want to dwell on the things I did with Katy. Fill my heart with love for my wife. For what You have in store for our future.

Second, he was to take authority over any thoughts not lining up with God's plan for his life. He did that, commanding his mind to think about good and pure things, according to First John 4:8.

Lastly, he was to fill his thoughts with good things about Liv. He pictured them kissing in the middle of their living room. He'd never forget how wonderful she felt in his arms, their lips pressed softly against each other's. He thought about the pre-proposal dream he had of kissing her, too. A real kiss was even better! He'd sure like to experience more of the romantic side of Liv North today.

A couple of hours later, after they ate a meal at a restaurant in downtown Spokane, Smith and Liv held hands and strolled along the Spokane River. He liked how she enjoyed walking in nature. That was something they had in common.

She pointed at some geese huddled together. "Are they early? Maybe they got the wrong message about it still being winter."

"A few usually stick around." He squeezed her gloved hand. "Huddled up like that, they'll be fine."

"Yeah?" She smiled at him flirtatiously.

"Sure." He met her lips for a brief kiss, and her eyes widened. "Is that okay?"

"It's okay."

"Good." He sighed and kissed her again.

He bought coffees for them at an outdoor vendor, then they sat on a bench in the park near the river. The air was cold, but holding his coffee, and the warmth of Liv's company, kept him feeling toasty.

"Thanks for inviting me on this outing. Was it your idea?" She met his gaze with a questioning look.

"Not exactly," he stammered over the answer.

"It was Trish's idea, right?"

"It was. But we both needed this, didn't we?"

"I guess."

She sipped her coffee in silence for a couple of minutes, but he could tell something was wrong.

"Does my mom making a helpful suggestion to me bother you?" Mom and Liv got along so well. What was at the root of her irritation or annoyance?

"Maybe we should keep walking." She stood. "My feet are getting cold."

"All right." He stood and walked beside her. "Do you want to look through some stores?"

"Not really."

Her previous happiness seemed to have vanished. He was frustrated their outing might end in hurt feelings. Far from how he hoped their date would turn out.

"Liv?" He clutched her elbow gently. "What is it? Did I say something stupid?"

Her usual sweet smile broke through whatever struggle or hurt she was experiencing.

"It's not that, but there are some things we should discuss." With the honesty he'd come to expect from her, she explained as they headed back in the direction of their car. "I'm concerned you have a specific idea of how our marriage should go. By this date on the calendar, we should be doing such and such."

He couldn't deny her words. Her insightfulness astounded him.

"Am I wrong?" She paused and met his gaze.

"No. I have been making more of an effort toward romance and spending time together. But isn't that good? I'm your husband. You're my wife."

"In a highly irregular union." Her cheeks flamed red. "Or a highly irregular non-union."

He chuckled. Again, her honesty and willingness to broach a touchy subject were endearing.

Suddenly, she shivered. "Do you mind if we go back to the car and warm up?"

"Not at all."

They dropped their cups into a trash receptacle, then Smith wrapped his arm around Liv's shoulders as they hurried back to the parking lot. "I want you to know I'm not being a fake about our relationship. I honestly care for you."

"Like friends. Good friends."

"Oh, Liv." He stopped walking and pulled her into his arms. "Much more than friends. The kiss we shared the other night ... I haven't been able to get it out of my mind." He gazed from her shining eyes to her lips which looked cold. "Come on, let's get you back to the car."

He clasped her hand and hurried back to the vehicle with her. He soon had the engine running and the heat turned up.

"I liked our kissing also," Liv said around a shiver. "It meant something to me. But when I thought your mom was behind today's outing, I didn't like it at all. I love her like crazy, but—"

"You don't want her planning our dates?"

"No, I don't." A smile crossed her mouth. "I want our relationship, our marriage, to grow and become real between us naturally, no matter how long it takes. Without anyone else interfering or offering advice. Just you and me falling in love. Do you understand what I'm trying to say?"

"I understand. Thank you for being honest with me. Are you ready to head back?"

"I am. I miss Lake."

A little let down that their date hadn't been more romantic, Smith sighed. "What now? I mean, if I kissed you again would you feel like I'm trying to force something to happen that we're not ready for?"

"When you kiss me, are you picturing Katy?"

He could have fallen twenty feet and not have felt as shocked as he did by her question.

"I'm sorry. But I have to know."

"Oh, Liv." He turned in the car seat, facing her the best he could in the small quarters. "When I kiss you, I'm thinking only of you. And when I'm kissing you"—he had to say this while he felt brave enough and vulnerable enough to express himself—"I want to be with you, stay with you, make love with you."

Her mouth opened as if he shocked her with his honesty this time. A sweet smile crossed her rosy lips. Lips he wanted to kiss again and again.

"May I kiss you?"

"You don't have to ask," she whispered. "As long as you're thinking of me, trying to get closer to me and what we have together, and it's happening because you want—"

"It is." He took her in his arms and kissed her, deeply and thoroughly, loving having this woman in his arms, near his heart. Her lips were sweet and warmly responsive as he kissed her again. She leaned her cheek against his shoulder, and he held her. They both sighed.

"Any doubts?" he asked.

"None. When would you like us to move into the same bedroom?" She shuffled back, gazing into his eyes with a dazed look.

"Any time you're ready."

She nodded slowly. "For me, it's important we're both in love, or close to that."

The way her face hued rosy was cute. He was so attracted to her.

"Is there anything I can do to help you fall in love with me?" he asked.

Her smile widened, brightening his spirits even more.

"Keep kissing me. Keep talking with me." She smoothed her gloved hand over his arm. "I feel like we're a family already."

"So do I." Brushing his mouth over hers, he enjoyed how she tasted of coffee and pie. "You are on my mind almost all the time, Livvy."

"Livvy?"

"Sweetheart. Darling. My Livvy."

Then he kissed her again. And he knew beyond any doubt, this woman who he liked so much was the only woman he wanted to be smooching and holding close to him for the rest of his life.

Chapter Seventy-nine

Liv had one thought on her brain. She was going to give cookie baking another try! She'd put the first batch of chocolate chip cookies, Smith's favorite, in the oven when Trish exited her bedroom.

"Mmm. Cookies. I can't wait."

"Anything could happen when I get a hankering for baking."

Trish laughed. "You are doing so well, Olivia. Both you and Smith." She put water in the tea kettle. "Say, I've been wanting to talk with you about something." By her tone, it was a serious topic.

"Okay." Liv leaned her hip against the counter and waited. Was Trish concerned about the kiss she walked in on the other night? Liv wasn't going to make any excuses about that. She was falling for Smith, and she couldn't wait to be in his arms again.

"I think it's time for me to move out and get my own place." Trish set the tea kettle on the front burner and turned on the element. "Maybe I should return to Spokane."

"Oh, Trish, no." She wanted to leave? Liv didn't want that. She'd already lost one family. She wasn't ready for Trish to go anywhere. "Why do you feel that way? I hope it isn't anything I've done. Or anything I said."

"Not at all. You have been a dream daughter-in-law." A gentle smile crossed Trish's mouth. "You and Smith need some time alone. A honeymoon, perhaps?"

Liv coughed. "That's not happening yet. We're not in love."

"Olivia, I don't mean to pry." Trish took down a cup and an Earl Gray tea bag. "I think there's more being in love happening here than you might think."

Liv held her tongue. Yes, she and Smith exchanged kisses. Great kisses. Trish had been an eyewitness to one of those. But a honeymoon? Her thoughts scrambled over what Smith told her on their date in Spokane. That he was ready to share a room with her anytime she was ready. How she'd told him they needed to be in love first. What Trish assumed was love between them was attraction and flirting, right?

Even though she didn't want to talk about private details with Trish, Liv wanted to make one thing clear. "You are welcome to stay here indefinitely, Trish. I mean it. You're the one who invited me into your home. You've been so helpful with Lake. You're the glue holding this irregular family together."

"I don't think I'm all that."

"Oh, you are. Please, don't leave." Liv clasped her mother-in-law's hand. "I asked you to stay with us. I still want you here. I promise I do."

Trish's eyes filled with moisture. "What about when you and Smith—" Her gaze flicked toward the back bedrooms.

"We're not there yet. Eventually—" Liv stopped herself from saying too much to Smith's mother. "You've raised a remarkable son. He's kind and honorable. We're both waiting to be in love first."

"Okay." Trish squinted at Liv. "You don't think you're in love with him?"

"I care for him. He cares for me."

"That's a fine starting place." Trish finished fixing her tea. "Need help with anything?"

"No. The cookies are coming along nicely."

The buzzer rang and Liv grabbed a hot pad and pulled out the cookie sheet. A delicious wafting of sweetened scents reached her. Good. They weren't burned. Nothing horrible had happened.

"Smells delightful." Trish left the kitchen and sat down in the living room.

An hour later, Smith came home for lunch. "What do we have here? Those cookies smell fantastic." He hurried over to the counter and picked one up. "Liv, did you make these?"

"I did. All by myself." She met him in the kitchen.

"So good," he mumbled around the food in his mouth. Then he guzzled down a glass of water.

She waited for him to finish. "I wanted to surprise you."

His eyes lit up and he looked questioningly at her.

"With the cookies, I mean."

"Right. Thanks." He clasped her hands and gave her a soft kiss. "It's nice to see you."

"You, too." She nodded discreetly toward Trish who sat in the living room with her back to them.

"Hi, Mom!"

"Hello, Smith. Welcome home." Trish turned on the couch. "Busy day?"

"It has been. And I'm famished." He winked at Liv then released her hands. "What do we have for a quick heat-up? I have to get back to the office for a one o'clock appointment."

"There's lasagna from last night."

"Perfect." He took the dish out of the fridge and served himself a generous portion, then tucked it in the microwave. "Have you eaten?" He held up the dish toward Liv.

"No. I'll fix something after a while."

"You sure? We could eat together." His words sounded spontaneous and inviting.

Wasn't his making romantic plans for them exactly what she wanted?

"What do you say?"

"Okay." She took the dish from him. "But I'll do it, since you have to rush back."

"Sounds good."

Trish brought her teacup into the kitchen and set it in the sink. "I'm going to take a walk." She bundled up and promptly left the house, probably giving Liv and Smith the privacy she thought they needed.

Liv was thankful for her thoughtfulness, again.

A few minutes later, she and Smith sat together at the table, eating lasagna, and he told her about his hectic morning.

A longing went through her for the days in the past when she was busy and had many tasks to face in the business world. The biggest challenge of her day was making cookies. And facing Trish's comments about her possibly leaving, and why.

"What are you thinking about?" Smith asked with a grin. "You blushed. You're cute when you blush. Was it a good thought about us? About me?"

She laughed. "No, silly."

"Indulge me." He took another bite of food.

"I was thinking about a conversation I had with your mom. She's thinking of moving out."

"What? Why?" He wiped his mouth with a napkin.

"She's concerned we might need more time alone."

"Well—"

"I don't want her to leave." Liv ran the tines of her fork back and forth over the lasagna noodles.

"Me neither. Not really." He touched the back of her hand. "Although, the part about us needing time alone sounds tempting."

"Smith." She batted his hand away.

"Just saying. I love my mom. But there are times when she's walked in on us hugging or kissing. It's awkward. But I'm not going to stop hugging and kissing you." He brushed his mouth against her cheek.

Too close to miss such an opportunity, she turned an inch and let her lips graze his.

"Aww, Livvy." He kissed her more fully. Then, grinning, he strode to the counter, grabbed a couple more cookies, and returned to his chair. After munching down the first cookie, he said, "Your baking has greatly improved."

"Thank you."

"You know how to make pies and cookies now. You're almost an expert baker."

"Far from that." She chuckled.

He held up the chocolate chip cookie between them. "Our relationship is kind of like your baking journey."

"How so?"

"When you first started baking, you were clueless about turning out cookies like this. Now, you know exactly what to do." He scooted forward on his chair, his knees touching hers. "In the same way, we dove into marriage without truly understanding how to be married." He linked his fingers with hers. "How about if you and I make a cookie pact?"

"A cookie pact?"

"Let's promise each other that just like you learned how to make this perfect cookie—"

"It's not perfect, Smith."

"It is to me." His gaze danced over her as if he was saying she was perfect to him. "Just like you, Liv North, pursued making cookies to the best of your ability, and succeeded, I, Smith North, promise to pursue you, to pursue a loving relationship with you, my wife, until we succeed at falling in love with each other."

His softly-spoken words simmered hope and joy in her heart. His grin drew her closer to him like a magnet. She got lost in his shining gaze. She felt like she was already so close to the precipice of falling in love with him.

"Will you pledge yourself to that too?" he asked, his lips about two inches from hers.

"All right. I, Liv North, promise to ..." She hesitated over the word "pursue."

Smith grinned in obvious expectation of her using the same word.

Never one to avoid a challenge, she said, "I promise to pursue you until we fall in love with each other."

"Come here, sweetheart." He leaned his mouth toward the cookie but didn't take a bite.

She matched his move, bringing her lips toward the cookie, too.

"Let's seal the deal by sharing this cookie." He bit into the outer side of the cookie but didn't bite down all the way until she did the same thing on her side. They both took a small bite of the cookie.

She finished her bite, loving the romantic mood between them and the promise she and Smith made to each other. Slowly, he took her in his arms and kissed her. He tasted of cookies and milk. Her heart pounded a wild cadence beneath her ribs.

Aww, Smith.

He stood, pulling her up beside him. "Did you mean it?"

"The promise?"

"Yes. I meant it with every breath in my body. I'm going to pursue you, Liv."

"Okay." Warmth rushed from her brain cells to her toes. "I meant it, too."

His lips brushed hers again, just a whisper of a kiss that left her wanting the type of kiss they exchanged a few nights ago. He was probably purposefully taking things slowly and honoring her wish for them to be in love before taking things further.

"Could you do something with me?" she asked.

"Anything." He set her back slightly, his eyes lighting up.

"I need to learn to bake something else." She toyed with the buttons on his shirt. "We have fun when we're making pies and cookies, don't we?"

"Yes, we do." He stroked a strand of hair back from her cheek. "I always have fun when I'm with you. You make me laugh. You make me want to be a better man. A better husband for you." His fingers lingered near her ear.

"Can we bake some more? Spend time together?"

"Yes. Absolutely." He moved his palms to her cheeks, holding her gently, gazing into her eyes. "What did you have in mind?"

She could barely focus since the urge to kiss him was so strong. "Brownies. I could eat brownies all day long."

"Sounds delicious."

He didn't close the gap between them. His twinkling eyes and his wide, welcoming smile called to her, wooing her closer to him.

"Smith—" She wrapped her arms around his shoulders and kissed him, pressing her mouth over his, softly then passionately then softly again.

"Sweet Livvy," he whispered. "I like it when you pursue me."

Chapter Eighty

Smith set down the phone in his office and groaned. Jubilee was demanding an audience with him this morning when he'd hoped to take an early lunch and spend time with Liv.

The nicer weather, even though it was still cold, made him antsy to get outdoors. He'd like to go for a walk with Liv. He enjoyed holding her hand and talking. Lately, it felt like they really were in a romantic relationship with each other.

At the most unexpected times, he found himself daydreaming about her. Picturing them kissing. Imagining what it would be like when she finally shared a bedroom with him. Things a pastor probably shouldn't be thinking about when he was supposed to be focused on his next appointment.

A knock at the door interrupted his thoughts.

Mrs. Scarlett strode to his desk. "Your schedule has altered."

"For the better?"

She quirked an eyebrow. "For the better, Pastor North?" There was a hint of scolding in her tone.

She probably wondered where his servant's heart had fled to today. Why did he feel this drawing away from his office, the urge to get outside, to find Liv and—

"Pastor? Are you okay?"

"Sorry. Just distracted." He clasped the sheet of paper she held out, his gaze skimming the schedule.

"Jubilee asked to see you before noon. It will mean taking a later lunch."

Not only was he not going to get out of here early, but he also had to stay late. "The afternoon looks full too."

"Yes. Was there something else you needed to do?" She gazed at him with a kinder look. While Mrs. Scarlett had a no-nonsense personality, occasionally she was extremely discerning.

"Spring itch." He peered out the window at the blue sky. "Are you eager to get outside after the winter, Mrs. Scarlett?"

"Indeed, I am. I can't wait to plant flowers and dig my hands in the dirt. I'm guessing you have something else tempting you." She tipped her head toward him, reminding him of his mother. "That bundle of joy must make you want to run home and scoop him up. I'm the same way around my daughter's twins. And you have a lovely new bride."

Smith grinned. "Yes, I do."

"How about if I clear your schedule for tomorrow afternoon? It would be easier than clearing things today. Especially with the way Jubilee said she must speak with you." She sighed as if she knew exactly what such a visit might entail.

"If you could rearrange things tomorrow, I'd appreciate it."

Mom could watch Lake. Perhaps, he and Liv could grab lunch and make a picnic of it.

"I'll do that." Mrs. Scarlett turned and left his office.

Smith glanced down his list and groaned. Amaryllis and Jubilee both scheduling appointments on the same day? That couldn't be good.

Chapter Eighty-one

Liv set the pan of brownie batter that she'd attempted on her own in the oven, then she strolled around the backyard, carrying Lake. She got distracted by pointing things out to him—the apple trees he'd climb someday, the garden space Granny Trish and Mama would make into a fine garden, the grassy yard where he'd play baseball and catch with his daddy and brothers when he was bigger, and the faucet where he'd cool off on sweltering summer days—and forgot all about her baking.

Lake cackled and cooed.

"Liv!" Trish called from the back doorway.

"Yes?" She held up her hand to block the bright sunshine.

"The buzzer was ringing. I shut it off, but—"

"Oh, no." She rushed for the door, Lake jiggling up and down. "I can't believe I forgot about the brownies." As soon as she entered the kitchen, the sharp scent burned her nostrils. "I did it again!"

Liv handed Lake over to Trish and then opened the oven door. Using a hot pad, she pulled out the pan and set it on the stove. The brownies were charred around the outer edges. She groaned.

"I'm sure they'll be fine," Trish said.

Her mother-in-law always had something nice to say. Surely, even she could smell the burned scent in the air.

But later, when Liv cut out a piece from the center of the brownies and tasted it, the flavor wasn't horrible. Perhaps, she'd trim off two inches around the edges and the middle part would be okay.

An hour later, Smith called to say his day was too hectic for him to come home for lunch. He'd grab food from the church refrigerator where they kept a few staples for sandwich makings.

Liv had a different idea. She wanted to bring his lunch over and surprise him like a girlfriend might do. More and more, she was thinking of him as her boyfriend. Well, her boyfriend-husband. She smiled.

After making a sack lunch, including two of her brownies from the center of the pan, she asked Trish to watch Lake. Then she hiked to the church, a mile away. The almost-spring air smelled delightful. The sun shining down on her felt wonderful, even though it was less than forty degrees.

When she reached the church, she jogged up the steps with a happy gait. Wouldn't Smith be surprised by her lunch delivery? Maybe she could do this more often.

She entered the receptionist's area, but Mrs. Scarlett wasn't present. She must have stepped out for lunch, or something. The door to Smith's office stood partially open, and voices reached her.

"I don't understand how things can go on this way!" The cranky female voice sounded like Jubilee's. "You are supposed to be an example to us! My husband says I don't have any cause for complaint against him when you and your wife are living as strangers in the same house!"

What? Liv backed up. She shouldn't be listening to this private conversation. She should go. Maybe run out the door. Yet she stayed, rooted to the spot.

"Jubilee," Smith spoke with a restrained tone in his voice, "I understand you're frustrated with your marriage. But there isn't any reason for you to be comparing your situation to mine."

"Why not? Aren't you and your wife living as strangers?" The woman's voice rose accusingly. "Not sharing the things a husband and wife in a normal marriage share? Not even the same bedroom?"

Liv clenched her jaw.

"Jubilee—"

"Doesn't scripture teach us that a married couple shouldn't keep themselves apart?"

Smith groaned.

Liv's face heated up by several degrees. She felt so embarrassed for him.

"Well, doesn't it?" Jubilee demanded.

Liv hated this. How could a person who professed Christianity be so cruel? So downright mean?

"Yes, of course, it does." Smith sighed noisily. "So, are things still not going well between you and Clay? Is that what this is about?"

"No, this isn't about us. This is about you, and the bad example you and your wife are setting for our church!"

That's it. Liv couldn't bear another second of hearing Jubilee's judgmental attitude without stomping in there and saying something she'd surely regret. She dropped the sack lunch on Mrs. Scarlett's desk. Then she grabbed a piece of paper off a notepad and scribbled, *Smith, here's lunch. Sorry about the brownies. Liv.*

She turned to leave but froze at Jubilee's next statement.

"Are you even planning to make yours a real marriage, Pastor North? Maybe Amaryllis would have been a better choice for you!"

Pain seared through Liv's heart. Before she could exit the office, Mrs. Scarlett stepped through the doorway, a sympathetic expression on her face.

"I, uh, brought Smith's lunch." Liv rushed past the older woman and ran from the building.

Did Jubilee really think Amaryllis would have been a better match for Smith? Did he? If not, why hadn't he disagreed with her?

Chapter Eighty-two

When Jubilee finally left, Smith covered his face with his hands and roared out a groan. He and Liv were trying their hardest to do things the right way. They'd been honest with the Board about their marriage from the start. They were learning to love each other at their own pace. Yet Jubilee's voice shouting at him that he should do better hurt like a fire burning in his spirit.

How had she even found out about him and Liv?

"Pastor," Mrs. Scarlett said quietly, "your wife left lunch for you."

"She did?" Liv stopped by but didn't talk to him?

"Yes, however, Amaryllis is here." She smiled compassionately. "Would you like her to wait until you've had a chance to catch your breath?"

"No, that's okay." He might as well face the next firing squad. How could he eat with this much tension churning through him anyway? "Let her in. Thanks, Mrs. Scarlett."

"Come in, Amaryllis. Pastor North will see you now."

He took a quick swallow of cold coffee. Sat up straighter.

"Thank you for fitting me in on short notice, Pastor." Amaryllis shuffled into the room and sat down, twisting a hanky between her fingers.

"What seems to be the trouble?"

Mrs. Scarlett left the door open. He appreciated her carefulness about these matters.

"I've done a terrible thing. I feel so guilty about it." Amaryllis dabbed her hanky to her nose.

"What's happened?"

"I'm sorry but I mentioned our possible marriage arrangement, and how you didn't choose me, to a couple of friends," she said and sobbed at the same time.

"You did what?" His voice came out sharply. Amaryllis had been spreading gossip about him and her?

"And about you and Liv. About your fake marriage." She cried again.

Smith groaned. "Amaryllis," he barely held his anger in check. "Our marriage isn't fake. I'll kindly ask you not to say that. And not to tell anyone else that!"

"Okay. If you say so." She sniffed.

No wonder Jubilee caught wind of their unusual marriage situation and got upset about it!

"We were hoping you'd keep that private information to yourself." He clasped his hands together and twiddled his thumbs, using up some of his restless energy. "After we are more settled in, we might share our story with the congregation. But that's our decision to make. Not yours."

"I know." She gazed at him with big sad eyes. "Have you ... settled in? You and her?"

"Yes. We're falling in love with each other," he said boldly. At least they were in the process of that beautiful eventuality.

"I was so hoping—" Amaryllis gulped. "I still wish things had worked out between you and me. That you could have cared for me. That's all." Her mouth arced into a silent wail.

Inwardly, he groaned. He had no idea what to say to that. Should he try to express something comforting or offer to pray for her?

Maybe this was his chance to take care of the emotional indebtedness he felt toward her, once and for all.

"Amaryllis, I am truly sorry for getting your hopes up during those times we met." He wished he'd never listened to Arnold about meeting up with his sister. If only he'd been more patient. "I appreciated your willingness to meet with me and talk things through."

"You're welcome." She hiccupped. "Jubilee asked me about it. What was I supposed to say? I told her the truth. But I didn't mean to cause you and Olivia any trouble."

"I'm sure you didn't mean any harm."

"I didn't. You are such a nice man. Liv has been kind to me too." Her chin quivered. "I'm sorry for adding to the gossip."

"Thank you. I appreciate your stopping by and explaining." He stood, eager for this meeting to be over.

Amaryllis didn't stand. "Are you going to stay with her?"

"Stay with my wife?" Why would she ask such a question? "Yes, of course, I'm staying with her. We're married. We took real wedding vows."

"Do you think you made the right choice?" She still wore a woebegone look on her face.

He was determined to set the record straight, peaceably, and kindly, if possible. "I chose Liv. She agreed to marry me. We're building a strong marriage that will last. So, yes, I made the right decision."

Amaryllis wept into her hanky.

Mrs. Scarlett stepped into the room. "Pastor, are you finished here?"

Bless her.

"Yes, I am."

"You have a phone call to return." She strode over to Amaryllis. "Come along, dear. Let's leave Pastor North to his ministerial duties." She escorted the woman to the door.

Amaryllis glanced back at him. "I would have enjoyed being your wife."

He bit back a groan, forcing himself to remain silent. He'd spend some time praying and asking the Lord for guidance before he ate the lunch Liv brought for him.

Chapter Eighty-three

Liv set the table with bowls and spoons for the vegetable soup Trish had tended throughout the afternoon. The scents of garlic and onions filling the room smelled delightful, but it wasn't enough to distract her from thinking about what Jubilee said. Her judgmental words still hurt. And it seemed weird that Smith hadn't called to check on her. Didn't Mrs. Scarlett tell him she overheard Jubilee's comments?

For the last couple of hours, she'd wanted to confide in Trish. But to do so meant gossiping. So she spent Lake's naptime knitting. Stewing and fretting, more like. But she kept busy.

A few times, Trish gazed at her with a concerned look, but she didn't pry.

Smith came through the door at five-thirty, hung up his coat, and greeted them in his usual jovial way. Liv didn't want to have it out with him in front of Trish, but as they sat down to eat, his not mentioning anything about her lunch delivery increased her irritation.

"How was your day?" Smith asked her.

"Tolerable." She put a bite of soup in her mouth and swallowed with difficulty. "This is great, Trish." She avoided Smith's gaze.

"Thank you."

"Thanks for the lunch. That was thoughtful of you to bring it over. Hit the spot." Smith smiled but there was a wariness in his eyes.

"You're welcome," she said tightly.

"And the brownies were ... great."

The hesitation in his voice was obvious. He hated them, didn't he?

Trish's questioning gaze flicked between Smith and Liv.

After dinner, Liv jumped to her feet and started the clean-up process. Smith picked Lake up from the baby carrier and sat down on the couch with him, playing with some toys off the coffee table.

Why didn't he mention Jubilee's visit? What if Mrs. Scarlett didn't tell him? He might think Liv dropped off the lunch and simply left. She had to explain, right?

"Everything okay?" Trish asked after she put the stewpot in the fridge.

Liv shrugged, still not wanting to discuss it with her.

"I'll take Lake in the bedroom for a while if that would help."

"Okay. Thanks."

Trish gave her a hug. "Everything will be okay, you'll see."

Liv appreciated her mother-in-law's positivity and lack of judgment. Sighing a few times, she finished washing the dishes.

By the time she dropped onto the couch next to Smith, Trish had taken Lake into Liv's room and closed the door.

Smith wove their fingers together. He seemed so relaxed as if he knew nothing of her inner turmoil. She hated bringing up a topic that might cause trouble between them. Yet if she played along as if nothing was bothering her, as if she hadn't heard Jubilee, she'd be lying to him, and to herself.

"I have something I need to talk to you about." She pulled her hand away from his.

"All right. What's wrong?"

"I stopped by your office today."

"I'm sorry I missed you. I had one appointment after another."

"It's okay." She took a breath. Maybe she'd use their cookie talk. "Sometimes one cookie speaks to another cookie in confidence, you know?"

Smith's eyebrows rose. "I'm listening."

"Another cookie might overhear what those two cookies were discussing and"—she bit her lower lip—"get her feelings hurt because the cookies were talking about her."

"Oh, Liv." His facial expression softened. "This cookie who over-heard one cookie talking to the other cookie, did she think the latter cookie should have spoken up for her?"

His gentle smile was nearly her undoing.

"Yes. Or at least mention something sympathetic."

He ran his smooth fingertips over the backs of her hands. "I'm sorry you heard what Cookie A said to Cookie B."

"Me too. Especially when Cookie A said Cookie C would have been a better match for Cookie B."

He closed his eyes for a moment. "That's what you overheard?"

"Is that what you think? Do you agree with her that someone else would have made a better match for you? Especially since we aren't sleeping together yet?"

"Oh, Liv. Never! What Cookie A said in anger about us is not true." He met her gaze steadily. "Sweetheart, I care deeply about you."

She knew that. Yet, he still couldn't say he loved her.

"Sometimes irate cookies say things in meanness that are hard to forget." He ran his hands over her arms. "But we must try to forgive and move on."

"I'm sorry I overheard any of it. I brought your lunch. Just trying to be wifely." She said the last part with some dry humor. "What she said hurts when I've tried so hard to go along with everything and make this arrangement work." She clenched her teeth to keep back a sob. She would not collapse into a puddle of tears. "I didn't like her saying the other cookie was better for you. That made me mad!"

He smoothed his fingers over her jawline, up her cheek, then his fingertips stroked her upper lip with a whisper-soft touch. "Can you picture me doing that to anyone but you?"

"No," she whispered, gaining some control of her emotions.

"Or this?" He brushed his mouth across the spot he'd touched, heating up her lips.

In the next second, they were wrapped in each other's arms, kissing, her melting against his chest, her previous sadness dissolving more with each movement of his lips searching hers, comforting her.

Letting out a slow breath, Smith settled back against the couch cushions, tugging her along beside him. She leaned her cheek against his chest, enjoying feeling his heartbeat and being wrapped in his strong arms.

"I'm glad you talked to me. You can talk to me about anything."

"Even about cookies?"

"Even that." He chuckled.

"Will Cookie A cause more problems?"

"I sure hope not."

They stayed in each other's arms for a few minutes. Liv smelled the spicy scent of his deodorant and him—scents that were becoming familiar.

He shuffled her chin up so she gazed into his eyes. "What does a man need to do to get more of those kisses of yours?"

"You'll have to figure that out yourself."

"Maybe I will." He kissed her again.

Chapter Eighty-four

Had Liv made a terrible mistake by agreeing to host the women's meeting in the parsonage? When Amaryllis called and nearly begged for the event to be held here on Friday, she didn't have the heart to say no. She'd been fretting about it all morning. Would Jubilee be attending?

Fortunately, Trish was available to make snacks and serve as hostess. But other than standing by Smith after church on Sundays, this would be Liv's first time doing anything in her official capacity as the pastor's wife.

Amaryllis arrived first. "Mrs. North, thank you for allowing us to meet in your home." She shook Liv's hand coolly, not meeting her gaze. What was that about?

"Of course. And it's Liv."

Amaryllis chuckled in a way that sounded like she was nervous or worried about something. Surely, she didn't know what Liv overheard Jubilee say.

A half dozen more women arrived, including some Liv felt more at ease with—Jenn, Candy, Brittany, and Mrs. Scarlett. Ten ladies filled the small living room, but Jubilee still hadn't arrived.

Thanks to Trish's warm hospitality, everyone got situated and was served coffee or tea and shortbread cookies.

"I want to welcome all of you ladies to our meeting," Amaryllis said in a strong voice. "And give a big 'Thank you' to Mrs. North for opening the parsonage for our gathering."

Liv wanted to correct her and say her name was Liv, again, but she refrained.

Several ladies made agreeing comments.

Amaryllis cleared her throat. "Today, I'm going to jump right in with my newest scheme to raise more funds for the orphanage."

A firm knock sounded. Liv strode to the door and opened it.

Jubilee stood on the porch, tapping her foot, a cross look on her face.

"Hello, Jubilee. Come in. Welcome. We're just getting started." She forced her tone to be welcoming, not allowing the tension she felt in her middle to infiltrate her words.

"I would have been here sooner if I didn't have to wait for Clay to drive me," she complained as she tromped past Liv. "The man's as slow as spring."

Taking a deep breath, Liv followed her back into the living room.

Greetings and small talk took up the next few minutes.

Trish asked Jubilee what hot drink she'd like, then hurried into the kitchen.

Liv wished that had been her task. Then she could avoid the new arrival's perturbed glances being shot in her direction. The woman's recent accusation rang in her ears. Would Amaryllis have made a better wife for Smith? Probably a better pastor's wife. A better choice for leading the women of the church.

But as Smith's romantic interest? As his wife? No way! Liv couldn't imagine the other woman in his arms the way he held her on the couch last night.

Sipping her coffee, Liv caught the tail end of Mrs. Scarlett's devotional.

"—so when the woman dropped off a basket of baby clothes on my doorstep, it meant the world to me. Sometimes doing even the smallest kindness for someone goes a long way."

"So true." Jenn nodded and smiled.

"Mama," Candy said, "I don't remember you telling me that story before. I guess I was raised on hand-me-downs."

"You sure were, honey." Mrs. Scarlett grinned. "You and me both."

Everyone chuckled except for Jubilee. For some reason, that woman looked like she was chewing on nails.

"Okay, ladies, let's discuss my idea." Amaryllis clasped her hands together. "Our presentation brought in some money and enthusiasm for our orphans. But we must figure out more things to do to raise funds and keep our church's, and the community's, focus on helping others in need."

"The Bible tells us to take care of widows and orphans," Brittany said.

"That's right!" "What are we going to do next?" "I want to help!" Comments came fast.

"Here's my idea." Amaryllis seemed like a natural at leading. "I want us to have a bazaar." She said "bazaar" like it was a magical word.

Oohs and aahs followed.

"What kind of bazaar?" Jubilee asked in a cranky tone.

"A spring bazaar!" Amaryllis gazed upward, still smiling like she loved being the center of attention.

As soon as the thought crossed Liv's mind, she regretted it. She didn't want to be spiteful and judgmental. She wanted to be graceful and caring to everyone. Even to people who'd hurt her or spoken badly about her. Even to Amaryllis and Jubilee.

Lord, help me to rise above any petty attitude I'm tempted to have. I want to be a blessing to others, especially to the people in Smith's church.

"Our bazaar will be more than a church fundraising event," Amaryllis said, sounding like an orator. "It will be a city-wide extravaganza!"

"What a great idea!" Brittany clasped her hands to her chest as if she had an epiphany. "We could rent spaces to other crafters and make even more money for our orphans."

"Exactly." Amaryllis nodded fast. "We could serve lunch and desserts."

The ladies chattered with each other, sharing a gaggle of ideas all at once.

Liv wasn't catching on to their eagerness. A bazaar sounded like a ton of work. What was the bottom line? How much work would they have to do in proportion to their profit? While the bazaar might be a fun social event, when it came to how long it took her to make a pair of knitted booties, she'd rather donate the five bucks.

Lake whimpered from the bedroom, and she took his cue to excuse herself and change and feed him. She left the door slightly ajar so she could still hear the discussions going on in the living room.

She'd just finished nursing Lake and stood to burp him when she saw Jubilee hovering outside her doorway peering in. A smug look crossed the woman's face as she glanced between Liv and something else. What? The twin bed? Liv recalled her accusation that she and Smith were living as strangers. Fighting annoyance, she returned to the group with Lake in her arms and sat down.

"If no one else has anything to add, we can adjourn," Amaryllis said. "We'll pencil in our spring bazaar on the church calendar. I'll make a few contacts about a place to hold our event. In the meantime, work on those craft ideas. Come up with baking ideas too! We'll finalize our plans at our next meeting."

Liv sighed in relief. The meeting was nearly over.

Jubilee raised her hand.

Uh-oh.

"Yes, Jubilee?" Amaryllis turned toward her with a wide-eyed expression.

"It's come to my attention that some of the younger ladies in our group might need a little guidance." Jubilee lifted her chin toward Liv.

Liv tensed.

"What kind of guidance?" Amaryllis questioned.

The room went silent other than Lake's gurgling sounds.

"Marital advice."

What?

"Jubilee, some of us aren't even married." Amaryllis patted her chest like she might be having heart palpitations.

A few of the ladies grimaced.

"I mean"—Jubilee's voice took on a lecturing tone—"the scripture says older women ought to teach the younger women how to behave. Some may need spiritual guidance about how a husband and wife ought to act toward each other. How they should live together." Her gaze drifted to Liv's bedroom.

Heat flamed up Liv's face. She wanted to march into her room and slam the door. How dare Jubilee bring up Liv and Smith's marriage? That's what she was talking about, right? That Liv needed "spiritual guidance" about her marriage to the pastor?

"I think our ladies' meetings should include times of teaching wives about marriage the way it's supposed to be." Jubilee shot another glance at Liv.

"Supposed to be according to whom?" Candy asked tensely as if she didn't like Jubilee's comments either.

"The scripture, of course. And the older women like it says."

Candy's face turned red, and she pressed her lips together.

Mrs. Scarlett cleared her throat and shuffled in her chair.

Liv felt sweltering hot in the stuffy room.

"Maybe we should leave this discussion for another day, hmm?" Trish stood and clasped her hands together in an obvious this-meeting-is-over gesture. "It was lovely having all of you here. Thank you for coming."

Most of the ladies stood, but Jubilee remained seated, arms crossed. "Doesn't anyone agree with me and the scripture that we ought to discuss the right concepts of marriage, especially when our own leaders are leading in a way that is unbecoming?"

Liv clenched her jaw and didn't dare look at Jubilee. If she did, she'd say something honest and rude. Something she might not be able to tamp down once she started telling the obnoxious woman what she thought of her suggestion and her unkind attitude. It took everything within her not to stand up and defend herself. The only thing keeping her seated was not wanting to embarrass Smith and Trish.

"Jubilee, come along." Mrs. Scarlett put her hand in the crook of Jubilee's arm and escorted her to the door. "Let's not discuss anyone's private affairs. We all have our own lives to live."

Liv stared at the floor, her vision blurry because of the angry tears she would not let anyone see. She'd learned about maintaining strong emotional control in her father's heated board meetings. She called on that strength now.

"Thank you for having us over, Liv," Jenn said in a subdued tone.

"You're welcome."

When only Liv and Trish remained, Liv blew out a trembling breath. Thank goodness she'd gotten through that meeting. Not unscathed. But it was over.

Trish came straight to her and hugged her. "I'm so sorry about that, hon."

"Me too."

Did all those women realize Jubilee had been talking about her?

Chapter Eighty-five

Later in the afternoon, Liv took Lake for a long stroller ride. He cooed and seemed to love the outdoor activity. It served as a tonic for beating back her frustrations and the embarrassment she still hadn't been able to shed.

Why did Jubilee think it was her business to comment on Liv and Smith's marriage? Why did she care whether they were sleeping in separate rooms? They were still married! They were nearly in love with each other. At least, Liv was nearly in love with Smith. They didn't have to explain or defend the marital path they were taking to Jubilee or anyone in the congregation.

What Jubilee suggested—that *she* should teach the younger women about marriage—still sent darts of anger and exasperation through Liv. What was she to do with these strong feelings of outrage toward the woman? Injustice, even? Especially since she'd already heard Jubilee's mean words in Smith's office.

Would she have to stay away from the church and the ladies' group for a while? No, that wasn't like her to back down from anything.

Lord, show me how to let the negative things go. Please help Smith and me to have wisdom. Fill us with Your grace so we can show grace too.

After she returned to the parsonage and put Lake in his baby carrier, she saw the light flashing on the answering machine. She hoped it wasn't any of the ladies calling to ask what Jubilee meant, or to apologize for the awkwardness in the meeting.

Punching the button, she listened.

"Hey, Liv." Smith's voice sounded tired or strained. "How about us making brownies after dinner? If you're interested, I'll pick up supplies." A pause. "Talk to you later."

Was that a gulp? Had Mrs. Scarlett filled him in on what Jubilee said?

She dialed the church number.

"Hello. Thunder Ridge Fellowship. Mrs. Scarlett speaking."

"Hi, Mrs. Scarlett. This is Liv. Is Smith busy?"

"I'm sorry, but he stepped out of the office." She made a sound like the shuffling of paper. "Can I take a message?"

"Tell him yes, will you? What he called and suggested is fine with me."

"I'll leave him a note. Oh, Olivia?"

Liv hesitated. "Yes?"

"I am sorry for what was said about marriage at the ladies' meeting." She took a breath. "Your private affairs, and those between you and Pastor North, are no one's business but yours and God's."

"Thank you." She was glad someone in the church understood that.

After dinner, Smith pitched in with washing dishes while Liv bathed Lake. Trish offered to spend time with the baby, freeing Liv to bake with Smith.

Liv strode into the kitchen and found Smith standing by the counter, his hands clutching the edges in what looked like a death grip. Ingredients were spread out across the Formica surface. He didn't turn at her approach.

"Smith?"

He released his hold on the counter's edge and let out a long sigh. "Here's the recipe I thought we'd try." He smoothed his hand over a page in the cookbook.

Thoughts of his hands smoothing over her cheeks when he kissed her the last time made her face flush.

One of his brows lifted. "Are you okay?"

"Better with you here."

"Oh, sweetheart. I'm so sorry."

He opened his arms and she fell into them, leaning her cheek against his dark green button-up shirt. His heart hammered beneath her ear. She liked being in this man's arms. The closeness between them had been happening slowly. But despite anything Jubilee thought about their marriage, their relationship was real, and it would get better, and it would last.

"Mrs. Scarlett explained what happened in the meeting," he said quietly.

Needing to see his eyes, she leaned back and smoothed her fingers over his cheeks the way she imagined him doing with hers moments ago. "It was awful."

He clasped her hands. "Jubilee had no right to bring up marriage and what she should be teaching about it. If anyone should not be speaking about marriage—" He groaned, silencing whatever he'd been about to say. "I'm here for you, Liv. Will always be here for you. We can talk about anything. I mean that. Although, we might have to do so with our cookie talk."

"Thank you." She drew in a long breath. "But some things have to work themselves out. I don't want you intervening every time there's a problem between me and someone in the church." She sucked in a breath. "You didn't already do that, did you? I mean you didn't call her or anything?"

"No. I almost did. You're my wife. I want to protect you. Stand up for you."

"That's sweet. Really." She let a small smile lift the corners of her mouth. "I like your being here with me now. I like us baking together. Working on being a couple."

"Me too." He exhaled like he might have been holding in his breath.

Perhaps her not wanting to go into detail about the meeting, her not wanting him to go to bat for her, was a relief to him too.

She sighed, releasing a little more frustration.

"Sounds like what I've been doing all afternoon." Smith chuckled.

"What's that?"

"Sighing."

"Before we start on the brownies, I have a weird idea I'd like to talk to you about," Liv said. "Feel free to disagree."

"Okay. Let's hear it."

"What would you say to us being a little affectionate after church on Sunday?" She grinned and licked her lip flirtatiously.

"Why, Mrs. North, what do you have in mind?" He took her in his arms as if he'd been doing so for years.

She laughed and toyed with a button on his shirt. Then she reverted to their cookie strategy for discussing members of the congregation. "Some cookies might need a little convincing that their pastor and his wife are a real couple. We have doubtful cookies among us."

"You mean I haven't been convincing enough that I'm a besotted husband?"

"Some convincing might be in order."

"Certain cookies might not approve of public displays of affection between the pastor and his wife." He made a slight scowl.

"Ah. I hadn't thought of that." She stepped back from him. "Bad idea?"

"Not at all." He clasped her hands again. "I agree with you that some convincing might be necessary."

Suddenly, he grinned and lifted her up, setting her on the counter.

"Smith! What are you doing?"

"Just practicing."

"You can't do this in church!"

"No?" His gaze sparkled up into hers. His arms came around her waist and he stroked her back. The ticklish sensations rushing up her spine exploded endorphins in her brain.

In a deep voice as if making a public announcement, he said, "Let it be known to all Thunder Ridge Fellowship attendees that I'm crazy about my wife!" His tone softened. "About you, Liv." He touched his lips to hers, increasing the pressure of his mouth on hers. After sharing a few smooches, he sighed. "I am so close to the precipice of loving you with all my heart, I can hardly stand it."

So close. But not there yet?

Still, when his lips met hers in another sweet kiss, her heart melted into a puddle of warmth and almost love for this man.

Chapter Eighty-six

Smith looked forward to Sunday morning even more than usual after his and Liv's brownie-making lesson—and the plan they concocted to convince certain church attendees of their genuine connection to each other. He hoped their scheme didn't backfire. Or that in his eagerness to prove he loved his wife—

Loved? Was it possible he loved her already?

As he tied his blue and gold striped tie around his neck, preparing for the Sunday morning service, he paused and forced an image of Katy and him into his mind just to test it. Not a single ounce of attraction or sorrow over missed opportunities hit him as it had in the past. Not one thought of wanting to kiss Katy came into his mind.

Yet when he thought of Liv, picturing their kissing last night, or he imagined making love with her, goodnight, his heart rumbled like a racecar engine. So many warm yearnings for his wife came to mind. The passion he felt when he held her in his arms and kissed her. His happiness when they laughed together. Their closeness and fun when they baked together. Even when he observed her being a mama to Lake, he felt so happy for the family they were making.

Maybe all those combined feelings were love.

When Mrs. Scarlett told him about the unkind things Jubilee said the other day, he wanted to stand up for his wife in front of the

whole congregation and defend her publicly. That his decision to
marry her quickly due to the church Board's expectations was causing
them trouble now irked him to no end.

But it was in God's hands. Daily, Smith entrusted their marriage
and family, and his church family, into God's loving care. He could
do that even with this, right?

He straightened his tie. Then he prayed today's plan would work
to temper whatever gossip or unrest was going on in the congregation.
Namely, with Jubilee and Amaryllis.

* * * *

All through Smith's sermon on the Beatitudes, Liv felt nervous.
Maybe she should send him a secret message telling him to drop her
idea. What if Jubilee got bent out of shape and said something even
more disrespectful to Liv?

She tried catching Smith's gaze a few times and shaking her head
discreetly, but he didn't glance her way. Maybe it took his full concentration to speak this morning.

"You okay?" Trish, sitting next to Liv, whispered.

"Uh-huh."

Her heart pounding against her ribs, Liv tried picturing what
Smith might do to be affectionate with her in public. They wouldn't
kiss deeply. Maybe just hold hands. Or he'd smooth his fingers down
her cheeks. Something sweet. That's all. Hopefully, that would be
enough to silence wagging tongues.

After the benediction, Trish held out her hands for Liv to pass
Lake to her like Smith had asked her to do. Of course, they'd let
Trish in on their little plan.

A couple of ladies came by and shook Liv's hand. A few averted
gazes demonstrated some of the women still felt awkward around
her following Jubilee's insinuations.

Smith's hand on the back of her waist made her jump. "Steady," he whispered in her ear. "Your lovely smile aimed adoringly at your husband will be more convincing than anything."

"Okay." She giggled and batted her eyes at him.

"That's better."

She met a couple of people's curious gazes. Did they think Smith was whispering romantically in her ear?

He kept one hand at her back while he shook hands with some congregants. During a lull, or maybe he saw someone approaching, he wrapped both his arms around her and kissed the side of her head. For the weirdest second, it felt like the whole group of exiting parishioners froze and stared at them.

Liv turned her face slightly toward Smith. He was so close. His mouth was so near hers. Their gazes locked and he smiled warmly at her. She could have kissed him. But they were in church. People were watching. But wasn't that the point?

The sound returned to the room. Parishioners continued moving out the door. Maybe that freezing sensation was all in her mind, anyway. Then Jubilee came into her line of sight. The woman squinted suspiciously at them.

Smith turned Liv slightly toward him, one eyebrow raised as if he were asking her something. And she went for it. She kissed him on the mouth. Not a long kiss. More of a wisp of a kiss. But she did it in front of Jubilee.

Smith smiled broadly. He lowered his arm from her shoulder, skidding his fingers down her arm. Leaning in, he whispered, "That should do it."

She grinned, too, glad he wasn't embarrassed by her kissing him.

The women in their vicinity smiled, almost as if they were cheering them on.

Trish nodded at her, seemingly giving her blessing on their little stunt.

After this, would anyone doubt Liv was in love with Pastor North?

Chapter Eighty-seven

A week later, Liv brought the baby swing outside beneath the shade of a bushy Mountain Maple and set Lake in it. He'd be content for fifteen or twenty minutes, giving her time to dig in the garden.

Picking up the shovel she found in the shed, she stabbed it into the earth over and over, working the soil. She'd never tried gardening before. Already, she loved the scent of the dirt and the gentle wind blowing across her face. She liked working hard and picturing the rewards of homegrown vegetables on their table.

What would her father say about her new endeavor? No doubt, he'd tell her she was wasting her talents. Raising babies and growing a garden? He hadn't sent her to college for this! But she was so thankful for her current life with Lake, Smith, and Trish.

She had grit and determination—things she learned from her father—and she'd put them to good use in figuring out how to be a good wife and mom. Maybe even a good pastor's wife. She pressed the tip of the shovel into the rocky soil and lifted it. Her arms ached, but in a good way. Hefting Lake around for the last few months had made her stronger.

A few more scoops of dirt and she made a dent in turning her garden space. Trish said it was better to start with a simple plot and expand when she had more gardening savvy. That's what she planned to do. But someday, she envisioned a grand garden for her family.

Lake fussed and gnawed on his hand, a sure sign of hunger. "Hey, baby," she called, trying to distract him.

She pressed the shovel into the ground a couple more times before he let out a full-on cry.

"There, there." She wiped her hands on her coat, cleaning them the best she could before scooping him out of the swing. "Everything's okay. Mama's here."

"Liv?" She turned at Trish's voice. "I came out to tell you there's been an accident. Mrs. Scarlett called with a prayer request."

"Oh? What happened?"

"It's Jubilee and Clay's daughter, Aimee." Trish shook her head fretfully. "She was hit by a drunk driver before the bridge coming into Sandpoint."

"Oh, no." Tremors raced through Liv. "What can I do?"

Trish set her palm on Liv's shoulder and led her back toward the parsonage. "Pray."

"And?" She kept jostling Lake. "Is Smith at the hospital?"

"Yes, I'm sure he's there."

Liv swallowed a wad of emotion. "You've taught me about being a pastor's wife and having a servant's heart. What would a pastor's wife who knew what she was doing do in a situation like this?"

"Hon, that isn't something I can teach you. You have to do what's in your heart." Trish tugged her toward the house. "For now, feed your baby. We'll keep praying for Aimee."

Inside, Liv dropped into the rocking chair and nursed Lake. Across from her, Trish sat down on the couch and folded her hands, her eyes closed, obviously praying. Still rocking Lake, Liv stared out the window and implored God to touch Jubilee's daughter and bring healing to her physical body. And for healing to take place in Jubilee's heart, too.

Later, after Lake was fed, changed, and taking his nap, and Liv had cleaned up from her digging in the dirt, she walked into the waiting room at the Sandpoint Hospital. She couldn't stay home when Trish was there to keep watch over the baby and not to check on Jubilee, and Smith too. How was he handling this crisis? His first as a pastor.

"Liv." He strode right to her.

She walked into his embrace and hugged him. He clung to her, his chin coming to rest against the side of her head. She felt him tremble. Oh, Smith. This must be agony for him. His arms around her were comforting, but she came here to comfort him. Stepping back, she clasped his hands and met his sad, weary gaze. "Are you okay?"

He nodded, tears filling his eyes. Warmth flooded her. How she loved this man! Loved his heart for people. How he sacrificed and cared for his congregation. She loved him for the tender way he treated her and Lake.

Ohhh. *Loved*.

"How is Aimee?" she asked.

"She had surgery on her broken leg. She's in ICU with a punctured lung and a concussion. Clay is with her now. Only one person at a time."

"And Jubilee?"

Smith nodded toward the waiting area. "She's being stoic, but it's been a rough day."

Liv turned and saw Jubilee bent over in a chair with her hands covering her face. She knew what she needed to do, but she had something to say to her husband first.

"I was so worried about you." She met his gaze, staring deeply into his dark eyes. "I wanted you to know … I mean, when I saw you just now … I knew."

"Knew what?"

"I love you, Smith," she said softly.

A tired grin spread across his mouth. "You just now realized that?"

She could tell he was teasing her.

"Yes. A moment ago." She kissed his cheek. "I wanted you to know as soon as I did."

Letting go of his hands, she felt his gaze on her as she crossed the room to reach Jubilee. "How are you doing?" She sat beside the woman who'd said some cruel things about her and Smith before, but at this moment, Liv felt only compassion for Jubilee and her mama's heart. She placed her arm over her shoulder. "I'm so sorry Aimee got hurt. I'm praying for her. So is Trish. We care deeply about what you're going through."

Jubilee shuddered and lowered her hands. Her tear-stained face crumpled. "We almost lost her."

"You must have been terrified to hear your girl was hurt," Liv said, imagining how she'd feel if anything happened to Lake. "We're praying. I want you to know you're not alone. We're here for you. I'm here for you."

Jubilee sobbed quietly and leaned against Liv's shoulder.

Liv wrapped her arms around the woman and held her, rocking her slightly. She whispered a prayer for peace for Jubilee and Clay, and for Aimee's healing.

When Jubilee relaxed and settled back in her chair, Liv stole a glance at Smith. He still stood where she left him. A soft smile played on his lips, and he stared right back at her.

She'd told him she loved him. And she did. She loved him with her whole heart, her whole being. He hadn't returned the words yet, but that was okay.

Previously, she worried about being in a loveless marriage. But that wasn't the case. She loved her husband. Maybe she'd loved him since she heard him singing to Lake in the middle of the night a couple of months ago.

But what if he never felt that way toward her?

Chapter Eighty-eight

That night, Smith got home late from the hospital. The lights were off except for a few night-lights. It had been a bear of a day, and he was exhausted.

He took off his coat, draped it over a hook, and trudged into the kitchen. Trying to be quiet, he opened the fridge and grabbed some leftover chicken. Anything would do. Fatigue made heading to bed more desirable than eating. But he needed sustenance too.

A sound made him still.

"Hungry?" Liv's soft voice washed over him. So did the remembrance of her telling him she loved him.

"Sure am. Sorry if I woke you."

"It's okay." She stopped between the living room and the kitchen, her arms crossed over her sweatshirt. She had on cute pink pajama bottoms and slippers to match. "How's Aimee?"

"As good as can be expected. I'll go back in the morning." He grabbed a saucer and set the chicken on it. Leaning his backside against the sink, he ate the meat cold.

"Don't you want to heat it up?"

He met her gaze. "The microwave is too noisy."

She smiled. He loved it when she smiled at him. Loved? He sighed. This was too rough of a day for them to talk about what she admitted to him at the hospital. To discuss what he didn't say back to her. Hopefully, she wasn't upset about that.

He appreciated her coming to the hospital this afternoon. How she hugged him. Then, how she embraced Jubilee, the same woman who'd spoken ill of her to others, offering her comfort and prayer. His wife's compassion and caring had been amazing to witness. If ever he questioned whether he made the right decision in marrying Liv, what he saw in her today reinforced the truth. He had made the best decision in the world by marrying this delightful woman!

In fact, if he could reset time, he'd go back and never have been in a relationship with Katy. He'd go straight to being with Liv.

The realization hit him like a powerful epiphany. He'd choose Liv over Katy? Yes! A thousand times yes! Liv was kind and beautiful and perfect for him. And he absolutely adored her. He loved her with his whole heart!

"Liv?" He set down his saucer.

"Yes?"

Their gazes met in the dim lighting.

"Oh, Liv."

He held out his arms and rushed to her at the same time she lunged for him. Arms wrapped around each other, they clung to one another in the middle of the kitchen. Kissing her deeply, ardently, he held her closer to himself than he'd ever held her or anyone else before. Her hands splayed over his back. He wanted to kiss her and then kiss her again. To take her to his room and spend the night in each other's arms, but he needed to talk to her first. To tell her—

"Oh, Livvy," he whispered. "Thank you for what you told me at the hospital."

She stilled in his arms, her hands stopping their movement. "Are you okay with that?" She leaned back. "With me saying I love you? With me coming to the hospital to be with you?"

"Sweetheart, yes." He took a deep breath and blew it out, controlling his emotions, his desire to kiss her like crazy. "When I saw you walk into the hospital lobby, I felt a breath of fresh air rush into me. Like life returned to my lungs, my veins, my heart. I was so tired and emotionally exhausted. Then you were there, hugging me. Saying you loved me."

"I do love you. I may have loved you for a while. But suddenly, I knew, without any doubts or hesitation about us being together." The smile he loved crossed her mouth. "I love you, Smith. You are my husband. I will always love you. My heart is yours."

"Oh, Liv." He kissed her gently, then more passionately. Heat and fire coursed through him. She loved him. Her heart was his. And he—

He pulled back, setting her slightly away from him, breathing heavily.

"What is it?" she whispered.

"I love you, too. With everything in my being, I love you! My heart is yours. You are my sweet, beautiful wife and I adore you. Will you be mine for all our days together?"

"Yes. Oh, yes!" She pressed her mouth against his, enflaming his senses.

But he had something else he wanted to say to her.

"I think I've known for a while too." He took a breath that rattled in his throat. "When I saw you walk into the hospital, even before you said what you said, I felt differently toward you. It was love, Liv. Even if I didn't recognize it at first, I love you with every breath in my body." He brushed his lips against hers, kissing her, wanting more.

Suddenly, she pulled back, chuckling. "Aren't you going to finish your food? You said you were hungry."

He grinned. "I'd rather kiss you and be with you."

"Even with the day you've had?" A cute smile crossed those lips he couldn't get enough of kissing. She smoothed her palms over his chest. "I understand if you just want to sleep."

"It has been a tough day. One of the worst. But I'm trusting God for a beautiful outcome for Aimee. And for her parents." He kissed Liv's cheek, leaving a trail of butterfly kisses down her jawline. "I'm trusting God for a beautiful outcome for us, too."

She leaned up as if to kiss him on the mouth. He touched her lips with his finger, stopping her kiss and smoothing his skin delicately over hers.

"What would you say to us sharing my room tonight?" He stroked some hair off her face, his fingers lingering near her ear. "And all our tomorrows?"

"I'd say, why did you take so long to ask?" She wrapped her arms around him, nuzzling her lips against his neck.

He chuckled then tipped up her chin and kissed her softly.

"Give me a minute, okay?" she said with a twinkle in her eye. "I'll check on Lake and leave the door open so we can hear him if he cries."

"Sure. I'll wait for you."

She started to walk away, then glanced back. "If I knew we were going to declare our love for each other tonight, I would have baked you something."

"Oh, yeah?" He grinned. "Apple pie?"

"Or cookies." She walked right back to him and kissed his mouth as if she couldn't get far without doing so. "Something sweet like me."

He muffled his chuckle. Marriage to this woman would be an exciting lifelong journey of romance and laughter, of them living together in the parsonage, and having a great big family.

Nine sons.

If God and Liv allowed him that dream.

Epilogue

Ten months later

Liv gripped Smith's hand tightly through the contraction. His other hand pressed hard against her lower back, providing counter-pressure. She tried to stay focused on her breathing, but she was so tired. How much more of this labor could she take?

"You're doing it! Keep breathing. Almost done," Smith said in a coaxing voice.

After the spasm ended, she sank back against the hospital pillow, breathing hard.

"You're doing great, Livvy. I'm so proud of you. Soon we're going to meet our little guy or gal."

She blew out a big breath. "This is the hardest work I've ever done."

"Even more than last time?"

"Yes. No. Maybe. I don't know." She focused on relaxing, preparing herself for the next contraction. Wishing this physical intensity was over already.

The nurse checked hers and the baby's stats. "Looks good."

"Won't be long now," the doctor said.

Smith leaned over Liv, kissing her forehead. "I love you, sweetheart."

"Love you too. I'm glad you get to be here with me this time."

"Me too." He stroked damp hair off her face. "I wouldn't have missed this for anything in the world."

"Boy or girl, you'll be happy, right?"

"Absolutely. Lake and I will let a girl be on our baseball team."

Liv's laugh was cut short by another contraction. "Oh, my. I need to push!"

"Go ahead," the doctor said, getting into position. "You're ready."

Taking a deep breath, Liv gripped her thighs and pushed through the contraction with all her might. She didn't need Smith rubbing her back now. But she was thankful he stayed right beside her, telling her she was doing a good job, whispering how much he loved her.

Exhausted, she sank back onto the pillow again.

A half hour later, the final push came, and she felt immeasurable love for God, Smith, and their family as another boy child passed from her body onto the sheets. He squalled loudly.

"He's so beautiful," she cried.

"Livvy, he's perfect." Smith leaned his head against hers, and they wept together.

Then the baby was in her arms, and she was kissing his soft, warm cheeks. "Hey, Coe," she whispered. "Just wait until you meet your brother, Lake. You two are going to have such fun times together."

"Best buddies forever." Smith held the baby's hand. "He has dark hair."

"Yeah, he does. Your chin dimple too. I love it!"

Chuckling, Smith leaned over and kissed Baby Coe's forehead just like Liv had seen him do with Lake a hundred times over the last year.

God had blessed her with a beautiful family. Two sons, a sweet husband, and a dear mother-in-law who was waiting outside her room. She couldn't wait to show Trish her new grandson.

"What to hold him?"

"You know I do." Smith's grin widened, if that were possible. He scooped up Coe and sat down in the chair beside Liv's bed, tenderly holding his son to his chest, just like he'd done with Lake a little over a year ago.

"Hey, buddy," he said softly. "Let me tell you a story about your namesake, Jack Coe. He was an evangelist in the 1940s. You and Lake are named after men of faith who I admire." He winked at Liv. "You and your brother, and your seven or so future siblings, are going to be named after special people."

Chuckling, Liv didn't have the heart or the energy to disagree with him. She loved this man. Would do almost anything for him. But nine babies?

Watching him holding their son, she couldn't wait to see what the next years, the next decades, brought to their marriage and their family. Maybe it would include nine children. Maybe two.

Two sounded just right today.

Smith stood and settled Coe back into her arms. "Here you go, sweet mama. Here's your boy."

"Thank you," she said with a gulp in her throat. "I mean it. Thank you, Smith."

"For?"

"Loving me. Loving us. Being my family."

"Oh, Livvy." He leaned over her, gazing deeply into her eyes. "I love you with all my heart. You are mine, and I am yours. We're family forever." He kissed her softly on the mouth.

Liv closed her eyes, letting his words sink into her heart.

Family forever.

Thank you for reading *Liv* & *the* PREACHER!

Author's note:

I hope you enjoyed Liv and Smith's story! For those who are wondering, Thunder Ridge is a fictional town located north of Sandpoint, Idaho. I hope to write more stories from that area in the future.

Blessings.

~Mary

Update:

Would you like to read a little more about Liv and Smith? To find out how they are doing five years later, you can download a Bonus Epilogue here:

https://BookHip.com/QFHVGHH

To access the epilogue, you'll be asked to enter your email, and you'll be subscribed to Mary's newsletter, but you can unsubscribe at any time.

**Lake* and *Hud,* Books 1 and 2 of The Preacher's Sons series—a spin-off from *Liv & the Preacher*—are available now.

Thank you to those who helped with this project!

Paula McGrew ... Thank you for believing in me and helping me fine-tune this story. You are a blessing to my writing journey!

Suzanne Williams ... Thank you for the fun cover! I appreciate your artistry so much.

Jason Hanks, Beth McDonald, and Mary Acuff ... Thank you for reading this story and giving me feedback. I appreciate your cheers and encouragement. You are a blessing to me!

This is a work of fiction. Any mistakes are my own. ~meh

If you are interested in hearing more about Mary's writing projects, sign up for her newsletter at

www.maryehanks.com.

Other Christian fiction by Mary Hanks:

The Preacher's Sons Series

Lake, Hud

Restored Series

Ocean of Regret, Sea of Rescue, Bay of Refuge, Tide of Resolve, Waves of Reason, Port of Return, Sound of Rejoicing. Shores of Resilience

Basalt Bay Series

Callie's Time

Second Chance Series

Winter's Past, April's Storm, Summer's Dream, Autumn's Break, Season's Flame

About Mary …

Married for 40+ years, Mary Hanks loves to read and write Christian fiction married romances. She has written twelve books in the second-chance inspirational Christian fiction genre so far. *Liv* & *the* PREACHER is her first marriage of convenience story.

Thank you for reading *Liv* & *the* PREACHER!

www.maryehanks.com

Made in the USA
Las Vegas, NV
20 September 2024

95553033R00219